ABOUT THE AUTHOR

Alan Hunt is a former British diplomat who served in the Middle East, Europe, Latin America and East Asia. He was Director of the Oxford University Foreign Service Programme for seven years and is now a Visiting Professor at the College of Europe in Bruges.

ALSO BY THIS AUTHOR

No Immunity
(Matador 2014)

Public Diplomacy – What It Is and How To Do It
(Unitar 2015)

A GAME THAT MUST BE LOST

ALAN HUNT

Matador
9 Priory Business Park,
Wistow Road, Kibworth Beauchamp,
Leicestershire. LE8 0RX
Tel: 0116 279 2299
Email: books@troubador.co.uk
Web: www.troubador.co.uk/matador
Twitter: @matadorbooks

ISBN 978 1785890 819

British Library Cataloguing in Publication Data.
A catalogue record for this book is available from the British Library.

Printed and bound in the UK by TJ International, Padstow, Cornwall
Typeset in 12pt Garamond by Troubador Publishing Ltd, Leicester, UK

Matador is an imprint of Troubador Publishing Ltd

For my family

AUTHOR'S NOTE AND ACKNOWLEDGEMENTS

The staff and their families (past and present) of the British High Commission in Singapore are innocent of the behaviour ascribed to the characters in this novel. So, too, are the inhabitants of Singapore and neighbouring countries, members of the Foreign and Commonwealth Office, and indeed all real-life individuals whose fictional counterparts are depicted here. For the sake of verisimilitude, the invented world they inhabit bears some relationship to that of early 2005. But the actions are imagined and any similarity of the characters to real persons, alive or dead, is unintentional.

I am indebted to Meredith Hunt, Charlotte Hunt and Victoria Leyman Hunt for their invaluable input when this book was in draft. Any inaccuracies or infelicities that remain are entirely my responsibility.

ACH August 2015

Philaster: *Oh, but thou dost not know*
               What 'tis to die.

Bellario: *Yes, I do know, my lord:*
               'Tis less than to be born; a lasting sleep;
               A quiet resting from all jealousy,
               A thing we all pursue. I know, besides,
               It is but giving over of a game
               That must be lost.

Francis Beaumont and John Fletcher, *Philaster*, Act III Scene I

OPENING MOVES

CHAPTER 1

Their guns were pointed at his head, and their faces hidden by gorilla masks like the one he'd worn to Kirsty's party.

He tried to speak, but his mouth remained clamped shut. He raised his arms in surrender, simultaneously becoming aware that a brass band outside the window was playing the National Anthem. He walked to the window, the attackers miraculously melting away, and looked out on to a fairy-tale land of castles and mountains, where children gathered flowers and newborn lambs leapt and played in the green fields. *I must climb through the window*, he thought, but his legs would not budge.

"It's time," said a voice behind him. He turned to see there was now only one gorilla in the room, which was suddenly his office: there were the maps on the wall, there his desk and neatly stacked in tray, and there his computer. On the screen he saw his own blood-stained body lying in a jungle clearing. In the foreground a young woman in fatigues spoke into a handheld microphone. Was it Kirsty? The answer was somewhere here in the room.

It's only a dream, he thought, but his eyes refused to open. He turned back to the gorilla. It had put down its gun and was lying on the floor with a second gorilla he had not previously noticed. They were fondling each other and kissing through their masks in such a lewd manner he felt his loins stir in envy. He snatched up the gun with a snarl of triumph.

"Now you can't stop me from speaking!" he shouted.

The first gorilla ripped off its mask and said, derisively: "You just don't get it, Andrew, do you?"

He saw it was Elena and screamed.

* * *

He lay on his back, sweating, still tense, for a minute or more. Then he began to relax. Beside him, Birgit lay naked, face down, motionless apart from the slightest of movements from her breathing, her hand resting idly along the inside of his upper leg.

He lifted Birgit's arm and slid his body silently sideways and out of the bed. He lit a cigarette and stood, unclothed, before the open window of the hut. Dawn was not far off. Through the mosquito screen the outline of the palm trees along the beach was just discernible against the dark sky. There was no breeze. Nothing moved. The only sound was that of the waves breaking unevenly against the shore.

The dream had been about retribution. It was not the first, nor would it be the last; he would never be free of Elena. But why had he suddenly thought of Kirsty? Whatever they had shared was finished thirty years or more ago, but the thought of her provoked in him a hopeless yearning. He swore softly to himself and pulled back the mosquito screen to flick his cigarette stub through the window.

Birgit stirred and turned on to her back. He drew back the sheets and knelt beside her. Sliding his hand beneath her waist, he turned her towards him and leant down to kiss the side of her neck at the point where her short-cropped, blonde hair curled below her ear. She murmured something and opened lazy eyes. *"Ach, Scheisse,* Andrew," she said, in mock irritation, as she extended her long legs in anticipatory pleasure. *"Bist du noch nicht satt?"*

"We're going to have to head back early," he said, "We'd better make the most of what time we've got."

Birgit considered him for a moment, as though weighing the significance of what he had just said. *"Du bist der Boss,"* she said at last, pulling him down on to her.

CHAPTER 2

The telephone of Mary Bennett, the Personal Assistant to the British High Commissioner in Singapore, rang as she was about to run out for a sandwich.

The High Commissioner was away travelling. Mary had hoped for a quiet couple of days to catch up on her emails, but Adam White had irrupted into her office the day before, full of apologies and with a series of urgent instructions to set up meetings and dinner for an unexpected ministerial visitor from London. There was no administrative support in the office, because Adam's secretary was absent, yet again – it seemed to Mary only a few weeks since Sophie had been off in Koh Samui with Susan and Siew Ling. Somehow, between them, Adam and Mary had cobbled together a programme.

Adam had left early on Friday morning to meet the Minister at Changi airport, leaving Mary to finalise the arrangements for the dinner that night. It had proved complicated and time-consuming telephoning around Singapore and pinning down the guests' acceptances, but she had just about tied up the final loose end.

Mary smiled at the recollection of Adam climbing hurriedly into the Rolls Royce, like a schoolboy late for class, his tie askew, his short, dark, hair still plastered to his forehead from his morning shower. He was the loveliest of men, his Glaswegian candour and good humour unspoilt by his years in the Foreign Office. Who knew what might have happened had he not already been committed to Alison? *But, then, who cares about that now?* she reminded herself.

Mary picked up the telephone. "High Commissioner's office," she said.

It was Muzafar. "Hello, my darling Mary," he said. She felt an uncontrollable surge in the pit of her stomach at the sound of his voice.

"Muzafar," she said. "What is it? Can't you make it tonight?" She cursed herself for asking such a pathetic question.

"No, my darling, of course I shall be there," he said. "But I shall be a little later than we agreed. Maybe around eight-forty-five or so – is that alright?"

"Of course, Muzafar," she said, relief flooding through her.

Siew Ling released the electronic lock to let Mary out of the secure area with a broad smile and the cheery greeting, "Have a most enjoyable and nutritious lunchtime break, Miss Bennett."

Mary negotiated a series of concrete barriers before finally emerging into the stifling midday heat of Tanglin Road. She hated the security and doubted its effectiveness. Since the discovery of the Jemaah Islamiyah plot to attack western diplomatic missions in Singapore, no embassy dared remain unprotected, but Mary herself was fatalistic about the risk. Nine-Eleven and Bali had demonstrated that nowhere in the world was safe.

Sitting in the air-conditioned cool of the Tanglin Shopping Centre, with a salad baguette and an orange juice, Mary went through the motions of reading the *Straits Times*. The lead story was about heightened tension in Indonesia following fatal clashes between Christian and Moslem groups in Sulawesi. But Mary could not concentrate on the news; she was thinking about Muzafar, as she did now virtually every waking hour of the day.

They had met shortly before Christmas at a British Council lecture ('Shakespeare's 'star-crossed lovers"). She had been immediately attracted by his youthful, dark-eyed intensity, and had been surprised and gratified that he should seem interested in her too. His first question had made her laugh.

"What work is your husband doing in Singapore?" he had asked politely.

"I'm not married," she said. "I work at the High Commission."

"I am truly astonished," he said. "Why is a beautiful woman like you not married?"

She blushed violently at his absurdly exaggerated compliment. "I was engaged once," she said. "My fiancé died."

"Oh, I'm so sorry," he said. There was an awkward silence. *Why did I have to say that*, she thought? It had been over ten years since Matt had driven his motorbike into the side of a taxi in a desperate attempt to avoid a child who had run into the road. Ten years during which she had seen her two younger sisters, like most of her friends, marry and have children, while she remained stuck in a self-imposed emotional limbo.

Meeting Muzafar had shaken Mary out of what she saw now was a kind of extended depression. During their early meetings they did little more than talk – about poetry, about their respective families and about his ambitions for the future. Mary tried to persuade Muzafar to come to the High Commission to play tennis, but he was too shy. Instead they met early in the morning, two or three times a week, to run together in the Botanical Gardens. On their third outing he had kissed her, tentatively, as they stood in the early morning light, hidden in the tropical rainforest. She could still taste the salt of his sweat on her lips. The first time they made love properly, at Mary's house, he had held her gently in his arms for a full five minutes, telling her over and over again how wonderful she was, that she was like a rose, a beautiful English rose, a flower too delicate for him to touch lest he crush her with his clumsy love-making. By the time he did, at last, kiss her lightly on the breast, she exploded with a ferocity of sexual desire of which she had never dreamed herself capable.

It was a hopeless relationship. He was younger than her,

employed as a clerk by a local ship's chandler – and he was a Moslem. Not that this worried Mary, who had abandoned all religious belief the day her fiancé was killed. But it worried Muzafar.

"My family will not understand," he said sadly, as they lay together in Mary's bed one evening. "They expect me to marry a nice Malay girl and live according to the teachings of the Koran." He turned on his side and traced a pattern across her milky skin with his lean, brown fingers until he reached the pink of her nipple.

She shivered now, as she sipped her juice, at the memory of that moment. Perhaps it was the impossibility of it all which made him so desirable. She did not care. She adored him. She would do anything for him.

* * *

The baby was awake. He had been crying for twenty minutes or so before Patrick finally gave up and dragged himself out of bed. Buffy grumbled slightly and tried to shift her position. Well over eight months into pregnancy, her options were severely constrained. "Will you go, love?" she said before lapsing back into sleep, but he was almost out of the room by that time.

It was gone six. The poor little beggar was hungry. Patrick fed and changed him. Then he sat looking out of the window at the unfashionable end of a cold, damp Streatham Common while he held his son to his chest, encouraging him with gentle pats on the back to disgorge the pocket of wind which was stubbornly refusing to come out. "Come on, Jamie," he said, holding the baby up before him. "A nice big burp for Daddy." Finally it came, with an improbably loud, belching sound, and Patrick laid the baby back into his cot with an exhausted laugh.

He made tea and took it back to bed. Buffy propped herself up on the pillows with a sigh which could equally well have been

9

an expression of domesticated contentment or of impatience at her prolonged confinement.

"Thank heaven you're home," she said. "I've been going mad."

It's not exactly been a picnic for me, he thought. With the bulk of the Foreign Office emergency consular staff diverted to help victims of the Asian tsunami, he had just spent three weeks having to deal, virtually single-handed, with the aftermath of a dance hall fire in the Dominican Republic which had killed fifty-seven people, many of them British. Co-ordinating the activities of the forensic experts, managing the expectations and emotions of the bereaved families and battling with the local authorities over a myriad bureaucratic procedures had sucked him dry of physical and spiritual energy. (Then there had been the business with the American Airlines stewardess. Would he never learn?) Thank heaven, indeed, that he was home. And, with a bit of luck, he could spin out production of his final report long enough to see the baby born and then claim his paternity leave.

"No more travelling for a bit, sweetheart," he said, snuggling up close to Buffy. "Not if I can help it."

They had ten minutes of quiet before Jamie began to cry again.

* * *

"So it's not working out for you, then?"

Turning from the kitchen window of her parents' house in Pinner, Alison Webster considered her mother's face. It was still undeniably beautiful, but it was showing signs of sagging. She wondered whether Ruth had deliberately chosen such an offensive formulation for her question or whether these things came naturally to her, much as a lioness unthinkingly rips the throat out of a wildebeest or a zebra.

"We're just taking a short break from each other, that's all,"

Alison replied, sitting down at the kitchen table and nursing a mug of coffee between her hands.

But the truth was that things were not working out. She loved Adam as much as she could ever love anyone, but her life had changed so absolutely over the last year that she desperately needed time and distance to take stock.

"You'll need a mat for that," said her mother, handing Alison a coaster to protect the table top, which glistened brightly, in common with every exposed surface in the kitchen. Ruth sat down, carefully holding a bone china cup and saucer. "You drink too much coffee," she went on. "Tea is far better for you."

Alison did not respond, but sat sipping her coffee. After a while, her mother said, "I knew he wouldn't marry you."

"That was my decision," said Alison.

"And very convenient for him it was, too," said Ruth. Alison knew that, in reality, her mother would have been even unhappier if she and Adam *had* been married. Ruth and Alison had fought about her relationship with Adam so many times. What, Ruth argued, could an impoverished diplomat – and , what was worse, a lapsed Roman Catholic – possibly offer the only daughter of a well-to-do Jewish family with her own successful career in law?

Never in a million years had Alison believed that Adam would propose to her. When he had done so, she knew it was in a moment of special vulnerability, so she had agreed in the first place only to move in with him. Six months of living together in his sparsely furnished flat off Archway had been a confusing blend of joy and domestic chaos. Given more time, they might have settled into an acceptable routine, but the sudden move to Singapore had proved a mistake.

She had tried to make it work. The heat and humidity had knocked her sideways on arrival, but she had not let this deter her from making a real effort. She had worked with disabled children. She had signed up with local clubs for archery and judo classes. She even allowed Adam to talk her into taking up tennis, although she was singularly useless at sports. But her unhappiness became worse. She missed her family. She missed her friends. And, more than she had expected, she missed her job.

It had been Alison's bad luck that her law firm was not represented in Singapore. There was no shortage of demand there for advice on British tax law, but the partners had recently decided to concentrate their immediate efforts overseas on Europe and the United States. Why, Alison wondered, had she not tried to get a job with another law firm, one with an office in Singapore? Was it because she was reluctant to burn her boats? Why else was she now planning to talk to Richard?

"Please, mother," said Alison. "Can't you give it a rest? I'm just visiting, okay? I haven't left him or anything."

The kitchen door opened and Alison's father appeared from the garden, where he had been planting spring bulbs. "Do I smell coffee?" he said.

"Harry, for God's sake, get those bloody boots off before you come in here," said Alison's mother. Her father complied with a conspiratorial grin to Alison and padded to the kitchen table in his socks.

"Here, I'll get you a coffee," said Alison.

"Good. Then I'll leave the pair of you to it," said Ruth. She gave Alison a look which managed to convey a poisonous combination of irritation and self-satisfaction. "If you're staying any length of time, I'll need to do a proper supermarket shop."

When she was gone, Alison and her father sat companionably at the kitchen table, drinking their coffee. The tension invariably created by her mother's presence had miraculously dissipated.

"Was she giving you a hard time?" asked her father.

"No more than usual," said Alison. "She seems incapable of thinking well of anything I do."

"She worries about you," said her father. "She just can't say it properly."

"You're too soft," said Alison. "Why didn't you walk out on her years ago?"

Harry Webster's face momentarily betrayed a hint of infinite sadness, as though this thought were one to which he was not a complete stranger. Then he smiled and shook his head. "Marriage isn't like that, Ali," he said. "There's so much that binds people together, you know."

They sat for a while in silence. Finally, Alison said, "Daddy, what am I going to do?"

"You love him, don't you?" said her father.

"Yes, of course I do."

"Then you must talk to him."

"That's easier said than done," said Alison. "He works so hard and he has so much responsibility. His boss is always travelling somewhere, leaving him to handle really difficult problems. I hardly ever see him."

"Then write him a letter. Write to him from here."

Alison laughed, despite herself. "Daddy, you've been reading too much Jane Austen," she said. "People just don't do that sort of thing any more."

"Write him a letter anyway," said her father. "Even if you don't send it, just writing it will help you sort things out in your own head."

Alison smiled at her father. "You're quite wise for an old fuddy-duddy, you know that?" she said. "I hope you're looking after yourself properly." This was not an idle remark. Both Alison's parents had aged subtly in the last year, and she detected signs of chronic tiredness in her father.

"Don't worry about me, Ali," he said. "Let's just try to get you properly sorted out."

* * *

The man standing, smoking a cigarette, in the corner of the gardens of the Sheraton Media Hotel in Jakarta, was very satisfied with his appearance. He might have been a businessman, possibly a sugar broker or a banker. He wore a dark tropical suit, a white shirt and a red and gold silk tie, which could have been bought on a recent visit to Thailand. His black shoes gleamed in the moonlight, courtesy of the shoeshine boy who plied his trade just outside the hotel entrance. The man knew himself to be handsome. His dark skin was smooth, his features neat, and his black hair hung thick around the collar and fell boyishly across his forehead.

The man pitched the cigarette end into the darkness, glanced casually at his watch and took out his mobile phone. With his back to the hotel lights he dialled a number and waited.

The phone was answered after three rings.

"It's me," he said. "We missed our chance this week, but I'm hoping for another very soon. I'll call you tomorrow."

He terminated the call and dialled a different number. "Can you speak?" he said. "Good, listen. I need more warning this time... Yes, I'm sure it's difficult, but you'll find a way."

The man switched off the phone and removed the sim card, which he stuffed into an empty cigarette packet. He strolled slowly back towards the hotel, tossing the cigarette packet absent-mindedly into the nearest waste basket. He would dispose of the handset at the airport.

CHAPTER 3

Someone died, who might have lived, because Adam White went for a drink on Friday night in the Long Bar at Raffles Hotel. He went there on a whim. He could have – he *should* have – gone straight home from the airport: he was exhausted enough. But Ali was away visiting her parents, and he badly felt the need to relax in company. So he decided he would have a beer. Just one beer.

And why the Long Bar? He might have asked the driver to wait, and had his drink at the airport. Or he could have gone to the penthouse bar at the Ritz Carlton, to gaze over his beer at the illuminated skyline of the Central Business District, a sight to rival Manhattan or downtown Los Angeles. He could have taken in some late night jazz at the Esplanade, or lost himself in a less fashionable venue in Chinatown or Little India. If he had wanted crowds, he could have mingled with the tourists at Boat Quay. But, for some reason he could not later explain, he told the driver to drop him off at Raffles.

A majestic bearded Indian in white uniform and turban whipped open the door of the Rolls Royce and greeted him with smiling courtesy, tactfully concealing his surprise that it was not the invariably immaculate High Commissioner who alighted from the highly polished car, but his slightly dishevelled Head of Chancery.

Even at this point, Adam might have chosen the first place he encountered, namely the Bar and Billiard Room, where according to legend a tiger had once been shot beneath the billiard table. It would have been far more relaxing to sip his ice-cold beer in the relative tranquillity of the historic bar, listening to the click of the billiard balls above the soothing rhythms of the resident musical trio.

But something impelled him to bypass the Bar and Billiard Room. Carrying his jacket over his shoulder, he traversed the interior courtyard of the hotel. He walked through the palms and frangipani trees, past the illuminated fountains, the boutiques selling Jim Thompson silk and Bulgari jewellery and the patio where the last, lingering diners sipped coffee under the stars, as they were serenaded by a Filipino band from an upstairs balcony. He ascended a flight of stairs, walked along a short covered walkway and pushed open the door to the Long Bar.

It had been a pig of a day. Adam had been wrenched from his bed at four o'clock in the morning by a call from the duty officer, who needed his approval to authorise the emergency medical treatment of a gap-year student who had contracted malaria during a visit to an uninhabited neighbouring Indonesian island. Adam had then been unable to get back to sleep, and had finally fallen into a troubled doze when his alarm went off to rouse him in time to go to the airport, with only a cup of black coffee to sustain him.

The ministerial visit was the absolute last thing he needed. Such visits were always nerve-wracking. If they went right, no one ever remembered, but there was no chance of anyone forgetting if they went wrong. Ministerial visits organised at twenty-four hours' notice were almost bound to go wrong. This one had been no exception.

Adam realised, with all the useless wisdom of hindsight, that he should have refused to take the visit on. The High Commissioner had been somewhere in Malaysia (Mary Bennett, loyally but infuriatingly, would not reveal the exact location). With the Chinese New Year only days away, people were already leaving town. And Adam himself was inundated with additional work, because the Commercial Counsellor was on leave and the Consul had fallen victim to the latest virulent strain of flu from north-east Asia.

But it would have been difficult to say no to the Foreign Office Minister of State responsible for Asia. He had been halfway through a regional tour when the Indonesian leg was cancelled because of a security alert. So what more obvious thing to do, but visit Singapore instead?

"We just want a call on the Prime Minister and the Foreign Minister," said the Minister's Private Secretary on the telephone from Bangkok. "You know, a general exchange about the region – Indonesia, Burma, EU-ASEAN, that sort of thing. The Foreign Minister will presumably give him lunch, so maybe he can have a late breakfast with local British businessmen, and the High Commissioner can give him dinner to meet the local movers and shakers. What do you think?"

"We can't guarantee the Prime Minister at a day's notice," said Adam. "In fact, I'm not sure it's appropriate even to ask." He made no mention of Andrew Singleton's absence. With luck, Mary could contact the High Commissioner soon enough to get him back to Singapore for the visit.

"Really?" said the Private Secretary, clearly unimpressed. "We've had no problem in Thailand. And the Indonesians were going to roll out the President. The Minister is, after all, carrying a personal message from the Prime Minister about the need to co-operate in the war on terror."

Adam forbore from pointing out that, if the Singaporeans really needed such a message, they should have been included in the original itinerary, not inserted as a last-minute substitute. "I'll ask," he said. "But they're pretty formal about these things here." *And your man is, when all is said and done, only a bloody, bollocking junior minister*, he thought. In the old days he would probably have said this out loud, but he was finally beginning to

17

learn the art of not saying literally everything that ran through his mind.

In the event, the Minister had had to make do with talks and lunch with his opposite number in the Singaporean Foreign Ministry. The Prime Minister was tied up with visiting United States senators. The Foreign Minister, a silken-tongued barrister of Indian origin, had long resolved to be out of Singapore whenever possible at Chinese New Year and had already left on a flight to London to visit his son, who was studying law at UCL.

The business breakfast was also very thin, and the High Commissioner's working dinner almost as bad. Mary had only been able to reach the High Commissioner by telephone late the previous evening, and Singleton had barely made it back in time for the meal. Adam had to admire the aplomb with which the High Commissioner, sun-burned, silver-haired and charming, had then taken charge. He explained, apologetically, to the Minister that he had been detained by meetings in Malaysia. He then went on, skilfully, to chair a round-table discussion which wrung the maximum possible information and insights out of the third-division experts Adam had been able to assemble in the time available. The Minister was to a degree mollified by this bravura performance. All the same, Adam had thought, Andrew was pushing his luck.

The atmosphere during the trip to the airport (from which the High Commissioner excused himself on the grounds that he needed to catch up on his paperwork) had been mildly strained. The Minister and the Private Secretary had discussed the Minister's London programme for the following week, leaving Adam to his chastened private thoughts. The final expressions of gratitude in the VIP departure lounge had been friendly enough, but Adam had not much liked the Private Secretary's parting shot. "We'll make sure a copy of the message on terrorism is emailed directly to the Prime Minister here," he said. "We don't want any further delays, and you clearly have a bit of an access problem."

Well, sod them, thought Adam. *At least they're out of the way and the weekend is coming.* He settled himself gratefully on to a bar stool and ordered a beer. Above him, serried rows of delicately carved, heart-shaped wooden fans flapped slowly backwards and forwards in unison. But they were only for decoration; the interior of the bar was heavily air-conditioned. Adam put his jacket back on as he felt the cold air penetrate his sweat-soaked shirt.

Adam looked around him as he waited for his beer. It was Friday night and the bar was packed and noisy. Virtually all the faces were white and most of them very young. It was curious, he thought. Walk into any other bar or restaurant in the hotel – Raffles Grill, for example, or the Tiffin Room – and you would find a true cross section of Singapore high society: Chinese and Indian businessmen and government officials; the occasional wealthy Malay; a Eurasian or two; and, in smaller numbers, affluent Japanese, Americans and Europeans, many of them permanent Singapore residents. But the Long Bar attracted a different group, most of them youthful expatriates. The noisy drinkers there were bankers, money dealers, lawyers, IT experts, junior diplomats or simply the well-heeled offspring of the older generation of permanent foreign residents. There were tourists as well. And occasionally a visiting cruise ship brought an older clientele, largely American, but they rarely lingered longer than the time it took to drink a Singapore Sling and have their photo taken with their arm around the ever-patient barman's shoulder.

The Long Bar was unashamedly over the top with its 1920s' decor: the bamboo furniture and ubiquitous palms, the peanut shells strewn across the wooden floor, the memories evoked of Somerset Maugham. And then, incongruously, there was the disco, Adam reminded himself, as the heavy rock music, which had been temporarily in abeyance, resumed on the floor above. Strictly speaking, it was not a disco, because the music was usually provided by a live band, but the effect was much the same. Even in the main bar, where he was sitting, conversation was rendered difficult by the pulsating sound coming through the ceiling. Upstairs in the disco itself, the only form of communication would be by wild gesticulation.

The barman had just handed Adam his beer when the door to the bar was thrust open and five uniformed policemen entered. This was a sufficiently unusual sight in Raffles Hotel for conversation to die rapidly around the bar. The music from the disco continued until two of the policemen went to the floor above and told the musicians to stop. The remaining policemen then moved from table to table asking people, very politely, to allow themselves to be subjected to a search. Adam showed his diplomatic identity card to the officer in charge, and asked what the police were looking for.

"Heroin," said the young Chinese police sergeant. "We've had a very reliable tip-off."

"I hope you catch them," said Adam.

"Thank you, sir," said the police sergeant. "We'll be some time yet. Please feel free to go, if you wish."

Adam drained the remains of the beer from his glass and looked at his watch. It was mid-afternoon in England. Ali would almost certainly be at her parents' house now. If he could stay awake, he would call her as soon as he got home. "Thanks," he said. "It's been a long day."

Adam was almost at the door when he heard sudden shouting from the disco above. He turned to see a young, dark-haired woman storming down the spiral staircase into the main bar, shaking off the hands of one of the policemen, who was trying hopelessly to detain her without seeming guilty of molestation. His difficulty was understandable, for very little of the girl's skin was unexposed. She wore a tight, strapless, pink top, which ended just before her navel, and a black mini skirt above bare legs and pink leather, ankle-length boots. She was also carrying a large

20

handbag, covered in some glittery material, with which she was aiming blows over her shoulder at the policeman.

The girl was in the main bar now and yelling at the top of her voice. "You can't search me! You've got no right to search me! Get your hands off me, you fucking fascists!"

The girl's physical appearance suggested Indian or Latin American parentage. But she spoke with the affected working-class accent of privileged British youth. Adam groaned to himself. "Calm down, Marina," he said. "They'll be fine once they've seen your ID."

The girl looked at him, wildly, for a moment before she recognised him. "Adam?" she said. "Fuck, that's lucky. Get me out of here."

"Just show them your card, Marina," said Adam.

"I haven't got it with me," she said.

"Do you know this young lady, sir?" asked the police sergeant.

"Her name's Marina Singleton," said Adam. "She's the British High Commissioner's daughter."

"You can vouch for her?"

"Yes, of course," said Adam.

"Then I suggest you take her home to her parents immediately," said the police sergeant.

"What about Dan?" said Marina, who appeared now to be more composed.

"Dan?" said Adam. "Who's Dan?"

"He brought me here," said Marina. "He's still upstairs."

"You can vouch for this person too?" said the police sergeant to Adam.

"I'm afraid not," said Adam. "I've never met him."

"Okay," said the police sergeant. "We'll search him. If he's clean, he can go with you."

"You've got no right to search any of us," said Marina, aggressive once more. "Just let him go, or my father will make an official complaint."

"Hang on, Marina," said Adam. "The police had a tip-off. They've legitimate cause to suspect anyone who's on the premises."

"Whose fucking side are you on?" shouted Marina. "I'm going to speak to my father right now. Give me your mobile."

Before Adam could respond to Marina's demand, a young man in jeans and a tee shirt was led, in handcuffs, down the spiral staircase into the bar. The policeman escorting him was holding a translucent evidence bag, which he showed to the sergeant.

Marina was suddenly very quiet. "Is he British?" Adam asked her. He was now alert, his tiredness momentarily forgotten. She nodded silently.

Adam spoke urgently to the police sergeant. "I'll need access to this young man," he said. "Are you planning to charge him immediately?"

The policeman looked at his watch. "It's late," he said. "First thing in the morning, I would think, if the substance he was carrying is what we believe it is."

"I'll be there," said Adam. He turned to the boy. "What's your full name?" he said.

"Daniel Charles Taylor," said the boy, white-faced and in a daze.

"Do you have parents here in Singapore?"

The boy was clearly terrified. "They're in England," he said. "I'm looking after the house while they're away."

"How old are you?" said Adam.

"Nineteen."

"Give me your parents' contact details and I'll try to get hold of them," Adam said. "In the meantime, say nothing until we can get you a lawyer. Are you happy for me to fix that for you?"

The boy nodded dumbly, then gave Adam the information he had requested.

The sergeant looked steadily at Adam. He appeared to be reconsidering the wisdom of his earlier decision to allow Marina to go, but in the end he simply said, "We shall need to ask Miss Singleton some questions in due course."

"Certainly," said Adam. "But, as you said before, the important thing now is to get her home to her father as soon as possible."

Adam regretted having let the High Commission driver go, but the Indian doorman rapidly spirited a taxi out of nowhere.

Once they were clear of the hotel, Marina rummaged in her bag and produced a mobile phone. Before she could begin to dial, Adam seized her wrist. "I thought you didn't have a phone with you," he said.

"Yeah, well," said Marina. "There was no way I was going to open my bag while the police were around."

"I should have realised," said Adam. "Your father would never let you leave the house without your identity card and phone. What gives, Marina?"

"Better you don't know," said Marina. "Now for fuck's sake let me make this call."

"Not until I've seen what's in your bag," said Adam, holding on to her wrist and pulling her closer, so that she could see the serious intent in his face. *Jesus, she's beautiful*, he thought. *Just like her mother must have been.*

"No way," she said. "Let me go or I'll say you tried to rape me."

"Grow up, Marina," he said. "Do you want me to take you straight back to the police?"

"You wouldn't."

"Try me."

"Alright then, fuck you," she hissed, and thrust the open bag into his face. The shock made Adam loosen his grip on her wrist; he was aware of her pulling away, dialling, and then speaking into the phone in Spanish. She spoke too fast for him to understand anything she was saying. Her tone was one of near hysteria. And every now and then she would interrupt an unintelligible stream of Spanish with the same apparently meaningless question in English. "Are we?" she would say. "Are we?" And, then again, "Are we?"

But Adam was only half listening to Marina's telephone call. He was staring, unbelieving, at the contents of her bag. Amidst the jumble of make-up, combs, tissues, sweets, notes and coins – and the diplomatic identity card Marina had claimed not to have with her – nestled eleven transparent sachets containing fine, white powder.

CHAPTER 4

The British High Commissioner's residence in Singapore sat on slightly elevated land, looking to the south-east across verdant gardens (whose extent had, however, recently been brutally reduced by the sale of part of the land to fund Foreign Office capital expenditure elsewhere in the world). It was a fine example of early twentieth-century colonial architecture which had been, in its time, a private home, a boarding house, a brothel and a billet for both Japanese and British army officers. At night, bathed in moonlight (augmented by powerful security lights), its grey and white decorated facade took on the appearance of a magical palace, conjuring up images of Britain's glorious imperial past.

It was well after midnight when the taxi arrived. Adam paid the driver at the gate and walked in silence with Marina up the long driveway. As they turned the bend leading to the final approach to the house, Marina suddenly began to cry and turned to Adam in supplication.

"Please, Adam," she said, sobbing. "You're not going to tell him, are you?"

"Are you serious, Marina?" he said. "How can I not tell him?"

She dragged him by the arm out of the light illuminating the driveway into the shadow of a massive palm. "You don't know him," she said. "He hates me."

"Don't be ridiculous," said Adam. "He's your father."

"It won't make any difference," she said. "He's always hated me. It would be a great excuse to get rid of me."

25

"This is crazy," said Adam. "Back at Raffles you were all for calling him to come and rescue you."

"Yeah, well, I wasn't thinking straight, was I?" she said. "Anyway, I could have got away with it so long as no one actually looked in my bag. Trouble is, *you* know now." Her expression switched to a combination of lasciviousness and entreaty. "But no one else needs to, do they, Adam?"

Adam tried to gather his thoughts. He faced a difficult enough dilemma as it was, without the improbable complication Marina had just thrown at him. Drug traffickers were the lowest form of criminal life, and part of his job involved co-operation with the Singapore authorities to thwart their activities. But Marina was the High Commissioner's daughter, towards whom he had a clear duty of care. His hope had been that Andrew Singleton would find a way through the moral quandary.

"Look, Marina," he said. "It could be a lot worse. At least you have diplomatic immunity."

"Yeah, right," said Marina. "And how long do you think that would last once he knew the full story?"

"The full story?" he said. "What do you mean?"

Marina looked evasive. "Forget it," she said. "Just forget it. *Please*, Adam."

"I'm sorry, Marina," he said. "I have a responsibility to tell your father."

"Then I'm as good as dead," said Marina. She moved closer to him and looked up into his face. "Do you want that on your conscience for the rest of your life, Adam? Wouldn't that be a terrible waste?"

She was much too close now and Adam backed away. "Stop that, Marina," he said. "We have to discuss this seriously."

"Well then," said Marina, spitefully. "How about this? I'll say I have no idea where the drugs came from — which means you must have planted them in my bag in the taxi. Oh dear, what would everyone make of that, I wonder?"

"Don't be absurd," said Adam, although he realised that she was perfectly capable of making such an allegation.

"Just don't say anything, Adam," said Marina, emollient once more. "It can be our secret."

"Are you forgetting your friend, Dan?" said Adam. "He could well be facing the death penalty."

Marina shrugged. "He won't say anything to get me into trouble," she said.

"And that's it?" said Adam. "What about *him*?"

"What about him?"

"You don't care if he hangs?"

"He won't hang," said Marina. "He didn't have enough on him."

"It only takes fifteen grammes, Marina," said Adam.

"I'm telling you," said Marina. "He's not in any danger."

"That still isn't the point, Marina," said Adam. "No, I'm sorry. Either we go straight to the police or we tell your father. One or the other."

"We can't talk to him now," said Marina. "He won't be there."

"I don't understand."

"He'll be… I don't know, he just won't be there."

"Let's see, shall we?" said Adam, consulting his pocket diary and punching in the residence phone number on his mobile. It was a new phone and he had omitted to transfer the local Singapore numbers from his old phone, an omission he resolved to remedy the following day.

The phone rang for around thirty seconds before cutting to the answer phone. Adam left a message asking that the High Commissioner ring him urgently.

Marina looked relieved. "Look, Adam," she said. "I'll talk to him first thing in the morning, I promise. Can't we just leave it for tonight?"

Looking back on the conversation later, Adam would identify this as the occasion of possibly the worst decision of his entire life. He could find reasons for what he did. He needed badly to speak to Ali. He was almost dead with tiredness. It was now very late and he faced a difficult Saturday morning. And wherever Andrew Singleton was, even if he could be reached, there was very little he would be able to do about anything before the morning. But none of these, Adam later realised, were sufficient excuse for his stupidity.

"Okay," he said. "Give me the stuff and we'll try to work this out in the morning. But you'll have to tell me where you got it, so I can figure out a way of putting things right."

"Are you kidding?" Marina said. "Do you think I'm going to give it to you, just like that?"

Adam finally lost his patience. "Hand it over, you stupid little idiot, or the deal's off," he said.

"Have it your own way," said Marina sulkily, opening up her bag and allowing Adam to transfer the sachets of heroin to his jacket pockets. "But somebody's going to want that stuff back before long – or the money for it."

"Who's that, Marina?" said Adam. "Who did you get it from?"

Marina began to cry again. "Please, Adam. Don't make me tell you."

If he had been less exhausted, Adam would not have listened to her. And a moment's reflection would have persuaded him that Marina's fear of her father's reaction made no sense: he should just track Singleton down and dump the problem where it belonged – into his lap. But he was rapidly succumbing to fatigue, so he simply said, "We'll have to talk again about this very soon, Marina. I'll be in touch in the morning."

"Thanks, Adam," said Marina, moving closer to him again. "I'm really grateful, you know that."

"Go to bed, Marina," said Adam, pushing her away. He turned on his heel and marched back down the driveway, turning only once to make sure that Marina was safely inside.

"Good night, sir," said the guard in the gatehouse, a dark-skinned Indian in navy blue uniform. He picked up his telephone. "Will you be needing a taxi?"

"No, I'll walk, thanks," said Adam, who had no desire to hang around making small talk.

Adam walked up Nassim Road towards the Botanical Gardens and then turned towards Napier Road and home. His jacket hung no heavier than usual on his shoulders, but the heroin in his pocket weighed hard on his mind. He could not help imagining the headlines in the *Straits Times* the following day if he were now to encounter a random police patrol.

* * *

Andrew Singleton could not sleep. Objectively, this was inexplicable. He had had little enough rest the previous night. And he had spent most of Friday racing down the Malay Peninsula, in order to get back to Singapore for the highly inconvenient ministerial visit arranged by Adam White. The journey had been complicated by the need to drop Birgit off in Johor Bahru, so that she could pick up her own car and cross the causeway into Singapore. He himself had then cut across country to join the main highway from Kuala Lumpur and enter Singapore by means of the second crossing, a vast bridge spanning the western arm of the Straits of Johor. So there was no question of him not being tired.

He had pulled out all the stops to impress the minister at dinner, but he had left it to Adam White to take the visitor to the airport. He had, instead, settled himself down on a bamboo sofa on the upper terrace with a brandy and soda, and read through the bundle of briefing papers Mary Bennett had assembled in his absence. After being virtually incommunicado for the previous two days, he needed to get up to speed with world events before the weekend. He could not afford to disappoint his Singaporean friends, who expected him to be a permanent source of wisdom on the interlocking crises that affected British and Singaporean interests in the region.

He had leafed rapidly through a series of telegrams about Iraq and Afghanistan, about a stand-off between the United States and Iran over the latter's nuclear programme, and about increased tension between Japan and North Korea. Closer to home there were reports of ethnic and religious strife in Indonesia, a high-level corruption scandal in Thailand, and the detention in Malaysia of a number of suspected terrorists under the Internal Security Act. By contrast, the main news in Singapore was that the central government budget had once more returned to surplus. *How apt*, he thought, *was the legendary Lee Kuan Yew's description of Singapore as a good house in a bad neighbourhood.* The final item in the folder was a circular telegram to all posts, warning of a new, but unspecified, terrorist threat to British interests.

He had gone to bed shortly before midnight, physically weary, and ready for a full night's rest to prepare him for an early round of golf in the morning. But sleep had eluded him. Now, at close to one o'clock in the morning, he lay wide awake, thinking about Kirsty. Not about Birgit, with whom he was engaged in a delicious, illicit affair. Nor – thank God – about Elena. No, he was thinking about Kirsty, when she was nineteen, in all her virginal unattainability.

She had walked into the Students' Union at the London School of Economics during freshers' week, arm-in-arm with a bearded boy in an anorak. Exercising all the overbearing authority of a second-year student, Andrew had rounded her up for a darts match. He had watched, already light-headed with excitement, as she screwed up her eyes and stuck out her tongue in concentration when her turn came to throw. He could never have described her as glamorous. Her dark brown hair was all over the place. Her pink, scrubbed, angelic face was devoid of make-up. She wore a shapeless sweater over corduroy jeans and sneakers and shouted, "Och, bugger!" every time a dart bounced out of the board or – on one occasion – thudded into the wall. But she laughed all the time, and exuded such innocent joy that he knew then and there he wanted her.

He invited Kirsty and her friend to join him for a curry, along with the girl he was then sleeping with (whose name and face, in the air-conditioned bedroom in Singapore, where he now switched on his bedside lamp and searched for a cigarette, he could no longer remember).

He had behaved disgracefully during the meal. He knew he was good-looking, and he had a self-conscious way of running his hands though his hair, which in those days was blond and thick. Girls liked this, he had found, and he turned the trick on full blast for Kirsty's benefit, all the time gabbling knowledgeably about politics and economics and offering to be her guide to the mysteries of university during her first term. Kirsty's companion, who had been at school with her in Aberdeen, ate in sulky silence while she and Andrew laughed and argued. Andrew's girlfriend (what the hell had been her name?) stood up after the main course and excused herself, stony-faced, on the grounds of an overdue essay. The boy sat it out, grimly, until the restaurant finally closed. They stood outside on the pavement, in slightly spitting rain.

"I've got some beers at my place," said Andrew.

"Not tonight, thanks," said the other boy, who had wearied of the game at last. "We'd best be getting back."

Andrew turned to Kirsty, whose face was shiny with excitement." How about you?" he said.

"I think Ian's right," she said. "It's been lots of fun, but it's pretty late."

He was unprepared for this response and had difficulty hiding his disappointment. "Okay," he said. "See you around in the Union, I guess."

He lay in wait for her in the bar night after night until she finally turned up, this time accompanied by two other girls (whose names and faces, over thirty years later, were also now lost to him). Ever

31

hopeful, he went through the same routine of suggesting that they all go out for a meal (this time Chinese, as he recalled). True to form, Kirsty went home with her girlfriends afterwards, but this time he at least obtained her telephone number.

He finally took her out to dinner, alone, six weeks after they first met. He over-did things, taking her to a ridiculously expensive French restaurant in Charlotte Street and showing off in his conversation with the wine waiter. She scolded him for his extravagance. "Andrew, you idiot," she said, when he paid the bill. "You've just spent the equivalent of my grant for the whole term." Still, she had had a good time; they laughed all through the meal, he remembered. But she held him away when he tried to kiss her on the doorstep of her hall of residence. "Don't, Andrew," she said. "Don't spoil it now."

Their relationship lasted six months, during which he suffered agonies of frustration but felt as if he was permanently walking on air. They went to restaurants, pubs, jazz clubs and a string of parties together. He introduced her to the National Film Theatre and his enthusiasms for Truffaut, Bergman and Hitchcock. He guided her through some difficult elements in her economics course (although it was soon evident that she was a far more assiduous scholar than him). They were the best of friends. But still nothing happened in the physical side of their relationship. Kirsty relented to the extent of allowing him to kiss her goodnight when they parted at night. But her strict Presbyterian upbringing gave her the strength to resist the temptation to go any further, even amidst the universal permissiveness of student life in London.

Finally, one night he could stand it no longer.

"Christ, Kirsty," he said, as she pushed him, laughing, towards the door of her room. "Do I have to ask you to marry me or what?"

She looked at him, evidently startled. "Andrew, we're friends," she said. "Isn't that good enough for you?"

Maybe he had had too much to drink. Maybe his patience would have been stretched beyond endurance in any case. But he heard himself saying: "No, it fucking well isn't, and you know it!" He grabbed her round the waist and pulled her to him, violently, but she strained back away from him and he saw the sudden terror in her face.

"Oh, shit, Kirsty, I'm sorry," he said, letting her go and kneading his knuckles into his forehead. "I'm just so frustrated!"

There was a terrible, interminable silence. Finally, white but calm, Kirsty broke it.

"Andrew, let's face it," she said. "We're different, you and I. And I don't think either of us is going to change."

She left the sentence hanging in the air, but he knew what she was saying.

"Okay," he said tonelessly. "I'll see you around."

It was just before the Easter break, and he did not see her again for several weeks. When he did catch sight of her one evening in the Union bar, he was already sleeping with someone else. Kirsty was in any case with Ian. Andrew lifted his hand in an ironic salute and turned his back.

He wondered again, as he stubbed out his cigarette and switched off the light, what would have happened if he had had the perseverance to sustain the friendship beyond that initial, frustrating phase. Could they have become lovers, or even more? He had fantasised about it often enough in the past. 'Do you, Gillian Kirsty King, take this man, Andrew John Singleton, to be your lawful wedded husband?' *Andrew and Kirsty Singleton. Andrew, the faithful husband.* It sounded good. Who knew? Her stubborn morality, allied to the constant joy of her company, might just have tempered his own baser instincts. There might have been no Andrew the womaniser, or Andrew the dedicated bon vivant. *And certainly no Andrew the cuckold*, he thought bitterly.

He turned on his side. It was extraordinary where Kirsty had ended up. But then again, maybe it was in the stars all along.

Almost asleep, Andrew felt a sudden need to relieve himself. He was in the bathroom when the telephone rang; by the time he had extricated himself the caller had given up. *I must get the answering machine fixed,* he thought. But in any case it was almost certainly a wrong number, of which there had been an inordinate amount recently.

Unless, of course, Marina had got herself into some kind of trouble; but then he heard the front door bang closed downstairs, and the inimitable sound of Marina's ridiculous fashion boots on the stairs. Marina must be home. He looked at his watch: just gone one; not bad by her standards. That was, at least, one less thing to worry about for another day.

But he did not want to think about Marina. He did not even any longer want to think about Kirsty, because it was pointless after all these years. *Concentrate on Birgit,* he thought. *Think about those legs, and those wonderful, supple shoulders and the evil grin on that flawless face. Think about Malaysia, think about where you'll be together again in a few days' time. And above all, never, never think about Elena.*

* * *

Marina hurled herself fully dressed on to the bed and beat the pillow savagely with both fists. *Fucking Adam White.* How the hell was she going to explain to Pepe?

She supposed she should be grateful to Adam for rescuing her at the Long Bar. But why did he have to be such a fucking do-gooder, *coño?* It was a mess. She had to get the heroin back somehow. In the meantime, she had to play for time.

Marina undressed and crawled under the sheets, without removing her make-up. With her knees almost up to her chin, and her arms clasped tightly around them, she imagined she was in her mother's womb, safe, untouchable, away from all her current troubles. Elena had always protected her, given her everything she wanted. She missed her terribly. *"Mamá, Mamá,"* she whispered. *"¿Dónde estás? Te necesito…"*

She slept, but in her dream she was no longer in her mother's womb. She was, instead, on a yacht, sailing through a calm, blue sea. Elena was by her side, holding her hand, telling her that everything would be fine, that Pepe would sort things out, that she would have some unspecified treat when they got home. Then suddenly the sky darkened, and her mother was no longer by her side. And who was at the helm? She caught a glimpse of silver hair, but the face was turned away from her. *Could it be…?* The sea grew rough, and black waves began to break over the bow of the boat, each succeeding wave higher than the one before. She struggled to hold on to the safety rail, but was swept away into the freezing waters…

She awoke with a start, cold from the air conditioning, the sheets in a jumble on the floor. She put on a night dress and pulled the sheets back over her. She felt a deep pang of nostalgia for her childhood, as intense as a physical pain. Unexpectedly, she slept again, this time to dream of Adam White and cascades of packets of fine, white powder and the pale, terrified face of Daniel Taylor.

* * *

Adam lived in one of a number of so-called 'black-and-white' houses in Ridley Park, a pleasant, wooded area, west of the city between Tanglin Road and Holland Road. The area was named after 'Mad' Henry Ridley, who in the late nineteenth century had introduced rubber from South America into Singapore in the teeth of his colleagues' ridicule and disbelief. Houses such as those in Ridley Park, with white-painted walls and black half-timbering, were still to be found throughout the island. They had been built in the nineteen-twenties and thirties for senior British administrators and army officers. Many were now expensively rented to expatriate businessmen, but a number had been retained for British High Commission staff.

Half an hour after he had left Marina, Adam closed the door of the house behind him with a sense of temporary relief. He had made it this far. But what did he do now?

His normal approach to difficulties was to tackle them head-on. For most of his life this policy had served him well, although as he advanced through his thirties he was beginning to moderate his customary recklessness. But this problem was different, because there was no correct solution. If he took the heroin to the police, he would have to explain how he came by it. If he then told the truth, Marina would be in serious trouble. If he lied, which was not in his nature, the police would probably guess that he was lying – even if Daniel Taylor did not break down under questioning and name Marina. If he destroyed the heroin, and was discovered to have done so, that would be the end of his career. Even in the unlikely event that he got away with it, he would have to live with the knowledge that he had suppressed vital evidence. And if he didn't destroy it, what else was he to do with it?

The real question he should be asking himself, thought Adam angrily, was why he had not found Andrew Singleton and placed the responsibility where it properly lay. But he had not, and now he had to deal with the consequences.

Too tired to think of anything else, Adam wrapped the heroin in a towel and put it in an empty suitcase, which he then locked and placed on top of the wardrobe. Then he called the Foreign Office to report Daniel Taylor's arrest and pass on his parents' contact details. Finally, he called Ali.

Ali's father answered the telephone, but passed it immediately to her.

"How's it going?" Adam asked.

"Oh, fine," said Ali. "You know…" She sounded as though she was in the next room, not halfway round the world from him.

"Are your parents okay?"

"Sure, they're fine. Anything happening at your end?" Her voice was curiously flat, almost as though she were reading a script.

"It's been busy," said Adam. He wanted to say more, but thought better of it. "We had an unexpected ministerial visit today. I've only just got home."

"It must be really late, Adam," said Ali. "What time is it there?"

"About one-thirty," said Adam. "Look, I'm pretty beat, Ali, and I've got an urgent consular case to deal with first thing in the morning. I'll call you again tomorrow – I mean tonight. Tomorrow for you. Okay?"

"Are you alright, Adam? You sound odd."

"I'm okay, Ali," he said. "I'm just a bit knackered, that's all. Speak to you later."

Afterwards, he sat reflecting on their stilted exchange. He had known Ali, altogether, for a year and a half. With her crooked nose and terrible temper, she had been an unlikely candidate for ending his bachelor days. "I've got my father's looks and my mother's temperament," she had warned him in their early days together. But she had got under his skin like no other woman he had ever known. Their six months living together in London had not been without problems, but he could not imagine his life without her. Singapore had changed things. Despite being worked off his feet, he had – at least until recently – thrived on it all, throwing himself into the local scene, playing tennis, coaching a local youth soccer team, and wanting to explore every corner of the island. But Ali had seemed diminished by the experience, even when she got over the initial shock of the climate and took up new interests. They had had no fights (there had been plenty in London, mainly because he did not share Ali's obsession for tidiness). She simply became progressively withdrawn.

If he had been less busy, they would have talked properly

about things long before now. Her announcement that she was going home to visit her parents had come out of the blue, but it had not really been a surprise.

Adam looked at his watch and winced. He hauled off his clothes, climbed into bed, set the alarm for six in the morning, and turned off the light. *Jesus*, he thought, *life's complicated – or rather, I've let it become complicated.*

CHAPTER 5

Mary Bennett lay in bed, watching Muzafar dress for work. He did so with precise, economical movements, which she found fascinating in a man. Soon he was ready, in grey slacks, black loafers and an open-necked white shirt. He came to the bed to kiss her goodbye.

"Do you really have to go so early, Muzafar?" she said. It was barely six-thirty and she had wanted him to lie with her for another half hour or so. "I can easily give you a lift."

"No, Mary," he said. "You mustn't do that." She knew that he was shy of being seen by her neighbours in Medway Park. He would rather slip out into the side road and walk through the back streets to the main road, where he would then catch a bus down to the port.

"Shall I see you tonight?" she asked, knowing already that it would not be possible; Muzafar invariably had a family commitment on a Saturday evening. For them to have met on the Friday evening – when Muzafar had told his parents he was joining a friend in prayer at a mosque on the other side of the island – had been daring enough for one weekend.

"I'm sorry, Mary," he said. He hesitated a moment and then said. "It would be so lovely if we could go away together over Chinese New Year, just for one night somewhere."

Mary frowned. "I don't think the High Commissioner's going away," she said. "He likes me to be around whenever he's here, in case something urgent crops up."

Muzafar looked disappointed. "So will he be here all week?" he said.

"I'm not sure," said Mary. "He's certainly not going anywhere on Tuesday or Wednesday, because he's accepted Chinese New Year invitations on those days. He did say something about possibly escaping for a couple of days at the end of the week."

"If he is, perhaps we could go away then," said Muzafar hopefully. "Can you find out for sure as soon as possible?"

"That would be lovely," said Mary. "Perhaps we could go to Tioman or somewhere like that. But will you be able to get time off?"

"I'll try," said Muzafar. "But I need to know if you're free before I ask."

* * *

The eighteenth hole of the old island course at the Singapore Island Country Club was a par three, but Andrew Singleton had never completed it in less than four. The tee and the green were at more or less the same elevation, but the fairway linking them ran through a steep-sided miniature valley, flanked on either side by unforgiving rough. If your ball was not struck straight, it would almost certainly be lost. If it was straight, but fell short of the green, it would roll backwards down the slope into the valley. If, in your anxiety to avoid this fate, you over-clubbed, your ball would play ducks and drakes across the green and disappear into a thick hedge behind. But worse was to come. The green was angled steeply towards the tee. So even if, with your second or third shot, you somehow managed to get the ball to come to rest on the green, you were faced with the prospect of a heart-breaking putt. From whichever direction you approached the hole, anything less than perfect accuracy and pace would be rewarded by an agonising parabolic curve that finally petered out into an unstoppable downhill roll, taking the ball off the green and, in the worst case, back down into the valley.

Andrew was not thinking about any of this when he struck the ball off the tee. Despite himself, he was thinking, again, about Kirsty. And so, in accordance with the perverse laws of golf, the ball rose, straight and true, to the perfect height. It fell almost vertically on to the far fringe of the green, where its backspin was sufficiently arrested by the slightly longer grass to ensure that it trickled slowly back down and came to a halt, a metre at most from the flag.

"Andrew, have you sold your soul to the devil?" said his partner, a slender Chinese with greying hair.

"I can still quite easily mess it up, T. K.," Andrew said.

"Better not," said Lee Tek Keng, who was busy reading a text message on his mobile phone. "Bill's given me ten to one against you getting a birdie. I've got a thousand dollars riding on this."

Bill Tan was managing director of Lee Tek Keng's shipping business and was playing in the four immediately behind them.

"US or Sing?" asked Andrew.

"No, Sing," said Tek Keng, with a laugh. "You've been pretty hot today, but I don't have *that* much confidence in you!"

Tek Keng's own shot hit the thick rough on the downside of the green and, against all odds, held its position on the brow of the hill. The two men stood back to allow their opponents – a Chinese heart surgeon and an Indian High Court judge – to take their shots. Tek Keng was furiously texting again, no doubt trying to tempt Bill Tan into accepting a further bet of some kind. Andrew never ceased to marvel at the Chinese compulsion for gambling. There were multiple bets of all kinds between him, Tek Keng and their opponents (who had both landed in the valley and were clearly in for a painful and expensive conclusion to their round). But Tek Keng was placing side bets with friends around the golf course on the progress of the individual players in their respective matches. How they kept track of everything was a minor miracle, but all debts would be settled one way or the other over beer and lunch after the game.

The other two golfers had now hacked their way on to the green and putted close to the hole. Tek Keng overhit his chip, and the ball disappeared into the hedge beyond the green to the accompaniment of vigorous Hokkien obscenities. "That's me out," he said to Andrew. "It's all down to you, High Commissioner."

Andrew's ball was uphill from the hole, but it was a straight putt. He closed his eyes as the putter briefly kissed the ball, and kept them closed until he heard Tek Keng's exultant and impenetrable cry: "One time!"

He opened his eyes and saw the ball hovering tantalisingly on the lip of the hole. Then, miraculously, it dropped. "I think I'll have lunch on you, T. K,." he said to his delighted partner, who was already texting the good news to the unfortunate Bill Tan (who had, however, won a forty-thousand dollar accumulator at the races the week before and would not be overly troubled by today's losses).

After they had showered and changed, Tek Keng and Andrew joined a group of friends for lunch on the terrace looking down over the lush, green, undulating course. In the distance, to the north, beyond the surrounding lakes and jungle, the high-rise buildings of Woodlands were visible. Behind Woodlands lay the causeway linking Singapore to Malaysia; on a clearer day than today it would have been possible to make out the tops of the higher buildings in Johor Bahru.

When they had all eaten their fill, and the good-natured banter and settling of bets had petered out, the group began to break up. Tek Keng took Andrew to one side and suggested that they have another coffee; he particularly wanted to pick Andrew's brain about developments in Indonesia.

"It's serious enough, T.K.," said Andrew. "But we certainly don't judge it to be terminal."

"What do you mean by 'terminal'?"

"The place isn't going to break up," said Andrew. This was

the nightmare vision for Singapore: a tide of anarchy washing on to her peaceful shores from the disintegrating giant to the south, disgorging refugees, agitators and violent criminals, and filling the surrounding seas with piracy and other unspecified mayhem.

"Maybe not," said Tek Keng. "But is it going to be taken over by Islamic extremists?"

"That's also a pretty improbable scenario," said Andrew, "particularly since the Indonesians have had a directly elected president, who seems to enjoy strong popular support. They may have been struggling a bit since the tsunami, but so have all the other countries affected. You can never rule anything out in Indonesia, but we're certainly not expecting radical Islamists to seize power."

"Do you think the armed forces would tolerate it if it happened?"

"I'm not sure the armed forces have a coherent position on the subject," said Andrew. "And if popular pressure was sufficiently strong, what could they do about it without risking all-out civil war? But honestly, T.K., that's such an outside possibility."

"It would be very bad news for us," said Tek Keng gloomily. "And it would give some people here funny ideas."

This surprised Andrew. "Really?" he said. "I'd say your Moslem community was a pretty contented bunch. We're always quoting Singapore as a model multi-cultural society."

"That's what we all thought," said Tek Keng, "Until Jemaah Islamiyah raised its ugly head."

"Well, okay," said Andrew. "That was a shock to us all. But surely that's all pretty well wrapped up by now."

"They've only got the ones they know about," said Tek Keng.

Andrew looked at his friend in frank disbelief. "T.K., are you seriously saying that your tiny Moslem minority could ever be a serious threat to stability in Singapore?"

Tek Keng looked at him grimly. "Look, Andrew," he said. "I employ a lot of Malay staff. I can tell you they're no longer as compliant and uncomplaining as they used to be. They sense their chance may be coming."

"Chance for what?" asked Andrew. "You don't think they're expecting some kind of takeover, do you?"

"Who knows?" said Tek Keng.

"Oh, come on, T.K.," said Andrew.

"I'm telling you, Andrew," said Tek Keng earnestly. "This is a very violent region. Just because things have been reasonably stable for a few years doesn't mean it's going to last. They've still got plenty of problems in the Philippines. Cambodia's pretty fragile. Who knows what could happen if things got out of control in Indonesia?"

Andrew was now genuinely perplexed. "Hang on, T.K.," he said. "You're letting your imagination run away with you. Maybe your staff are more assertive than they used to be, but that's just a sign of the times. Your own government's encouraging a move away from the old rigid disciplines. People pick up on these things."

"It's more than that," insisted Tek Keng.

"But are your Malay employees any different from the Chinese or the Indians?"

Tek Keng shrugged, suddenly strangely quiescent after his outbreak. "Maybe not. Maybe I'm imagining it all. But Indonesia makes me nervous, Andrew, I can't help it."

* * *

Adam was thankful to have the pool to himself. Saturday morning was usually a quiet time, when High Commission staff and their families were doing their weekly shopping. He had only half an hour or so to spare, but had decided that a vigorous swim would help him get his thoughts in order.

It had been a grim morning. The ringing of his alarm clock had interrupted a vivid erotic dream involving Marina, fragments of which kept returning while he showered, despite his efforts to dismiss them. He had managed to contact the High Commission Legal Adviser before the latter left for his Saturday morning golf. Adam had persuaded him to detail one of his criminal lawyers to meet Adam at the jail where Daniel Taylor was detained.

The boy had seemed even more terrified than he had the night before. Adam and the lawyer, a mournful young Indian called Inderjit Singh, had spent two hours watching Daniel protest his tearful innocence under interrogation. His story, from which he would not be shaken, was that he had no idea how the packet of heroin had come to be in his pocket the previous evening.

Finally, the police called a halt, and Daniel was led back to his cell. The lawyer told Adam that the boy could be held for a maximum of forty-eight hours without charge. If he was charged, Singh would apply for bail once he had had a chance to speak to Daniel's parents, but he was not hopeful of success. "There were fifteen point three grammes of heroin in the packet, Mr White," he said. "So the presumption is that he was trafficking. You know what that means."

"But he's patently not a trafficker," said Adam. "They must be able to see that."

Singh gave Adam a weary look. "I know of only one recent case in Singapore where someone caught knowingly in possession of that amount of heroin has escaped the death penalty," he said. "His defence was that he was an addict and had the drugs exclusively for his own consumption. Amazingly, the judge accepted the argument and he got away with a prison sentence."

"You said 'knowingly in possession'," said Adam. "But he claims he didn't know he had the heroin."

The lawyer gave the faintest of smiles. "That is indeed what he claims," he said. "I just hope we can find some way to prove it."

After leaving the lawyer to talk again to Daniel about his possible defence, Adam had come to the High Commission to send an e-mail to the Foreign Office with a detailed report, the gist of which he also gave by telephone to a sleepy night duty officer in London. Then he rang the High Commission duty officer to instruct him to let the High Commissioner know what was happening and to refer any press enquiries to Adam.

As Adam thrashed his way up and down the pool, he continued to wrestle with the impossible, and unnecessary, dilemma he had created for himself. Why should Marina survive unscathed while her hapless boyfriend was in such danger? He should take action now, before it was too late. But he had foolishly undertaken not to talk to Marina's father until she had had an opportunity to explain herself. And now, inevitably, she was not answering his telephone calls.

Adam was no nearer resolving his problems when he became aware that someone had entered the pool area. He paused and looked up to see Mary Bennett, dressed chastely in a one-piece swimming costume, smiling down at him as she pushed a wayward strand of light brown hair under her swimming cap.

"Leave some water for me, Adam," she said, and dived in, still laughing. He watched Mary swim slowly up and down the pool using an easy crawl, and wondered why he couldn't be in love with someone like her. Someone sweet-natured and athletic, someone who, at one time, he had even thought might be attracted to him.

Mary stopped swimming and hung on the edge of the pool, waving her legs idly back and forth in the water. "Do you feel like a game of tennis later on, Adam?" she said.

"I can't, Mary," said Adam. "I told Jane I'd look in on her and then I've got football training. And I promised the High Commissioner I'd show my face tonight at a children's concert in the Prime Minister's constituency." *As if that was all I had to worry about,* he thought.

"You do too much," said Mary. "You need a break. You should have gone back to England with Alison for a bit."

Adam did not reply, and for a while they lounged lazily in the pool, thinking their own thoughts.

"By the way," said Mary after a while. "Did the High Commissioner say anything to you about going away next week, at all?"

"He may be planning to go off somewhere on Wednesday evening," said Adam. "He passed on one of his Chinese New Year invitations to me."

"Any idea how long he'll be away?"

"Not really," said Adam. "You're the keeper of the diary, Mary. You'll be the first to know when he makes up his mind."

* * *

Golf and several beers at lunch had left Andrew convinced that he would sleep a peaceful siesta, but the telephone rang before he had even closed his eyes. It was the duty officer bringing him briefly up to speed with a consular case Adam White was handling. He then felt so sleepy that he switched the phone through to the duty maid, with instructions not to call him except in an emergency. He closed his eyes, but this time it was his mobile which rang. It was Birgit.

"This is rather daring," he said. Their normal rule was to call from outside telephones, usually at a restaurant or a club. Birgit was calling from her mobile to his.

"I can't get out of the house this weekend," she said. "Dieter's got friends staying and we're all playing some stupid tennis marathon." She laughed wickedly. "In case you're interested, I'm in the shower room now with nothing on."

He was instantly aroused. "When can you get away?" he said.

"Dieter's away somewhere in Central Asia all next week. You choose."

"I'm free from Wednesday afternoon. Maybe we can manage two nights again."

"Maybe. Where shall we go?"

"Malaysia again?"

She groaned. "No, Andrew, please," she said. "Not another of your primitive islands."

"Well, you suggest something," he said.

"I want a bit of luxury," she said. "What about Bintan?"

"That's a bit close to home, Birgit," he said.

"Not if we're careful," she said. "We could travel separately. We don't even have to book into the same hotel. Just as long…" She paused, and he could imagine the grin spreading across her face. "Just as long as your room has an enormous bed and twenty-four hour room service."

It was tempting. The ferry from Singapore took only forty-five minutes to reach the Indonesian island of Bintan, along the north-east shore of which stretched an array of luxury resorts looking out over white sands and palm trees towards the South China Sea. Because of its proximity, he had never before seriously considered it for one of their sexual encounters. But Birgit was right. If they were careful, why not?

"I'm half convinced," he said. "I'll call you tomorrow to confirm."

"*Verdammt noch mal,* Andrew," she said. "Decide now. I'm already weak with anticipation. The uncertainty will kill me."

He knew her well enough to know that instant capitulation would be a mistake. "Tomorrow," he said. "Now put your clothes on and be a good little *Hausfrau* while your husband's around."

* * *

In normal times, Jane Rosendale was a plump, rosy-faced and bubbly woman, full of energy and enthusiasm, ever helpful to the distressed British citizens who beat a regular path to her door, a vigorous chairperson of the High Commission Social Club committee and, in what spare time she could carve out, an inveterate traveller around the region. It had been during a trip to southern China, her doctor in Singapore suspected, that she had contracted the influenza which had now laid her low. Adam was shocked at her haggard, yellow face and the weakness in her voice.

"Jesus, Jane," he said. "You look like hell!"

"Thanks a bunch, Adam," she said feebly, as she adjusted her pillow. "You always were good at cheering me up."

"Have you got everything you need?" he asked. He had brought the usual cargo of fruit and magazines, but Jane had shown little interest in them as he placed them on her bedside table alongside assorted medicines and glasses of fluid.

"A new pair of lungs would be nice," she said. "What's happening in the outside world? I've not even had the strength to listen to the radio."

Adam told her the main world news and then mentioned the drugs case. "Oh, Lord," she said. "That sounds really serious. Tell me all the details."

When Adam had finished, Jane looked worried. "Adam, did you actually appoint his lawyer for him?" she said.

"Yes, of course," said Adam.

"That's not strictly according to the book," she said. "You're supposed to give him a list of lawyers and let him choose."

"We didn't have time for any of that," said Adam. "And surely he can't go wrong with the Legal Adviser's man?"

"That's not really the point," said Jane. "It's supposed to be his choice. If he doesn't feel he was adequately defended, it could come back on to us."

* * *

The flat was far more cheerful than Alison remembered it. There were brightly coloured scatter cushions on the neatly made bed, flowers in a glass vase on the table by the gas ring, where Janet was busying herself over making coffee, and an intriguing set of Victorian prints hanging on the walls. An Indian rug covered much of the small floor area and a plain pine bookshelf held a full complement of books. What looked like a brand new fan heater directed a steady stream of warm air towards Alison's legs, where she sat on one of the two chairs in the tiny basement bedsit flat.

Alison picked up a framed photo from the bedside table. It was of her, Adam and Janet, sitting cross-legged on the grass, somewhere on Hampstead Heath. It was summer. They were all grinning broadly and raising their glasses to the unknown photographer (a passing dog-walker, as she recalled). Janet was painfully thin in the photo, but she looked happy. *As do we*, thought Alison, looking in wonder at the beautiful, sunny-natured man into whose hands she had committed her life only weeks before the photo was taken.

"Would you like a doughnut with your coffee, Ali?"

The Glaswegian accent was no less strong. But something had changed. For one thing, Janet had definitely put on weight. You could never describe her as anything other than thin, but there was an undeniable aura of healthiness about her which had not been there six months ago. Yet it was more than that. She seemed more confident, almost assured.

"Janet, you know about my hips," said Alison. "How can you ask me such a thing?"

"I'll take that as a yes," said Janet, handing Alison a mug and a plate.

"You look really well, Janet," said Alison.

"I feel great," said Janet. "You look absolutely terrible."

"Oh, I'm just a bit jet-lagged," said Alison. She was taken aback by Janet's directness.

"Come on, Ali," said Janet. "I'm not that dim."

Alison said nothing. Adam was the single most important person in the world for Janet, and she did not want to cause her any distress.

"No, really," she said. "It's colder than I'd expected and I'm feeling pretty tired."

"Alison, listen to me," said Janet. "You and Adam saved my life."

"*Adam* saved your life, Janet," said Alison.

"You both did," said Janet. "You did it together. And I'm cured now. I'm clean. Have you any idea what that means to me? I've a job. I'm playing squash. I've started making other friends." She paused, suddenly shy, and then went on. "I've even got a boyfriend now. And it's all thanks to you."

"I thought so," said Alison. "I could see there was something about you. Tell me about him."

"That can wait," said Janet. "Tell me what's up with you and Adam."

"There's nothing up," said Alison, but she knew she did not sound convincing.

Janet said nothing. Unblinking, she looked at Alison and waited.

Suddenly, without warning, Alison was crying and saying things she had only half-thought until now. "Oh, Janet, I've been so unhappy," she said. "I've been homesick and miserable, and guilty because I felt disloyal to Adam, and it's all mixed up in my mind and I don't know what to do. Oh, bollocks, I'm sorry, I didn't mean to unload on you like this. Oh, shit, what a mess… "

Janet crouched next to Alison's chair and put an arm around her shoulder.

"Listen, Ali," she said. "I've known Adam all my life. When we were teenagers, I kidded myself he'd marry me one day, although I don't think I ever really believed it. He's the best man in the whole wide world, but I doubt that he's the easiest to live with."

"It's not that," said Alison.

"It's part of it," said Janet. "He's not the tidiest of men."

"That's true," said Alison, laughing despite herself. "But, honestly, that's not really it. I just missed so much of my life here."

"Did you tell Adam?"

"No, not properly," said Alison. "He was always so busy and it didn't seem fair to trouble him."

"He'll understand," said Janet. "He loves you, we both know that. Talk to him, you silly girl."

"Okay," said Alison, now more composed. "I promise I will. I really will." She wiped her face with a handkerchief and blew her nose. "I'm fine now, really I am," she said and took a bite from her doughnut. "Now tell me about this boyfriend."

* * *

The man selected a mobile telephone from the six remaining handsets in his briefcase and dialled a number. Through the window of the first-class lounge at Ninoy Aquino International Airport, he surveyed the lights of three aircraft taxiing in line along the approach runway in preparation for take-off. His name – the name he was currently using – was on the passenger manifest of the leading aircraft, which was scheduled to depart from Manila for Bangkok in twenty minutes. But he was a no-show, a fact which would be rapidly registered by any intelligence service whose attention he might, despite his scrupulous care, have attracted in the previous forty-eight hours. With luck, therefore, they would shortly be looking for him anywhere but in Bangkok.

The telephone was answered. "Can you talk?" he said. "Good. Any news?… That's unfortunate. I was hoping we would know by now. Don't let me down again. I'll call tomorrow."

The lounge was virtually deserted. The man picked up his briefcase and suit bag and strolled towards the lavatories. He locked himself in a stall and removed his wig and all his clothes, except his underpants and socks. He donned a pair of combat jeans and trainers and a UCLA tee-shirt, and covered his shaven head with a baseball cap. Then he packed his suit, shirt and tie and black leather shoes, together with the wig, neatly into the suit bag, which in turn he placed in a large, scruffy holdall. He removed a Filipino passport from the hidden compartment at the back of his briefcase and put the current Indonesian one in its place. He then placed his briefcase in a cabin bag as scruffy as the hold-all. Finally, he removed the sim card from the phone he had just used and flushed it down the toilet. The phone itself, wiped clean, he placed inside the cistern.

There was a flight out to Ho Chi Minh City first thing in the morning which connected with a midday flight to Bangkok. He had checked availability, using an airport pay phone. He would buy his ticket with cash an hour before departure.

The continuing uncertainty was irritating. He could not keep the team on standby indefinitely. One more day was about as long as he dare wait.

CHAPTER 6

Exercise was Adam's unthinking cure for stress, and so he found himself jogging through the Botanical Gardens shortly before seven o'clock on Sunday morning.

Saturday had not gone well. First, one of Adam's star players had strained a groin muscle in football practice. Adam had then arrived late for the children's concert, because of confusion about the address on the part of the duty driver. The latter was an elderly Malay, whose astonishing anticipation and skill on the tennis court – Adam had yet to master his delicate top spin lobs – was not, sadly, matched by any navigational ability once he sat behind the wheel of a car. Worst of all, the telephone call to Ali had again been unsatisfactory, although the news about Janet had cheered him up a little. "Look, I'll write to you, Adam," said Ali finally. "I can't talk to you about anything properly on the telephone."

He ran along the side of the lake towards the conserved area of rainforest. A collared kingfisher, its plumage a flash of blue and white, sped low across the surface of the water in pursuit of breakfast.

What was Ali trying to tell him? Adam found himself analysing every word she had spoken, as though they contained a message beyond their literal meaning. Was she leaving him? Would her letter open with a treacherous formulation to the effect that this was the most difficult thing she had ever done in her life? Or would the dismissal be effected with tough love? *Adam, you and I both know things haven't been working out...* Or – please God, yes – did Ali simply mean what she said – that there were things she needed to get off her chest which she could not say on the telephone?

He also had the more immediate problem of Marina. He had called the residence several times to try to speak to her on Saturday, but each time the Filipino maid had said that she was out. If the High Commissioner had been home, Adam would have felt obliged to break his word to Marina and speak to him. But Singleton had been playing golf in the morning and when Adam called in the middle of the afternoon, he was told that the High Commissioner had given instructions that he was not to be disturbed. Adam could now think of no further plan than to go to the residence, after his run, in the hope of finding either Marina or Andrew there.

He entered the rainforest without breaking gait. In a typically thoughtful, Singaporean way, a labyrinth of discreet concrete paths, gently distressed by moss and algae, had been laid between the towering trees and attendant creepers and undergrowth, so that visitors might enjoy the wonders of nature without falling prey to poisonous snakes.

Adam turned a bend and saw, some way ahead, a couple walking side by side, their arms around each other's waist. They were dressed in shorts and vests, and had clearly also been running. But now they had slowed to a walk, engrossed in each other as they talked and laughed. She was slightly taller than he was and, as she turned to kiss him on the cheek, she ran her hand affectionately through his black hair. Adam slowed to a halt and turned off down a side path. *Good for you, Mary,* he thought. *And it's none of my business, but I hope you know what you're doing.*

* * *

Andrew Singleton ducked beneath the boom as he went about in the small racing dinghy. The boat paused, momentarily, in a windless interlude, before surging away, sails taut once more, as he pulled in the sheets and leant back, as far as he dared, to balance the force of the wind. *I'm getting a bit long in the tooth for this*, he thought, seeing that his opponent had gained several metres with a snappier tack, and could not now be caught before the finishing line. *What the hell*, he thought, easing the sheets slightly and coming a fraction off the wind to make the remainder of the run more comfortable. *The sun's shining and the lunch will be good.* And anything was better than being stuck in the house with Marina all day – always assuming that she was there and not already engaged in some unimaginable mischief elsewhere.

Andrew had not seen Marina since she had sallied forth on Friday evening looking like a cross between her mother and Britney Spears. "What a very striking girl," the Minister of State had said when, in defiance of Andrew's injunction, Marina appeared just as the Minister was climbing into the Rolls Royce. Thank God, the car had moved away before he was subjected to any of Marina's highly personal views on the Foreign Office in general, and her father in particular. This absence of contact did not alarm Andrew; they could often go for days without seeing one another. Marina was rarely out of bed before noon, and frequently began her evening socialising long before he returned home.

Marina was a problem to which Andrew saw no solution. She had her mother's looks and deviousness, but not, apparently, her ambition or intelligence. All her schools had complained that she was a disruptive influence, but Elena had defended her savagely against all criticism. Elena was not around to shield her any more, but her absence had made things worse. After several warnings, Marina had finally been expelled from boarding school on the eve of her A Levels, caught in possession of enough cannabis to keep the entire sixth form stoned for a month. Somehow the school had managed to keep the police out of the affair, but Andrew had then had no choice but to bring Marina out to Singapore with him and pray that she keep out of trouble. Singapore's notorious prudery and relative absence of crime was a double-edged sword: the dangers and temptations were relatively few, but the full weight of a harsh penal code fell on those who succumbed, irrespective of their nationality or parentage. No British citizen had been hanged or flogged since his arrival in Singapore, but he knew it was only a matter of time.

Marina was of age, beyond his control and clearly loathed him. He didn't exactly hate her himself: he regarded her with a kind of revolted fascination. He was not to blame, he kept reminding himself, for the beautiful monster Elena had left behind in his care.

* * *

Adam drove through the gates of the residence with no clear plan in mind, other than to force the truth out of Marina. He found her lying on her back by the swimming pool, wearing a skimpy, bright yellow bikini, designed to show off her golden-brown skin and jet-black hair to optimum effect. She opened one eye as he approached.

"Well, well," she said. "Sir fucking Galahad himself."

"Why didn't you answer my calls?" said Adam.

"I'm not your mistress," she said, rolling over on to her stomach and resting her chin on her hands so that he got the full benefit of her cleavage. "Although that could always be arranged."

"Marina, don't mess around," said Adam, pulling up a plastic chair and sitting down. "I need some straight answers from you."

"Or what?"

"Or I take the drugs to the police and tell them where I got them," he said. He had not planned to threaten her quite so directly, but it seemed as good a ploy as any.

"Yeah, right," she laughed, sitting up. "And I'll deny it and it will just be my word against yours."

Adam was determined not to get stuck in this impasse again. "They'll do DNA tests," he said. "They'll be able to prove you handled them."

"But you'll still be involved," she said, although now with less conviction.

"I don't care," said Adam. "I want this sorted out once and for all."

Marina said nothing for several seconds. She was clearly debating with herself how serious Adam was.

"Okay," she said finally. "This is all I know, okay?"

Adam said nothing, allowing her to marshal her thoughts.

"I'm not into this stuff, you understand," Marina said. "I smoke, but I don't touch anything hard."

"That's good to know," said Adam, not entirely ironically.

"It was just that this friend wanted me to do him a favour, right?" Marina said.

"What friend, Marina?"

"I can't tell you that," she said.

"I need to know, Marina."

"No, you don't," she said. "Just let me tell the story, okay?"

Adam sighed. "Go on," he said.

"This friend called me from Kuala Lumpur and said he wanted me to carry something for him to Changi," she said. "I had to take the train to Johor Bahru and pick up a package from someone I'd meet in a restaurant there. Then I had to bring it back to Singapore, hang on to it for a few days, and then go out to the airport to meet someone who'd be in transit there and give the package to him."

"That sounds all very neat, Marina," said Adam. "But the stuff was in open packets in your bag."

There was silence for a while. "Yeah, well, you know me," said Marina finally, in what Adam took, perhaps too charitably, to be a rare moment of critical introspection. "Curiosity killed the fucking cat and all that."

"You opened up the package?"

"Well, I guessed what it was, and I thought I'd just have a bit of fun."

Adam could not believe he had heard her correctly.

"*Fun*, Marina?" he said. "Are you mad?"

"I couldn't see there was any real risk," she said. "Me being diplomatic and all that. And I got a real kick out of parading around Singapore with the stuff in my bag."

Adam looked at Marina in total disbelief. There had to be something else behind her outrageous statement. "Did it never remotely occur to you that you might get caught?" he said.

"Who was going to suspect me?" Marina said.

"Jesus, Marina," said Adam. "What kind of world do you live in? The police had a tip-off."

"Yeah, that did kind of change things," she said.

"And how did Daniel get involved?"

"Yeah, well I panicked, didn't I?" said Marina. "I had a packet of the stuff in my hand when I heard the police arrive and I slipped it into his pocket while we were dancing."

She was studying Adam's face to see whether he believed her. "I'd have taken it back from him afterwards," she added, as though this mitigated her criminal stupidity.

"Why, Marina?" said Adam. "Why did you have the packet in your hand?"

Marina shrugged. "I was having a little dare with myself," she said.

"Are you serious?" said Adam. He could not decide whether Marina was lying or terminally idiotic.

"It's the truth," she said defiantly.

"And are you telling me Daniel doesn't know the packet came from you?" said Adam.

"He hasn't a clue," said Marina. "So, you see, I've got nothing to worry about."

Adam was almost rendered speechless. "He could hang because of you, Marina," he said at last.

"No way," said Marina. "He didn't have enough on him."

"Yes, he did, you little idiot," said Adam. "He had over fifteen grammes."

Marina shook her head. "He can't have," she said. "They're very careful about these things."

"Well whoever 'they' are, they ballsed up this time," said Adam.

Marina was silent for a long time. Then she said, very slowly, "You got him a good lawyer, right? He'll get him off, won't he?"

Adam was praying that she was right, that the lugubrious young Indian would find some flaw in the police case, some forensic detail no one had picked up, some procedural omission; anything, anything which might get the case thrown out. But he said, "No chance, Marina. No chance."

Marina was silent again. Then she began to moan to herself. "Fuck, fuck, fuck, fuck, fuck." she said.

"Who supplied the drugs, Marina?" said Adam.

"Look," said Marina, recovering now and in negotiating mood. "I can tell you what the guy in Johor Bahru looked like and where he hangs out. I can tell you when and where I was going to meet the courier at Changi and give you his description. But there's no way I'm telling you who my friend is."

"Well, it's a start," said Adam.

Marina was warming to her story now. "Maybe I could tell the police that I overheard all this from someone else in the disco," she said.

"How would that help Daniel?" said Adam.

"I could say I saw this other person stick the stuff into his pocket or something," said Marina.

"That's fantasy land, Marina," said Adam. "The police would ask you to describe this other person. They'll have records of all the people who were there. You might wind up incriminating someone totally innocent."

Marina became sullen. "Okay," she said. "So what's your plan?"

"Come clean," said Adam. "Tell the police the truth, or as near as damn it. We'll hand over the drugs. You'll tell them everything you know, but say you had no idea what you were carrying, that you opened the package in the disco out of curiosity. You were so shocked by its contents that you panicked when the police came, and put it in Daniel's pocket."

"Great," said Marina. "So that's Dan out of trouble. Where does that leave me?"

"If you collaborate one hundred per cent, and your diplomatic immunity holds good, you might get away with just having to leave Singapore," said Adam.

Marina was quiet again. "Okay," she said. "I'll do it." Then, after a pause, "But can I at least tell my father first? I haven't been able to see him all weekend."

Adam knew he should say no. He should say that he had allowed Marina to prevaricate for far too long already, that they had to go the police immediately. But he heard himself saying instead, "Alright. But we go to the police tomorrow morning without fail." Then, as an afterthought, "When's the pick-up at Changi scheduled for?"

"What? Oh, yeah, Tuesday evening," she said.

"Okay," said Adam. "I've got a couple of things to take care of first thing. I'll come by to collect you at eleven. Where is your father, by the way?"

"Probably off somewhere with his German bitch," said Marina.

"I beg your pardon?" said Adam, taken aback.

"You heard me."

"I don't understand."

"No, you wouldn't," said Marina. "He's very discreet – or he thinks he is."

Adam had no time to delve into this latest bone of contention between Marina and her father. "He absolutely has to be told," he said. "As soon as you see him."

"Don't worry about that, Adam" said Marina, who did not appear disposed to argue. "I'll talk to him when I see him tonight. That's a promise."

"Good," said Adam, who was beginning to feel a little happier with life, although there was still something nagging away at the back of his mind that he could not quite put his finger on. "I'll see you tomorrow morning."

Marina, climbed to her feet as he stood up. "Why don't you stay for a swim and a drink, now you're here?"

"Sorry, Marina," said Adam. "I don't have my costume with me."

"I don't really see that as a problem," she said, reaching behind her for the catch to her bikini top, but Adam was already halfway to his car.

* * *

The Argentine Ambassador had collected his pennant amid scattered applause from the small group of weekend sailors who had stayed for the presentation. Now, he and Andrew made their excuses, and headed off together from the Changi Yacht Club for their pre-arranged lunch at one of the many open-air seafood restaurants along the East Coast Parkway.

"You seemed to have your mind on other things today, Andrew," said the Ambassador, as they settled down with beers and waited for their food to be served.

"Not really, Guillermo," said Andrew, although the Argentine was in fact close to the truth. "You're just too bloody good, that's all."

Guillermo roared with laughter. "That's also true," he said. "I am exceptionally fast in every sense of the word."

The Argentine Ambassador was one of those larger-than-life characters who gave diplomacy a terrible name, and for whose existence Andrew gave fervent thanks. No one had ever seen him do a stroke of work. He drank, chased women while his wife was away in Buenos Aires (although, as far as Andrew could determine, his dalliances were entirely innocent), and was frequently out of Singapore, pursuing expensive hobbies such as motor racing and hang-gliding. He was a former eight-handicap polo player and had once played, in a personal invitation match, as part of a team formed by the Sultan of Brunei, whose country was among Guillermo's many regional accreditations. He was also, as he had just demonstrated, an accomplished racing sailor.

Guillermo was famous in Singapore for his inimitably Argentine dinner parties. It was not just the free-range steaks and the vintage Mendoza wines. There was always music, laughter and dancing, and everything was done with an unmistakably Latin extravagance that eluded even the most hospitable of Andrew's other diplomatic colleagues.

Andrew had met Birgit at one of Guillermo's parties. She was there because her husband's company was engaged in a convoluted deal, financed by undisclosed European bankers, which brought together Argentine grain exporters with Malaysian traders, whose end buyer – but not their immediate customer – was the Chinese Government. Guillermo was explaining all this when he introduced them, but Andrew scarcely paid any attention. Nor, he was sure, did Birgit hear Guillermo's feeble joke about Andrew's most eligible bachelor status among the senior members of the diplomatic corps (he was in fact the only ambassador in Singapore without a wife at the time).

Andrew had been with many women in his life, but only twice before had he experienced anything resembling this kind of shock. With Kirsty it had been love. The first sight of Elena's exotic beauty had triggered an instant infatuation. This was different.

He knew she felt it too. She stood before him, unsmiling, tall and slender in close-fitting black silk, her shoulders bare, a pearl choker at her throat, her short blonde hair breaking very slightly over the forehead of her perfect face.

"High Commissioner," she said, still not smiling (the lazy grin would not manifest itself until much later).

"Frau Berger," he said in response.

For slightly longer than was wise, they stood silently looking at each other, after Guillermo had excused himself to greet some newly arrived guests. Then Andrew spoke, in as neutral a tone as he could achieve.

"Is your husband not here this evening?" he said.

"No," she said. "He travels a lot during the week." The accent was slight, but he guessed she was from northern Germany, possibly Hanover.

"That must be very boring for you," he said.

Still she did not smile. "I have a jewellery business," she said. "It keeps me occupied."

"Jewellery? That might interest my daughter," he said. "Perhaps you could give me your card?"

"I thought you were not married." So she had, after all, been listening to Guillermo's jocular introduction.

"My wife is dead," he said

"I'm sorry," she said, extracting a card from her bag.

"It was some time ago," he said.

He took Birgit's card and gave her one of his own in return, writing Marina's name on the back. "So that you know who she is when she calls," he said. *And*, he thought, *so that your husband does not ask what you're doing with the High Commissioner's card, when he inevitably stumbles across it one day.*

Guillermo had come back with more people for him to meet, and Andrew did not speak to Birgit for the rest of the evening. After the driver had dropped him off at the residence, he removed his jacket and tie and sat on the terrace for ten minutes or so, drinking a brandy and soda. Then he took out Birgit's card and called her mobile number.

"Berger," she said.

"Singleton," he replied. There was silence at the other end.

"Please say if this is inconvenient," he said.

"Unfortunately, I've given the maid the evening off," she said.

"I fully understand," he said and terminated the call. After briefly consulting a street atlas, he drove in his own car to the Swiss Club, where he parked and walked for five minutes through winding streets of detached houses of varying levels of luxury. The Bergers' house stood back from the street, the front door conveniently in the shadows.

He rang the doorbell and waited. Nothing. He rang the bell again. It crossed his mind, fleetingly, that there had been a misunderstanding. Then the door opened and she stood there, wearing a kimono, and he knew there had been no mistake.

"Chilli crab twice, mixed rice, green salad. You want more beer?"

Andrew nodded affirmatively to the waiter, and he and Guillermo set upon their lunch with the appetite earned by their morning's activity.

"Seriously, Andrew, what's up with you?" said Guillermo twenty minutes later, as he sucked the last of the chilli sauce from his fingers and wiped his chin with his napkin. "You're so goddamned quiet, I think maybe I've hurt your feelings or something. *¡Maldito sea!*" He cursed as a drop of sauce fell on to his otherwise immaculate chinos.

I'm quiet because I'm remembering the first time with Birgit, thought Andrew. He had felt like a heroin addict taking his first hit. It would never be quite the same again, but he could not stop himself from coming back, time after time, for more. And, like addicts, he and Birgit had created a secret world of deceit and subterfuge in which to indulge their compulsion undetected.

Singapore was too small for an affair to survive undiscovered for long. Servants gossiped, friends would spot you in the most obscure of restaurants, the hotel owner with whom you played golf would bump into you in the lift as you ascended to a midday tryst. So, after that first time, they had established a firm rule: they met only outside Singapore, travelling independently, and in places no one could expect to find them. A rule, he reflected, from which they were about to depart, if only slightly, thereby injecting an extra element of danger into a relationship already rendered that much more seductive by the risk of discovery.

He was also, perversely, yearning for his first, lost love, even though he knew that she was today a bespectacled, middle-aged bureaucrat. Her Highlands accent – like her now iron-grey hair – had long been tamed, her once lithe figure broadened by thirty years of a sedentary career. And her meticulous, logical mind was currently untroubled, he was sure, by any thought of the idiot youth who had come perilously close to raping her so long ago.

"Don't worry yourself, Guillermo," he said. "I'm just a bit preoccupied, that's all."

Later, he went to the lavatory and stopped off on the way back to call Birgit from the telephone behind the bar.

"Can you believe it," she said "We're all still playing tennis. I'm going crazy."

"Where are you?"

"I'm sitting this one out."

"Can Dieter see you?"

"Yes," she said. "But he's far too interested in winning to take any notice. He'll think you're just an importunate client." He wondered again at the precision of her English.

"I've decided you're right," said Andrew and gave her the details of the Bintan resort where he would arrange to meet her, together with his planned arrival and departure times.

"Excellent," she said. "I'll get there on the first ferry the following morning and leave on Friday evening. That gives us almost two whole days."

He was mildly disappointed. "You can't stay until Saturday and leave after me?" he said.

"It's too dangerous," she said. "Dieter's back at lunchtime on Saturday. I need to be home and all cleaned up in plenty of time. Besides, I'll need a rest to cope with him after a week away."

For the first time, he felt a stab of unreasonable jealousy at the mention of her husband.

"Okay," he said. "We'll just have to make every second count."

"If it's any help, my tennis shirt is soaked in sweat at the moment."

"It might if I weren't in a public place," he said. She laughed and cut him off.

* * *

Marina lay on her back by the pool in the heat of the late morning sun, her eyes closed. To the casual observer she would have looked asleep.

She was not asleep. Her mind was a ferment of fear and confusion. Pepe had told her that all would be well if they could get the heroin back, for then it would simply be her word against Adam's. She had even half thought that she might seduce Adam into an act of indiscretion, something with which she could buy his silence, but he had not seemed interested. What the fuck he saw in that prissy cow, Alison, she had no idea...

But what if Adam was right about her DNA being on the packet? She had watched enough television to understand that it was possible. Could the police oblige her to provide a DNA sample? Or could she refuse on the grounds of diplomatic immunity? Would they even think to ask for one? Dan wouldn't say anything to incriminate her, because he knew nothing. But would he then be found guilty of dealing rather than simple possession? Pepe had at first said that would not happen. Now he was saying it would tidy things up neatly. This wasn't what she had signed up for. Drug smuggling was one thing. It was a laugh, a thumbing of the nose at authority, a chance to make some easy cash. Nobody was supposed to die.

Marina suddenly remembered the day Elena had taken her to one side and talked to her about men. She must have been barely twelve. She could smell her mother's perfume, intermingled with the scent on her breath of whatever extravagant cocktail Elena had been drinking, something rum-based, with tropical fruit. She could see the diamond necklace around Elena's beautiful neck, the exquisite silk blouse and high-fashion slacks, the designer boots. She could not, distressingly, picture her mother's face, although she knew objectively that it was beautiful. But she could remember her mother's exact words.

"Most men are bastards," Elena had said. "The rest are fools. The bastards will give you a good time and the fools will pay for it."

Young as she was, Marina had had no idea what her mother was talking about. At the time, it had sounded profound, but so far in her short life all the men she had encountered had been fools. Maybe Pepe was the bastard…

Marina opened her eyes and sat up. Pepe had instructed her to find a way of getting safely out of Singapore and back. She had no time to waste.

* * *

Mary had been surprised, but delighted, when Muzafar rang early on Sunday morning to suggest they meet in the Botanical Gardens. They had run only briefly, because he had to get back to his family for the rest of the day. But he had promised to try to get away to spend some time with her in the late afternoon.

They were still shy of each other. The idea of going to

bed in the afternoon was just a little too much at this stage in their relationship. So they sat on her sofa, hand in hand, talking and kissing gently, making no plans (for neither of them dared look beyond the immediate future), just exploring each other's emotions and recounting stories from their very different pasts.

The telephone rang. It was the High Commissioner, apologising for interrupting Mary's Sunday.

"Mary, I'm going to Bintan on Wednesday evening and staying until Saturday," he said. "Could you get on to the bookings first thing in the morning, do you think? It will be the last day before the holiday and I've left it a bit late."

She took careful note on her message pad of the ferry timings and the resort details he dictated to her. "Make sure you get a villa with a pool," he said. "I'm going to be revising the draft human rights strategy and I'll need a bit of peace and quiet." He paused, then added, "Make sure you tell Adam that last bit – he's been on at me for weeks about it."

Mary put the telephone down and gave Muzafar a triumphant thumbs up. "The High Commissioner's away on Thursday and Friday," she said. "If I can square it with Mr White, we can go away too. It shouldn't be a problem – Sophie's back in the office next week."

Muzafar smiled at her. "That is wonderful news," he said. "I will speak to my boss in the morning and see if I too can be given leave."

"I'll make us some tea," said Mary, moving towards the kitchen.

"That would be lovely," said Muzafar. "Can I quickly use your phone to tell my mother what time I shall be back tonight?"

* * *

Half listening to one of the more melancholy tracks on Dido's latest CD, Alison sat staring at the screen of her laptop. Her brain was devoid of any coherent thought. Impatiently, she closed the lid of the computer and looked out of the window. Down below, at the end the wintry garden, she could see her father forking over the compost heap. She watched him for a full minute, willing him to stop and look up and wave to her. But he did not cease the regular rhythm of his movements. Over and over again, he dug into the mound of damp, rotting leaves and grass, lifting and turning repeatedly. Harry Webster had been in Shell's senior management structure, with responsibility for a large budget and hundreds of staff. Now all he seemed to want to do was tend his garden.

Ruth was at a bridge coffee morning. She had half-heartedly invited Alison to go along as well, but Alison knew that she would be happier on her own. Ruth had a particular circle of friends, all close to the – for them – terrifying age of sixty. Alison guessed that they spent most of their time complaining about the shortcomings of their husbands. Certainly, her mother had frequently relayed to her family over Sunday lunch the minor scandals and misfortunes affecting her friends, usually as the result of a sin of omission or commission by their spouses. It would be unlikely, and uncharacteristic, if Ruth was not giving as well as receiving in this gossip mongering.

Dido had finished singing. Alison changed the CD for a vigorous Haydn string quartet, hoping to be inspired to greater decisiveness. It had no effect. She stood up and wandered aimlessly around her room. Strictly speaking, it had not been 'her' room since she moved out to the flat in Earl's Court, three years previously. Her mother used it now for ironing and, when the mood took her, the occasional bout of sewing, but it remained otherwise unchanged. It had the same white-and-blue wallpaper she had chosen when moving back home after completing her law degree, the same (she grimaced) Laura Ashley mock-Victorian bed, with matching bedside table and chest of drawers, and the same framed prints of works by Klee and Klimt

– deemed by her to be too clichéd for her new flat, which she had decorated instead with cheap originals by an unknown artist she had discovered in a scruffy gallery in Camden Lock. *What a difference three years can make*, she thought. *Or six months, come to that.*

She flipped open the laptop, and typed very fast:

'Adam, you know how much I love you.'

She stared at the screen for several seconds, then deleted the sentence and typed instead:

'*I love you I love you I love you I love you I love you*'

She deleted all the words again and snapped the laptop shut once more. Maybe she would wait until she had seen Richard. Adam had sounded very busy on the telephone yesterday, almost as though he had no time to talk to her. Another twenty-four hours would make no difference.

* * *

Andrew was surprised to find Marina waiting for him on the terrace with afternoon tea when he got back to the residence. He and Guillermo had spun their lunch out well into the afternoon, exchanging titbits of information about who was on the ascendant (or not) in the relatively serene world of Singapore politics and – as they downed ever more beers – what the latest diplomatic scandal might be. The newly arrived Austrian Ambassador had a beautiful young Laotian wife who had attracted the attention of the French Cultural Attaché. Otherwise everyone seemed to be on relatively good behaviour, always excepting Guillermo himself, whose transgressions were so blatant they were rarely the subject of gossip.

The Austrian Ambassador had, however, caused a stir by complaining to the Foreign Ministry about the ERP: the electronic road pricing system. Every car registered in Singapore was fitted with a device containing a re-chargeable cash card, from which the appropriate toll was deducted when the car drove under the gantry marking the entry point to the ERP zone. The Ambassador had claimed that this was a tax, from which he should be exempt. He also said that the Singapore authorities were using the road pricing system to conduct covert surveillance. The Singaporeans had advised him politely to get lost, but Guillermo had some sympathy.

"I tell you, *ché*," he said. "They know where we are every hour of the day. Each time we drive in and out of the city centre – click! – into the records we go. The same if we travel at peak hour on the Pan-Island Expressway. And don't give me this bullshit that they destroy the records within twenty-four hours. I just don't believe it."

Andrew had laughed. "Listen, Guillermo," he said. "I drive around most of the time in the back of a chauffeur-driven Rolls Royce flying a bloody great Union Jack. Anyone who wants to know where I am only has to stand on top of the Ritz Carlton with a pair of binoculars." *All the same*, he had thought, *it's as well that Birgit and I stick to our rule.*

Marina was wearing the nearest thing she possessed to a modest outfit: a sleeveless, high-necked, white cotton shift. She did not look remotely demure, which was the effect she was no doubt seeking to achieve. But she was clearly on her best behaviour, which meant she must want something.

"How was Guillermo?" she asked, as he sat down. Guillermo had made a pass at Marina at their first meeting, but Andrew was reasonably confident she had not taken it seriously.

"Same as ever," said Andrew, taking the cup she had handed him.

"And the sailing?"

"Good, thanks. I didn't win, but it was enjoyable. What have you been up to?"

"Nothing much," she said. "I've been by the pool all day."

This was more small talk than they had exchanged for months. He did not think she would be able to keep it up for much longer.

They drank their tea in silence for a while. Then she said, "I was wondering…"

He looked at her expressionlessly.

"I was just wondering," she said. "Is there any chance I could have the car for a couple of days?"

The car to which she was referring was his personal vehicle, a second-hand Land Rover Discovery he had bought from his predecessor. He rarely used it during the working week, but preferred it to the Rolls at weekends and holidays, when he invariably let his driver take time off. Since his first meeting with Birgit the mileage on the Discovery had increased exponentially.

"A couple of days?" he said. "What for?" He had not meant to sound ungracious, but his instincts told him she was up to something. He had occasionally allowed her to use the car, and miraculously she had not crashed it, but the general rule was that she used the excellent public transport for which Singapore was rightly famous.

"The gang are going on a diving trip," she said. "They need a bit of space for the gear."

This sounded so plausible that he assumed it was a fabrication. *But*, he thought, *what the hell?* If he refused, she would turn nasty. And when she turned nasty, the subject of Elena would sooner or later be raised. "My mother would never have treated me like this," she would say. And he knew what she would be thinking. *My mother, who you killed by your carelessness, by your gross negligence, because you did not love her properly, because you did not care enough. Because you wanted her dead anyway.*

"I'll need it by Wednesday," he said.

Her face clouded at this news. "What for?" she said.

His first reaction was to say that it was none of her business, but he wanted to avoid unpleasantness and there was, in fact, no point in not telling her where he was going. The very act of booking the ferry would put his trip into the public domain. He had even mentioned his destination to Guillermo, when the latter had asked about his plans for the Chinese New Year.

"I'm off to Bintan for a couple of days," he said. "I'm leaving on Wednesday evening."

Marina looked sullen. "Why can't you use the Rolls?"

The truth was that he could use the Rolls, but he preferred not to. "I've given the driver the afternoon off," he said.

"Can't you change that?"

"Not now," he said. "He's already made his plans."

She seemed on the verge of arguing further, but changed her mind. "What if I get the car back by four in the afternoon?" she said.

"I'd sooner it was back by lunchtime," he said. But when he saw the ugly expression forming on her face, he relented. "Okay," he said. "Four – but no later."

"Cheers," said Marina. She looked at her watch. "I've got to go," she said, her mission clearly accomplished. "See you."

* * *

Some 200 miles south of Bangkok, shortly before Chumphon, he had stopped the hire car by the side of the road. It was already dark.

"It's not good enough," he said into his mobile. "If I don't have the information by tomorrow it will be too late. And you know what that means."

He listened for several seconds. "Okay," he said. "This is your last chance. Call me any time in the next twenty-four hours on this number. Use a Thailand dialling code. But make sure you have what I need when you call."

He checked his watch. He would make it as far as Krabi tonight. That meant he could be in place and ready to go by midday on Monday.

ALARMS

CHAPTER SEVEN

"Good morning, Siew Ling."

"Good morning, Your Excellency. Have a nice day, as far as it goes."

When he first arrived in Singapore, Andrew Singleton had toyed with the idea of sending the High Commission receptionist to remedial English classes. But he had decided that, on balance, her linguistic idiosyncrasies were not seriously infelicitous. He had been reinforced in his decision by the disproportionate irritation Siew Ling's relentless and inaccurate cheerfulness appeared to cause the Third Secretary in Chancery. The latter was a humourless young man called Benjamin Kendall, who visibly resented any request (such as to check the account or arrange taxis for departing visitors) which he deemed intellectually beneath him. Adam White had somehow charmed him into being more of a team player in the last few months, but Andrew avoided all contact with him if possible.

"All okay, Mary?" asked Andrew, as he strode into his office. *She's looking well*, he noticed. Andrew had originally thought his personal assistant rather colourless, but recently she seemed to have a lot more spark. He realised, with a faint twinge of conscience, that he had little idea how Mary occupied herself outside office hours.

"Nothing much new in the telegrams, High Commissioner," said Mary. "But there's a message from the Foreign Ministry. The Permanent Secretary would like to see you this morning. They said it was urgent."

"What's the diary look like?"

"You're free between ten and twelve thirty."

"Make it eleven forty-five, if that suits him," said Andrew. "Then I can go straight on to lunch. Any idea what it's about?"

"'Urgent and personal' was all they said," said Mary.

"Sounds mysterious," said Andrew. "Any luck with Bintan?"

"The ferry's reserved," said Mary. "And I've booked the resort. But they've got to call back to confirm the pool."

"The pool's important, Mary," he said. "Let me know if I need to lean on anybody."

Andrew opened up his computer and scrolled rapidly through his telegrams, making a brief note of any action required of the High Commission. His staff were good at taking the initiative on most things; he had made clear, on first arrival in Singapore, that he would be travelling frequently and would expect people to get on with their work in his absence. All the same, he liked them to know he was monitoring their activities.

When he turned to his emails, he found little official traffic. He rapidly deleted copies of exchanges between ambassadors in neighbouring countries about the timing and location of the next heads of mission regional conference (the subject was of supreme indifference to Andrew, but his colleagues were falling over themselves to host the meeting). The other emails were, for the most part, circulars about budget cutbacks or planned structural changes in the Foreign Office. He deleted these, along with a number of ephemeral private messages, mostly from his golfing friends. That left a characteristically terse communication from his older brother, demanding to see Andrew in Oxford to discuss his latest piece of research when he was next in England.

Despite a shared teenage enthusiasm for sailing and cinema classics, the two brothers had grown steadily apart in adult life and had little in common these days. Roger Singleton, ascetic and cerebral, regarded his younger brother as a dilettante and a shameless apologist for American neo-imperialism. Andrew himself enjoyed their periodic intellectual sparring matches. But they would never see eye-to-eye, not least because Roger was forever seeking to impose complicated conceptual structures on what Andrew insisted was the irredeemably messy reality of international relations.

Next, Andrew turned to his in tray. At the top was a pile of invitations, which he riffled through rapidly, marking some for acceptance, some for regrets and a third category to be passed on to other High Commission staff according to their area of expertise. Then he worked his way through a series of draft letters and reports prepared by various of his subordinates, approving most of them after a cursory glance and the occasional manuscript amendment. A dense draft economic report, left behind by the currently absent Commercial Counsellor, he set aside for further work later in the day. At the bottom of the tray, where it had sat now for several weeks, lay Adam White's draft human rights strategy. Despite what Andrew had said to Mary Bennett the previous day, he had no intention of taking this with him to Bintan. He resolved instead to tackle it at home over the Chinese New Year Holiday.

Adam White put his head round the door and asked if Andrew was ready for the Heads of Section meeting. He looked strained. Andrew could only attribute this to a combination of post-ministerial visit fatigue and the absence, in England, of Adam's partner, a young woman who seemed permanently cross, but with whom Adam was clearly besotted.

Andrew beckoned the group waiting in Mary's office to come in. They sat in a tight group on the sofa and armchairs around his coffee table. Andrew remained behind his desk.

"Right, Adam," Andrew said. "What have you got? Something exciting to lighten up our Monday morning, I hope."

Adam gave him a strange look. He briefly described Daniel Taylor's arrest, which had been reported factually in Sunday's *Straits Times*, although with no mention of the boy's name. Then he worked his way through a list of current activities, from time to time consulting his notepad. Andrew nodded and crossed the items off his own checklist, one by one, thanking his lucky stars for sending him such a conscientious and hard-working Head of Chancery. (Adam's predecessor, whom Andrew had inherited, had been rather too keen on suggesting things for Andrew to do, rather than getting on with them himself.) The final item on Adam's list was an instruction received over the weekend to seek Singaporean support for a planned British initiative at the United Nations on money laundering. Adam suggested this be carried out after the Chinese New Year holiday.

"I'm seeing the Permanent Secretary this morning," said Andrew. "Why don't I do it then?"

"If it's all the same to you, High Commissioner, can we do it in slightly slower time?" said Adam, who was again looking at Andrew in a decidedly peculiar way. "There's a lot of supporting written material to prepare and I'm a bit tied up this morning."

"When's the deadline?"

"They've given us two weeks."

"Fair enough," said Andrew. "Susan?"

Susan Hyde was the First Secretary Commercial. The young wags in registry had nicknamed her Dr Jekyll, partly because she did, in truth, suffer from something of a split personality. In the office, as today, she seemed perpetually frightened, glancing nervously around as she spoke, fiddling with a strand of her reddish, curly hair and clutching her file box like some pale imitation of Dante Gabriel Rossetti's *Pandora*. But after a couple of drinks she could become, to put it kindly, a good deal more relaxed. As far as Andrew knew, Susan had never met Guillermo, but this was almost certainly an accident waiting to happen.

"Nothing from me, High Commissioner," she said, averting her gaze. She seemed particularly agitated today. Andrew recalled that there was a major trade mission due in two weeks' time, but he was unconcerned. For all her nervousness, Susan was a thoroughly competent officer and would have made meticulous preparations for the mission. The Commercial Counsellor would, in any case, be back by then to take charge of the event.

Nick Childs, the Defence Attaché, was a diminutive, super-fit Wing Commander who had in his time played fly-half for the RAF. He reported, in clipped, efficient sentences, on arrangements for a visit by the Chief of the Defence Staff the following month. The Management Officer, a fair-haired young man bearing the unlikely name of Robert Redford, gave warning of the danger of an overshoot on the local budget, which Andrew asked Adam to sort out in a separate meeting later on.

The last member of the group was Quentin Asquith, who ran the section in the High Commission which in the old days nobody used to speak about. It was impossible to tell Asquith's age. He had the appearance, at first sight, of a gangling schoolboy, but his straggling, sandy hair was streaked with grey and the skin around his neck was almost lizard-like. Asquith was unmarried, and considered by some to have been lucky to survive the early stages of his career, in a period when only the robustly heterosexual were regarded as trustworthy. Andrew's guess was that Quentin was not bothered either way. His idea of excitement was exploring caves in Brunei or looking for orangutan in Borneo.

Asquith spoke now with a slightly halting, rather pedantic, voice, looking over the top of rimless glasses.

"I've nothing of general interest, High Commissioner," he said. "But may I have a quick word with you afterwards, please?"

"What is it, Quentin?" said Andrew when the others had left.

"I thought I'd better give you a heads-up on your call at the Foreign Ministry this morning," said Asquith.

It mildly irritated Andrew that Asquith frequently knew his business before he did himself. But he did not let the irritation show, for fear that Asquith would cease telling him things, a situation which would be far worse. "That would be jolly helpful, Quentin," he said.

"The Singaporeans have been picking up the odd snippet or two in the last week, which lead them to believe someone is going to try something very soon," said Asquith.

"Really?" said Andrew. "What sort of thing?"

"They're not sure," said Asquith. "All they've got are reports of a number of people being on the move, people who've previously been sitting tight for some time."

"On the move?" said Andrew. "Where from?"

"Various places around the region," said Asquith. "But the point is, they seem to be heading this way."

"Singapore?"

"Or points nearby."

"Who are these people?" said Andrew.

"The press would probably describe them as 'suspected terrorists'," said Asquith. "But there's no hard evidence. They just fit a certain profile, so they've been under surveillance for several months."

"Who by?"

"Certainly not by us," said Asquith. "We don't have the assets in this neck of the woods. But the Indonesians do. So do the Australians – and quite possibly the Malaysians."

"And they share information freely with the Singaporeans?"

"Since Bali, yes."

"What do the Americans think?" asked Andrew.

"I'm still trying to get hold of them," said Asquith. "I only got this over breakfast this morning."

"Keep trying," said Andrew. "They must have some kind of collateral."

When Asquith had left, Andrew tried to work on the Commercial Counsellor's draft report, but Asquith's news made it difficult to concentrate. He was tempted to telephone the American Ambassador, but decided to let Asquith deal with the professionals first. He would, if necessary, speak to the Ambassador after he had been to the Foreign Ministry.

Mary Bennett came in to say that the travel agents had called back to confirm the availability of a pool villa. Andrew had a subliminal flash of Birgit, naked, draped lazily across a sunbed, before he returned dutifully to the complex detail of Singapore's GDP growth prospects for the second quarter of the year.

* * *

The portrait of Elena Singleton hung in a prominent position in the main reception room of the residence. Adam stood looking at it and wondered what this incredibly beautiful woman had been like in real life.

The painting, by an unknown Panamanian, had very little artistic value. But, knowing Elena's daughter, Adam could see that its near-photographic quality accurately conveyed how Elena must have looked as a young woman. The enormous eyes, the silky, black hair, the voluptuous lips had all been passed on to Marina. There was also a hint of the arrogance and wilfulness which characterised Marina's prevailing attitude to life. Only the formality of the clothes betrayed the inescapable difference in time and place. Elena was wearing a scarlet evening dress and black shawl, with a diamond necklace and earrings, and she carried a decorated fan, open across her left breast. Marina would not have been seen dead in such an outfit.

"What can I do for you, Adam?"

Adam turned to see Sarah Childs standing in the doorway. The Defence Attache's wife was a tall, rather forbidding woman, who always gave Adam the feeling she did not wholly approve of him. She worked part-time at the residence as Social Secretary, bullying all the High Commission staff with whom she dealt, while allowing the cook and the maids to run rings around her.

"I was supposed to be meeting Marina," said Adam.

"She's not here, I'm afraid," said Sarah. "I don't know where she is. She left before I arrived this morning."

Adam began to get a very bad feeling. He had been willing Andrew Singleton to say something about Marina earlier in the morning, but he had not done so. Was it possible he still knew nothing?

"What time was that?" asked Adam.

"Just before eight."

"Before eight? That's early for Marina," said Adam.

"That's what I thought," said Sarah, not bothering to conceal her built-in antipathy towards Marina.

"Have you any idea when she's due back?"

"None, I'm afraid," said Sarah. "Would you like to leave her a message?"

Adam thought for a moment. "No," he said. "I'll catch up with her later. Just say I was here if you see her."

She gave him a look suggesting that she thought he and Marina were up to no good. "I'll be sure to do that," she said.

Adam sat in his car outside the front door of the residence, trying to work out what to do next. Inderjit Singh had telephoned earlier in the morning to say that Daniel Taylor had not yet been charged, but that the police had sought exceptional authority to keep him in custody for a further period.

"Is that usual?" Adam had asked.

"No," Singh replied. "There's some delay in getting the forensic results, so they can't charge him yet. Their argument for holding him was that he could be a link to a major narcotics gang, and that he might make a run for it if they release him now."

"But surely they're holding his passport?"

"They think he could have access to false documents."

Adam decided he must speak to Andrew Singleton at once. He could see Sarah Childs fiddling with a flower arrangement in the front hallway while she watched him through the glass panes with undisguised curiosity. Rather than give her any further cause for speculation, he drove down the drive and out of the grounds. Halfway along Nassim Road he parked on the verge and telephoned the High Commission.

"Good morning, one more time, Mr White. I hope you are having a fruitful and instructive visit, wherever you may currently be located."

"Thank you, Siew Ling," said Adam. "Can I speak to the High Commissioner, please?"

"Certainly, sir. It will be my great pleasure and privilege to put you through without any further delay."

It was Mary who answered the telephone. "The High Commissioner's just about to leave for the Foreign Ministry, Adam," she said.

"Two minutes, Mary," said Adam. There was a muffled exchange, then Singleton came on the line.

"Make it quick, Adam," he said. "You know what a stickler for punctuality Michael Seng is."

"High Commissioner, I'm sorry to be a nuisance," said Adam. "I'm at the residence. I was supposed to be meeting Marina at eleven o'clock and she's not here."

"She's gone diving," said Andrew. "What did you want her for?"

"Diving?" said Adam. *Holy shit*, he thought. *What the hell is she playing at now?* "Did she talk to you last night, by any chance?" he said.

"Yes, of course," said Andrew.

"So you do know?"

"Know what?"

"What did she say to you?"

"She asked to borrow the car."

"Nothing else?"

"No, nothing else." A distinctly peevish note was creeping into Andrew Singleton's voice. "Now, I've got to go, Adam. Whatever it is, talk to me about it later."

Adam sat in the car, reflecting on his next move. As he did so, he went over Marina's story in his mind again and suddenly realised what had been worrying him. The heroin she had been carrying was sufficient to hang her ten times over. But it was worth, at most, around 50,000 Singapore dollars – a relatively small amount for the elaborate courier arrangement she had described. Was the heroin stashed in his wardrobe only a small part of a much larger consignment? Or was she lying about the whole affair? For another thought had belatedly struck him. The division of the heroin into smaller packets suggested a retail operation, or possibly a deal with local pushers. Marina could not be the ignorant courier she had claimed.

* * *

Andrew travelled to the Ministry of Foreign Affairs by car. Since the completion of the Ministry's new building at Tanglin Circle, many of his staff walked to their appointments there. But Andrew preferred to arrive with a clear head, fresh from his air-conditioned car, rather than sweating and untidy from the heat and humidity.

He was greeted by a tiny Chinese girl, who led him past the inner reception desk, where a young Malay woman in a headscarf smiled shyly at him, and into a VIP receiving room. Almost immediately the Permanent Secretary joined him and they sat sipping tea and exchanging pleasantries for a minute or two. Unlike most of his Chinese colleagues, who were Buddhists or Taoists, Michael Seng was a Methodist. He had reached the rank of Brigadier-General in the Singapore Armed Forces before becoming a diplomat, a fact betrayed by a slight stiffness in his bearing. When he turned to the matter in hand, his tone was grave and measured.

"High Commissioner," he said. "We've had some rather alarming reports and I felt I must share our analysis with you as soon as possible."

"That sounds serious, Michael," said Andrew, noncommittally.

The Permanent Secretary would almost certainly know that he had already been tipped off, but they both had appearances to keep up.

"We think there will be some kind of terrorist act this week."

"Here in Singapore?"

"We don't know," said Seng. "The possible perpetrators have not yet tried to enter Singapore, but they are almost certainly close by."

"Almost certainly close by?" said Andrew. "Could you unpack that phrase a little for me, Michael? Do you actually know where they are?"

"We knew with reasonable confidence where three of them were just before midnight last night," said Seng. "Now we seem to have lost them. We also think there's a fourth, although we have no idea where he is."

"This all sounds a little alarming, Michael," said Andrew. "What do you suggest we do?"

"I've advised the Americans to close their embassy temporarily," said Seng. "Perhaps you should do the same."

I see, thought Andrew. *So you spoke to the Americans first*. Well, why not? The world's only hyper-power ranked higher than everyone else, the former colonial power included. "That's easy," he said. "We'll be closed over Chinese New Year anyway. We can easily extend that arrangement until the weekend."

"I think that would be sensible," said Seng. "Although... " He paused for a moment, as though choosing his words carefully. "Although we think the balance of probability is that the act — whatever it is — will take place outside Singapore."

Andrew, in turn, chose his own words carefully. "Are you suggesting I advise my staff to avoid visiting neighbouring countries over the Chinese New Year?" he said.

"No, no," said Seng. "I think that would be going too far. But you should ask them to exercise great care, avoid crowded bars and discos, that sort of thing." He hesitated and then turned to the

Chinese girl, who had been busy taking notes. "Ah Fong, would you see if there's any chance that we might have some more tea, please?" he said. Ah Fong looked a little surprised at this request, but obediently went in search of the tea lady.

"This is off the record, Andrew," said Seng, when they were alone. "We have no hard intelligence for this particular dimension to our analysis, you understand. It's just gossip we've picked up around the streets."

"And what is this particular dimension, Michael?" said Andrew.

Seng looked down briefly and then raised his head and looked Andrew straight in the eye. "The threat, whatever it is, appears to be specific either to you personally or the American Ambassador," he said.

* * *

For nearly an hour after the High Commissioner had left for his appointment at the Foreign Ministry, Mary resisted the temptation to telephone Muzafar. She was not by nature superstitious, but somehow she felt she would be tempting fate if she did not patiently await his call. So she busied herself with routine activity, responding to the High Commissioner's invitations, typing up the letters he had approved, and distributing the various tasks he had delegated around the High Commission.

Finally she could control herself no longer and called him.

"Muzafar," she said. "The High Commissioner's arrangements are all confirmed now. Have you had any luck?"

"Oh, Mary," he said. She knew immediately that something was wrong. "Mary, I'm so sorry. I was just going to call you, my darling."

"Is there a problem, Muzafar?" she said. A heavy weight seemed to be pressing on her chest.

"I'm afraid so, my darling," he said. "I can't get away at all this week."

"What a shame," she said, striving to make her voice sound conversational. "Maybe we can try again the next time the High Commissioner goes away." They would, after all, not have to wait too long, judging by the frequency of Andrew Singleton's travelling in recent months.

"Yes," he said. "I hope that will be possible."

Was it her imagination or did his voice suggest that he did not realistically expect anything of the kind? She waited for him to say something else, but there was silence at the other end of the line. Finally, she spoke herself. "So, when shall I see you?" she said, straining hard to avoid appearing plaintive.

"I'm not sure, Mary," he said. "We're very busy at work and everyone's having to work long hours."

"Oh, Muzafar, poor you," she said. "But what about the holiday?"

"I have to work all through the holiday," he said.

"Surely that's not legal?" she said, conscious that she was grasping at straws.

"Mary, my darling. I don't want to lose my job," he said. "I'm sorry, my darling. I must go now."

"So, will you call me when you can?"

"Of course, my darling."

Mary sat and stared out of her office window, which looked down on to the High Commission tennis court. Two of the boys from registry had taken an early lunch and were playing a quick game of singles to work up a thirst for their first beer of the day. But Mary was not really watching them, although she was vaguely aware of the muffled sound of the ball being struck and distant whoops of triumph. She was picking over the bones of her conversation with Muzafar. Despite his constant use of terms of endearment, he had seemed somehow distant. And, for the first time ever, they had spoken on the telephone without making a firm arrangement for their next meeting. Was she being unnecessarily sensitive? Or had some subtle shift taken place in their relationship?

* * *

"Doesn't anyone here share my feeling the judicial killing machine's moving into overdrive?"

The *International Herald Tribune* correspondent, Murray Parker, was a tenacious young New Zealander who had come close on several occasions to being invited by the Singapore authorities to practise his journalistic skills elsewhere. That he was still around – and a regular participant in Andrew's periodic lunches with the local press – was largely because Singapore was relaxing its censorship policy, in order to enhance its image as a place for talented foreigners to live and work.

"I don't think you should read too much into the statistics, Murray," said the *Straits Times* foreign editor, an improbably long-haired young Chinese. "We're just nabbing more rascals, that's all."

Andrew had considered cancelling the lunch and closing the High Commission immediately, keeping back only Adam White and Quentin Asquith, so that the three of them might, together, compose a telegram to London reporting the Singaporean warning. But he had inferred from Michael Seng's calculated indiscretion (which he had decided to keep to himself) that the Singaporeans saw little real danger of an attack on the High Commission building. He also did not want to put off the lunch, which had already been twice postponed for one reason or another. So instead he had telephoned Mary Bennett from the car on the way to the residence, to ask her to arrange a meeting with Adam and Quentin in his office at two-thirty.

"It's not as simple as that," said Murray. "The judges are getting tougher, I reckon."

"Is that a problem for you?" asked the *Agence France-Presse* representative, a wizened Frenchman who had lived in Singapore for nearly twenty years.

"No trial by jury? Hanging judges? Kids being flogged for painting the odd slogan on a wall?" said Murray. "No, of course it's not a problem. What do you think?"

"I think I like the idea of being able to walk the streets at night without being mugged," said the *Asia Wall Street Journal* correspondent, a Taiwanese girl who clearly did not understand what all the fuss was about.

"Yeah?" said Murray. "Well you can do that in Wellington and we don't have the death penalty there."

"Murray, you know why that is," said Andrew, in a bid to lower the temperature. "All your criminals would be tucked up in bed with a glass of warm milk long before Lucy goes out to play."

There was ragged laughter around the table. Andrew noticed that Adam White, who was seated at the end of the table, barely cracked a smile. There was definitely something worrying him. There had been no chance to continue their conversation about Marina before lunch, and Andrew decided he must try to remember to have a word with Adam afterwards.

"Seriously, though," said the *Straits Times* man. "Increasing numbers of people are trying to bring drugs into Singapore. We have to be firm with those we catch, to deter others from trying to do the same."

"Hang on a minute, Kuan Loong," said Adam, who seemed now to be taking more of an interest. "If hanging is supposed to be a deterrent, why are more and more people bringing in drugs?"

Kuan Loong was not to be swayed. "Just think how bad it would be if we didn't hang the ones we caught," he said.

"Well, you're certainly cutting down on repeat offences," said Andrew. "But I rather take Adam's point. It's very difficult to demonstrate the deterrent effect of the death penalty if crime is actually rising."

"But it isn't," said Kuan Loong. "Not in general terms, at least. We have very few violent crimes, as you well know, High Commissioner. It's just the drugs, for some reason, and mainly in the last few months."

Adam was frowning and looked as if he was about to say something, but Andrew spoke before he could do so. "Well, I think we may all have to agree to differ on this," he said. "Now, can we talk about Indonesia? I'd be interested to know your views on what's been happening in the last couple of weeks."

* * *

Adam realised he had missed his chance again. There had been no time to talk to Andrew Singleton immediately after lunch, because they had travelled separately to the meeting with Quentin Asquith at the High Commission. Once they were all in the High Commissioner's office, and Singleton had described his meeting with the Permanent Secretary, thoughts of Marina were temporarily pushed to the back of Adam's mind.

"I spoke to the Americans," said Asquith. "They've broadly the same picture as the Singaporeans. But they seem to think their man may be a particular target."

"Do they now?" said Singleton, with a hint of a smile. "Well, best not to take any unnecessary risks, for all that. Let's keep the High Commission closed on Thursday and Friday unless we get the all clear by then."

"And the British Council?" said Adam.

"Yes," said Singleton. "Tell them to do the same."

"What about British companies?" said Adam. "We issued a general security awareness warning last week. Do we need to do any more?"

Singleton thought for a few seconds. "Get Susan to ring

round with a slightly stronger message to the high-profile ones like British Airways and Shell," he said. "And we need to remind our own staff to take special care if any of them are planning to travel to neighbouring countries. Can you handle that, please, Adam? I'll draft the telegram for London. We'd better copy it to everyone around the region. You and Quentin can give it the once-over before sending it off."

It was nearly five o'clock by the time Adam had discharged the tasks arising from the meeting, and added his initials to the draft telegram shown to him by an uncharacteristically subdued Mary Bennett. The High Commissioner had already left to attend a lecture by the visiting Thai Defence Minister at the Institute of Strategic Studies. Adam knew that Andrew had two further social engagements that evening. So he decided, yet again, to put off talking to him. He turned to his in tray and set about clearing up whatever he could before the holiday began.

Shortly before seven o'clock, he decided to call it a day. He was locking away his papers when the telephone rang. Everyone else had long gone home, and he hastened to pick up the telephone before it cut automatically into the standard recorded message.

It was Peter Coles from Consular Department in the Foreign Office. "I thought you'd be having your supper by this time, old son," said Coles. "But I'm glad I caught you. We've finally made contact with Daniel Taylor's parents."

"Thank the Lord for that," said Adam. "Where'd they been?"

"Skiing, apparently. Some spur of the moment decision they omitted to tell their son about."

"Are they coming straight back to Singapore?"

"Yes," said Coles. "But the father wants to speak to you first. I promised I'd get you to ring him." He paused and then added, "I have to say he was pretty chewed up about it."

Adam rang the number Coles gave him. There was no answer and no recorded message. He rang Coles back.

"I was just off to lunch," said Coles. "What's up, old son?"

"The Taylors aren't answering their telephone," Adam said. "Can you give them my mobile number when you next speak to them and get them to call me direct?"

Adam let himself out of the High Commission through the series of security barriers and stood, momentarily undecided, in the car park. It was still very warm, but the humidity had dropped and it was not uncomfortable. He needed to call Ali. But he could not face the empty house in Ridley Park – at least not yet. Lunch at the residence had been relatively light fare. He decided he would treat himself to a couple of beers and something Italian at an open-air restaurant in Holland Village.

* * *

All through lunch, Alison had been waiting for Richard to make his pitch. But he had resolutely stuck to polite questions about life in Singapore, small talk about former colleagues, or minor laments about the Chancellor of the Exchequer's most recent offensive against corporate taxation loopholes. She had gradually allowed herself to relax, as she ate her way through a series of exquisite fish dishes, accompanied by a vintage Chablis and followed by a chestnut parfait of incredible delicacy, which Richard had insisted should be complemented by an intriguing Hungarian dessert wine he had recently persuaded the restaurant to add to their list. By the time the coffee came, she was bathed in a vague, warm glow, and had more or less persuaded herself that he was not going to make a move of any kind.

Richard Sheinwald was the youngest managing partner the firm had had in its existence. He was brilliant, personable and unfailingly courteous. Ruthless in his business dealings, he was protective of his staff and fellow partners, and a tireless advocate of charitable causes. He was also, perhaps surprisingly, unmarried, though rarely to be seen without a female companion.

"Will you have a small brandy, Alison?" he asked solicitously.

Alison considered his dark, fine-boned face. He was the last of a central European legal dynasty that had escaped the gas chambers by months, to survive and prosper, transplanted, in England. When she had first begun to work with him, Alison had fantasised about their entering into some kind of relationship. She had rapidly decided that his intellect and glamour were too powerful for her taste. Sitting opposite him now, however, in the disarming intimacy of the discreet restaurant he had selected just off Leadenhall Market, she could not deny his attractiveness. Nor could she deny that, in anticipation of their meeting, she had spent two hours at the hairdresser and half an hour in front of the mirror perfecting her make-up.

"Why not?" she said, conscious, as she spoke, that she might be slipping across some kind of line.

Richard summoned the waiter and ordered two brandies.

"So," he said. "How's it *really* going in Singapore?"

"Not as well as I'd hoped," Alison heard herself saying. The pain she felt at the treachery implicit in those simple words was only partly anaesthetised by the effects of the food and alcohol.

"I'm very sorry to hear that," said Richard. On a personal basis he probably was genuinely sorry, she thought. But she suspected that his mission today was strictly professional.

"I didn't think I'd miss so much of my life here," she said.

"I see," he said, his delicate features studiously impassive. *Ask me about Adam*, she thought. *Ask me if I still love him*. But this was not why Richard had invited her to lunch.

"Do you think, maybe, that you need a little more time to adjust?" he asked. "How long has it been now? Three months? Four?"

"Nearly six," she said. "Nice to know how much you've missed me." This was the alcohol talking. She would never have spoken to him like that before.

He laughed. "I'm sorry," he said. "We've been very busy. I don't know where the time's gone to." He paused for a moment, then continued. "Six months," he said. "Well, I assume you know by now what you want to do."

Alison was silent. She did not know what he expected her to say. She was also beginning to feel very sleepy. It was a pleasant sensation, but not one conducive to intelligent conversation.

"Do you want to come back?" he asked.

It was the question for which she had been waiting, but it still took her unawares. She did not respond immediately, seeking to gather her thoughts. "Do I have that option?" she said finally.

"If you come now, yes," he said. "But every month you're away makes it that much more difficult. You know how rapidly things move on."

"I don't know," she said, now suddenly listless. "I just don't know."

The waiter arrived with a box of cigars, but Richard waved him away. "Look, Alison," he said, marginally more briskly. "Here's the way it is. You were one of our best tax specialists, almost certainly destined for a partnership. We'd take you back tomorrow if that was what you really wanted. But no half measures, please. We need you to be sure."

Alison now wanted nothing more than to crawl up into a ball and go to sleep. "Give me until the end of the week, Richard," she said. "Can you give me that long, please?"

* * *

Simon Taylor rang as Adam was parking his car outside the house in Ridley Park. Adam sat in the car to take the call.

"Mr White, I should be grateful if you would tell me exactly what has happened," said Taylor, the strain in his voice apparent. Adam told the story as fully as he dared, omitting only Marina's role in the affair.

"It's totally unbelievable," said Taylor. "He's never touched drugs of any kind in his life."

"Daniel says it was planted on him," said Adam, wincing inwardly at the inadequacy of this bare truth.

"Of course it was planted on him," said Taylor angrily. "And I'll find a lawyer who can prove it."

"We already have a lawyer working on that," said Adam.

"Has he got my son out of prison yet?" said Taylor.

"No," said Adam. "The police have sought authority to detain him beyond the normal forty-eight hour period."

"But the charge is rubbish!" said Taylor. "Any halfway competent lawyer would simply get it dismissed."

"Mr Taylor," said Adam. "You're free to appoint any lawyer you want to represent your son. But Inderjit Singh has an excellent reputation. I'm sure he's doing all he possibly can."

"It's not good enough," said Taylor. "For Christ's sake, man, this is my son! Don't you understand?"

"Yes, of course I do," said Adam

"No, you don't," said Taylor. "Or you'd be doing more to sort things out. Where's the High Commissioner? What's *he* doing about all this?"

"The High Commissioner's been kept fully informed," said Adam. "He's taking a very close interest in the case."

"What the hell is that supposed to mean?" Taylor was shouting now and clearly no longer in control of himself. "What's he *doing* about it?"

"Unfortunately, there's nothing he can do at this stage," said Adam. "If it comes to a trial, we shall, of course, make clear at the highest level where we stand on capital punishment." Even to Adam's own ears this sounded incredibly wooden. Taylor became nearly hysterical.

"Capital punishment? Are you mad?" he screamed. "If any harm comes to my son – any harm at all – I'll destroy you... and your High Commissioner, do you understand?"

"Mr Taylor, I think the best thing, for your son, would be for you to get back to Singapore as soon as you can," said Adam, as calmly as he was able.

"Don't worry," said Taylor. "I'm on the next flight."

Adam let himself into the darkened house. *Is there anything else that could possibly go wrong?* he asked himself. At least the exchange with Simon Taylor had finally shaken him out of his temporary torpor: he would take the heroin to the police first thing in the morning and tell them everything, whether or not he had, in the meantime, managed to speak to Andrew Singleton.

Adam was aware, as he switched on the lights, of a faint, unfamiliar draught of fresh, warm air on his face. As he moved to the back of the house, it became stronger. He turned on the lights in the living room. It was a complete shambles: furniture was overturned, the contents of drawers and shelves scattered over the floor. He swore and walked across the room to close the French windows, which had been forced open by the intruders.

The main bedroom upstairs was in as bad a mess: the bedside drawers yanked open, the wardrobe door hanging loose, and bags ripped apart all over the floor. His tennis and squash rackets, and Ali's archery equipment, had been hauled out and dumped on the bed, chairs had been turned over, and the back of an ornamental clock torn off. Adam hardly bothered to look for the suitcase he had left on top of the wardrobe. There was no way these people would have left without taking what they came for.

* * *

The information had come very late. It would be tight: some of the team would have to fly when it might have been safer to travel by boat. No matter, there was no way they could be connected with him before it was all done. What happened afterwards was in the hands of Allah – at least, that was what he would tell them.

The chartered motor yacht chugged slowly out from the tiny harbour in southern Thailand, where it had been sitting at anchor most of the day. He sent a trail of sim cards over the side, to be followed a few minutes later, one by one, by the four handsets. Two phones left, plus a laptop and a digital camera. That was all he had need of now. And the gun, of course.

CHAPTER 8

Andrew was awakened by the liquid rattle of a black-naped oriole calling to its mate from the mango tree just beyond the balcony. For several minutes he lay motionless, trying to recapture the details of his dream. Kirsty had been involved again, somehow both as a nineteen-year old and in her current, middle-aged identity. So, too, had Elena and Marina, merged into one person, but speaking alternately as their individual selves. The overall tone of the dream had been menacing, but his waking brain could not articulate the nature of the threat. He had a momentary recollection of Michael Seng, shaking his head disapprovingly, but then the image evaporated and, with it, his grasp on the entire dream.

He rolled out of bed and performed thirty push-ups before going into the bathroom. It was an ingrained habit he could not shake. Later he would run three laps of the garden, even though it left him short of breath. One day, he promised himself, he would give up smoking.

After he had run and showered, Andrew dressed in shorts and a tee-shirt and ate a breakfast of fruit on the balcony while he browsed through the newspapers. Within minutes, the sudden burst of a pneumatic drill had interrupted his reading, and he cursed the pusillanimity of his predecessors for not resisting London's decision to sell such a large slice of the garden: even on the first day of the holiday, the developers were pressing ahead at full speed with the house-building project on the land that had been sold. Andrew lit a cigarette and took his tea down into the garden on the other side of the house to sit in the shade by the pool, as far away from the building noise as he could get. It had rained in the night, releasing the scent of the heliconia which grew thickly close by where he sat. The gardener was always warning Andrew that it was a perfect nesting ground for cobras, but Andrew took the view that, if he did not bother them, they would not bother him.

Andrew's first Chinese New Year's engagement was not until late morning. He should really have been devoting the next couple of hours to the human rights strategy, but he was not in the mood. If the High Commission remained closed until the weekend, there was no point in finalising the document before Monday. In any case, given the atrocities being committed elsewhere around the world, London were not especially anxious to learn his plans to coax the Singaporeans into greater tolerance towards Jehovah's Witnesses or gay relationships. On the issue that really mattered – the death penalty – there would be no budging them under any circumstances. So he abandoned the thought and indulged himself in day-dreaming about Birgit.

Before long, however, he found himself thinking about Marina and wondering what was bugging Adam White so badly.

* * *

Adam sat on his own modest terrace, eating his way automatically through a bowl of cereal. For a man whose normal disposition was irrepressible cheerfulness, he was experiencing something close to depression.

Adam had tried to call Ali just before midnight, but her mother had told him she had yet to return from lunch with Richard Sheinwald. It was still only late afternoon in England, but somehow Ruth Webster had managed to imply that her daughter's continuing absence was laden with significance. Adam had put the phone down and sworn violently for several seconds. Then he had made a half-hearted attempt to tidy up the mess in the house, establishing in the process that nothing else seemed to be missing. He had fixed the French windows as best he could, reflecting, as he did so, on the discrepancy between the appalling lack of security at his house and the extravagant protection afforded to the High Commission offices. He had decided there was no point in calling the police.

During the night, he had slept surprisingly well at first, but had awakened early with a wave of ill-defined anxieties crowding in on him. Stupidly, he had not got up and gone for a run, but tried instead to go back to sleep. As a result, he tossed and turned for an hour before finally falling asleep some time after six o'clock in the morning. Now, at eight-thirty, he felt woozy and unsettled.

Someone had once told Adam that writing down one's worries was the best way of diminishing their destructive properties. It was important, apparently, to let the mind and hand run free and not to delete anything once it was in writing. He had never before felt the need to resort to this device, but now he found himself reaching for a ballpoint pen and a sheet of paper. He wrote continuously for several minutes and then surveyed the list:

1. Ali doesn't love me any more.
2. She's having an affair with Richard Sheinwald. *(No, that's bollocks, he thought. Consider that crossed out, whatever the bloody rules of the game.)*
3. I have a nineteen-year-old British citizen as good as on death row.
4. Marina could save him, but I've no idea where she is.
5. I haven't told the High Commissioner a bloody thing about Marina's involvement.
6. I've suppressed criminal evidence – which has now gone missing.
7. Daniel Taylor's father is going to hang me out to dry.

So this is supposed to make me feel better, he thought. *Well, at least I can see the full awfulness of the situation.* He screwed the piece of paper into a ball and shoved it into the waste bin in the kitchen. Then the High Commission duty officer rang to say the *Daily Express* wanted to talk to him.

* * *

"*Gong Xi Fa Chai!*"
"*Gong Xi Fa Chai!*"

Andrew placed his two oranges in the growing row on the dining table, and kissed his hostess on both cheeks as they exchanged the traditional Chinese New Year's greeting. From his jacket pocket he produced a handful of thin, bright red packets, each containing a new ten-dollar bill, which he distributed to the young boys who were running excitedly around their mother's legs.

"How are you, Mei Lin?" he said. "I must say, you're looking terrific." He spoke no more than the truth. His hostess looked stunningly beautiful in a cream *cheong sam,* with a single flower tucked behind her ear.

"And so do you, High Commissioner," said Mei Lin, smiling in that unmistakable way of women paid a compliment by someone in whom they are not remotely interested. "Come on through. Boon Wang's in the sitting room."

Cheng Boon Wang was probably the richest man Andrew had ever known. He had built his commercial empire from scratch after his father, a modest rice trader, had died when Boon Wang was only sixteen. He had taken over his father's business, diversified into other commodities and had initially invested everything he earned in equal proportions in property, cash and the stock market. The business grew steadily under Boon Wang's strong stewardship. But he had made his real fortune by knowing when to switch his assets around. His rivals thought he was either very lucky or guilty of insider trading. Andrew suspected his secret was a combination of painstaking research, a formidable network of well-informed contacts and the guts to seize the turning of the tide. Whatever his methods, Boon Wang was always heavily invested when the markets soared, but, miraculously, already into property when they collapsed. If property and shares should be simultaneously depressed, he was suddenly long on United States Treasury bonds and cash deposits. But he had always escaped the constraints of cash in good time before interest rates came down and stock markets began to pick up. "Never wait for the top or the bottom of the market," he once said to Andrew (on whom, with nothing more than an overdraft to manage, the advice was sadly wasted). "Let some other fellow have his kicks and risk losing his shirt at the same time."

The house had been especially designed for Boon Wang. The architect had collaborated with a *feng shui* consultant to ensure that every feature of the building would bring good health and fortune to the inhabitants. A series of spacious interlocking rooms, arranged over different levels, enclosed a waterfall and intricately designed pools, in which exotic fish wove their way around giant lilies and water ferns. The furnishings were traditional Chinese mixed tastefully with European antiques. Eighteenth and nineteenth century masterpieces hung on the walls alongside modern works by Singaporean artists. The overall effect was one of elegant opulence.

Mei Lin led Andrew through the house, which was filled with people eating, drinking and chattering. Like Andrew, many of them had already been at another party that day, sometimes more than one. He recognised a large number who had been with him earlier at the Singapore Chinese Chamber of Commerce (among them Lee Tek Keng and Guillermo, whom he saw now vainly trying to chat up the Austrian Ambassador's wife). At the Chamber of Commerce, the Interior Minister, a normally rather jovial man, had taken Andrew to one side and assured him earnestly that no damned rascal of a terrorist would get past his tight security to do any harm to the British High Commission.

There were also one or two people who had been at a more select gathering at the house of a former President of Singapore. But lovers of good food and fine wine always made a point of arriving at the home of Boon Wang and Mei Lin at lunchtime, because the Chengs had a well-deserved reputation for lavish hospitality.

Boon Wang, resplendent in an open-necked gold silk shirt with white trousers and handmade brown leather casual shoes, was sitting on a sofa, with his younger brother and business partner on one side and the American Ambassador on the other. Assorted millionaires and cabinet ministers filled the other chairs surrounding an enormous mahogany coffee table, on which stood wine bottles and glasses.

"Welcome, High Commissioner," said Boon Wang, waving Andrew to the place beside him on the sofa, which his brother had vacated with a smile and a wave before disappearing into another room. "We're just trying this latest consignment of Margaux. Get yourself a glass."

Andrew shook hands all round and made himself comfortable on the sofa with a glass of wine.

"We were trying to get these fellows to give us a clue about their plans for government land sales," said Boon Wang. "But for some reason they're not telling us anything."

"I can't blame you for trying, Boon Wang," said the Minister for National Development, a chubby Chinese whom Andrew had last seen performing a very creditable version of 'I Shot the Sheriff' late one night in Boon Wang's cellar bar. "And I don't deny that we're a mite concerned about land prices overheating. But all I can say, for now, is that this is an exceptionally fine vintage."

"Bob thinks I should be getting out of some of my property, Andrew," said Boon Wang. "What do you think?"

Robert Paderewski, the American Ambassador, was a self-made millionaire who had played college football with George Bush. He looked at Andrew with an expression of polite interest on his beefy face.

"Far be it for me to contradict someone with Bob's track record for making money," said Andrew. "But I suppose it's just possible that, if you sold a significant proportion of your land, you'd be doing the government's job for them. That wouldn't do the rest of your land portfolio much good."

Boon Wang laughed. "You could be right, High Commissioner," he said. "In that case, maybe I'd better sell it all – or none of it!"

The conversation continued in this vein for several more minutes. Andrew contributed nothing further: it was, in truth, a subject which interested him very little. But he obtained a certain vicarious pleasure from watching Boon Wang in action. He strongly suspected that Cheng knew exactly what the Government's plans were. And, if they involved releasing large tracts of publicly owned land in the near future, Boon Wang would already have taken the necessary countervailing action well before the holiday. His high-profile assets – the shopping malls and five-star hotels – would remain untouched, because they were integral to his public image and generated a handsome income. But he would have discreetly disposed of every spare parcel of land in his speculative portfolio, using a range of intermediaries to disguise the transactions from the market watchers until it was too late for them to do anything about it.

Guests came and went from the inner sanctum and, after a while, Andrew excused himself to go to look for some of Mei Lin's legendary food. He was surprised to find the bulky figure of the American Ambassador at his shoulder as he circulated around the buffet table.

"That was a smart observation you made back there, Andrew," said Paderewski. "Do you have a background in real estate?"

Andrew added a selection of salads to the beef, chicken, pork and rice already on his plate. "Not at all," he said. "It was just a passing thought." He spooned relish on to his plate. "But I've no doubt it had already occurred to Boon Wang."

"I expect you have substantial properties in England," Bob said, with no apparent hint of irony, as he heaped his own plate with food.

"Not really," said Andrew. His finances, or lack of them, were no concern of the American, and he was not going to get drawn any deeper into that particular conversation. "Look, can we change the subject a moment? I wanted to ask you what you made of this stuff the Singaporeans have been passing on to us."

Paderewski looked at him sharply. "Maybe we'd better go outside," he said.

At the back of the house was a large swimming pool and an extensive patio, where some of the guests were sitting and eating at tables under sun umbrellas. The heat hit the two men like a wall as they stepped out of the air conditioning, and within seconds Andrew was bathed in sweat. *This had better be good*, he thought, as they took seats at an unoccupied table.

"There may be something going down this week, but it's definitely not in Singapore," said Paderewski.

"You sound very sure," said Andrew. "Michael Seng thought it unlikely, but he wasn't that emphatic."

"It's somewhere in Indonesia," said Paderewski. "Trust me."

"I'd heard that your people expected something aimed at you," said Andrew.

"Well, it seemed like too much of a coincidence," said Paderewski. "We were planning to take the yacht around the Riau Archipelago over the holiday. That's where we think something's cooking."

"Planning to?"

"Yeah," said Paderewski. "Abby put her foot down. We're staying in Singapore now."

Paderewski's wife, who had been a criminal lawyer in New

York before her marriage, was a formidable woman with whom every conversation felt like a cross-examination. Her will invariably prevailed over that of her husband.

"So where does that leave the threat?" asked Andrew.

"We still think something's going to happen," said Paderewski. "I guess Abby's right. We're better off staying here until it's cleared up, one way or another."

"That would certainly seem to be the wisest course," said Andrew. But he was thinking of the smoothness of Birgit's thighs and how pink her tongue was, and the amazing things of which it was capable, and he knew it would take more than vague warnings to prevent him from boarding the ferry to Bintan the following night.

* * *

"Easy does it, Adam, it's only a game, you know!"

With his mind on other things, Adam had volleyed the ball with all his strength straight at Mary Bennett. Luckily, she had moved swiftly to one side and avoided otherwise certain injury.

"And I always thought you were a gentleman, Adam," said Murray Parker, picking the ball up and knocking it back to Adam. "It's the game that counts, old chap. Isn't that what the British always say?"

"You're full of shit, Murray," said Mimi Parker, who was partnering Adam. "Win at all costs is your motto. Mine too. If Adam needs to kill Mary in the process – nothing personal, Mary – I say go right ahead, Adam."

"I'm really sorry, Mary," said Adam. "I don't know what I was thinking of."

He served, very gently, to Mary, who struck a powerful passing shot down the line, which left Adam groping and stumbling.

"I'd say honours were pretty much even now," said Murray with a grin.

They played for a further twenty minutes, before, by common consent, abandoning the blazing heat of the tennis court for the shade of the British Club terrace.

"So, Adam," said Murray, once they were all settled with beers and soft drinks. "What's the low-down on this drugs case? Is it going to give you a serious problem?"

Where would you like me to begin? thought Adam. "Off the record, Murray?" he said.

"Of course, you dope," said Murray. "You don't think I play tennis with you for professional reasons, do you? I just like winning, that's all."

"It looks very bad," said Adam. "He's innocent, but it's going to be difficult to prove it."

"They always are innocent – that goes without saying," said Mimi, who did not share her husband's liberal conscience.

"No," said Adam. "He really is innocent. Someone planted the stuff on him."

"Not the police, surely?" said Murray.

"God, no," said Adam. He had had a similar exchange earlier in the day with the *Daily Express* journalist, whom he had telephoned, with some reluctance, after the duty officer confirmed that the Foreign Office was happy for him to do so. It was after midnight in London, which he knew meant the *Express* believed they had some kind of a scoop. He had assumed they had belatedly picked up the piece in the *Straits Times*, so was momentarily knocked off balance when the reporter mentioned Daniel Taylor by name.

"All I can say is he's suspected of possession of heroin," said Adam. "He hasn't yet appeared in court."

But the journalist had not been content to let things go. He had tried to suggest that the boy had been framed by the Singaporeans, and that the British Government were not doing anything to protect him. It had gradually dawned on Adam that Simon Taylor had been speaking to the press in England.

"We're doing all in our power to ensure he has a fair trial," Adam had said, but he knew the words sounded hollow.

When the reporter began to ask about the British Government's policy on the death penalty, Adam had said, more curtly than he had intended: "You know full well what it is, because the Foreign Office will have briefed you in London."

It was an irritable note on which to end the conversation, and Adam suspected the reporter would have his revenge when he wrote the story. But it would have been even worse if Adam had said something which could have been twisted to suggest there was any difference of view between London and the High Commission.

"Who, then?" said Murray.

By the High Commissioner's daughter, thought Adam. *The High Commissioner's daughter, who's disappeared off the face of the earth.* His first thought after speaking to the *Daily Express* had been to call off his tennis date with Mary and the Parkers and to set about trying to find Marina. But he did not know where to begin. Devoid of inspiration, he had decided to stick to his schedule. Nothing would happen to Daniel Taylor over the holiday. Maybe some bright idea would occur to him during the course of the day.

"It was someone in the disco," said Adam, conscious, as never before, of what it meant to be economical with the truth. He saw the incredulity on Mimi Parker's face. "I know it's a long shot," he said. "But his lawyer's working on it."

Mary looked at her watch and said she would have to be going. Adam thought she seemed a little down, although there was nothing he could really put his finger on. She had played well today, but not given the impression of deriving much pleasure from the game.

"Are we on for Sunday?" Adam asked.

"Sorry, guys," said Murray. "I've got to cover the Commonwealth Finance Ministers' meeting in Kuala Lumpur next week. I'm flying up on Sunday."

"Yeah, but I'm not," said Mimi. "So if you can find some handsome young hunk from the High Commission to take Murray's place, I am most definitely on."

"I'll ask Lim Beng Seng at the Foreign Ministry," said Adam. "He's usually up for it."

Murray made a ribald remark, but Adam was not really listening. Murray's mention of Kuala Lumpur had triggered a train of thought. He was replaying, in his mind, his conversation with Marina on Sunday. "This friend called me from Kuala Lumpur and said he wanted me to carry something for him to Changi," she had said. "I had to take the train to Johor Bahru and pick up a package from someone I'd meet in a restaurant there. Then I had to bring it back to Singapore and hang on to it for a few days and then go out to the airport to meet someone who'd be in transit there and give the package to him."

What else, Adam? What else did she say? When's the pick-up at Changi scheduled for? What did Marina say? "… Oh yeah, Tuesday evening." Was it possible? Could she have been telling the truth this time? Could she be going to meet the courier at Changi that very evening?

He looked at his watch. It would almost certainly be a flight to Australia, or possibly to London, but that would be even later. He had enough time.

* * *

Alison awoke early, dehydrated and with a throbbing headache. A faint, grey light penetrated the room through the gap between the curtains she had drawn, too carelessly, on going to bed the previous night. She had no recollection of drawing them at all, nor of changing into her pyjamas, but she had apparently done both of these things. What she had not done, on the evidence of how the inside of her mouth felt, was clean her teeth.

She lay for several minutes gathering her thoughts. It had

been a mistake to arrange to meet Janet and her boyfriend on the same day as her lunch with Richard. With so much alcohol already in her system, she had become rash after the first couple of glasses of wine and had soon lost track of what she was drinking. Janet herself drank only mineral water throughout the evening while her friend, Barry, drank draft lager from half-pint glasses.

Alison had liked Barry at once. He was a radiographer at Wittington Hospital. Janet had met him when she went for a routine chest x-ray after coming out of the rehabilitation centre and, as Barry cheerfully acknowledged, had bullied him into asking her out. He was unassuming, straightforward and had a nice sense of humour. Most important of all, he clearly adored Janet. So the three of them had spent an easy, laughter-filled evening together, first in a pub in Highgate Village and then in a nearby Italian restaurant. Once, briefly, Alison had caught herself thinking of the times she and Adam had spent with Janet before going to Singapore, and was almost overwhelmed with sadness at his absence. But the evident happiness of her companions had soon jollied her out of herself.

The latter part of the evening was now very hazy in her memory. She recalled that Barry and Janet had insisted on driving her back to Pinner, and that it had taken a long time, with a lot of giggling, to open the front door of her parents' house. Her mother and father had presumably already been in bed, but she had no real memory of anything once she was inside the house.

Alison had never in her life been this hungover. She looked at her watch through half-closed eyes: it was not yet seven. She had to get something for her headache. With her eyes still half-closed, she got out of bed, gingerly, and groped her way in the gloom, down the corridor towards her parents' bathroom, which, luckily, was not en suite. She switched on the light, wincing, and began to search the bathroom cabinet for aspirin.

Like everything in Ruth Webster's house, the cabinet was

forbiddingly tidy. Various soaps and shampoos were stacked carefully along the bottom shelf. The next one up had assorted hand and face creams and lotions. Then came a shelf with Harry's shaving equipment neatly arranged. (*By Ruth, of course*, thought Alison. Her mother was as compulsively tidy as Alison herself. Harry, like Adam, would have left everything lying around on the washbasin.) The next shelf up contained a range of toothpaste and mouthwashes. Finally, on the top shelf, sat a small first-aid box and alongside it a row of pillboxes.

If Alison had chosen to look in the first-aid box, she would have found a packet of aspirin immediately. But she tried the pillboxes first. She found no aspirin in any of them. She found anti-inflammatory pills for her father's arthritis. She found milk-of-magnesia tablets for his indigestion. She found pills for eliminating haemorrhoids. She found a whole range of treatments for minor ailments of one kind or another. And then, on the label of the final box, sitting, unmenacingly, at the far end of the shelf, she at last found, in capital letters, the word 'ASPIRIN'. But it formed part of a sentence which at first made no sense to her: 'NOT TO BE TAKEN IN COMBINATION WITH ASPIRIN'. She opened the box and looked, uncomprehending, at the pills within. Then she turned the box round and saw the single word: 'WARFARIN'.

Alison put the pills back on the shelf and closed the cabinet door. She switched out the light, went back to her bedroom and crawled under the covers. Her head was pounding now, worse than ever before. And it pounded rhythmically over and over again. *Why, why, why, why?* said the pounding. *Why didn't you tell me? Why are you fussing around over me and my stupid emotional crisis, when all the time I'm the one who should be looking after you? Why, why, why, why, why...?*

CHAPTER 9

Changi regularly wins the title of 'the world's favourite airport'. It is efficient, clean and beautiful, with waterfalls, aquariums and abundant greenery to complement its state-of-the-art design. There are luxury shops, selling everything from diamond necklaces to home-grown orchids, and restaurants to suit every taste. The volume of traffic is prodigious. And yet, first-time visitors to Singapore can be forgiven for thinking that theirs is the only flight of the day, so quiet and unhurried is the process by which the airport handles its over 100,000 passengers arriving and departing every twenty-four hours.

At two o'clock in the morning Changi was not, however, Adam's favourite airport. Marina had not come – or, at least, he had not seen her. Not knowing where she was to meet the courier made it difficult to decide where to lie in wait. If Marina had wangled some kind of airport pass, the handover might have been planned for the transit lounge. This seemed the most probable arrangement, with the courier having boarded the aircraft in another country. But the lounge was vast and there were hundreds of potential locations for a meeting. It was even possible that the courier was not in transit and that the exchange had been arranged in the check-in area. Worst of all, there was no knowing, for sure, which terminal was involved. Thankfully, the projected third terminal was not yet operational, but even keeping track of two buildings was a challenge. Not for the first time in his life, Adam realised that he had embarked on an enterprise without giving it enough advanced thought.

In the end, he decided to focus on the various points of entry into the two departure terminals, patrolling on foot along the inside of the buildings. He calculated that, if he kept up a reasonably brisk pace, he would return to the same spot every five minutes or so. If Marina arrived in his absence, the chances were that he would see her car parked outside the relevant terminal entrance. (Parking in this zone was illegal, but Marina was not one to worry about such things.) He would know then that she had, at most, only a few minutes start on him. Unless, of course, she came in a taxi. Or chose the arrivals entrance. Adam's plan was full of holes, but he could think of none better.

Adam became aware, as he strode up and down through the terminals, that there were more police around than usual. At one point, he recognised a plain-clothes member of the Central Narcotics Bureau and turned rapidly away to avoid being seen. *What the hell are you doing?* he thought to himself. *You're not a criminal. You're trying to avert a crime, for God's sake.* But he did not want the complication of having to lie about why he was at the airport. He supposed they had received another tip-off. If he did not get to Marina before they did, she would be beyond saving.

He need not have worried. Shortly before two, the police abandoned their watch. After a further twenty minutes, Adam also admitted defeat.

There was, realistically, only one other line of enquiry to pursue. "This friend called me from Kuala Lumpur..." *Please, no,* thought Adam. *That really would be too much like looking for a needle in a haystack.*

But what else could he do? And why should he not at least try? The High Commission would be closed until Monday. He was not even formally in charge of the post – Andrew Singleton never bothered to notify anyone in London or Singapore when he disappeared on one of his impromptu expeditions. And, according to Inderjit Singh, Daniel Taylor's court appearance would not be before Monday: Adam could brief the duty officer to call him on his mobile if the boy's father made contact in the meantime. *One last throw*, he thought, *to try to sort things out.* And, if it failed, he would somehow find Andrew Singleton and tell him the whole truth and let *him* worry about the consequences.

* * *

Andrew was experiencing mixed emotions as he boarded the ferry for Bintan at the Tanah Merah terminal. The anticipatory pleasure at his imminent reunion with Birgit was temporarily marred by his fury with Marina for failing to return the car, as promised. Using the Rolls would broadcast knowledge of his movements more widely than necessary. The trip was not exactly a secret, but he could have done without the explanatory small talk with the duty driver, who had been summoned at short notice. The latter had, for example, remarked on the fact that Andrew was not taking his golf clubs with him. He made some excuse about a bad back, at which the driver nodded enigmatically, almost as though he knew what Andrew really planned to be doing for the next forty-eight hours.

The ferry pulled away from the shore, and the distant grey of the Singapore City skyline receded further into the distance. Andrew settled himself into a seat alongside a young Chinese couple and glanced through a copy of the *Economist*. But his anger with Marina persisted. He could not decide whether she was worse than her mother. Their selfishness and capacity for damage were of the same order, but they were very different people. Marina was aimless and casually destructive. Her mother, by contrast, had been extraordinarily calculating.

Elena's father had been one of the youngest of the generation of Panamanian politicians swept aside by the Torrijos revolution at the end of the 1960s. His relationship with the deposed

President had been sufficiently distant to spare him from exile, but the ban on political activity imposed by the National Guard when they seized power obliged him to seek an alternative source of personal enrichment. He had chosen offshore banking, at the time a rapid growth activity in Panama, and highly profitable for those who asked no questions about either the provenance or the destination of the money expensively committed to their temporary care.

After Torrijos's death some twelve years later in a helicopter crash, there was speculation, premature, as it turned out, that the old political parties might be allowed to re-form. As the number two in the Embassy, Andrew had taken it upon himself to cultivate the potential leaders of the future, among whom Enrique Castro was one of the more prominent. A better description would have been 'notorious', because many of Enrique's dealings were very shady. A Swiss banker friend of Andrew's had warned him that a number of people who came too close to the truth about Enrique's activities had mysteriously disappeared. But Andrew was undeterred. If anything, the rumours made him more curious.

Castro had taken to the athletic, blond young Englishman and invited him to spend a weekend at his beach house in Playa Coronado. There, Andrew had met Elena. She had clearly decided that he was her passport to respectability, because she had set out to seduce him by every conceivable means.

At the time, Andrew had no idea of Elena's true character. He did not know that, following the death of her mother, when Elena was barely three years old, her father had indulged her beyond all reason. Or that, by the time she was fourteen, she had had a string of servants sacked for various alleged crimes, when their only real offence had been to seek to temper her awesome selfishness. That, at sixteen, she had shot Enrique's chauffeur in the foot with her father's hunting rifle when he had refused to take her to a local night club without her father's permission. Or

117

that she had become pregnant at seventeen by one of her father's gardeners, a pregnancy terminated in highest secrecy in a Miami clinic, while the life of the boy involved was terminated in equal secrecy in a back alley of Colon City.

These facts emerged later, after they were married. Andrew learned of them, as husbands do, from well-meaning friends, from jealous women, and through Elena's own behaviour once she had secured her catch. But the Elena with whom Andrew believed himself to be in love was sweet, playful and passionate, and flattered him with her admiration for his intellect and what she regarded as his exalted status. (Andrew had briefly been in charge of the Embassy in the Ambassador's absence.) He had fallen for it. Having drifted through a series of half-hearted relationships, he was ready for something more permanent. He was mesmerised by Elena's beauty and fooled by her apparent love for him. And, in his more honest moments of reflection, he acknowledged that her father's wealth had completed a very attractive package. He proposed to Elena one evening as they sat, entwined in each other's arms on the beach, watching a deep red sun sinking into the Pacific. Three months later they were married in the Cathedral in Panama City. Within a year, he had borne her back to England with him.

Even before they left Panama, Andrew detected signs of what he would soon learn was the real Elena. She was rapidly bored by his Embassy duties, and insisted on late night outings to clubs and expensive restaurants. When he was away from their flat at an official function, she would invite in groups of her old friends, who stayed on, drinking and dancing, long after he had returned and gone to bed. One of the regular visitors was a sardonic young man called José, who wore a great deal of gold jewellery, and seemed to Andrew to be excessively familiar with Elena. He had remarked upon this once to Elena, who had laughed dismissively. "*¿José? ¿Eres loco?*" she said. "*Es maricón.* He's gay. *Todo el mundo lo sabe.*" She was, he discovered later, an impressive liar.

Back in England, things deteriorated rapidly. Elena was not prepared for the reality of living in London on a Foreign Office salary. And she could not believe Andrew was serious, when he showed her the terraced house in Stockwell where he proposed they should live. After she had thrown a monumental tantrum, he agreed to look at properties in central London, buying in the end a ludicrously short lease on a flat in Kensington with the maximum mortgage he could negotiate. When, at one point, Andrew had suggested that Elena's father might want to help them out financially, Elena had thrown a screaming fit, accusing him of not being able to support his own wife to the standard she had been led to expect.

Then, suddenly, she was pregnant. Andrew was faced with mounting medical bills to add to the sums Elena was spending on lavish furnishings and clothes – or on entertaining her friends, who regularly came through London, many of them staying for several weeks before moving on to some other free watering hole in Europe.

Marina's birth momentarily slowed down Elena's social activities, but it did not stop her spending Andrew's money. No amount of remonstrating from Andrew had any effect. By the time they went on their next overseas posting, to Caracas, he was heavily in debt.

The extra money from being abroad – they went straight on to further postings in Rio de Janeiro and Bangkok – eased his financial situation to some degree. But the marriage was characterised by terrible fights, and he suspected that Elena was unfaithful to him more than once, although she was clever enough to give him no proof. All during this time, Elena kept Marina jealously to herself and a series of expensive nannies, frustrating all Andrew's attempts to bond with the child. He had, in any case, found it difficult to relate to Marina, whose sulky and spiteful nature was reinforced by Elena's extravagance.

Their relative affluence and intensive social life overseas

masked the serious cracks in the relationship. When Andrew was posted back to London again, there was nothing to prevent the marriage from disintegrating. The lease on the flat was almost expired and, at Elena's insistence, Andrew borrowed heavily to extend it. Elena continued to spend his money and chose the most exclusive schooling for Marina. The fights between them grew ever more frequent and violent. Until the last fight of all. The fight he strove not to think about.

The boat had encountered a heavy swell during the crossing, but now it entered the calmer waters of the ferry port in Bintan. The television screens, which had been showing tourism advertisements and, bizarrely, an old episode of *Mr Bean*, went suddenly blank as the vessel turned in a wide arc and slowly made its approach.

Andrew picked up his holdall and made his way with the other passengers towards the gangplank. On the dockside a group of men, barefoot and dressed in shorts and ragged shirts, worked together to lash the ferry firmly into position alongside. *Forget Elena*, he told himself. *Get to the resort. Book in and eat dinner, alone, in full view of everyone at the outdoor restaurant. Have a late-night stroll along the beach and then turn in early. And if you dream, dream only of Birgit.*

* * *

It was beginning to get dark as Adam turned off the motorway and headed towards Kuala Lumpur. Throughout the five hours of the journey from Singapore he had done his best to concoct a plan of action for finding Marina, but inspiration had eluded him. Once again he found himself playing things by ear.

He had been tempted to chase after Marina straight from the airport, but he had recognised the wisdom of getting some rest first. He had slept until eight o'clock and had then spent an hour telephoning various people to seek their help. First he spoke to

Stan Murdoch, his opposite number in the High Commission in Kuala Lumpur, explaining in confidence that Marina had gone missing, and that he was trying to reach her to talk some sense into her before her father found out where she was. (All of which was true, if not exactly the whole story.) Murdoch took the details of Marina's car and undertook to seek the assistance of the local police, promising to emphasise the need for absolute discretion.

Then Adam rang Murray Parker. "Murray, I'll have to ask you to trust me on this," he said. "I need some discreet eyes and ears in Kuala Lumpur and I can't tell you why." Murray had come up with the name of a Malaysian photographer with whom he had frequently worked, and offered to call to prepare him for Adam's visit. "I'll take a very large beer in payment when you get back," Murray said.

Adam had then rung Susan Hyde, who was the duty officer of the week, to ensure that she knew what to do if Simon Taylor called. She had sounded nervous at the prospect, but he had persuaded her that there was unlikely to be a serious problem. Adam's final call was to Mary Bennett, to ask her to relay some plausible excuse to the host of the Chinese New Year's party at which Adam was supposed to be representing the High Commissioner that evening. "Say I've been called out of town on business – that should do it," said Adam. "If you'd like to go in my place, feel free. But it's not really that important." Mary's reply had surprised him. "Why not?" she had said. "I've got nothing better to do."

When his calls were completed, Adam had scrutinised the Central Narcotics Bureau website. He studied the pattern of arrests made in the last twelve months for some clue to the operations of the people Marina had somehow become involved with. Johor Bahru seemed to be the starting point of most of the smugglers arrested, but Adam could trace no connection with Kuala Lumpur. Should he be looking for Marina instead in Johor Bahru? No, he decided. It was a long shot under any circumstances, but if Marina was in trouble he would expect her to look for help from her so-called friend, not from an anonymous link man in Johor Bahru – if such a man had ever existed.

Balancing a Kuala Lumpur city map on the steering wheel, Adam turned off the ring road and into a network of tree-lined streets running along the western edge of the Royal Selangor Golf Club. After two false starts and one overshoot he found the English-style detached house where Stan Murdoch lived. Fran Murdoch opened the door of the house, as he climbed out of the car.

"Good timing, Adam," she called, gathering up into her arms the twin toddlers who were trying to make a break for freedom past her legs. "Stan's just been trying to ring you. He thinks he's had a sighting of your wayward girl."

* * *

By mid-afternoon, Alison had finally composed her letter to Adam. She had made no attempt to write it the previous day, which she had spent recovering from her hangover and wrestling with her conscience about whether to tell her father she had discovered his secret. She had not done so, on the grounds that he clearly did not want her to know about his illness, and would be happier believing she was still in ignorance. She had thought, fleetingly, of talking to her mother, but could not bring herself to do so.

Alison looked down into the garden, where, as usual, her father was working. Today he seemed to be preoccupied with waterproofing the garden shed. Her mother had gone to a meeting at the synagogue – an unusual event, in Alison's experience, for a family which normally wore its religion lightly.

The letter read as follows:

Dearest Adam

I love you. I always will. But I have to stay in England for the foreseeable future. First, because my father is seriously ill and I must spend as much time with him as possible. And second, because I have the chance to get my old job back and I realise now how important that is to me. Please don't be angry with me. Singapore was simply a step too far too soon. I shall miss you dreadfully and when you come back to England I am yours if you still want me. Nobody can ever replace you.

With love

Ali'

It was not much of a letter, but all her attempts to explain her feelings in more detail had sounded as if she was making either excuses or complaints. In fairness to Adam, she wanted to do neither of these things. She had also thought of saying nothing about her job. Her father's condition alone would have kept her in England, so why complicate things? *Because this is Adam,* she reminded herself. *Because we swore we'd always be honest with one another. Because the easy way is invariably the wrong way.*

Ali toyed with the idea of telephoning Adam to tell him what she had decided. But their long-distance telephone calls had been unsatisfactory, and she did not want to break down and cry, particularly if he began to remonstrate with her. She also thought of emailing the letter, but felt that would be too soulless. She sealed the envelope and went downstairs for her coat. She called briefly to her father, who waved cheerfully from the end of the garden, as she let herself out of the side gate and set off for the Post Office.

* * *

"Patrick? How's it going, old son? It's Peter here."
Patrick Young was in Brixton Market, his son strapped into

a papoose on his back. It was cold. Father and son both had woollen hats, pulled down over their ears, and scarves wrapped around the lower halves of their faces.

Peter Coles had called him on his mobile. It must be something urgent.

"What's up, Peter?" he said.

"Patrick, I'm sorry to fuss and all that," said Coles. "But the boss is asking when your Santo Domingo report's going to be ready."

"Give me a break, Peter," said Patrick. "I've barely been back a week."

"Yes, sure, I know," said Coles. "But you know what he's like. Any chance of a sight of it by Friday?"

"Monday," said Patrick. "I'll be in the office on Monday, as agreed. I'll bring the report then."

"Monday it is then, old son," said Coles, who had clearly been expecting no different.

Patrick looked around him at the mess of colourful stalls. *It's funny*, he thought. *We bust a gut to get out of Brixton, stretching our finances to the limit to buy a flat somewhere different. And where do I go to do the shopping? Brixton, of course.*

Patrick's grandfather had come to England from Jamaica in the 1950s to be a bus driver. Patrick's father, an electrician, had married a girl from Dublin. They had had seven children, of whom Patrick was the oldest. When, against expectation, Patrick did exceptionally well at his A levels, there had been no money for university. He had got into the Foreign Office in a junior capacity and his parents had wept with pride. If they had only known, thought Patrick, how boring and badly paid his first job in London had been.

Still, it's looking up a bit now, he thought. The Foreign Office had recognised his native talent. He had had two overseas postings and two promotions. And meeting Buffy – a teacher in the local primary school – had given him an extra sense of direction, an edge to his ambition. His current job could be the stepping stone to even greater things. On reflection, perhaps he should try to get the report in before the weekend. He looked at his watch. If he could get Jamie down as soon as he got home, and if Buffy was still resting, he could get in a quick hour on the computer.

* * *

Despite the difficult nature of her errand, Alison had enjoyed the walk to the Post Office. The sudden cold snap had required her to wrap up in winter clothes. Her nose and ears were stinging and her cheeks were flushed. Six months in the sticky heat of Singapore had almost made her forget the simple pleasures of the English climate.

Ali let herself in by the side gate. She was feeling sad, but relieved, to have taken her decision and conveyed it fairly to Adam. She would be miserable without him. But better that than to be resentful in his company and sour their relationship for all time. *Who am I kidding?* she thought. *I'm going to be beside myself with longing for him.*

She looked up the garden to greet her father. When she did not see him, she thought for a moment that he must be taking a break for a coffee. Then she saw something sticking out from behind the garden shed and realised, with a sickening shock, that she was looking at the ends of her father's wellington boots. She cried out and ran up the garden, seized by fear and incipient grief. She rounded the shed and saw her father lying on his side on the concrete, facing towards the back wall of the shed, one hand outstretched and clutching the far end of the wall, the other wedged between his body and the shed.

Alison cried out again and knelt beside her father, touching him on the shoulder.

He looked up, surprised. "Hello, Ali," he said. "What's all this about?"

Alison looked at her father, stupidly. She saw now that he had been fiddling with an awkward piece of waterproofing material to try to plug a knothole in the wood low down on the shed wall.

"I thought… " she said.

"Did you think I'd fallen over or something?" laughed her father, clambering up and squeezing her round the shoulder.

"No. Yes. No, I don't know what I thought," said Alison. He looked so cheerful that she felt completely idiotic. Might he have guessed that she knew? If he had, he was an exceptionally good actor.

CHAPTER 10

The pool was surrounded on three sides by the villa, which was constructed from seasoned tropical wood, in a subtle variation on a traditional Indonesian style. On each side of the pool was an air-conditioned bedroom, forming the arms of a U-shape, the linking section of which was a raised *al fresco* dining area sheltered by a high, timbered ceiling, roofed in thatch. This area could be further protected, if desired, by releasing rattan blinds, but it was now open front and back. Beyond was a small enclosed garden with a pathway leading over an ornamental pond to the entrance gate, which was set in a high stone wall. The gate was closed, but not locked.

The open end of the pool looked straight out to the South China Sea through the fronds of coconut trees. With the taste of his breakfast coffee and the first cigarette of the day still lingering in his mouth, Andrew stood, with his knees slightly bent, up to his neck in the pool. He watched the distant smudge of a container ship working its way across an otherwise clear horizon, where the faint blue of an almost cloudless sky merged with that of the sea. Raising himself on tip-toe and leaning forward, he could see, some three feet below, a concave ledge filled with decorative stones designed to catch and filter the overflow from the pool. Beyond and below the ledge there was a near-vertical drop to rocks some fifty feet or more below, where the sea swirled and foamed, dark green and scattering spray. The villa was perched on the edge of a cliff, with access only from the front, and was supported at the rear by concrete pillars overgrown with vines and orchids. Andrew knew there were a number of similar villas on either side of him, but they were all cunningly positioned to give the impression to the inhabitants that they were totally isolated.

The resort was exclusive and catered mainly for wealthy Singaporeans seeking a few days of tranquil respite from the hurly-burly of their daily lives. Its main attraction was its seclusion, although it had many other things to offer: a spotless beach, where a variety of water sports was possible; a golf course designed by a former United States Open Champion; an artistically landscaped pool area; a luxurious massage salon; and three restaurants, offering haute cuisine to satisfy both Asian and Western tastes. Andrew had no intention of sampling any of these attractions. Nor, as he had on past visits, would he be venturing further afield to seek out the sunbirds and silverleaf monkeys that inhabited the still unspoiled areas of forest on the island. From this point on, he would not be leaving the confines of the villa. He had his own pool. The refrigerator was stocked with champagne, and the restaurants would deliver food on demand. He needed only one more thing to complete his pleasure, for which, by his calculation, he now had barely half an hour to wait.

* * *

Stan Murdoch's news the previous evening had not, in the event, been quite as good as Adam had hoped. Marina's car had been sighted close to the Petronas Twin Towers in central Kuala Lumpur earlier in the day. The car, driven by a young woman accompanied by an older man, had been heading south. Without explicit instructions, the police had not sought to detain the vehicle. Adam had telephoned Murray's friend, a young Chinese Malaysian called Yong Pung How, but they had agreed that at this stage there was little Pung How could do to help.

With only a single sighting, the direction in which the car had been travelling told them nothing. They did, however, exchange mobile telephone numbers and agree to keep in touch.

Over dinner, with the twins safely in bed, Adam had given the Murdochs a suitably edited account of the reason for his search for Marina. Stan, who had played football with Adam when they were both posted in London, was keen to help in any way he could. But Fran, a sturdy former hockey international (who had met Alison on a visit to Singapore a couple of months earlier), asked Adam rather pointedly why he felt it was his responsibility to find Marina.

"Good question," said Adam. *Bloody good question actually*, he thought. "I suppose I feel sort of responsible for her with the High Commissioner being away."

Fran looked unconvinced. "And what does Alison think about it all?" she said.

"Ali's away at the moment," said Adam. Fran had given him a thin smile and the conversation moved on to other things.

Later, prompted by Fran's question, Adam had tried to telephone Alison. Her father had answered the telephone to explain that she was visiting an old girlfriend who had just had a baby. "But I think she's written to you, Adam," said Harry. Adam took this as a hint that Ali's father thought it best that he not try to reach her on her mobile. "Is she okay, Harry?" said Adam. "She was pretty down when she left Singapore."

"She just needs time to sort herself out, Adam," said Harry. "Be patient with her."

Eating breakfast now, alone on the Murdochs' terrace the following morning, Adam tried not to think about Ali's letter. It would probably have arrived by the time he got back to Singapore. There was no point in torturing himself further about its possible contents now.

A common myna suddenly arrived on the terrace rail, brown plumage bristling, black head on one side, casting a speculative, yellow-bespectacled eye over the remains of Adam's breakfast. It was joined immediately by its mate and hopped, emboldened, on to the back of the chair opposite Adam. Grateful for the momentary diversion, Adam tossed the bird a piece of toast. This was a mistake, because the other bird suddenly swooped down on to the table and began strutting brazenly among the plates, jabbing its beak randomly at anything that looked remotely like food.

"Cheeky little bastards," Adam muttered, shaking his napkin at the birds, who retreated, clicking and squeaking in protest to the terrace rail. At that moment, Stan Murdoch telephoned from the High Commission, bringing Adam's thoughts abruptly back to Marina.

"It looks as though she's on the move," said Stan. "The police have seen the car three times in the last hour."

Adam took a note of the details and times of the three sightings and telephoned Yong Pung How to seek his views.

"The car seems to be headed north-west now," said Pung How. "And it's already in the north of the city."

"Assuming they're leaving town, what would be your guess about where they could be going?" asked Adam.

"If they keep on their present trajectory, I'd say there were two basic options," said Pung How. "Either they're heading up the west coast to somewhere like Ipoh or Taiping. Or they could be going across country to Kota Bahru on the east coast."

"If they're going to the east coast, why not Kuantan?" said Adam, looking at a large-scale map of Malaysia that Stan Murdoch had given him.

"That's less likely," said Pung How. "The last sighting is farther west than the normal turning off the ring road for Kuantan. But, of course, it's not entirely impossible."

"If you had to choose between east and west coast, which would it be?" asked Adam.

"Impossible to tell," said Yong Pung. "You'd need another

130

sighting after the road divides to be absolutely sure." He paused, then added, "Of course, there is another possibility, whichever route they're taking."

"Which is?"

"That they're on their way to Thailand."

* * *

The sun had climbed higher in the sky. Andrew submerged himself in the pool to cool his head. As he came to the surface, he heard behind him the faint sound of the latch of the outer gate being opened. Perversely, he did not turn, but remained looking out towards the sea, savouring expectation until the final moment.

For a few seconds, nothing happened. Then he heard footsteps, followed by a further few seconds of silence. Then something landed with a crash in the pool behind him. Before he could turn, an arm came round his neck and a hand went over his mouth. As he was dragged backwards under the water, Andrew saw, in a subliminal flash, the image of Michael Seng shaking his head as in his dream of two days ago. Water ran up into his nose and he lashed out wildly in an attempt to free himself, but the grip was firm and unrelenting. For what seemed like a very long time, he struggled to hold his breath. Then, miraculously, the restraining arm released him and he surfaced, choking and cursing.

"I hope you're not getting too old for this sort of thing, Andrew," said Birgit. He turned and saw her before him in the pool, the disturbed water lapping backwards and forwards across her nipples.

Andrew looked at her, breathing hard. Behind, at the pool edge, he could see her sandals, an overnight bag and the cotton shift she had moments before pulled off her otherwise naked body.

"You're going to pay for this, Frau Berger," he said.

Birgit waded slowly towards him until her mouth was only inches away from his. *"Gut,"* she said, reaching one hand down between his legs. *"Das hatte ich mir eigentlich gedacht."*

* * *

Adam drove north at high speed along the main highway between Kuala Lumpur and Ipoh. To his right, the Cameron Highlands bulked dark against a grey and threatening sky. To his left lay wetlands and mangrove swamps.

He had no idea where he was going. He could not be sure that Marina was not, in fact, headed for the east coast, or even that she might not still be in Kuala Lumpur. The elusive fourth sighting had not materialised; there was a limit to what Stan could ask the police to do, on an informal basis, outside the capital city itself. Choosing the west coast route had been a gamble, but one which Adam had felt obliged to take. He had lost Marina completely for two days. To be this close and do nothing would have been intolerable. Pung How's mention of Thailand had clinched things. Marina had only about an hour's start on him. If he could keep up this speed, and had guessed her route correctly, he could still, just, catch her within Malaysia. *That's if she keeps to the highway*, he reminded himself. There were countless towns and villages along the way where she might turn off. She could go up into the hills. Or she could easily hide up in a town the size of Ipoh. *Don't think about it*, he said to himself. *Concentrate on driving.*

Adam's mobile telephone lay on the passenger seat beside him. He had left it switched on for the best part of two hours in case Stan or Pung How rang with any further information. Now the battery was running low and, like an idiot, he had not checked to see if the charger was in the car before he set out. He debated whether to keep the phone switched on in the hope of some final piece of intelligence coming through, but decided that he could not reasonably expect to hear anything further now. He switched the phone off to preserve the battery for an emergency.

The sky had become darker and one or two spots of rain were falling by the time he reached the run-down outskirts of Ipoh. Once a thriving tin mining centre, the town had stagnated economically in recent years and looked sad and shabby in the greyish light. Adam resisted the temptation to search for Marina's car in the town, and drove straight through as fast as he dared and on towards Taiping. Just west of Kuala Kangsar, he hesitated momentarily when he saw a sign to a road leading to Kota Bahru. (Why hadn't Pung How warned him about this?) But he decided to stick to his plan and push on to Taiping, and beyond towards Butterworth and Penang.

There were distant flashes of lightning now behind the thick clouds massed over the highlands to his right. Thunder grumbled belatedly and the rain spots became heavier and more regular. It was dark enough for Adam to need to put on his headlights. As he did so, he rounded a bend and saw a car on the road ahead, no more than a mile distant.

Adam accelerated and rapidly overhauled the vehicle, which was travelling very slowly. To his disappointment, he saw that it was not Marina's car, but a battered Ford pickup truck, filled with sacks of seed, driven by a young Malay. On an impulse, Adam sounded his horn and wound down his window as he drew alongside, gesturing to show that he wanted to ask something. The other driver obligingly pulled into the side of the road, and looked expectantly towards Adam as the latter leaned across to speak to him through his open window. The man was dressed in farm overalls and wore a straw hat pushed on to the back of his head.

"*Selamat pagi, encik,*" he said, smiling. "*Bagaimana saya boleh tolong?*"

"*Selamat pagi,*" said Adam. "*Terima kasih.*" Then he hesitated, trying to structure in his head a sentence to convey his question as accurately as possible. He rarely needed to use Malay in Singapore; although a keen student, he lacked spontaneous fluency.

When he had the sentence worked out, Adam embarked upon the process of delivering it. Halfway through, the man interrupted him. "If it's easier in English, please don't hesitate to say so," he said. "I can pretty much get by without too much trouble."

"Bloody hell," said Adam. "You'll have to forgive me for murdering your language."

"Some people wouldn't even try," smiled the man. "But I sense you're in a hurry, so let's have your question."

"I'm looking for a green Land Rover Discovery," said Adam. "Driven by a young girl, possibly accompanied by an older man."

"Oh, yes," said the man. "They nearly drove me off the road about ten minutes ago."

Ten minutes ago. At last Adam felt his luck had changed. "That's fantastic," he said. "Thanks so much."

Adam put the car into gear, but turned to the man before pulling away. "If you don't mind me asking… " he said.

"Five years at King's, Canterbury," said the man. "And three studying agronomy at Reading. Drive carefully, old chap – it looks as though we're going to have quite a storm."

* * *

Andrew absently massaged the sole of Birgit's foot as they lay, head to toe, on the double bed in the air-conditioned room. They had made love first, very fast, in the pool, then later, after champagne, on a sun lounger. Andrew had then taken delivery of their barbecued lunch, while Birgit kept out of sight. They ate, wrapped in towels, sitting opposite each other in the raised dining area. Andrew had then placed the tray with dirty plates outside the entrance gate, which he locked to ensure no further interruption, and they had retreated from the fierce midday heat into the cool within.

Their afternoon sex had been slow, imaginative and exhausting. Now, for the first time that day, Andrew found himself thinking about something other than the wonder of Birgit's body. She lay on her stomach, close to sleep, her face pressed into the pillow. He was on his back, his head by her feet. He moved his fingers lightly up and around her incredibly slim ankle.

"How did you meet Dieter?" he asked.

She lifted her head and looked at him over her shoulder. Her short, blonde hair was slightly mussed and there was the beginning of a crease line in her face from the pillow.

"Why do you ask me that?" she said.

"Why not?" he said, sitting up and resting his hand on the small of her back. "You know all about Elena."

"But I didn't ask you about her," she said, her face back down in the pillow.

He said nothing for a while. He sat cross-legged, running his fingers gently up and down her spine, and listening to her little grunts of appreciation. What she had said was true. He had drunk too much during one of their early meetings and had told her the whole story. Well, not the whole story, but enough.

"Don't you want to talk about it?" he said.

"Not particularly," she said, still into the pillow.

"Why not?"

She turned on to her back, reaching for the rumpled sheet and pulling it over her, up to her neck. "Can you lower the air conditioning?" she said. "I'm getting cold."

"Don't change the subject," he said.

"Look, Andrew," she said. "We've known each other for what? Something like half a year now, and you've never once before asked me a single question about Dieter. Why now, suddenly?"

"I don't know," said Andrew. "Perhaps I've started to feel jealous."

"That's ridiculous," she said. "You don't want to be married to me."

"Of course not," said Andrew. Just for a moment the idea made him curiously excited, but he knew it was impossible. She was barely thirty. Today her clever fingers had played across a hard and muscular body. But in five years' time he would be sixty, and he was already aware of the inevitability of his physical decline. The episode in the pool had shocked him. She was young and strong, and had had the advantage of surprise. But he was disturbed that a woman had, even temporarily, overpowered him.

"That doesn't mean I enjoy sharing you," he said.

"Nothing in this world is perfect," she said, her eyes closed. Then she opened them. "*Scheisse*, Andrew, it really is cold in here."

He continued to look at her without moving. With a gesture of impatience, she swung her long legs out of the bed and disappeared into the bathroom. She returned a few seconds later, wearing baggy, long-sleeved cotton pyjamas and brushing her hair. Unaccountably, Andrew felt the stirrings of desire once more.

"Give me a cigarette," she said.

He lit two cigarettes and handed one to her. She sat cross-legged on the bed facing him, their toes almost touching.

"Can't you keep that thing under control for more than five minutes?" she said. She thrust a pillow into his midriff. "At least cover it up while we're talking."

"Talking? Are we going to talk?"

She exhaled smoke with a resigned sigh. "That seemed to be what you wanted to do."

"Okay," he said, reaching for his shorts and tee shirt and pulling them on. This time he sat beside her on the bed, not looking at her. "Tell me about Dieter."

"I met him on the rebound," said Birgit. "I was in a mess, emotionally. Dieter was in the right place at the right time."

Andrew had met Dieter only once, by accident, at the races

soon after he had embarked on the affair with Birgit. All three had been the guests of Cheng Boon Wang. Despite Andrew's discreet efforts to surround himself with Singaporean friends, they had been seated together at lunch. In his late thirties, Dieter was conventionally handsome, but he was already beginning to run to fat, and his carefully styled, black hair was thinning at the back. He had been boisterous and extravagant in his betting, and had cracked a lot of anti-German jokes, which had clearly been designed to amuse Andrew. He seemed impervious to the electric tension between Andrew and Birgit as they conducted polite conversation, and commiserated with each other over their gambling losses.

"You didn't love him?" said Andrew. "You *don't* love him."

Birgit did not respond immediately. Then she said. "I'm not sure I know what that means. He gives me security. He provides my material needs. He's amusing and considerate. The sex isn't bad."

"That doesn't sound like love to me," said Andrew, experiencing a mild sense of loss at the thought of Birgit and Dieter in bed together.

"Maybe not," she said. "But I was in a contented enough groove until you appeared. That was a shock."

"It was a shock for me too," he said. He paused, and then said: "Do you think *this* is love?"

She stubbed out her cigarette in the ashtray on the bedside table, and turned her head to look at him. "Why does it have to have a label?" she said. "Why not just enjoy it for what it is?"

He did not return her look. He had strayed too far into territory which neither of them was anxious to explore.

"You still haven't said how you and Dieter met," he said.

"At a fashion shoot."

"In Germany?"

"In Hamburg. Dieter was an old school friend of my agent."

"You were a model," he said. "I might have guessed."

"That was strictly part-time," she said. "I was a lecturer in international politics." He could not tell from her tone whether this was a rebuke or a simple statement of fact. He deserved the admonishment. He knew every square inch of her body, which areas to touch to stimulate desire, which to induce relaxation. He knew her tastes in food and drink, what music she liked, what sport she played, which books she read, which films she saw. They had even had, he now recalled, an intriguing discussion on one occasion about the peculiarly successful political, economic and social structures of Singapore. But, in six months of making love to her, he had never once asked anything about her life before she came to Singapore. Neither, he reminded himself, had she expressed any curiosity about his own past.

"Lucky, lucky students," he said. "And now you run a jewellery business."

"Dieter didn't want me to get involved in anything remotely political in Singapore," she said. "I set up the business to give myself something to do while he was travelling."

Andrew could think of nothing to say immediately. Finally he said, "I still don't understand. Why Dieter?"

She took his cigarette from him and squashed it into the ashtray next to hers. "Can I have a drink?" she said. "Something a bit stronger than champagne."

He rummaged in the mini-bar and found two miniature vodka bottles. He poured one each into two tumblers from the bathroom and dropped ice cubes into them. He swirled the ice around with his finger and handed her one of the glasses. He sensed that she was about to tell him something of which she rarely, if ever, spoke.

Birgit took a sip of her vodka. "I'd been involved with another man," she said. "Someone I met at Oxford."

"You read international politics at Oxford?" he said. "Good God, don't tell me you knew my brother."

Birgit looked momentarily startled, and then something

seemed to dawn on her. "I never made the connection," she said. "Dr Singleton, of course. I attended some of his lectures." She smiled, as if in recollection. "I found them somewhat obscure, as I recall."

Andrew grinned. "Some things haven't changed," he said.

Birgit still seemed to be taking in the extraordinary coincidence Andrew had just revealed. "I might have seen you on one of my visits," he said. "That opens up an interesting line of thought."

Birgit grimaced. "I doubt I'd have made quite the same impact on you during my grunge period," she said. Then she closed her eyes and said nothing for a minute or more. Andrew thought she might have fallen asleep, but she finally opened her eyes and sipped her drink again. "What about this man?" he said.

"We'd had no contact for several years," she said. "Then he turned up, out of the blue, in Lübeck, where I was teaching. It became pretty serious."

"This man, you did love," said Andrew.

"Please don't use that word, Andrew," she said. She drank once more, this time a generous slug, which she swilled around in her mouth before swallowing. Her tongue worried the edge of her lip, where a stray drop of vodka had escaped. "We were heavily involved. Maybe I thought it was love. He certainly didn't."

"Did he leave you?"

"No, in the end I left him."

"In the end?"

Birgit was silent for several seconds. "I was pregnant," she said. "He told me to have an abortion. Like a fool, I did what he said."

"You stayed with him after that?"

"Yes. Until I discovered he'd been unfaithful."

"With a friend?"

"With half the women in Lübeck, as far as I can judge."

"What an idiot," said Andrew. He found it difficult to imagine a man who would not be satisfied with Birgit alone.

Birgit had misunderstood him. "Yes," she said, "I was an idiot."

"No, I meant him."

She did not seem to have heard him. She drank again and held out her empty glass. "My parents had been right all along, although for the wrong reasons." she said. "They thought he was 'unsuitable'."

"Unsuitable?" He took her glass and poured the contents of his own into it.

"Not white," she said, taking the glass back and holding it against her chest with clasped hands. "He was from Malaysia."

"Ah," said Andrew.

"You know what he said when I told him it was over?" she said. "That I attached disproportionate value to the concept of monogamy."

"He sounds like an exceptionally cool customer," said Andrew.

"He was a bastard," said Birgit. "But he was irresistible. I cried for a week after he left. Then my agent bullied me into doing the fashion shoot and there was Dieter, just like Prince Charming, ready to pick up the pieces. We were married within three months."

"Did Dieter know what had happened?"

"I never told him about Hussein, or the abortion. I suppose I was ashamed. But he knew I'd had a bad experience."

"How long ago was this?"

"Four years. We came to Singapore less than a year after we were married. Dieter had some big deal he needed to mastermind from the region. Once he looked into the tax advantages in Singapore, he decided to make the move permanent."

"Singapore's less than a stone's throw from Malaysia," said Andrew.

Birgit finished her drink with one swallow. "I remember thinking that at the time," she said. "But I'm pretty sure he's not living there. Anyway, I lost touch with him after we moved from Germany."

"You still had contact after you were married?"

"Only once. He got hold of my phone number from one of my friends. He said he was concerned that my husband should treat me properly, which I thought was pretty ironic. He asked me all sorts of questions about Dieter: where he came from, how he made his money, where he travelled on business, that sort of thing. I should have told him to go to hell."

"But you didn't?"

"I was listening to the sound of his voice," she said. "It didn't matter how badly he'd treated me. I didn't want the conversation to end. How stupid can a woman be?"

"I'm sorry," said Andrew. "I didn't realise this was going to be so painful for you."

"I try my best not to dwell on the past," she said. "It's now that counts."

"An admirable sentiment," he said, rolling over on his side towards her. He ran his finger lightly down her nose and on to her lips. She seized it gently in her teeth and gnawed on it, her eyes closed. He pulled his finger free and turned her face towards him. Her breath was sweet with vodka fumes. She opened her eyes and gave him a faint smile.

"I'm a bit pissed now," she said, as he reached inside her pyjama shirt. "Be gentle with me."

* * *

Adam saw the Discovery in front of him just as the storm broke over both cars. He had been driving for nearly five hours and had decided Pung How was right and that Marina was headed for Thailand. They had left Butterworth behind them half an hour previously. The border could not be much more than an hour away.

141

The rain was suddenly descending like a massive waterfall and there were dramatic flashes of lightning, followed almost immediately by vicious cracks of thunder. The Discovery had been forced to slow down by the torrent of water sweeping across the road, and Adam had to brake to avoid coming up too close behind it. He took a few seconds to adjust to the slower pace, but then settled into a speed that kept him some fifty metres behind the Discovery. He dared not drop back further lest he lose visual contact in the storm. But he had to be far enough away not to alert Marina to the fact that he was following her. He could scarcely make out her number plate at that distance, and hoped that the same would be true of his own car if she looked in her mirror.

They passed some twenty minutes in this fashion, buffeted by wind and rain. Adam's windscreen wipers, at double speed, afforded him momentary glimpses of the road ahead through the blinding rain. Only the rear lights of the Discovery guided him forward.

And then he lost them. A slight bend in the road took the Discovery momentarily out of sight and when his own car rounded the bend, the lights had disappeared. He cursed and accelerated, believing that they had somehow got away from him, but just as he did so he saw the exit from the highway, the sign for which had been obscured by the torrential rain. He slammed on the brakes, skidding badly and almost turning the car over. He was past the exit now and had to reverse, praying that no one was coming up the highway behind him. Now he could see the sign: *'Kuala Kedah'*. It meant nothing to him. *Damn*, he thought. *Maybe they have gone up the highway after all and I'm losing valuable time.* He sat, frustrated, trying to decide what to do, conscious of the seconds ticking away and of Marina escaping him once more. Then, as rapidly as it had begun, the rain abated and he saw through the afternoon gloom another sign, beyond the original road sign, bearing the words: *'Feri ke Pulau Langkawi'.*

Feri ke Pulau Langkawi. Pulau Langkawi. Langkawi. Langkawi? Something about the rhythm of the word set adrenalin running through his system. He was back in Singapore. It was the small hours of Saturday morning. He was sitting in the taxi staring, unbelieving, at the contents of Marina's bag, while she spoke rapid, unintelligible Spanish into her mobile phone. What had he heard her say over and over again? A burst of impenetrable language and then the question, in English: "...Are we?... Are we?... Are we?" Except that now he saw that this was not what she had been saying at all. She had been saying "Langkawi". Langkawi, holiday resort island and political stronghold of the former Malaysian Prime Minister, Mohamed Mahathir. A destination as far north as you could get in Malaysia, without actually entering Thailand. That was where Marina was bound, where she had been planning to go from the very beginning. He still had no idea what she was up to, or who she was involved with. And he suspected that most of what she had told him previously was lies. But he was right behind her now. One way or another he was about to learn the truth.

CHAPTER 11

At just before six in the morning the light breeze along the shore was still cool enough to be refreshing. Andrew had not planned to run while in Bintan. But he had slept badly and awoken early from yet another nonsensical dream, in which now the images of Kirsty and Birgit were confused, while the ghost of Elena stalked his unconscious, unseen but relentless. Unable to sleep again, and not wishing to disturb Birgit, he had slipped out of bed and left the darkened villa to make his way down to the beach.

An unusual tenderness had informed their lovemaking the previous evening. Later, Birgit had slept in his arms, which had never happened before. *This will not do*, he said to himself, as he turned at the far end of the beach and began to jog back, barefoot, through the shallow waves. *This is an affair, nothing more. Neither of us can afford an emotional entanglement.* And yet something had changed, and he could not deny it. Birgit had revealed an unsuspected vulnerability which had affected him more than he had guessed possible.

The sky was growing lighter. Day would arrive rapidly at any moment, in the way it happened in the tropics. The horizon was now clearly visible and Andrew could just discern the masts of an approaching motor yacht in the middle distance. Closer to the shore, the buzz of an outboard motor heralded the return of a fisherman. An osprey wheeled and dived into the choppy waters at the base of the cliffs. Andrew replaced his sandals and made his way back up towards the villa as the first shaft of sunlight appeared.

* * *

Mary Bennett was a methodical person. She liked both her office and her home to be neat and tidy. Her maid came only once a week, but Mary herself kept her house spotless in the intervening period. She was also an early riser, and, most mornings, ran before going to work.

Today, however, she lay in bed at past eleven o'clock, staring listlessly into space. Several half-empty coffee cups stood on her bedside table. A mess of newspapers spread across the floor, and the shirt and shorts she had been wearing the previous day lay tangled in her underwear at the foot of the bed. Downstairs in the kitchen, the unwashed dishes of the past three days sat in the sink, and the remains of several makeshift meals littered the working surfaces. The sitting room, alone, was as tidy as ever, because Mary had not ventured into it for three days.

Muzafar had not called since their telephone conversation on Monday. It was unprecedented for them not to speak over such a long period. With each successive day, Mary had become more convinced that something was wrong between them. Perhaps if she had been working she would have had sufficient distraction to prevent her from falling so rapidly into despair. But the two-day Chinese New Year holiday, followed now by the enforced closure of the High Commission, had left her with little to do but dwell on her loneliness.

Since playing tennis on Tuesday she had left home only once, to attend the Chinese New Year party Adam White had missed on Wednesday evening. Across the room, at one point, she had recognised Lee Tek Keng, owner of the shipping group of which the company where Muzafar worked was part. She had thought of telling him how unfairly his managers were treating his employees, but her courage had deserted her at the last minute. Lee Tek Keng was a golfing partner of the High Commissioner and she did not want to create any awkwardness.

When the telephone rang, Mary grabbed it before the second ring. It was not Muzafar but Susan Hyde, who was evidently under some stress.

"Mary, I need your help," she said. "Have you any idea how I can get hold of Adam? It's really urgent."

"Didn't he leave you his mobile number?" said Mary. "He said something about going up to Kuala Lumpur."

"It doesn't answer," said Susan. "I gave it to Daniel Taylor's father and he called me back in a terrible rage. It was awful."

"Have you called Kuala Lumpur? I think he may have been staying with the Murdochs."

"No. I suppose I'd better do that now." Susan hesitated. "Mr Taylor was also demanding to speak to the High Commissioner."

Mary's professional protectiveness kicked in. "I don't see what good that would do," she said. "Adam's the person you really need to find."

"I'll keep trying," said Susan. "But I'll have to come back to you if I have no luck. He's an awful man – he just kept shouting at me."

Temporarily energised by this exchange, Mary took a shower and pulled on her shorts and a clean tee-shirt. She cleared up the mess in her bedroom and went downstairs to tackle the kitchen. When she had everything more or less tidy, she took a deep breath and walked to the telephone. She had decided it was absurd to languish in uncertainty. She dialled the number of Muzafar's office.

A woman answered the telephone.

"Muzafar's not here," she said.

He must have taken an early lunch break, Mary thought. "What time will he be back?" she asked.

"He won't be here before next week," said the woman.

"Has he taken the afternoon off?"

"Afternoon, no, la," the woman said. "He's not been here since Monday."

* * *

Adam sat at a balcony table of the bar of the Sheraton Perdana looking out to the south-west across the Kuah Straits towards the jungle-clad islands of Pulau Dayang Bunting and Pulau Tuba. The storm of the previous day had cleared the air. The sun shone down from a cloudless sky on the sailing boats tacking lazily backwards and forwards in the gentle wind which rippled the surface of the blue water. A ferry, similar to the one which had brought Adam from Kuala Kedah the previous day, made its way slowly towards the southern exit from the Straits. The perfume of hibiscus and frangipani drifted up from the hotel gardens to where Adam sat, nursing a beer.

Adam was wearing a large straw hat and a pair of fake Gucci sunglasses, both of which he had bought cheaply, and in a hurry, at the ferry terminal at Kuala Kedah the day before. His sports shirt, shorts and sandals he had purchased, at much greater expense, in the hotel boutique. The combined effect was faintly ludicrous, but it served Adam's purpose, which was to make himself totally unrecognisable.

Some thirty feet below, a group of the younger hotel guests were playing a makeshift game of water polo in the swimming pool. Other guests lay on sunbeds, some soaking up the sun, others sheltering under giant blue umbrellas. They were reading, or sleeping, or drinking iced drinks and idly chatting.

Marina and her companion appeared to be fast asleep. Their sun beds were at the far end of the pool, sheltered by one of the many giant palms surrounding the pool area. The couple had established themselves there shortly after breakfast, and gave every impression of intending to make a day of it.

After his initial rush of adrenalin the previous day, Adam had found himself once more in a state of indecision when he pulled into the ferry terminal car park in Kuala Kedah. Marina's car was there, so it was a safe assumption that she would be taking the next ferry to Langkawi. Should he confront her, immediately, in the terminal? Should he do so on the ferry itself? Or should he follow her to Langkawi in order to discover what she was up to? The latter was a risky option, because he might lose her again when she left the ferry in Langkawi. But it was the one he chose.

Keeping out of sight on the crossing had not proved too difficult. The rain had continued to fall, albeit with less intensity. The inclement weather had confined most people to the interior of the ferry, and Adam had been able to remain on deck, close to the disembarkation point, without attracting attention. It had been wet and uncomfortable, but he had felt he had little alternative.

As the ferry approached Kuah, the giant statue of an eagle loomed suddenly and dramatically out of the rain. With his straw hat pulled low over his face, Adam bent down and made great play of tying his shoe lace as the passengers began to disembark. As soon as he spotted Marina he moved swiftly to join the queue some three or four people behind her. From here he could get a reasonable look, for the first time, at Marina's companion. He looked to be in his late forties. His hair was grey and swept back, lying curled around his collar. His complexion was dark and his slightly effeminate looks seemed somehow familiar to Adam, although he could not explain why. He wore a thick gold chain around his neck, and on the wrist of the arm slung casually around Marina's shoulder he wore an expensive-looking gold watch.

Marina and her companion took a taxi as soon as they disembarked. Adam shoved his way past the passengers in front of him and jumped into the next taxi, leaving a young Australian couple, encumbered with diving equipment, protesting loudly as the taxi pulled away.

"I'm with them," said Adam, pointing at the taxi ahead. The driver seemed used to this sort of occurrence and accelerated away with a cheerful "Okay, sir!"

It had been a short journey to the hotel, which was only just outside the town limits. Luckily there were rooms available. Adam had checked in, and then sat in the lobby until it was late enough for him to be confident that Marina and her companion were not going anywhere that night. He had then gone to his room, ordered dinner from room service and arranged a wake-up call for five in the morning.

At a reasonably civilised hour, Adam had tried to call Susan Hyde to let her know where he was. But a freak lightning strike the previous day had cut all external telephone connections from the hotel. He had rung Susan from his mobile, but the line was engaged and he rang off immediately: he was afraid his battery would not survive the long and elaborate message on her answer phone. He had decided to try again later.

For the time being, he could now only watch and wait. He had imagined any number of possible scenarios to explain why Marina had come to Langkawi. But he had not bargained with the possibility that she was going to lie in the sun all day. It looked as though it was going to be a long vigil.

* * *

Andrew leaned on the rail of the terrace alongside the pool, smoking and looking out to the darkening sea. Birgit had just left on the early evening ferry and now he had time to himself to reflect on the thirty-six hours they had just spent together. He was booked on the first ferry out in the morning. He had settled his bill, and ordered a private taxi to avoid the excessively early start involved in using the resort transportation. Now he planned a light supper of fruit, followed by an early night.

It had been a strange day. Birgit had awoken like a woman

refreshed. She had swum ten rapid lengths of the pool and then demanded a large cooked breakfast. After breakfast, she had insisted on giving Andrew a lengthy back massage, to compensate, she said, for having inflicted her 'miserable past' on him the previous day. When he pointed out that it had been him who had pressed her on the subject, she gave a broad grin and said, "Andrew, I'm offering you the sensation of a lifetime – don't argue about it."

The massage, combined with the tiredness from his broken night, had sent him to sleep. He must have slept for two hours or more and awoke to the sound of a champagne cork; Birgit had organised lunch of fish, salad and fruit. "Wasn't that a little risky?" he said, still befuddled from sleep. She laughed. "I didn't want to wake you and I knew you'd be hungry. No one will remember – and who's going to ask them anyway?"

They had made love only once, again in the cool of the air conditioning. It had been the old Birgit: artful, adept and arousing him to sublime heights of sexual pleasure. And yet he could not entirely shed the memory of the previous day. At times he detected in her a wildness which hinted at hidden desperation. She had touched his cheek lightly with the tips of her fingers when they had kissed before her departure, but was gone before he could say anything.

It was dark now, and cloud had partly obscured the rising moon. He could make out lights on the motor yacht he had seen earlier in the day, which was moored now at the edge of the bay. Down below, near the rocks, the creak of oars and muffled splashes betrayed the presence of a fisherman setting his lobster pots. An animal rustled in the undergrowth at the base of the creeper-clad pillars, and then there was silence. Andrew sent his cigarette spinning into the darkness and turned to go inside.

ENGAGEMENT

CHAPTER 12

The Foreign Office is good at many things. Contrary to the popular image, it is not the preserve of Oxbridge classics scholars, and it does not see its function as being nice to foreigners. Nor do its diplomats overseas spend all their time at cocktail parties. The Foreign Office is a lean machine, which works non-stop to promote British interests around the world. It persuades, cajoles and bullies foreign governments into understanding, accepting and contributing towards the United Kingdom's security and economic objectives. It also helps British businessmen export and invest overseas, and extends protection every year to tens of millions of British citizens living or travelling abroad.

What the Foreign Office does best, however, is crisis. By the very nature of its responsibilities, it is geared up for action twenty-four hours a day. A former Foreign Secretary, in less politically correct times, is quoted as saying (although it is doubtful he ever used these precise words): "How can we sleep when somewhere in the world Johnny Foreigner is getting up to mischief the moment we switch off the light?"

So, when war or revolution threaten, when British citizens are taken hostage, when earthquake, tidal wave or other natural calamity strikes, the Foreign Office moves into well-oiled action. Situation rooms are opened, staff pulled off their normal duties, the Cabinet Office, the Ministry of Defence and Number Ten alerted in case wider emergency measures may be called for, and a buzz of controlled excitement runs around the corridors of Downing Street and King Charles Street.

At seven minutes before noon on Friday morning, when Dame Gillian King summoned the Head of South East Asia Department to her office overlooking a bedraggled, late winter St James's Park, she did not yet know she was facing a crisis. In the brief time available between a courtesy call by the new Brazilian Ambassador and an office meeting on Afghanistan, she aimed to initiate action which would avert what she expected, at worst, to be an embarrassment for the Foreign Office. Beneath the controlled exterior with which she invariably faced her staff, her dominant emotion was irritation, and its target was Andrew Singleton.

"Paul, what exactly is going on in Singapore?" she said.

"I'm sorry, Permanent Under Secretary?" Paul Burrows was a rotund, pink-faced man with a sharper intellect than his jovial appearance might suggest. He appeared to have no idea what Dame Gillian was talking about.

"One of the first things I read this morning was a carping minute from Private Office about last week's ministerial visit," she said.

"I thought that was a bit unfair," said Burrows. "The Minister landed on Singapore at zero notice. Under the circumstances they didn't do that badly."

"But that's not all, Paul," said Dame Gillian. "About half an hour ago I received a telephone call from Adrian Stringer, the senior partner in a London law firm representing Mr Simon Taylor. He claimed the matter was urgent and personal. So my Private Secretary put him through – which was just as well in the circumstances."

"Oh, yes," said Burrows. "Simon Taylor. His son's on a drugs charge in Singapore."

"I know that," said Dame Gillian, taking care not to communicate her impatience. "It's been in all the newspapers. The *Express* are saying he's been framed."

"I don't think we necessarily believe that," said Burrows.

"Be that as it may," said Dame Gillian. "Mr Stringer was ringing to express his client's dissatisfaction with the way things were being handled in Singapore. He said he hoped it wouldn't be necessary to take the matter up through Mr Taylor's MP."

"I haven't seen all the correspondence," said Burrows, looking suitably concerned. "But Consular Department haven't given any indication they're worried."

"Well, they are now," said Dame Gillian. "Mr Taylor has been unable to speak to the High Commissioner. In fact, he's been unable to speak to anyone all day except a Duty Officer, who gave him a mobile number for the Head of Chancery which didn't respond."

"The High Commission's technically closed, of course," said Burrows. "They had a security alert from the Singaporeans."

"Closing the office temporarily does not entail total withdrawal of labour," said Dame Gillian. "I asked Consular Department to investigate. They tell me the Consul is sick. The High Commissioner, the Commercial Counsellor and the Head of Chancery are all out of the country. And MI6 are apparently off down a cave somewhere in Brunei. The most senior member of the High Commission available is the Defence Attaché, whose knowledge of consular procedures is probably on a par with my ability to fly Eurofighter. And on top of all this, the Duty Officer seems to be afflicted with terminal timidity and confesses to have broken down under Taylor's bullying."

"I had no idea," said Burrows, looking very unhappy. "It's been Chinese New Year, but that's no excuse."

"No, it's not," said Dame Gillian. "And we need to do something about it – fast. First, and most urgently, we need to make sure Simon Taylor is satisfied. Someone authoritative in Singapore has to speak to him within the next hour, to persuade him everything's under control. I've instructed Consular Department to get the Consul out of bed, even if it's only for twenty minutes or so. Make sure that happens, will you please? I've told Adrian Stringer I'll call him back by one-fifteen at the latest – he's planning to speak to Taylor again at nine-thirty local time in Singapore."

"Yes, Permanent Under Secretary," said Burrows, making a rapid note.

"Second," said Dame Gillian. "Get the High Commissioner and the Head of Chancery back to Singapore at once. I don't care how you do it. And when you speak to Andrew Singleton, tell him he's risking disciplinary action for leaving the country without notifying London first."

* * *

"It's Alison, Elaine. How are you?"

"Now there's someone I haven't heard for a very long time," said Richard Sheinwald's personal assistant, a twice-divorced chain smoker with a voice to prove it. "How the hell are you?"

"Good, thanks," said Alison. She remembered that Richard had called her direct when inviting her to lunch earlier in the week. Maybe Elaine did not know about their discussion. Alison did her best to sound casual. "Is Richard there, by any chance?"

"He's just off to lunch, Ali," said Elaine. "But I expect he'll take a call from *you*." The implication of Elaine's tone was clear. *She does know,* thought Alison. *Or she thinks she knows.*

Richard came on the line almost immediately. "Alison," he said. "I was hoping to hear from you."

"Richard, I'd like to accept your offer… "

"Excellent."

"… but on one condition."

"We can talk about your package when you come in," he said. "Would next week be too soon for you?"

"Next week's fine," said Alison. "But I must be sure of this one thing now."

"Of course," he said, divining her mood with his customary sensitivity.

"I shall need to take two weeks off, without fail, three times a year to visit Adam in Singapore."

"That's a tall order, Alison," he said. "You know how unpredictable the timing of our jobs can be."

"It's my only condition," she said.

He paused, but only briefly. "Okay," he said. "We'll work something out. But you have to do me a favour in return."

Alison could hardly contain her relief that he had acceded to her request so easily. "I'd be happy to," she said.

"I have two tickets for *La Bohème* tonight," he said. "I need someone to take."

Alison hesitated momentarily before she spoke. "You know I can't resist Puccini," she said, truthfully, but with a slight feeling of misgiving.

"Terrific," he said. "Get yourself to Covent Garden by six forty-five, and we'll crack a quick bottle first to celebrate your return to the firm."

* * *

As soon as Paul Burrows had left, Gillian switched her concentration to the meeting on Afghanistan, for which people were already filing into her room from the outer office. Her ability to focus exclusively on the current priority (which, in this case, was how best to deploy the slender British resources in Kabul to help the fragile Afghan administration control opium production) had earned her the affectionate nickname of 'old laser-brain'. For forty-five minutes she did not think about Singapore. But, as she was about to leave for lunch with the German Ambassador, she received a call from Burrows.

"I'm afraid it's worse than we thought," said Burrows. "Apparently the High Commissioner went to a resort on Bintan."

"That means nothing to me," said Gillian.

"It's an Indonesian island a short ferry ride from Singapore," said Burrows. "The High Commissioner's personal assistant made the arrangements, so she knew how to contact him."

"Well, thank heaven for small mercies," said Gillian.

"Except that they've been unable to speak to him," said Burrows. "The people at the resort where he's staying can't locate him, and his mobile doesn't answer."

"When is he expected back?"

"He's booked there tonight and the residence staff in Singapore were instructed to prepare lunch for him tomorrow."

"What about Adam White?"

"Apparently he's in Malaysia trying to find the High Commissioner's daughter."

"Find her? Is she lost?"

"We don't know the details," said Burrows, who sounded uncomfortable about being the purveyor of such unsatisfactory information.

"Where exactly is he in Malaysia?"

"He was last seen by Stan Murdoch in Kuala Lumpur on Thursday morning," said Burrows. "He was heading north. Stan thought he might be going to Thailand."

"God give me strength," said Gillian. "Has anyone spoken to Simon Taylor yet?"

"Consular Department have reported to you by email," said Burrows. "They didn't want to interrupt your meeting. Jane Rosendale's calmed Taylor down somewhat. But she's really unwell and has had to go back to bed."

Gillian looked at her watch. She was already five minutes late. She would have to speak to Adrian Stringer from the car, once she had read the full report from Consular Department.

"Alright, Paul," she said. "Here's what I want you to do. First, you must get the Defence Attaché to take over from the Duty Officer. She's clearly not up to it."

"Strictly speaking, of course, I can't actually instruct him to do that," said Burrows.

"Now, Paul," said Gillian, employing the quiet, patient tone which warned her staff that she expected them to do exactly as she asked. "I'm sure he's a reasonable sort of chap, and that you're an accomplished enough diplomat to get over that minor technicality. After all, our political masters are constantly enjoining us to practise joined-up government."

"Of course, Permanent Under Secretary," said Burrows, sounding appropriately chastened.

"Good," said Gillian. "Then I want Singapore to redouble their efforts to contact the High Commissioner and Adam White. They must keep calling every conceivable number until contact is established."

"I've already told them to do that," said Burrows.

"Well, do it again, on my explicit authority," said Gillian. "Next, who's the Commercial Counsellor, remind me?"

"Vincent Greenfield."

"Fine. Get hold of him, wherever he is, and put him on notice to return to Singapore in forty-eight hours if neither Singleton nor White materialises over the weekend. And, whatever happens, get Consular Department to fix some kind of emergency reinforcement in Singapore before the weekend's out. I want their top gun there in action by Monday morning without fail."

In the car, Gillian read Consular Department's email on her Blackberry. It looked as though a reasonable stand-off with Simon Taylor had been achieved, thanks to Jane Rosendale's experience and diplomatic tact. Gillian rang Adrian Stringer and gave him a carefully edited account of the situation. She added, without offering any further detail, that it was regrettable that the High Commissioner and the Head of Chancery had been unexpectedly called away at the same time, but that they would be back in Singapore very soon.

Gillian sank back into the leather upholstery, and began to compose her thoughts for the lunch. She and the German Ambassador, who were old friends, were planning to explore ways of bridging the gap between their governments on the next stage of a common European Union security and defence policy. Gillian had held a brainstorming session with her European experts the previous day, and had a number of ideas up her sleeve to help clear what was threatening to become a damaging impasse. But before she locked her intellect firmly on to the process of rehearsing the intricate set of arguments she was planning to deploy with the Ambassador, she allowed herself one fleeting moment of personal anguish. *Jesus wept, Andrew*, she thought. *This time, you've finally gone too far.*

* * *

"Patrick? It's Peter Coles, old son. How's Buffy bearing up?"

"Hello, Peter," said Patrick, tucking the phone under his chin and shifting the baby, who was on the verge of sleep, to a more comfortable position on his left arm. "She's resting at the moment. It can't be too soon as far as she's concerned."

"I can imagine," said Coles. "Look, Patrick, I'm sorry to bother you, mate… "

"Bloody hell, Peter, if you're still fussing about my report—"

"No, no, it's not that," said Coles. "It's not that at all."

Patrick sat down on the sofa and repositioned Jamie once more. He sensed unwelcome news. "Spit it out," he said.

"Look, Patrick, old son, I'm really sorry about this," said Coles. "They want you to go to Singapore."

"Singapore? When?"

"By Monday, I'm afraid."

"You've got to be joking!" Patrick kept his voice low in a bid to avoid disturbing Jamie. But the sudden tension in his body transmitted itself to the child, who stirred and began to cry.

Patrick stood up and jiggled the baby around gently on his arm, making soothing noises.

"It's a bit of an emergency," said Coles. "They've got a serious consular case on their hands, and the Consul's sick and the High Commissioner and the Head of Chancery have gone missing."

"Peter," said Patrick, rocking the boy more vigorously as his crying grew louder. "My wife's expecting a baby any day now. I can't leave her alone. I've only just got back from Santo Domingo."

"You're the only person available," said Coles. "You know how stretched we are, what with the tsunami and all the rest of it."

The baby was screaming now. "You'll have to find someone else," said Patrick. "I can't go. It's as simple as that."

Patrick put the telephone down and turned his full attention to calming the baby. But Jamie had got himself into a self-reinforcing circle of misery and was shrieking and sobbing beyond all consolation. Buffy came into the sitting room, bleary-eyed, her dressing gown tied loosely around her swollen belly.

"Patrick, for heaven's sake, what are you doing, man?" she said. "It sounds as though you're torturing the child."

She took Jamie from him, and immediately the boy's wailing diminished. He snuggled into his mother's neck, as she turned awkwardly from side to side with him in her arms. Momentarily, he lifted his head to stare accusingly at Patrick before subsiding in contented silence into Buffy's arms.

"What set him off?" said Buffy.

"I was on the phone," said Patrick. "The office wanted me to go somewhere, but I told them I couldn't."

Buffy stopped rocking the baby. "You told them you couldn't do a job they wanted you for?"

"Yes. I said it was impossible, with you being so close."

"Call them back."

"What?"

161

"Come on, Patrick," she said, rocking the baby once more, but gently now. "You know what they said. Do well in this job and the next promotion will come that much faster. Besides, we need the money."

"Buffy, they want me to go to Singapore this weekend," he said.

She seemed momentarily taken aback at this news. But then she said, "All the same, you have to go. I'll get mum to come and stay."

He wanted to argue. He wanted to say that being with her for the birth of their child was more important than money or promotion. He had a dangerous urge to say that he could not trust himself to be away from her again so soon. But he suppressed his doubts. Buffy was right; the consular standby job might be disruptive and arduous, and the workload unpredictable, but the overseas duty allowances were generous. With a crippling mortgage, and a second child on the way, they needed every penny he could earn.

"Okay, Buffy," he said, picking up the telephone. "If you say so, sweetheart."

* * *

"Would you like a little light supper to round off the evening?" he had said. Still in a half-trance from Puccini's glorious tragedy, Alison had murmured her assent, without thinking.

Now they sat in a discreet corner of the Savoy Grill and she was eating smoked salmon and partridge eggs with caviar. She had declined the champagne he had offered to accompany the meal. But, even sipping mineral water, she had a sensation of nagging disloyalty.

Richard had just come to the end of a typically witty anecdote when, unable to help herself, she glanced at her watch.

"Are you alright for time?" he said.

Alison knew she would almost certainly miss the last tube. She would have to grit her teeth and take a taxi. "I'll be fine," she said. "But maybe I should be making a move."

"Sometimes I stay over here when it gets late and I can't be bothered with travelling," he said.

"Good heavens," said Alison. "It surely can't take that long to get back to Hampstead." She realised this had sounded rude, but he took it in his stride. "It's just sometimes – more convenient," he said.

Alison pondered the significance of what Richard had just said. She considered his dark, handsome face. The slightest of smiles played around the corner of his mouth as he returned her gaze. Alison felt suddenly hot, and very nervous.

"I really must get back," she said, listening to the sound of her voice as though it came from a complete stranger. She suddenly had an absurd vision of her mother witnessing their conversation and expressing wrathful incredulity that she should have rebuffed a proposition from the scion of one of the wealthiest and most influential Jewish families in London.

His smile became broader. "If you must," he said. "Let's see about a taxi for you."

What a strange man he is, she thought. *He's had any number of women far more beautiful than me, and yet he feels compelled to play this game. But it is only a game – and he is, at least, gracious in defeat. He might even have been disappointed if I had accepted.*

He spoke again, interrupting her thoughts. "Oh, by the way," he said. "I meant to tell you. I had lunch today with an old friend, Adrian Stringer. He was saying rather uncomplimentary things about the High Commission in Singapore. I wondered if you knew anything about it."

CHAPTER 13

The telephone connection between Langkawi and the outside world was restored in the early hours of Saturday morning. Adam discovered this when he awoke, again at five, but decided against ringing the duty officer in Singapore at that hour. He waited instead until he was satisfied that Marina and her companion had once more settled themselves by the pool, shortly after nine, and then went rapidly to his room.

Susan Hyde's home telephone did not respond and, curiously, did not default to an answering machine. Adam then called the duty officer's mobile number and was surprised to hear the eager-beaver voice of Nick Childs.

"Adam? Good Lord, old chap. We've been hunting all over for you."

"I'm in Langkawi," said Adam. "The phones went down in a storm on Thursday night and my mobile battery's flat."

"There's been an enormous kerfuffle here," said Childs. "The High Commissioner's gone missing. And that Simon Taylor chappie's been kicking up rough."

"Oh, bollocks," said Adam. "I'd better call him."

"No, I'd leave it," said Childs. "Jane sorted him out temporarily, bless her, and a chap's coming out from London to take over until she's better."

"Bloody hell," said Adam. "I'll be back by Monday. Someone in London must have panicked."

"It was your Permanent Under Secretary, apparently," said

Childs. "And it's not just you. The High Commissioner's missing as well."

"He's not missing," said Adam. "He's in Bintan. Mary knows how to contact him."

"Well, that's what we thought," said Childs. "But the resort where he's staying haven't seen him since yesterday."

* * *

At one-fifteen in the morning Alison lay, wide awake, in her parents' house in Pinner. The taxi had dropped her off shortly before one. She had been so tired that she had expected to sleep immediately, but could not do so.

Richard's account of his conversation with Adrian Stringer had painted a picture of slovenly ineptitude in the High Commission in Singapore. Alison knew this was false, but she did not think Richard was wilfully exaggerating what he had been told. He was altogether too grand and accomplished to want to hurt her simply because she had declined to respond to his casual advance. There had to be at least a germ of truth in what he had said.

Alison had promised herself she would not call Adam before he had a chance to read her letter. But now she decided she must warn him of the criticism she had heard from Richard Sheinwald. She reached for her mobile and dialled their house in Singapore. When she got no response, she called Adam's mobile, with the same result. Then she called the High Commission, where a recorded message gave her a mobile number to call if she faced a genuine emergency. After examining her conscience for a few seconds she called the number, but it was engaged.

Finally she called Mimi Parker.

"Mimi, I know this sounds silly," she said. "But have you any idea where Adam might be? I need to speak to him urgently."

"It's not silly at all," said Mimi. "It must be bloody urgent if it's what time I think it is in London. Murray said something about Adam going to Malaysia. Hang on a second, I'll get him."

After a few seconds delay, Murray Parker came on the line.

"He took off for Kuala Lumpur some time on Thursday, Ali," he said. "I haven't heard from him since then."

"Do you know what for?"

"Well, he didn't actually say at the time," said Murray. "But he did ask me to give him a contact there, so I put him on to a photographer friend of mine. I was talking to him yesterday and he said Adam was following some girl he thought might be going to Thailand."

"A girl?"

"That's all he knew, Ali," said Murray. There was a pause, as though he was thinking back over what he had said and realised how bad it sounded. "No. Ali," he said. "It's nothing like that. You know Adam."

* * *

Mary Bennett dialled the High Commissioner's mobile telephone number for, perhaps, the thirtieth time since her conversation with Nick Childs at eight o'clock that morning. In his inimitably disciplined way, Childs had allocated tasks around the High Commission staff and instructed them to call him every hour at slightly staggered times to report progress. Mary was to keep calling Andrew Singleton. Susan Hyde had been calling Adam White. Robert Redford was interviewing the residence servants and the duty driver to see if they had picked up any hint that the High Commissioner might have changed his plans. And Childs himself was periodically telephoning the Bintan resort, in case Singleton had unexpectedly turned up there again.

The ringing sound ceased and Singleton's automated message began. Mary terminated the call. The first three times she had left messages. That was surely more than enough.

Mary was beginning to experience mild concern for the High Commissioner. But that was nothing as to the anxiety induced by the knowledge that Muzafar had lied to her. His mobile did not respond whenever she called. A second telephone call to his manager, the previous day, had revealed that he had asked for a week's special leave on Monday to visit a sick relative in Malaysia. Why had Muzafar not told her this? It made no sense, and it made her ill with unhappiness.

She rang Nick Childs to report no progress. It was some relief to hear that Adam White had finally made contact, but nothing could alleviate her overwhelming misery.

Outside, her tiny garden was a riot of tropical plants and flowers. But her eyes were sightless as, sitting before the window, she picked up the telephone and once more punched in Andrew Singleton's number.

* * *

Late on Saturday afternoon, Adam was on the verge of accepting that Marina and her companion were engaged in nothing more exciting than spending a long weekend together. For nearly two days he had observed them relaxing by the pool. At midday on both days they had eaten a sandwich lunch without moving from their sun loungers. The previous evening they had dined al fresco in the hotel restaurant. Not once had they indicated any intention of leaving the hotel grounds.

Now, fighting sleep in the sticky, perfumed heat of the bar terrace, Adam wondered whether he should not cut his losses and make his presence known. He could not stay away from Singapore indefinitely waiting for Marina to make a move. It was time to confront her. He stood up to make his way down the steps to the swimming pool area.

Just in time, Adam saw that Marina and her friend were packing up their things in preparation for leaving the pool. He retreated rapidly from the top of the steps and made his way to the reception desk, where he ordered a taxi. He suffered an anxious ten minutes waiting for the car to arrive. But, in the event, a full forty-five minutes elapsed before Marina and her companion emerged from the hotel, carrying their overnight bags, to climb into another taxi, which had just drawn up.

Adam gave rapid instructions to his driver, who had been happily reading a newspaper while the meter ticked away at Adam's expense. The car pulled away from the cover of the trees at the edge of the hotel car park and followed the second taxi.

The ride was not long. They drove through a brief stretch of forest back towards Kuah, past the entrance to the harbour and some kind of memorial park. Then suddenly the taxi in front stopped. Both Adam and his taxi driver were taken by surprise and the car overshot by thirty metres or so before coming to a halt.

Adam stuffed a wad of cash into the driver's hands and told him to wait, all the time straining to keep visual contact with Marina and her companion as they crossed the road and merged with the stream of pedestrians on the other side. Almost immediately they turned off the main pavement into a side road, which seemed also to be the destination of most of the other people.

Adam ran across the main road and positioned himself a few yards back from Marina in the crowd. They were in a market, which seemed to consist of a single, narrow road, flanking a canal, running at right angles from the main road. On either side of the road were stalls selling clothing, footwear, belts, bolts of cloth, kitchen utensils, fake branded watches and sunglasses, and a bewildering variety of foodstuffs. Fruit and vegetable stalls were laden with oranges, pears, grapes, jack-fruit, pineapple, potato, ginger root and many more varieties Adam could not name. The inimitable stench of sliced durian momentarily turned his stomach, and he hurried on past wet fish stalls where shrimp and crab feebly waved their feelers, past a man selling sexual potions made from extract of snake venom, his snakes writhing blackly in a bucket of water at his feet, and then past kiosks selling satay, chicken balls and pancakes. Between the two rows of stalls, a mass of people jostled up and down the narrow road, some stopping to bargain and buy or eat, others simply enjoying the sociability the market afforded. There was only a handful of non-Malaysians in the crowd, which made Adam's task of keeping track of Marina both easier and more dangerous. He had only one really bad moment, when Marina stopped unexpectedly to look at an expensive-looking, but undoubtedly imitation, Prada handbag. Adam turned his back and studied a selection of beans and root vegetables, until Marina's companion pulled her roughly away with some angry words of Spanish.

At the far end of the market, a footbridge crossed the canal. This seemed, at first, to be Marina's destination. But, after pausing briefly at the base of the bridge, she and her companion turned and came back into the market. Adam slipped behind a meat stall, before they could see him. Once they had passed, he followed them again. Finally, they stopped in front of a stall selling fake leather luggage. The stall owner, whose appearance was otherwise unremarkable, appeared to have been in an accident of some kind, because his right hand was missing. After a brief conversation, Marina's companion bought a dark green sports holdall and they went on their way.

Adam followed them out of the market and across the main road. He watched with horror as they approached his taxi and tried to persuade the driver to take them. Adam hid behind a tree to watch, helpless to influence events. There were no other taxis around and Marina's companion was being very insistent, pointing at his watch and gesticulating. He pulled out a fistful of notes and waved them in front of the taxi driver. The driver, who must have thought it was his lucky day, made a big show of scouring the crowds leaving the market, then shrugged and gestured to Marina and the man to get in. *Bloody bollocks*, thought Adam. There was not another taxi in sight.

The taxi did a U-turn and headed back towards the port. Adam emerged from his cover and sprinted after it. *Thank God for football training*, was all he could think.

* * *

Whenever her schedule allowed – which was not nearly often enough – Gillian King escaped to the house she had inherited from her parents in a small village twenty miles to the north of Aberdeen. There she struggled with an unruly garden, practised amateur carpentry, walked in the hills and shared simple meals with childhood friends who still called her Kirsty. The house was not large, but it contained almost everything which was dear and personal to her.

The flat just off Victoria Street, by contrast, was little more than a place to sleep between working and socialising. She had friends in London, but they called her Gillian. She went with them to the theatre and the ballet and was invited to their houses for lunch and dinner. But when she reciprocated, she did so in restaurants.

The flat was not austere. It was comfortably furnished and equipped with modern television and high-fi equipment, and with the fastest broadband currently available. There were plants, some decent antique prints on the walls, and photos of family and friends all around. But it was a tiny apartment, a necessary evil in which she had been loath to invest more, either financially or spiritually, than she absolutely had to. It was a place to work quietly, and to rest alone. And, most important of all, it was a place from which she could walk to the office in ten minutes. Whether she liked it or not, this was where she was to be found most weekends.

The telephone rang while she was sitting at her computer,

refining the wording of a detailed analysis, for the Foreign Secretary, of German wriggle room (or lack of it) on the European Union common security and defence policy. The drafter of the paper, a disturbingly brilliant young man, had dissected the German position with awesome precision and deep pessimism. While not wishing to contradict the intellectual logic of his analysis, Gillian was trying to inject an element of human psychology which left room for hope in spite of the objective difficulties.

It was her Private Secretary on the telephone, calling to update her about a range of issues on which major developments were expected over the weekend. When he had finished, he added: "Oh, by the way, there's still no sign of the High Commissioner in Singapore. It's been over twenty-four hours since anyone has seen him. Personnel have authorised Singapore and Jakarta to bring in the local police."

"That's very bad news, Hilary," said Gillian, her voice deliberately even. "We'll need a press line."

"We're simply planning to say that he's overdue from a visit and that we're anxious for his safety."

"That might hold things for twenty-four hours or so," she said. "But if he's not turned up before then we'll need something more substantive. Get people to put their thinking caps on. And keep me advised of any news. Anything at all, Hilary, understand?"

Gillian put the telephone down and allowed her suppressed anxiety to emerge in a long sigh. For thirty years and more, she had observed Andrew Singleton's progress through the diplomatic service. While she had been slogging her way around the inner circle of Paris, Washington, Bonn and New York, he had travelled the more exotic and leisurely route of Latin America and the Far East. Kirsty had turned into Gillian, but Andrew had remained resolutely Andrew. He had not exactly neglected his duties, but he had rarely let them come between him and the pursuit of pleasure. His personal file was little more than a catalogue of affairs, punctuated only briefly by the early years of his ultimately catastrophic marriage. (Gillian had met Elena only once and had known immediately that she was poison.)

Sometimes, just very occasionally, Gillian had allowed herself to wonder what might have happened if she had slept with Andrew at university. God knew, she had been tempted. But would it have lasted? If they had married, she would have had no career: female officers back then were automatically required to resign on marriage. That seemed unimaginable now, but would she have missed what she had never known?

She stirred herself from her reverie and went into the kitchen to make coffee. In any case, it hadn't happened, she reminded herself, as she waited for the kettle to boil. She doubted Andrew ever gave her a single thought these days. But this did not prevent her from feeling something much stronger than professional concern about the fact that he was missing. She told herself that her anxiety was almost certainly misdirected. He was probably off on some sexual adventure; it would not be for the first time. But still she could not stop the nagging sensation at the corner of her mind that, this time, he could really be in trouble of some kind.

* * *

Patrick could find no film to tempt him in the selection available on the British Airways flight. He had eaten, but was not yet ready to sleep. So he made a virtue out of necessity and read his briefing pack.

He skipped through the routine information about living conditions and local customs in Singapore, and looked first at the High Commission staff list. It was longer than he might have expected, but he saw that there were several staff members with regional remits and others whose activities were no business but their own. Then he studied the papers on Daniel Taylor. Apart from the slightly unorthodox decision to take it on themselves to appoint the boy's lawyer, Singapore appeared to have handled everything properly. On the face of it, Taylor looked guilty. His father's outbursts, while entirely understandable, did not seem to have any objective justification. All the same, there was something about the whole story that did not quite ring true. Patrick could not put his finger on anything in particular, so he placed the papers to one side and moved on. Experience told him that whatever it was would be more likely to come, unprompted, to the surface of his mind if he concentrated on something completely different.

The final papers were biographical notes on the High Commissioner, the Head of Chancery and the Consul. Patrick had wheedled these out of a friend in Personnel who happened to be working late on Friday evening. They were not, strictly speaking, part of his official briefing, but he had felt the need to know something in advance about the people with whom he was most likely to be concerned. He noted, among other things, that Andrew Singleton had been at the London School of Economics, and Adam White at Glasgow. Jane Rosendale did not appear to have a degree but to have entered the Foreign Office, like Patrick himself, after A levels. At least he would not have to put up with any Oxbridge bullshit on this assignment.

Nothing extraordinary emerged from the biographies, except the fact that Adam White had been awarded an MBE the previous year when working in Security Department. Patrick had a vague recollection that this was linked in some way to the assassination of the British Ambassador in Buenos Aires, but he could not now recall the details, if he had ever known them (he had been helping clear up after a plane crash in Russia at the time).

Patrick put the papers back in his briefcase and did his best to sleep. As he was drifting off, a thought slid, unbidden, into his head. Why would a nineteen-year-old English boy be on his own in the Raffles Long Bar with a packet of heroin in the back pocket of his jeans? Did he have no friends? Was he really on his own? Or had there been someone else there whose existence was not acknowledged in the High Commission's account of events?

* * *

Luckily for Adam, the taxi was not going far. Within a quarter of a mile, it turned into the entrance to the harbour and made for the terminal building. By this time, Adam's lungs were bursting and sweat was streaming off him. But at least he had not lost contact.

Now, however, he was faced with a further problem. Marina and her friend were clearly returning to the mainland. Adam had no choice but to follow them, but most of his things were back at the hotel, where he had not settled his bill. *Too late*, he thought. *I can't stop now.*

The return ferry journey, by contrast with the stormy outward journey, was across calm waters and against a spectacular sunset. People were wandering freely around the ship, and Adam locked himself in one of the toilets to avoid the risk of premature discovery. When he emerged for disembarkation he immediately saw Marina, but could not see her companion. She was carrying the green holdall. After leaving the ferry, she walked to the parked Discovery and climbed in, but made no attempt to drive away. Adam made his way carefully around the outside edge of the car park until he came to his own car, where he waited, crouched behind the bonnet, to see what would happen next.

Ten minutes passed. Nothing happened. There was still no sign of Marina's companion. Was he not planning to accompany her? Had he returned to Langkawi? Another ten minutes. There was now no one else in the car park. Adam decided to seize the moment. He ran between the rows of parked cars, swung open the passenger door of the Discovery and jumped in beside Marina.

"What's in the bag, Marina?" he said, reaching for the green holdall on her lap.

"Oh shit, I might have known it was you," Marina said, moving the bag beyond his reach. "What the fuck kept you, by the way?" There was a look of resigned exasperation on her astonishingly beautiful face, now deeply tanned from two days in the sun. Adam had not been expecting such a greeting and simply stared at her.

"Money talks, Adam," she said. "So do taxi drivers."

"What are you playing at, Marina?" he said. "What have you got yourself mixed up in?"

"It would all have worked out so well if you hadn't insisted on being so virtuous," she said. "And so fucking nosy."

"You seem to be forgetting that I saved you from being arrested," he said.

She shook her head, as though faced with a recalcitrant child. "And I'm grateful, Adam. I really am. But why couldn't you just have left it alone after that?"

Before Adam could respond, he saw the expression on her face change to one of alarm and she shouted urgently in Spanish. Adam started to turn as the door was pulled open behind him, but he was too late. Something hit him hard on the side of the head, and then he felt nothing more.

* * *

In the late morning, Alison managed finally to get through to Mary Bennett, who gave her the telephone number of the hotel in Langkawi from where Adam had last made contact. "I can't talk, Ali," said Mary. "The High Commissioner's missing – we're in full crisis mode here."

Alison called the hotel, to be told that Adam was not in his room. She asked how long he had booked to stay. 'Two nights', they said, and asked whether she by any chance knew if he would be needing the room for a further night, as this was a very busy time of year. If not, there might be a penalty charge, because it was long past check-out time…

Alison was at a loss. She left a message at the hotel for Adam to call her urgently. She left the same message with Mary Bennett and Mimi Parker. All she could do now was wait.

* * *

Marina watched fearfully, as Pepe hauled Adam's unconscious body from the back of the car and rolled it into the ditch at the side of the road by a pile of recently felled timber. He dragged one of the logs to the edge of the ditch and pushed it in on top of Adam, then went back to the pile for a second log.

Marina leapt from the car. "I thought we were just going to warn him off," she shouted. "He has no proof. He can't hurt us. Pepe, please stop, it's not necessary."

Pepe smiled at her unpleasantly. "You are very stupid, Marina," he said. "You were stupid to get caught with the drugs, and you are stupid if you think this *hijo de puta* is going to stop causing us trouble." He began to drag the second log towards the ditch.

Pepe had always been Marina's favourite uncle, spoiling her as a child with extravagant presents and making her laugh with his dancing and his silly jokes. He had made the whole drug smuggling idea seem like a great adventure, a bit of fun, something to do for kicks. She did not recognise this ruthless Pepe. She did not know what to do.

The second log followed the first, and Pepe returned a third time to the pile. In desperation, Marina scrambled back into the car, revved the engine and began to move off. "Come on," she cried. "Let's go, before someone sees us."

Pepe hesitated, then shrugged and ran after the car and jumped in. "I'll be gone after this consignment anyway," he said. "And if you have any sense, you'll be coming with me."

CHAPTER 14

Sunday was a day of waiting.

The British High Commission in Singapore – now reopened with a skeleton staff – waited for news of their High Commissioner, as did the duty team in the Foreign Office and Gillian King in her flat in London. The Singapore police authorities had formally requested an investigation by their Indonesian counterparts, and there had been parallel communications between the High Commission and the British Embassy in Jakarta. The intelligence services in both countries were tasked with producing any information which might be relevant, and Quentin Asquith had been extracted from his cave in Brunei to sit permanently at the end of a telephone line from his liaison contact in the Singapore services. So far, there had been no substantive news. A thorough police search of the resort where Andrew Singleton had been staying had revealed no trace of him beyond the few personal effects he had left in the villa. No one had seen him leave. No one had seen him at all since lunchtime on Friday, when a waiter delivering a meal had observed him, apparently asleep, lying on a sun lounger. The Indonesian police were still interviewing the resort staff, local taxi drivers and workers at the Bintan ferry terminal. A full report would not be available until this process was completed, probably early on Monday morning. In the meantime, the High Commissioner's disappearance had been featured on Indonesian television and an appeal made for anyone who had seen him to come forward.

Mary Bennett, who had volunteered to work in the High Commission, waited for Muzafar to telephone her. But she waited without hope, and he did not call.

Alison Webster waited for news from Adam, not knowing whether to be concerned or angry.

And Adam White waited, semi-conscious and blood-stained, prostrate in a ditch off the road out of Kuala Kedah. He was waiting to be rescued. And in his more lucid moments he realised that, if no help came within the next twenty-four hours, his great adventure would be over for all time.

CHAPTER 15

At dawn of the third day of his captivity, Andrew Singleton saw light for the first time. His captors hauled him roughly up from the cramped compartment in which he had been confined, and tied him round the waist and legs to a chair. They removed his blindfold and the shackles on his wrists, and thrust into his hands an open laptop computer with the screen facing away from him. He felt a gun against his temple as his eyes struggled to adjust to the light, to get some sense of where he was. He had barely time to see that he was in a cabin lined with dark, varnished wood before he was blinded by a camera flash. Within seconds he was stuffed back down into the compartment, blindfold and shackled once more.

It had been nothing like the dreams. He had not even seen them at the villa. There had been the slightest of noises behind him, an arm around his neck – not smooth and fragrant like that of his mistress, but rough and hairy and smelling of sweat – and then the needle went into his upper arm. After that there were long periods of blackness, interspersed with periodic pain and discomfort. He had sensed the movement and smell of the sea and experienced nausea, which he fought to overcome. His hands and ankles were bound, and he was obliged to lie in a foetal position to fit within the compartment where they had put him. But he had sufficient freedom of movement to bring to his mouth the plastic bottles of water they brought him periodically, and the meagre handfuls of boiled rice. Thankfully, he seemed to be constipated, but they had left him to urinate where he lay. After more than two days, the combined smell of bilge water and stale piss was unbearable.

Despite all this, he felt curiously calm, as though this was how it was meant to be. He had always half feared an ultimate reckoning, some final payment for the easy pleasures of his life. Since Elena's death, the fear had become a near-conviction.

This was as bad as he could have expected, but at least the waiting was over.

* * *

For Adam, as he felt the first rays of the sun on his neck, the waiting was still not over.

He had had one piece of good fortune. Sunday had been overcast and he had not, therefore, run the risk of sunstroke or immediate dehydration. Late in the evening it had rained hard and he had become fully conscious. By twisting his head and shoulders he was able to swallow enough rain to slake his thirst. Thus refreshed, he made an effort to turn further. But something heavy was pinning down his lower body, and in the end he gave up.

He had heard several cars pass during the day, but no one had stopped. He was obviously invisible from the road.

Having drunk, he had then felt hungry, which he supposed was a good sign, as was the fact that he was capable of rational thought. He must be only slightly concussed, although his head hurt like hell. But from now on he would become progressively weaker. If he was to do anything to get himself out of this mess, now was the time to act.

He had tried, again, to move the weighty object holding him down, which seemed to be a fallen tree trunk, although in the black of night he could not be sure. It was impossible.

He had one last option. He had felt for the mobile in his pocket and with an enormous effort switched it on, depressed the first speed-dial button and brought the phone to his ear. A woman's lilting voice informed him pleasantly that the number he had dialled was unobtainable. Of course, he was in Malaysia. Both his and Ali's mobiles were Singapore-based. But Ali was in England. Which international code did he need to dial? Singapore or the UK? He could not risk getting it wrong; he probably had only one more shot before the battery died. Should he try the High Commission in Singapore? Or in Kuala Lumpur? But, late on a Sunday night, he would get only an answer phone message. And he did not have any staff home numbers in his head, nor, stupidly, in his mobile. They were neatly listed in his diary, which was sitting, uselessly, in the pocket of his jacket, which in turn was hanging in the wardrobe of his room at the Sheraton Perdana Hotel in Langkawi.

Desperately, he had searched his memory for the telephone number of Ali's parents. Painfully, he punched in the digits and prayed as he hit the dial button. With a sense of enormous relief he heard the dialling tone, but it cut immediately into a recorded message. Mercifully, it was brief. He spoke as fast as he could: "Ali, it's Adam. I'm badly hurt. Call Stan Murdoch in Kuala Lumpur. I'm in a ditch somewhere near Kuala Kedah. That's K-U-A-L-A new word K-E-D-A-H. I can hear seagulls and cars, so I can't be far from the port. It's urgent. Call Stan Murdoch, Ali. Call him."

That had been nine hours ago. The sun was warmer now, and he was terribly thirsty again. He tried to lick moisture from the wild grasses in the ditch, but it was rapidly evaporating in the growing heat. His mobile lay by his head, battery flat, its blank display mocking him. *I'm dead, laddie*, it said. *So will you be soon.*

* * *

Gillian King's telephone woke her at three-thirty in the morning. It was her Private Secretary.

"We have confirmation that Andrew Singleton's been kidnapped," he said. "The Singaporeans have received a demand."

"Oh sweet Lord," said Gillian, her stomach suddenly knotted. "What do they want?"

"The release of all Jemaah Islamiyah detainees within three days."

"The Singaporeans won't do that," said Gillian. "Who's in the office, Hilary?"

"Paul Burrows is on his way and someone from Consular Department. Otherwise it's just the duty staff so far."

"Get the Heads of Personnel and Security there at once." She looked at her watch. "I want a meeting at four-thirty. Then I'll talk to the Singaporeans. Does the Foreign Secretary know yet?"

"Someone is calling the duty minister now. We thought we'd let him decide whether to wake the old man up."

"Fair enough. Have we spoken to the Cabinet Office?"

"That's my next call."

"Good. I'll see you in the office in half an hour, Hilary."

Her words were crisp and decisive. She was taking action, action for which all her operational experience had prepared her. Everything which could be done, would be done. No effort would be spared to secure Andrew Singleton's release. But, deep inside her, Gillian suspected that she was generating activity for the sake of activity. If Jemaah Islamiyah had Andrew, there would be no negotiating with them. Which meant that, if the Indonesians did not get to him soon, Andrew was as good as dead.

* * *

The meeting room in the British High Commission in Singapore was too cold. The Management Officer had muttered something about getting a faulty thermostat fixed. Meanwhile the assembled group shivered in their lightweight clothes, while outside the mid-morning sun beat down relentlessly on the traffic in Tanglin Road.

The meeting was chaired by Nick Childs. It was a small group. Apart from Patrick himself, there was only Quentin Asquith, Robert Redford, Susan Hyde and Mary Bennett. Patrick had not expected to be there. But, for some reason, the prosecuting authorities had requested a postponement of Daniel Taylor's court appearance. Patrick had therefore found himself in Susan Hyde's office when the meeting was called. Susan, who had been deputed to look after him, had brought him along with her. Although initially surprised, Nick Childs had not demurred at his presence.

"I'll keep this brief," said Childs, his voice clipped and authoritative. "The Singaporeans have informed us the High Commissioner's been kidnapped. We're awaiting instructions from London. In the meantime, we're trying to keep everything under wraps. So, no talking to the press, please. If – and only if – any of your staff ask, we stick to the line that the High Commissioner's return has been unavoidably delayed."

The meeting sat in stunned silence. Both women were white with shock. Then Mary Bennett managed to ask: "What about Adam? Where's Adam?"

"He should be here any time," said Childs. "When I spoke to him in Langkawi on Saturday he expected to be back this morning."

Patrick began to wonder what kind of slipshod organisation he had joined. "Do we know what the kidnappers want?" he asked.

"Something the Singaporeans won't give them, I'm afraid," said Childs. "Look, I'm sorry, people. There's not much more I can say at this stage. But can Quentin and I have a quick word with you afterwards, Patrick, please?"

Patrick remained behind when the others, except for Asquith, had left.

"Patrick, I think there's something you should know," said Childs. "As you're the senior Foreign Office person at post, at the moment."

"We've had the Indonesian police report from the Singaporeans," said Asquith, pulling awkwardly at the lobe of his left ear. "It includes the testimony of the man at the resort who last saw the High Commissioner. He seems to think he had a woman with him."

* * *

"A woman," said Gillian King, sitting at the meeting table of her office in Downing Street. "I can't say I'm surprised. But is there any corroborating evidence?"

Paul Burrows looked solemn and, for a plump man, extraordinarily haggard in the harsh artificial light. "They found some female deodorant in the villa bathroom," he said. "And a number of blonde hairs in different places. They've sent the bedclothes and towels for forensic testing, but they're pretty clear there was a woman there."

Gillian saw the Head of Personnel, immaculately dressed despite the awful hour, shaking his toad-like head in disapproval. She wondered at the hypocrisy of men. Until his recent marriage, Julian de Crespigny had probably held the Foreign Office record in serial philandering.

"Do they think she was kidnapped too?" Gillian said.

"They doubt it," said Nigel Meyer. The Head of Security, normally a flashy dresser, was looking uncharacteristically scruffy in jeans and an old sweater. "All the physical evidence points to only one body being dragged along the ground by the pool area. After that, they must have used a sling of some kind, because there are traces of rope on the balcony and the villa's supporting pillars, and heavy trampling in the undergrowth below leading down to the rocks near the beach."

"Do they think she was involved?"

"It's possible," said Meyer. "Either that, or she was no longer in the villa when the kidnapping took place. The police are investigating all the other people staying at the resort at the time, but we won't get much more on that for another twenty-four hours or so."

"Alright," said Gillian. "Let's look at the demand now."

They all had before them a hard copy of the email the kidnappers had sent to the Singaporean Prime Minister. It was devoid of any rhetoric. Andrew Singleton would be executed at 1800 local time on Thursday, if the Jemaah Islamiyah prisoners had not by then been released and given safe passage to the country of their choice. There would be no negotiation and no further communication.

The attached photograph showed Andrew Singleton, unshaven, grey-faced and unkempt, grimacing with one eye half-closed at the camera. He was clutching to his chest an open laptop, on the screen of which appeared the front page of that day's online version of the *Asia Wall Street Journal*. Behind him stood two men in shorts, their upper bodies cut off by the top of the picture. One of them was holding a gun at Singleton's head.

"Well, there's no doubt they have him," said Gillian. "Any guesses where they might be?"

"The Singaporeans and the Indonesians are having their experts look at the photo in case there are any clues," said Meyer. "MI6 are looking at it too. But it's a close-up and the background doesn't seem to have any distinguishing features."

"We should get Scotland Yard in on it as well," said Gillian. "And the Americans." She turned to the Head of Personnel. "Julian, who's Andrew's next of kin? Presumably his daughter."

"Yes," said de Crespigny, who seemed to have difficulty keeping awake. "I assume the High Commission are taking care of her."

"Unfortunately they don't know where she is," said Burrows.

"Hasn't Adam White found her yet?" said Gillian.

"They've lost track of him too," said Burrows. "They had contact with him on Saturday, but seem to have lost it again."

Gillian bit back the remark which first sprang to her lips. "What about family in this country?" she said to de Crespigny.

"His parents are both dead," de Crespigny said. "He has a brother. Teaches at Oxford."

"So he does," said Gillian. "I think I met him once. You'd better speak to him, Julian. Tell him we're doing all we can, but to be prepared for the worst."

Gillian turned to her Private Secretary. "I thought you said someone from Consular Department was here."

"He's on his way," said the Private Secretary. "He's coming from Chatham."

"My God, whoever commutes from Chatham?" said Gillian.

"You'd be surprised where people live these days," said de Crespigny, who had himself driven in from Chelsea.

As if on cue, Peter Coles appeared, red-faced, at the door. "I'm terribly sorry," he said. "I came as fast as I could."

"Is your man in Singapore yet?" said Gillian, by-passing the niceties.

"He arrived yesterday," said Coles. "He should be seeing Daniel Taylor and his father today."

"He may have rather more than that to worry about now," said Gillian. "Alright, there's enough collective wisdom round this table. Does anyone think there's any prospect of the Singaporeans complying with this request?"

There was silence. "I thought not," said Gillian.

"We wouldn't do it ourselves," said Meyer.

"And we all serve overseas in that knowledge," said de Crespigny, somewhat pompously.

"I agree," said Gillian. She turned to Burrows. "Paul, we need a telegram to Singapore and Jakarta – copied to all the usual people – instructing them formally to ask for maximum efforts to secure

Andrew Singleton's release, and offering any help the two governments need. We may want to reinforce that later with a personal message from the Foreign Secretary, but let's not lose any time now. We also need to get the Americans and our EU partners on side as soon as possible. I suggest a message from the Political Director to his opposite numbers. Have you established an emergency unit yet?"

"They're opening up now," said Burrows, looking up from his notes. "I thought I'd better run it myself."

"Report any major developments direct to me," said Gillian. "And just ask Julian if you need any extra people." She turned to her Private Secretary. "Hilary, get Singapore to patch me through to Michael Seng," she said. "I want to hear what's happening first hand before I speak to the Foreign Secretary."

* * *

It was eight o'clock, the time Alison had been planning to arrive at the office and greet old friends before getting down to the serious business of discussing her package with Richard. Instead, she sat in a state of tearful tension by the telephone. Her bags were packed, her ticket paid for and awaiting collection at the airport. Despite the entreaties of her parents, she had not slept at all throughout the night. Now, after too much coffee, she was exhausted, but incapable of sleep.

Stan Murdoch had her mobile number and would be able to call her at any time up until the moment she boarded the plane. But why did he not call her now? She knew why. Because they had not found him. Because he was dead. *Oh, dear God*, she thought. *How could I ever have thought of not being with him?*

* * *

In the early evening, the hatch was opened once again and Andrew was helped to climb out into a standing position.

He felt the shackles on his wrists and legs being removed and was escorted across the cabin and through a door, which closed behind him. When nothing further happened after a few minutes, he took off the blindfold. He was in a toilet and shower room. Light entered through a porthole just above the level of his head, but it was too dirty for him to identify anything clearly beyond. He saw that there were clean towels, soap and shampoo – but not, he noted, a razor. On a hook behind the door hung clean shorts and a polo shirt. Gratefully, he showered and changed.

The door to the shower room was not locked. When Andrew emerged he saw a man seated at the table in the cabin, dressed in slacks and a casual shirt. He was dark-skinned and handsome, probably in his mid-thirties, and his head was smooth and entirely devoid of hair. He wore a pistol in a shoulder holster.

"I hope you're feeling a little better after that," said the man.

"Much better, thank you," said Andrew.

"Good. Come and have something to eat. I'm afraid you'll still have to use your hands. There's a limit to how far I can take this, you understand."

"Of course," said Andrew. On the table, beside the laptop Andrew had briefly held in his hands that morning, was an opened can of beer and a plate of grilled fish and rice. Andrew sat down, and ate and drank while the man watched.

"That was excellent," said Andrew. "I hope it wasn't the last supper."

The man smiled. "Not quite yet," he said. "We have until Thursday."

"Thursday? What happens on Thursday?"

The man opened the laptop and swivelled it round so that Andrew could read the email sent that morning. Andrew laughed in disbelief. "You might as well kill me now," he said. "They'll never agree."

"You're right, of course," said the man. "But it's a little game I have to play. Can I offer you anything else?"

"Would a cigarette be out of the question?"

"Of course not," said the man. He proffered a pack, taking one himself and lighting both their cigarettes with a disposable lighter.

"You know what I smoke," said Andrew, savouring the taste of the cigarette and letting smoke trickle from his nose before exhaling.

"I know a lot of things about you," said the man.

"I don't get it," said Andrew. "Why am I suddenly getting the deluxe treatment?"

"I'm sorry we had to keep you cooped up before," said the man. "It was a little dangerous for the first day when we were negotiating waters where the coastguard regularly patrol. Now there's less need to keep you hidden." He paused, then added, "Also, to be perfectly honest, my collaborators expected me to treat you badly, and I couldn't disappoint them."

Andrew was trying to work out the man's provenance. He looked Indian. But the accent was cultivated upper class English. "They've gone — the others?" Andrew said.

"Yes," said the man. "It's too risky for them to be away from their regular jobs for too long. I don't want any of them getting fired."

Andrew took this to be a joke. "That doesn't worry you, though," he said.

The man smiled. "I'm on extended leave of absence," he said. "No one will be missing me."

The two men smoked in silence for a while. Then Andrew said, "Look, I'm feeling very tired now. If it's all the same to you, I'd like to sleep."

"But of course," said the man. "Use the bunk over there. I'll be up on deck if you need anything. We can talk further tomorrow." He gathered up the dirty plate and beer can and walked to a flight of steps leading up to the deck. He paused and turned before ascending. "I'll save you a lot of trouble. There's no way to escape."

When the man was gone and the door to the deck had been closed and bolted from the outside, Andrew inspected his surroundings. It was soon clear that his captor spoke the truth. There were only two ways out of the cabin, either through the locked door or through a ceiling hatch over the bunk area, which was also bolted from the outside. The windows did not open. Even the hatch to the bilge area, where Andrew had been imprisoned, was now padlocked. And there was no loose object in the cabin which Andrew might have used to break a window or force the padlock. He went into the shower room and searched in vain for anything which might be of use. He fantasised, momentarily, about dismantling the shower to use it as a weapon of some kind. But he had no tools to do this, and in any case doubted that he would stand any chance in hand-to-hand combat, even with the advantage of a piece of metal tubing.

There were storage cupboards with sliding doors by the table, but they contained only charts and log books. A quick glance at these revealed that the boat was registered in Thailand and was on charter. Andrew then turned his attention to cupboards above the bunks, but they were locked and too strong for him to force without some kind of tool.

He looked out through each of the windows in turn. As far as he could see, they were surrounded by nothing but ocean.

Now he really did feel tired, and suddenly apprehensive. The switch in his treatment had unsettled him, had momentarily given him the barest of hopes that there might be some way out for him after all. Now he could see there was none, or none that was immediately apparent. He lay down on the bunk and was soon asleep, to dream of swimming through an endless sea, pursued by Birgit in the guise of the Angel of Death.

* * *

The final call for the Air Malaysia flight had just been announced when Alison's mobile rang. For several seconds, after all the waiting and anxiety, she was afraid to answer it. Then she took a deep breath and punched the green button.

"It's Stan Murdoch, Alison. We've found him. He's not in great shape, but he'll be okay."

CHAPTER 16

Much though she ached to do so, there had been no question of Mary calling Muzafar on Monday. The intensity of telephone, telegram and email traffic between London, Singapore and Jakarta had been such that all those in the know in the High Commission had had to work non-stop late into the night. Following the conversation between the Permanent Under Secretary and her opposite number in the Singapore Foreign Ministry, there had been a further exchange between the two Foreign Ministers. From these discussions had flowed a number of mutually agreed tasks for each side. The Singaporeans had also asked that selected High Commission staff be interviewed by the police, and Mary had been detailed to set up the individual appointments. Late in the evening, the news that Adam White had been found injured in northern Malaysia had generated a further stream of traffic with Kuala Lumpur. Mary had finally gone home after midnight and fallen, exhausted, straight into bed.

On Tuesday, at around nine-thirty in the morning, there was, unexpectedly, a brief let-up. Most of the people involved in London were snatching a few hours' sleep. There was, for the moment, nothing new coming from the Indonesians. And the first of the police interviews was not scheduled for another fifteen minutes. Mary took a deep breath and called Muzafar.

He answered the telephone almost as soon as it began to ring.

"Is that you, Mary?" he said.

She felt weak at the sound of his voice. "Muzafar, where have you been?" she said.

"I knew you would call, my darling." he said. "I'm so sorry to cause you all this worry."

"Where were you, Muzafar?" she said, fighting tears of anxiety and relief.

"I had to visit a sick relative," he said.

"But why didn't you tell me?"

"I don't know," he said. "I didn't want to worry you."

"But that's silly, Muzafar," she said.

"I know," he said. "I have been very silly. But, Mary, listen, my darling. I don't think I should see you any more."

Mary felt sick. "I don't understand," she said.

"I think it would be better for both of us."

"What do you mean?" she said, crying now. "I love you, Muzafar. What do you mean?"

"Oh, Mary," he said. "This makes me so sad. But it is for the best, I promise you."

"No," she said. "No, Muzafar. You have to explain. You can't just say it's for the best."

"But it is, my darling. I promise you. Goodbye."

He had cut her off before she could speak again. She stared out of the window, past the bougainvillea, at the empty tennis courts, trying desperately to come to terms with what Muzafar had said. The telephone rang again.

"Good morning, Miss Bennett, I hope your morning is being highly fruitful and fulfilling."

"What is it, Siew Ling?" said Mary, her voice unintentionally brusque.

"I have great pleasure in informing you that Detective Inspector Ow Suan Yew of the Singapore Police has arrived," said the receptionist. "Could you please be so kind as to arrange for him to be escorted on high?"

* * *

193

Andrew sat on a canvas chair under a sun awning. He was drinking what, in the circumstances, was a very passable cup of coffee and smoking his first cigarette of the day. His companion, also smoking, sat on a similar chair on the other side of a folding table, on which stood the remains of a breakfast of rice and fish. "I'm sorry about the monotony of the diet," the man had said. "The catering logistics are somewhat constrained, as you can imagine."

Andrew said nothing, as he smoked and sipped his coffee. He was trying to remember what little he knew about the technology of mobile telephones. The yacht appeared to be riding in open sea, with no land in sight. And yet his kidnappers had sent an email to the Singaporeans the previous day. He doubted that they would have been so careless as to use a satellite phone for this purpose. They must have used a mobile, which meant that in the last twenty-four hours the yacht had been within a network area of some kind. Not just close enough for the other kidnappers to reach land safely in a small boat, but some place where it was possible to obtain a strong signal. This must mean that an inhabited island of some description could be only just over the horizon.

"I trust you're fully rested now," said the man.

"Yes, thank you," said Andrew. "I feel much better."

"That's good," said the other. "Because I should like to ask you some questions."

Andrew said nothing. Whatever game the man was playing, he would let him make the running. But he was not expecting the first question.

"Do you feel guilty?" asked the man.

"Guilty? About what?"

"Don't tell me you're not nursing a guilty secret," the other said.

Yes, curse you, Andrew thought. *But how the hell do you know about that?* "I don't know what you mean," he said.

"Oh, I think you do," said the man.

"I have a question for you," said Andrew, deciding attack was the best form of defence.

The man smiled, but said nothing.

"Do *you* feel guilty?" Andrew said.

"Not in the least," said the man. "Why do you think I should?"

"Because you belong to an organisation whose avowed purpose is wholesale murder."

The man laughed. "You presume to know more about me than you actually do," he said. "In any case you wouldn't understand. You're from a degenerate and godless culture. You can't conceive of the conviction of those prepared to sacrifice their lives in the service of Allah."

"Actually, that's not true," said Andrew. "I understand the hatred of young Palestinians raised in the camps. I can even see how a suicide bomber might believe he'll earn an instant ticket to paradise."

"Such empathy is admirable."

"But I'm not talking about them," said Andrew. "I'm talking about you. You don't exactly give the impression of being under-privileged. What motivates you?"

"This is going to be more interesting than I had expected," said the man. "Can I get you some more coffee?"

Andrew shook his head. "No," he said. "Answer the question."

"I will, don't worry," said the man. "But you must promise to tell me about your own guilt in return."

Andrew was irritated. "To hell with you," he said. "You're going to kill me, whatever I say or do. I have no need of your absolution."

The man's eyes widened slightly and he spoke in a tone hinting at mild disappointment. "I was hoping we could at least have a civilised exchange," he said. "I'd confess if you'd confess, that sort of thing."

"Except that you don't regard your crimes as crimes," said Andrew. "Which makes it a bit one-sided."

"So you do have crimes to confess," said the other.

"Touché," said Andrew. "But not for your ears."

"We shall see," said the man. He tossed his cigarette end into the sea. "So, you want to know what motivates me?"

"Yes."

The man settled himself more comfortably in his chair. "Have you read Samuel Huntington?" he said.

"No, but I'm familiar enough with his thesis – I've argued enough about it with my brother."

"Do I take it you don't agree with Huntington?"

"Well, I don't agree with my *brother*," said Andrew. "He believes the clash of civilisations is the key to all future international conflict. I think the world's a much messier place than that."

"Huntington's right," said the man. "But he's been overtaken by events. The struggle between Islam and western imperialism is already under way."

"Well, honestly," said Andrew. "That's so much bullshit."

"On the contrary," said the man. "It's the simple truth. The decadent forces of the West are fated to be crushed by the faith-inspired armies of Allah."

Andrew looked in frank disbelief at the well-fed, handsome features of the young man opposite him. "You're making this up," he said.

The other shrugged. "Well, maybe I'm laying it on a little thick," he said. "It's the sort of thing my people like to hear."

"Your people?"

"Yes, the people I work with." He smiled, mirthlessly. "You met some of them this week."

"But what do you personally believe?"

"There is a fundamental conflict, of that there's no doubt," said the man. "I aim to be on the winning side."

Andrew was now exasperated. "There is no conflict," he said. "Except between terrorists like you and the rest of mankind."

"Really?" said the other. "What about Bosnia and Kosovo? Palestine? Afghanistan? Iraq?"

"Bosnia and Kosovo are bad examples," said Andrew. "The West intervened in both places to protect Moslems from being killed by Christians."

"That was the action of hypocrites," said the man. "You stood idle long enough for the Serbs to achieve what they wanted."

"We've made plenty of mistakes," said Andrew. "It's an imperfect world, for God's sake. That doesn't mean Islam and the West have to be at war with each other."

"You have to choose one side or the other," said the man.

"You *don't* have to choose," said Andrew. "Not so long as moderate people are prepared to promote dialogue."

"This is a little disappointing," said the other. "I'd hoped for a full-blooded debate on the values of the West versus Islam."

"Well, you won't get it from me," said Andrew. "I have far too great a respect for Islam to become embroiled in that game."

"I suppose I should have realised you believed in nothing," said the man. "Knowing what I know about you."

And what exactly do you know about me? thought Andrew. *And how?* "Not accepting the inevitability of conflict between people of different religions and cultures doesn't mean I believe in nothing," he said.

The man sat silently, with an interrogative smile on his face, waiting for Andrew to continue.

"I believe in tolerance," said Andrew. "In live and let live."

"Hardly the most visionary of creeds," said the man.

"No, it's not," said Andrew. "And that's what makes it a good creed. The problem with visionaries is that they're blind to the rights of those who don't share their vision."

"But if you have no vision, you just live from day to day with no purpose."

"There's a lot to be said for living from day to day."

The man sighed. "Oh dear," he said. "I can see this is going nowhere."

"My creed causes no suffering," said Andrew. "I can't say the same for yours."

"I thought you weren't prepared to criticise Islam," said the other.

"I'm not talking about Islam," said Andrew angrily. "I'm talking about your perversion of it."

The man roared with laughter. "Good," he said. "Passion at last."

"Actually, it's just come to me," said Andrew. "You don't believe in anything either. It's a game to you, isn't it? You manipulate your own people. You play hide-and-seek with the security services of a dozen countries. You toy with the life of the hostage you're going to kill whatever happens. It's the exercise of power that fascinates you."

"That's a very bold analysis," said the man, who seemed stung by Andrew's outburst. "But you're missing the point. I'm going to inflict appalling damage on you and your kind. Others will follow my example. We'll keep going until the whole rotten edifice comes tumbling down. And I shall be the one who started it all. That, my friend, is power."

"With all due respect," said Andrew. "I rather think it was Osama bin Laden who started it all."

The man smiled, relaxed once more. "Believe me, Mr Singleton," he said. "I'm talking about something far bigger than Osama bin Laden ever dreamed of."

* * *

"Your first visitor's arrived," said Sophie Smith, the Chancery Personal Assistant. The expression on her deeply sun-burned face suggested that she was not too sure about the interloper sitting behind the desk in Adam White's office.

Patrick rose to greet Inderjit Singh.

"Thanks for coming a little early," he said. "I've read all the papers, and I had a quick session with the boy yesterday, but I'd welcome your personal impressions before the father turns up."

"On the face of it, things look pretty damn hopeless," said the melancholy young Indian. "He was caught in possession. End of story."

"Then why aren't they pressing ahead with charging him?" asked Patrick.

"They've obviously hit some problem with the physical evidence," said Singh. "I hope so, but I don't want to raise Mr Taylor's hopes too far."

"You know he's likely to want to bring in his own lawyer now," said Patrick.

"That's his privilege, of course," said Singh. "I'm certainly not going to fight anyone for this case, I can assure you."

Their conversation was interrupted by the arrival of Simon Taylor, who was accompanied by an impassive Chinese, whom Taylor introduced as Chin Beng Seng, the senior partner of a leading Singapore criminal law firm.

"Now we have a bit more time, I thought it would be helpful to have this meeting to take stock," said Patrick, when Sophie had left after serving coffee. He turned to Taylor, who was sitting stiffly, formal in a dark suit and plain blue tie. "I know you had difficulty speaking to anyone in authority at the High Commission before the weekend, Mr Taylor," he said. "I apologise unreservedly for that. Both the High Commissioner and the Head of Chancery were unexpectedly absent and the Consul is sick. I've come from London to take charge of the case personally." *Sorry about that, Adam,* he thought. *But it's no more than the truth.*

"I finally got some sense out of the Consul," said Taylor grudgingly. "I'm sorry she's not well." He seemed to be implying that he'd be happier if Jane Rosendale were handling things. *Why should I be surprised?* thought Patrick. Taylor did not strike him as a man who would be content to have his son's life dependent upon the combined skills of a very young Indian and an Irish-Jamaican from Brixton.

"Mr Singh and I were talking about the delay in charging Daniel," said Patrick. "We think the prosecutors may not be satisfied they have sufficient evidence to proceed."

"It's a possibility," said Singh.

"You should have got the whole thing thrown out from the word go," said Taylor angrily. Patrick assumed this was aimed at Singh, but the lawyer said nothing in response.

"Can't we ask the prosecutor why there's a delay?" asked Patrick, turning to Singh. "And surely they can't detain Daniel indefinitely?"

Singh began to speak, but Taylor interrupted him. "It's totally outrageous," he said. He turned to the expressionless Chinese beside him. "Surely we can do something about this, Beng Seng."

"Leave it with me," said Chin.

"My lawyer will be taking over the case from today," said Taylor to Inderjit Singh. "Make sure he has all the information necessary."

"Of course," said Singh, apparently unmoved by Taylor's rudeness. "I have a set of all the papers with me today for that very purpose."

"Mr Taylor," said Patrick. "There is one question I wanted to ask you. Has your son said anything to you about being accompanied by friends the night he was arrested?"

"Friends?" said Taylor. "No. Why do you ask?"

"It just struck me, looking at the reports, that it was inherently unlikely that a young man like Daniel would be on his own in the disco of the Long Bar at Raffles."

"You think he may be protecting somebody?"

"I don't know. It's a possibility."

Taylor looked thoughtful, his anger momentarily diminished. "He has a gang of friends," he said. "But lately he's been mainly going out with a girl he met recently. He could have been with her."

"Do you know who this girl is?"

"We've never been introduced," said Taylor, now somewhat subdued. "We don't get too much insight into our son's personal life. But I'm pretty sure her first name is Marina."

* * *

Detective Inspector Ow was younger than Mary had imagined – or at least he looked very young. He wore a shirt and tie and neatly pressed slacks, but was without a jacket. He carried a palmtop computer.

Mary was Ow's last interviewee. He had spoken to Nick Childs, Quentin Asquith, Robert Redford and the duty driver. He had also had a brief meeting with Patrick Young, before the latter had excused himself for his meeting with Simon Taylor.

It was still very cold in the meeting room, and Mary pulled her cardigan around her shoulders as she sat down.

"It is rather chilly, isn't it?" said Ow.

"It's the thermostat," said Mary, automatically.

"Miss Bennett," said Ow. "My main concern, as I've explained to your colleagues, is to find out exactly who in Singapore knew the High Commissioner was planning to be in Bintan last week."

"You think someone in Singapore had something to do with the kidnapping?" said Mary. The vaguest sensation of dread began to make itself felt at the back of her mind.

"Well, actually, no," said Ow. "The most probable explanation is that a member of the resort staff tipped the kidnappers off. The Indonesian police are interrogating them all very thoroughly, but so far no one has confessed. The Indonesians have asked us to follow up any possible leads at this end, mainly to eliminate them from the enquiry."

"You have some leads?"

"Well, we have the names of everyone from Singapore who was staying at the resort at the same time as the High

Commissioner. We're interviewing all of them, although mainly with a view to discovering if they saw anything suspicious while they were there."

Mary thought for a moment. Then she said, very carefully: "I was the first person to be told, I'm pretty sure of that. The High Commissioner asked me on the Sunday to make his bookings first thing the following morning."

"Did you make the bookings direct?" said Ow, tapping the keys of his palmtop.

"Yes," said Mary.

"So, no one else could have known at that point."

"I don't think so," she said. "No one in the High Commission, at least."

"What about the ferry bookings?"

"I made those direct as well," said Mary.

"Did they know the booking was for the High Commissioner?"

"Well, I made the booking in his name, and they knew I was from the High Commission," said Mary.

"We'll have to follow that up," said Ow, making a further note "So, who else knew?"

"Adam White, the Head of Chancery."

"Who I understand is not here at the moment," said Ow.

"No," said Mary. "He had an accident in Malaysia at the weekend. He's in hospital in Kuala Lumpur."

"I'd better speak to my colleagues there," said Ow. "Anyone else?"

"No," said Mary. "Not that I can think of. Unless the High Commissioner told them himself."

"You weren't aware that he had a… " Ow paused, as though searching his vocabulary. Then he went on, "… a travelling companion?"

Despite her anxiety, Mary had to suppress a smile at the detective inspector's choice of words. "No, I booked him on his own," she said.

"But you wouldn't have been surprised if someone had gone with him?"

Mary struggled with her natural loyalty to Andrew Singleton and the gravity of the situation. Then she said, "The High Commissioner went off on trips on his own quite a bit. I think it's possible he was meeting someone when he was away."

"Have you any idea who?"

"No," said Mary. "He was extraordinarily discreet – and it was none of my business."

Detective Inspector Ow looked pensive. "You say he went off on trips frequently?" he said.

"I'd say every couple of weeks or so over the last few months," said Mary. "Usually to one or other of the islands off the east coast of Malaysia."

"Did you make the bookings?"

"Mostly, yes."

"Could you let me have a list of the places Mr Singleton stayed during that period?"

"Of course," said Mary.

Ow scrolled back up the screen of his palmtop and read his notes again. "Can we come back to the booking arrangements for Bintan?" he said. "Is it absolutely impossible that anyone else could have had knowledge of them?"

"Well, I certainly didn't tell anyone," she said, once more uneasy.

"Were the bookings confirmed there and then on the telephone?"

"The ferry booking was," said Mary. "They had to call back to confirm the pool villa."

"Did the call come straight through to you?"

Mary thought for a moment. "No," she said. "Siew Ling put it through."

"Siew Ling?"

"The receptionist. She takes all calls that come in through the switchboard."

"I see," said Detective Inspector Ow, making a note. "Well, I'd better speak to her as well." He handed over his visiting card. "Perhaps you could email the list of resorts and the dates of the High Commissioner's visits," he said. "And if you do think of anything else… "

"Yes, of course."

Mary returned to her office to find that the temporary lull had passed. Someone, somewhere, had leaked the news of the kidnapping to the press. Nick Childs was striding up and down the corridor with a harassed expression on his face. He looked disproportionately relieved when he saw Mary.

"Mary, bless you," he said. "Someone who can spell and type. We're a bit inundated here, so I think it's all hands to the pump, old thing, if you don't mind."

Mary took a sheaf of handwritten notes from the Defence Attaché and began working through the text methodically on her computer to turn it into a telegram format that would be recognised in London. But she was thinking all the time of her conversation with Detective Inspector Ow. She had told him the truth. She had given no one other than Adam White any information about Andrew Singleton's plans for Bintan. Of course, Siew Ling might have picked up something from the return telephone call from the resort. But the idea that Siew Ling was involved in a conspiracy to kidnap the High Commissioner was as quaint as her grasp of the English language.

No, Mary had told no one. Above all, she had not told Muzafar, the man she loved and who had just been mysteriously absent from Singapore for a week; the man who had only that morning told her, without explanation, that he could no longer see her. Of course she had not told him. If she had, she would have confessed to Detective Inspector Ow, there and then. There was no way, she tried to persuade herself, that Muzafar could have known the High Commissioner's travel plans.

But she could not prevent an image flashing into her head, an image from the Sunday when she had taken the call from Andrew Singleton asking her to make the Bintan bookings. It was an image of Muzafar crossing to the telephone in her house, Muzafar standing by the table on which lay the notepad where she had written every last detail of Singleton's instructions. "Can I quickly call my mother to tell her what time I shall be home tonight?" he was saying, as she disappeared into the kitchen to make tea.

* * *

Adam opened his eyes. For the first few seconds he could not relate what he was seeing to any rational thought. Then he realised he was looking at a face. It was a lovely face, even though it defied all notions of conventional beauty. The nose was crooked, the eyes slightly too close together, the mouth a shade too generous. It was also a face that frequently looked cross. But at this moment it was tight with exhaustion and suffused with such agonised tenderness he could hardly bear to look at it.

"That was quick," he said, listening unbelievingly to the hoarse croak which emerged from his mouth.

Alison began to cry. "Thank God," she said, bending down, carefully so as not to disturb the saline drip attached to his arm, and kissing him gently on the lips. He smelled her hair as it brushed his face and gave his own silent prayer of thanks.

"What time is it?" he said.

"I don't know," she said. "Late afternoon some time."

"How did you get here so fast?"

"Adam, it's Tuesday," she said.

He lay for some time with his eyes closed, digesting this information. Then he opened them and tried to lift himself off the pillows, but the effort was too much and his head was suddenly hurting. "Bloody hell," he said. "I'm in a bit of a state."

"Concussion, an infected scalp wound, dehydration, multiple insect bites and mild sunburn are the things I can remember," said Alison, "The doctor will have a few more to add to the list when he speaks to you. What the hell happened, Adam?"

"Someone bashed me on the head and threw me in a ditch," said Adam. "Then I think they rolled a tree on to me or something."

"Logs," said Alison. "It was logs. Apparently they meant to bury you, but for some reason they didn't finish the job."

"Jesus," said Adam.

"Who was it, Adam? Murray said something about you chasing after a girl."

Adam's head was hurting worse now. "It's a long story, Ali," he said. "Can you get me some water?"

Ali held a paper cup to his lips and gently tilted it so that he could drink. When he had finished, Alison sat by the bed and took his hand in hers.

"Adam, we promised each other. No secrets, remember?"

Adam knew she was right. He had nearly lost her at the very beginning of their time together by concealing his relationship with Janet, even though it had been wholly innocent.

He told her everything, and as he did so a sense of astonishing relief came over him. Why he had kept the whole thing to himself for so long he could not imagine. Because he was an idiot, he reminded himself, a bone-headed, stubborn idiot.

He had spoken out loud without realising it.

"You're not an idiot," she said. "You were trying to do the right thing."

"I must speak to the police," said Adam.

"Don't worry," said Alison. "They want to speak to you as well. The doctor tells me he's been keeping them at bay all day."

"But I should telephone Andrew Singleton first," said Adam. "That's only fair."

"I'm afraid that's going to be difficult, Adam," she said.

* * *

206

As Gillian King welcomed Roger Singleton into her office, she was aware that she was involving herself far more closely in Andrew's kidnapping than was proper for someone in her position. Permanent Under Secretaries were supposed to advise ministers, set strategy and allocate resources, not micro-manage individual crises.

To be fair, she had recognised this after her initial actions in the early hours of Monday morning. She had withdrawn from the fray, leaving Paul Burrows and his team to make the running and draw guidance from the relevant senior officials in the office as necessary. She had held back from the debate about whether or not to open the Cabinet Office briefing rooms or involve the Prime Minister, noting, however, with approval that her staff had in both cases won the argument for retaining the handling of the kidnapping in-house, thereby starving the terrorists of publicity. And, aside from a quick telephone call to her opposite number at the Ministry of Defence, she had even kept out of the negotiations for getting an SAS team attached to the Indonesian special forces searching for Andrew.

But when Roger Singleton had asked to see her personally, she had not hesitated in cancelling a call by the new Uzbekistan Ambassador to free up the necessary time.

Paul Burrows had extracted himself from the emergency unit to give Gillian an oral update on the latest situation and sat now, slightly awkwardly, to Gillian's right, on the sofa. Singleton sat in an armchair to Gillian's left, and her Private Secretary, Hilary Price, sat in an upright chair to Burrows's right.

Gillian had met Roger Singleton, although she was sure he would not remember her. He had attended Andrew's twentieth birthday dinner in a Spanish restaurant in Soho and had clearly felt out of place. Already established in his academic career, he appeared uncomfortable with the juvenile behaviour of Andrew's undergraduate friends. Gillian had attempted a half-serious discussion with him about the role of the United States in Vietnam, but they had been interrupted by a spontaneous toast to Andrew from another member of the party and the thread of the debate had been lost.

Other than the grey, thinning hair and incipient double chin, Roger had changed remarkably little. He was unmistakably Andrew's brother, but he lacked Andrew's vivacity, and there was a hint of barely suppressed anger about him.

"I'm so very sorry about this desperate situation, Dr Singleton," she said. "We're doing everything possible to try to secure Andrew's release, but the signs are not immensely hopeful."

"I suppose there's no chance of the Singaporeans giving the kidnappers what they want," said Singleton.

"No," said Gillian. "I'm afraid that's out of the question."

"Have you put any pressure on them?"

"No," said Gillian. "Our policy is the same as theirs. We don't give in to blackmail."

Singleton looked at her sourly. "You would if it was the Queen they were holding."

Gillian sighed inwardly. "Thankfully, the policy has not so far been put to such a severe test," she said.

Singleton's expression was inscrutable. "Do you have any idea where he is?" he said.

"The Indonesians have identified an area in the Riau Archipelago that is almost certainly where the kidnappers' email was sent from," said Burrows. "But there are hundreds of islands within that area. There's no way of searching them all thoroughly before Thursday."

"Don't you have any other clues?"

"The experts have been poring over the photo sent with the kidnappers' message," said Gillian. "But they've had no luck so far."

"May I see it?"

Gillian paused. It was a distressing photograph, one which she would not wish on any close family member. Thankfully, it had not been placed on a website, and the Foreign Office had decided against releasing it to the press. But Roger Singleton had every right to ask to see it. "Yes, of course," she said. "Paul?"

Burrows pulled the photograph out of a translucent folder of key papers he had brought with him and handed it to Singleton.

"He's on a boat," said Singleton.

"How can you possibly know that?" said Gillian, startled by the conviction of Singleton's statement.

"Because he's telling me he is," said Singleton. "That's why he's winking at the camera. To get us to look for the message. Why didn't you tell me about this before?"

"I'm truly sorry," said Gillian. "We didn't realise it was deliberate. But where's the message?"

"Look at his hands," said Singleton, placing the photo down on the coffee table between them. "See how he's holding the computer."

Gillian and Burrows studied the photograph. Gillian saw that the fingers of Andrew's right hand were making an inverted 'V' sign, while the thumb of his left hand was vertical. "I don't get it," she said.

"It's a code," said Singleton. "He's on a boat with a mast, a yacht of some kind."

"How can you tell?" said Burrows.

"Because we made the code up together, when we were learning to sail as kids," said Singleton.

* * *

The interview with the Malaysian police had been more straightforward than Adam had feared. They were content to leave it to the Singapore authorities to pursue the irregularities in Adam's behaviour. Their immediate interest was in getting as much information as possible about the rendezvous in Langkawi, and a detailed description of Marina and her companion. They also asked questions, at the request of the Singapore police, about Adam's knowledge of Andrew Singleton's trip to Bintan.

When the interview was complete, Adam was told he was free to travel to Singapore as soon as the doctors gave the green light. Stan Murdoch had personally guaranteed that Adam would return to Kuala Lumpur, if required for further questioning.

"The doctor says you'd better spend another night here before travelling," said Alison. "Do you trust me to drive? Stan's driver's bringing the car to Kuala Lumpur this evening."

"Ali, I'd trust you to do anything," said Adam. "Now go to the Murdochs and get some rest."

"I'm not sure it's safe to let you out of my sight," said Alison.

"Relax, Ali," he said. "I'm not going anywhere without you ever again."

* * *

Roger Singleton telephoned from Oxford, just as Gillian was winding up a meeting with senior staff to agree the final budget allocations for the coming financial year. It had been a difficult meeting, occasioned by a harsh settlement for the Foreign Office in the annual negotiating round with the Treasury.

"He says it's personal," said Hilary Price.

"Dame Gillian?" said Singleton. "Look, I'm awfully sorry to disturb you, and I hope you won't think this is silly."

"Of course not," said Gillian. "We need every scrap of information you may have."

"No, it's nothing like that," said Singleton. He sounded awkward, almost embarrassed. Gillian waited.

"This is very stupid," said Singleton. "But I have to ask. You're Kirsty, aren't you?"

"Good grief," said Gillian. "You have a phenomenal memory."

There was silence from the other end of the line. Then Singleton said: "Andrew was such a bloody fool."

CHAPTER 17

The dawn brought a grey sky and an uneasy, rolling sea. The yacht was moving faster in order to match the rhythm of the swell. Andrew lay on the bunk, seeking to compose his stomach, and to decide whether the deterioration in the weather might work to his advantage. Motoring in calm, open seas was a relatively easy task for one person to manage. If there were a storm, life would become more complicated.

Andrew had been confined in the cabin since his late afternoon meal of rice and dried meat the previous day. Would he now be allowed out for breakfast? If so, there might be the slightest of chances he could profit from the situation.

The debate of the previous morning had continued for several hours. Round and round the argument had gone between them, with Andrew advocating tolerance while his captor preached ideology and activism. Andrew had tried, unsuccessfully, to draw the other man further on his threat to inflict catastrophic damage on the West. At first, he had thought the threat was empty bragging. Gradually, he had come to the conclusion that the man was deadly serious.

What Andrew could still not understand was why his captor was prolonging the agony over his own execution. They both knew the Singaporeans were not going to release the detainees. The man might as well have put a bullet in Andrew's head two days ago.

Andrew's thoughts were interrupted by the opening of the

door at the top of the steps. "Come up on deck," said the man. "It's more comfortable in the fresh air."

They sat, as before, under the awning, which today flapped intermittently in a gusting wind.

"More dull fare, I'm afraid," said the man, doling out a pile of rice and beans. "And this is the last of the coffee. But the cigarettes should last us."

Andrew ate and smoked in silence, watching the sea for tell-tale white flashes of foam. But, if anything, the wind seemed to ease off slightly, although the yacht continued to pitch as it drove forward through the oncoming waves. The sky remained overcast, but the transition from cloud to sea was clearly visible. At one point, Andrew thought he saw another vessel dead ahead on the horizon, but after about half an hour it had moved off to the right. Later, as the yacht began to roll, Andrew realised that the boat was set on auto-pilot to describe a large circle. The unpleasant movement lasted for three quarters of an hour, then eased off as the waves began to come from behind the boat.

"Well," said the man. "Let's talk, shall we, while conditions are suitable?"

Andrew had decided he would try a different ploy. "You were right about one thing," he said. "Now my time is running out, I do have an urge to confess."

"Splendid," said the man. "I knew you'd come round."

"And then you must tell me exactly what you're planning to do."

"But, of course," said the man.

"I killed my wife," said Andrew.

The man's eyes widened. "Well now, that really is something to feel guilty about," he said.

"It was an accident," said Andrew.

"I read about it," said the other.

"But I could have saved her."

"Then why didn't you?"

212

Andrew took another cigarette from the proffered pack and smoked for a while before replying.

"It was a sailing accident," he said. "Or yachting, to be more accurate. Elena wasn't exactly the sailing type."

He saw it in his mind, as clear and bright as on a newly minted DVD. The yacht and crew rented at ludicrous expense to impress Elena's visiting Panamanian friends. Elena, dressed as expensively as some latter-day Jackie Onassis, teetering around on absurd heels and putting away champagne like lemonade. The sudden squall as they motored out of the Solent. The look on Elena's face as the boat lurched unexpectedly and she found herself thrown against the safety rail. Her brief, terrified gesture of supplication as the stanchion, rusted at the base, snapped under her weight. (The coroner had savagely criticised the owner of the yacht hire company at the inquest, but Andrew had not had the stomach for the subsequent civil suit his negligence would certainly have justified.) And then – his body turned cold in the humid heat as he spoke of it – Elena's outstretched hands, the imploring look, the frozen horror of the fateful moment when he might have leaped forward and grasped her wrist. A moment informed by all the poison and malice she had directed towards him throughout their marriage. A moment resonating, above all, with the triumphant act of cruelty she had inflicted on him in the car on the way down to Portsmouth.

And then the moment had passed and she was gone. He had dived into the choppy, green-grey sea and swum himself to exhaustion searching for her, before the coastguard arrived and pulled him out. Her body was not recovered until the following day.

"You could have saved her but, you chose not to?" said the man. "That's as good as murder."

"It wasn't that simple," said Andrew. "I was physically incapable of saving her. My brain was telling me to do it, but my body was paralysed."

"And why was that?"

They had been fighting in the car, as always, about money – this time another extravagance Elena wanted to buy for Marina.

"Elena, it's no use screaming at me," he said. "We simply don't have the money to buy a horse."

"Money, money," she said. "*¡Coño!* Why don't you have the money? We need it."

"Because you've spent it all," he said. "You've spent everything I've ever earned. More than spent it."

"What about your parents' money?" Andrew and his brother had inherited a small house in Windsor when their widowed mother had died. They had sold the house and split the proceeds between them.

"That went long ago," said Andrew. "If you want money, why don't you ask your father?" This was a low blow, because he had recently discovered that some years previously Enrique had lost everything in a mining scam in Mexico that had backfired disastrously. He had moved to Miami (because of the climate, according to Elena), leaving money owing to some very nasty people in Panama. He was desperately trying to build a new business, and in no position to indulge his daughter's excesses.

Elena did not know Andrew knew the truth about her father. "You have no pride," she said. "It's your responsibility to meet my needs. And my daughter's needs are also mine."

"She's my daughter too, Elena," said Andrew. "And I say she doesn't *need* a horse. Christ, woman, I can't even keep up the mortgage payments on the flat."

"You have no say in the matter," said Elena.

"That's bullshit, of course I do," said Andrew.

Elena's lip curled with impatience. "You just don't get it, Andrew, do you?" she said.

He could only guess why she chose that moment. How she must have wanted to throw it in his face so many times before and yet somehow controlled herself. Perhaps she was disposed to keep the secret so long as she believed Andrew was destined for the top, and it was clear now that he was an also-ran. She would never swagger through the diplomatic salons of Paris or Washington. She no longer had anything to lose.

He brought the car to a swerving halt on the hard shoulder.

"What did you say?" he said.

"You heard me, *coño*," she said.

He stared at her, still struggling to understand. Then, suddenly, he did. "José," he said.

"You were so easy to fool," said Elena. "We laughed so much at how easy it was."

"You evil bitch," he said.

"Fuck you too," she replied.

"Does Marina know?"

"No. I didn't want her saying anything to you before I was ready." Her beautiful face was ugly with derision. "I'll tell her now, of course."

He put his head in his hands on the steering wheel and said nothing for several seconds. Then he straightened up and looked at her. "This is the end for us, Elena," he said. "It's been a long time coming. Now we're finished."

"Good," she said. "You can move out tomorrow."

Andrew threw his cigarette stub into the sea, which had become calmer. He too felt calm now. Talking about Elena's death had been a device to soften up his captor. But, to Andrew's surprise, it had actually proved therapeutic.

"Your daughter never knew?" said the man.

"She's not my daughter," said Andrew. "And, no, Elena never had the chance to tell her."

"Could she not have guessed?"

"I don't think she has the intelligence," said Andrew. "She'd certainly have thrown it in my face by now if she had done."

"So, you killed your wife because she had betrayed you," said the other. "Or maybe it was just so that you could keep your property?"

"No," said Andrew. "It wasn't like that at all."

"But it was very convenient, wouldn't you agree?"

"I can't deny my life has been a good deal easier since Elena died," said Andrew.

"Then I'd say you were guilty of murdering her," said the other.

"You need me to be guilty?" said Andrew.

The man smiled. "You're right, of course," he said. "It makes no difference one way or the other."

* * *

The thermostat had been repaired and the temperature in the meeting room was now much more tolerable. Detective Inspector Ow seemed perfectly comfortable. Mary, however, felt herself perspiring very slightly.

"Thank you for agreeing to see me again so soon," Ow said. Mary said nothing, trying to ignore the sick feeling in the pit of her stomach.

"I just wanted to check again who you might have talked to about the High Commissioner's movements," said Ow.

Mary heard herself speaking, as though from a distance. "I can't think of anything to add to what I've already told you," she said.

"I see," said Ow. "Are you quite sure about that?"

"Yes," said Mary.

"The reason I ask is that we've had some information from our colleagues in Johor Bahru," said Ow. "Two weeks ago they detained a man under the Internal Security Act on suspicion of terrorist activity. Last week this man received several visits from his cousin. The cousin's name is Muzafar Nasser – he works for a subsidiary company of Lee Tek Keng here in Singapore. We ran a routine check on Nasser's telephone calls over the last couple of months and found that the High Commission number occurred rather frequently. I wondered if you could explain that for me, please?"

No, thought Mary, *I can't explain it. I don't know anything about a man called Muzafar Nasser. Please don't ask me to say I know him, or that he's used me and sullied our love and made me feel stupid and dirty and guilty.*

But then she realised that the next person Detective Inspector Ow would talk to was Robert Redford, who would show him the telephone log demonstrating that all the calls had come to her extension. Or he would talk to Siew Ling, who would cheerfully explain that whenever Muzafar called during Mary's absence she would take a message to pass on to Mary, whose face would light up, without fail, at the mention of his name 'just like a most illustrious New Year's lantern, Inspector'.

"Yes," she said. "Muzafar was my lover."

* * *

The yacht had completed a full circle and was once more headed into the wind. The sea had become much calmer now, but the sky remained overcast and there was a sultry heaviness to the air. Neither man had spoken for some time. Andrew began to suspect that his captor was not going to tell him anything.

When the other finally spoke it was as though he had been rehearsing something in his mind. "You're an Alfred Hitchcock fan, I believe," he said.

Is there anything this man does not know about me? Andrew thought. "You've done your research," he said.

"Then you're familiar with the central idea in *Strangers on a Train*?

Where the hell is this leading? thought Andrew. "Of course," he said. "Two people meet by chance. One offers to kill the other's wife if the other will kill his father in return."

"Very succinctly put," said the man. "But what is the essential point of the agreement?"

"It's a random meeting," said Andrew. "There's nothing to connect the two men. So no one would suspect either of them."

"Precisely," said the man.

"I don't get it," said Andrew.

"I'm one of the strangers on the train."

"You've lost me completely," said Andrew.

"Alright," said the man, "Let's try a different track. Why do you think I haven't already killed you?"

"I've been trying to figure that out," said Andrew. "I've no doubt all this talk about guilt and the clash of civilisations has been enormously interesting, but it hardly seems worth the risk you must be taking in hanging around for so long."

"So, what could be the reason?

"I don't know."

"Could it be that I'm waiting to receive something in return?"

"I thought you were hoping to secure the release of your comrades-in-arms," said Andrew.

"Naturally I should be delighted if they were freed," said the man. "But that would be in return for *not* killing you. And we both know that's not going to happen."

Andrew was becoming increasingly confused. "If I have the analogy correct, you're planning to kill me in exchange for someone else's murder," he said.

The other man laughed. "I shouldn't strain for too exact a parallel if I were you," he said.

"In exchange for what, then?"

"Something I need to fulfil my plan."

"There's no reason for you to be so bloody coy," said Andrew. "I'm as good as dead already."

Andrew could tell from the man's expression that he was enjoying himself. "Let's just say that it's a very complicated and costly requirement," said the other.

"Why not just tell me what it is?"

"Don't worry," said the other. "I promise to tell you before I kill you."

* * *

"I think the doctors would describe this as nothing less than a miraculous recovery," said Alison.

"Thanks entirely to Nurse Webster," said Adam, as he kissed the nape of Alison's neck and ran the fingers of one hand lightly up and down her naked thigh.

Alison turned in his arms and looked him straight in the face. "You weren't faking, were you?" she said.

"It's very difficult for us chaps to fake it, Ali," said Adam.

"No, before, you idiot," she said.

He laughed and then grimaced involuntarily. "No," he said. "That was for real, I promise you."

She nestled closer to him. "You're hopeless when I leave you on your own," she said. "I don't think I'd better do it again."

Adam said nothing. But she was right. Virtually everything he had done while Ali was away in England had been ill-judged or gone wrong through some stroke of ill luck. Now that she was back, everything seemed to be flowing in the right direction again.

He had still to face the Singaporean police to give them a first-hand account of his behaviour. But his doctors had advised him to rest on returning to Singapore and put off any taxing interview until the following day. Alison had driven directly to their house after the journey down from Kuala Lumpur, and had insisted that Adam go straight to bed after they had eaten a sandwich lunch. He had argued, but had finally capitulated when Alison, still tired from her plane journey, had made clear she was joining him.

"It seems like a very long time since we did this," she had said.

"Too long," he had said. Although still in pain, he had made a special effort to do all the things he knew pleased her best. She, in turn, had responded with a combination of vigour and tenderness.

Now she was asleep. But Adam could not sleep. His enforced stay in hospital and a car journey spent in intermittent dozing had left him too well rested. He began to have a bad conscience about lying in bed while the High Commission was under such pressure, and he felt badly cut off from events after being out of Singapore for several days. He looked at his watch. It was just after four. The least he could do was go to the office and read himself in, so he could hit the ground running the following morning.

He gently eased his arm out from underneath Alison's shoulder. She complained to herself and turned on to her side as he tiptoed from the bedroom.

* * *

Patrick received a telephone call from Chin Beng Seng in the late afternoon.

"I thought you'd wish to know Daniel Taylor's been released," said the lawyer. "All charges have been dropped."

"That's amazing news," said Patrick. "What happened?"

"The prosecutor acknowledged there was no physical evidence to demonstrate Daniel was knowingly in possession of the heroin."

"But the police found it on him," said Patrick.

"Quite so," said Chin. "But his fingerprints were not on the packet and there was no DNA match."

"So someone must have planted it on him," said Patrick.

"As both he and his father insisted from the very beginning," said Chin.

"Well, thank you very much for letting me know," said Patrick. "This is a great relief for everyone."

"Yes, it is," said Chin. "But I think I should warn you that the police are now turning their attention to the young woman who was with Daniel Taylor the evening he was arrested."

"The girl called Marina?" said Patrick.

"Correct," said Chin. "It turns out that she's the High Commissioner's daughter. And the police seem to be very anxious to discuss her whereabouts with your colleague, Mr White."

* * *

Gillian delayed the daily morning meeting with her senior staff to take a call from Paul Burrows.

"Some news has just come in," he said. "The Indonesians have narrowed the search area down considerably. They picked up a man who admitted he was involved in Andrew Singleton's abduction."

"That's a real breakthrough," said Gillian, allowing herself a momentary sensation of hope.

"Well, it is and it isn't," said Burrows. "All he can tell them is where the yacht was on Monday."

"Did he have no idea where it was headed?"

"No," said Burrows. "He said it was kept secret from him." He paused, then added, "I'm pretty sure that's genuine. The Indonesians' interrogation methods are very thorough."

Gillian preferred not to think too much about Indonesian interrogation methods. "Well, at least if they know the yacht's maximum speed they can calculate the distance it will have travelled in two days," she said.

"That's true," said Burrows. "But they don't know in which direction. And it's still a lot of ocean to explore in not much less than twenty-four hours."

* * *

It was shortly after five when Adam walked into his office. He could tell at once that something was wrong, but it took him several seconds to realise what it was: everything was far too neat. His desk was clear, apart from a clean notepad, alongside which lay a sharpened pencil. The chaos of post-it stickers on his computer screen had been rationalised into one sheet of notes, which lay by the keyboard. The photos of Ali and of his parents had been moved to a side table, together with a batch of personal mail. The piles of newspapers which normally littered the table had been tidied into a single stack, which on further inspection turned out to be carefully arranged in reverse date order.

"You might have watered the plants while you were about it," Adam muttered to himself. He went to look for Mary, but she had left unexpectedly early. Sophie Smith was in the cypher room. Nick Childs was on the telephone to London, and Quentin Asquith had been called down to the headquarters of the Singaporean Security Service for a detailed briefing on the most recent intelligence on the kidnapping.

Adam asked the registry for the files on the Daniel Taylor case and the High Commissioner's abduction. He read the first while the latter was being brought up to date.

He was astonished, and mightily relieved, to learn that Daniel Taylor had been released, but he became increasingly irritated as he read Patrick Young's report to the Foreign Office. It was factually accurate, but it contrived to convey the impression that Adam had not handled things well, and that Young had stepped in to save the day. Adam read, and re-read, the key passage:

'I agreed with Simon Taylor that it would be sensible to appoint a new legal representative (Chin Beng Seng, a leading Singaporean criminal lawyer) to replace the one originally chosen for his son by the High Commission. I suggested that, in the light of the delay by the prosecution in bringing the case to court, there might well be grounds for challenging the validity of the physical evidence. I also

suggested that the police should be encouraged to investigate more closely the person accompanying Daniel Taylor on the night he was arrested (see my separate email, personal for the Deputy Head of Personnel). Happily, as a result of this new approach, Taylor was released today without charge.'

Well, thanks a million, Patrick Young – whoever you may be, thought Adam. *There goes my promising career down the drain.*

But the burden of his anger was directed at himself. If he had simply turned Marina in that first night, all this trouble would have been avoided.

* * *

Patrick had left the High Commission as soon as he had finished his report. He had agreed with Nick Childs that he would focus on the Taylor case while the rest of the senior staff in the High Commission – such as they were – dealt with the kidnapping. Now that Daniel Taylor was released, Patrick was temporarily at a loose end. There was no point in inserting himself into the kidnapping work at this stage; everyone was, in any case, far too busy to take time out to brief him. No doubt there was a host of routine consular work to be done, but Robert Redford seemed to have things under control, and there was nothing that could not wait until the morning. In any case, Patrick was still mildly jet-lagged, and had felt his concentration waning severely as the afternoon wore on. So he left a message with Sophie Smith to say where he could be found if required, and went to his hotel for a swim and a drink.

He was lying on his bed, wrapped in a bathrobe, balancing a glass of whisky and water on his stomach and half-watching television, when there was a knock at the door. He assumed it was room service and shouted to them to come in, but there was a further knock and a woman's voice called through the door. "Can you let me in, please, Patrick? It's Susan."

She had come straight from the office and was dressed in a demure skirt and blouse. Her freckled, frightened-rabbit face was strained and she seemed very close to tears.

"Oh, I'm so sorry," she said, seeing that Patrick was not dressed. "I shouldn't have burst in on you like this."

"Don't be silly, Susan. Come and sit down," he said, turning down the sound on the television. "Here, have a drink." He opened the door of the mini-bar, but she shook her head.

"I'd better not," she said. "Really."

"What's the problem?" he said.

"I've messed everything up," she said, looking down into her clasped hands.

"Messed up? How?"

She made agitated movements with her hands, but still did not look up. "I just have," she said.

Patrick had read all the back papers in the Daniel Taylor file, including the record of the exchange Susan had had with Simon Taylor. "No, you haven't," he said. "Adam White had no right to leave Singapore the way he did, leaving you to face the flak from Daniel Taylor's father."

She looked at him blankly for a moment. "Oh, that," she said. "Yes, that was awful. He was so *angry*. No one's ever shouted at me like that."

"He's just a bully," said Patrick. "Anyway, it's all sorted now, so there's nothing to worry about."

She looked up at him, still nervous. Then a fresh thought seemed to occur to her. "They made you come all the way out here when you should be at home looking after your wife and baby," she said.

"I've told you," said Patrick. "That's Adam White's fault, not yours."

There was a further knock on the door. This time it was room service, with the club sandwich Patrick had ordered. "Here," Patrick said. "This is too much for me. Have some. And for heaven's sake have a drink and relax."

She refused the drink again, but took half the sandwich. They sat for a while, eating in silence. Then she said, "You're very kind. I shouldn't be bothering you, but I had to speak to someone."

The whisky and general tiredness was making Patrick very sleepy now. Common sense told him that he did not want to encourage a virtual stranger to pour out her heart to him. But there was something very sympathetic about Susan, a kind of emotional fragility that made it impossible for him to be unkind. As she spoke, he could not help contrasting her insecurity with the tough confidence of his own Buffy, who possessed a steeliness born of fighting for survival in a poor black family in Brixton.

He must have dozed off for a while, because he suddenly heard her saying, "Forgive me, Patrick. I shouldn't be troubling you with any of this." He shook himself awake and said, "Don't be silly, Susan. I'm just a bit jet-lagged that's all. Come on, have one drink before you go. One for the road."

Her pert little face seemed tortured with indecision. "Okay," she said at last. "One drink won't hurt, I suppose."

* * *

The kidnapping file, even shorn of ephemeral material, already ran to four fat volumes and several annexes. Adam glanced briefly at the latest situation report, which included the mildly encouraging news of the arrest of one of the kidnappers. Then he read the files in chronological order to try to get a feel for the crisis as it developed.

It was gone seven by the time he had finished reading the main files. He debated whether to call Alison, but decided she would probably still be asleep. He had left a note to explain where he was, so there would be no harm in leaving her in peace for a while.

The annexes were, for the most part, copies of police and

intelligence reports that had come from the Singaporeans, the Malaysians and the Indonesians. The bulkiest document was the first full Indonesian police report following interrogation of the staff at the Bintan resort. Its contents had been succinctly summarised on the file in a reporting telegram to London. Adam riffled through the report, and found his eye running down a list of the guests who had been staying at the resort at the same time as Andrew Singleton. Somewhere on the main file Adam had seen something to the effect that the Singapore police had interviewed all those resident in Singapore, but had come up with no fresh evidence. Some of the guests remembered seeing someone answering Singleton's description dining alone on his first night in the resort, but none recalled seeing him later.

Around half the names on the list meant nothing to Adam: they were of people who had come from other parts of the region. Of those from Singapore, Adam recognised the names of two leading bankers and their wives, a local television actress and the Deputy Chairman of the Singapore Tourism Board. He did not know the others, but his guess would be that they were businessmen or senior civil servants. They were mostly Chinese or Indian, although he spotted one Malay name. There was one other name, at which he found himself looking and wondering. It rang a vague bell at the back of his mind, but he did not understand why. He looked at his watch: eight-thirty. He would call it a night. Maybe it would come to him while he slept.

* * *

Back down in the cabin, lying on his bunk, Andrew Singleton tried in vain to sleep. Tomorrow he would die, unless his captor made a serious mistake, or he was rescued, or – or what? Unless the other partner in the sinister pact his captor had described failed to deliver his side of the bargain? No, that was a forlorn hope. The man might claim to be holding out for final confirmation, but in the end he would have to kill Andrew, whatever happened. Andrew had seen him, could identify him, knew too much already about his plans.

Andrew feared death. But he saw it as a final reckoning which was not without a certain justice. He had lived well, far better than most. He had lived selfishly. And, although he had never sought to hurt anyone, he was guilty of allowing Elena to die when he might have saved her.

The remaining question that haunted him was the identity of the person who wanted him dead so badly that they were prepared to provide material assistance to terrorists in return. He could think of only one person who hated him enough – and that person was Marina.

CHAPTER 18

Buffy had given birth and was holding the baby towards him with both hands. At the same time, somehow, she was pointing accusingly at the person lying next to him. He could not turn to see who this person was. But his gaze was in any case fixed upon the baby, whose freckled face and reddish curls were those of a young woman.

He awoke with a start, feeling her weight against his back. *Jesus, no, not again*, he said to himself. *I promised myself, never again. What the hell's wrong with me?*

"Just have one drink," he had said. She had had the first – a gin and tonic – and become suddenly garrulous, sweeping her hand extravagantly through her hair as she spilled out her life story to him. Then she had helped herself to a second – which had gone down with one gulp – and then a third, before muttering something about needing the bathroom. Patrick had closed his eyes momentarily in silent prayer. When he opened them, she was standing in the doorway, wearing only her underclothes, her lips slightly parted, her hair awry where she had pulled the still buttoned blouse over her head.

He could not deny that it had been good. Buffy's two pregnancies in quick succession had severely constrained their lovemaking. That was why he had strayed before on overseas trips. That, and the need to alleviate the stress of dealing with human catastrophe. After the American girl in Santo Domingo, he had resolved to call a halt. So much for that.

She stirred and opened her eyes. In the pale, flickering light of the silent television, with her red, tangled hair, she reminded Patrick suddenly of a woman in a pre-Raphaelite painting he had seen on his first ever visit to the Tate Gallery. "What happened?" she said. She sat up rapidly, pulling the sheets around her when she realised she was naked. "Where are my clothes?" She looked at him with horror. "Where are yours? Oh my God, what time is it?"

Patrick looked at his watch. "It's just after four," he said.

She put her hands over her face. "What have we done?" she said.

"What do you mean?" said Patrick.

She looked at him, distraught. "I can never remember anything after the first drink," she said. "That's why… " Her voice trailed off.

"Are you telling me you get drunk on a regular basis?"

"Only since I've been in Singapore," she said. "I never used to drink at all. The boys in the Registry got me going one night on Singapore Slings."

Despite himself, Patrick felt strangely aroused by Susan's crumpled dismay. "Look," he said. "It's probably not a good idea for you to go home at this hour. Why don't you wait until seven-thirty and leave then. There'll be a lot of people checking out. No one will notice you."

She looked at him, uncertainly. "You don't mind if I stay?"

"Of course not," he said. "I want you to stay."

"You feel sorry for me," she said.

"No, I mean it," he said, lifting a stray curl and kissing her gently on the forehead.

* * *

Alison could see Adam sitting at his desk. She looked over his shoulder. He was reading the letter she had sent him the previous week. But someone had crossed out all the words and written across them in large letters: 'IT'S ALL OVER'. Desperately,

229

she tried to snatch the letter away, but Adam's broad shoulders impeded her attempts. "No," she cried. "It's not fair!"

She was suddenly awake, lying in the dark, momentarily disorientated. Adam lay on his back beside her, his hairy chest moving to the regular rhythm of sleep. She groped for her watch and could just make out the time: shortly before five in the morning. She had slept for over twelve hours.

In all the drama of the previous two days she had forgotten about the letter. Thankfully, she had sent it to the High Commission address, so Adam would not yet have seen it. Somehow she would have to get to his office before him in the morning and intercept it.

* * *

Andrew had not dreamed. Or rather, he could piece together nothing coherent from the fragmented images which had accompanied the fitful snatches of sleep he had managed during the night. But he had thought a lot. He had thought of Kirsty, the one major sin of omission in his life. He had thought of Birgit. He had, inevitably, thought about Elena, although with greater tranquillity than before. And, most of all, he had thought about Marina, and the hatred that had brought her to strike such a terrible, and incredible, bargain.

Still confined to his cabin at seven in the morning, he became aware of a more purposeful sound to the engine and judged that they were now bound for a specific destination. *Keep your wits about you*, he said to himself. *You're not dead yet. He could still make a mistake.*

* * *

One of the conceits of the Foreign Office was that official telegrams, irrespective of their authorship, were personal communications between the Head of Mission and the Foreign Secretary. As a new entrant, Adam had been told of one Ambassador who had insisted that telegrams be drafted without exception in the first person singular. When the Ambassador suffered an accident, his number two had despatched a telegram to the Foreign Office containing the immortal words: '*I regret to inform you that I have fallen downstairs and knocked myself unconscious.*'

The demise of the old guard and the ubiquity of email had largely eroded this tradition. But telegrams despatched from an overseas post still bore the surname of the Head of Mission. When reading the kidnapping file the previous evening, Adam had observed that outgoing telegrams on Monday and Tuesday had still carried the signature: 'Singleton', as though Nick Childs and his colleagues had been anxious to preserve the fiction that Andrew would turn up at any moment. But on Wednesday the signature had changed to 'Young'. Drawing on his dwindling reserves of good nature, Adam had limited himself to making a mental note to issue a corrective telegram first thing in the morning.

In the event, he received a telephone call over breakfast from Sophie Smith to say that the Central Narcotics Bureau had asked to see him in their office at eight-thirty. He decided to go straight there, dropping Ali off at the High Commission on the way, so that she could collect something she said Mary Bennett was holding for her.

The meeting with the Central Narcotics Bureau was difficult. There were three officers present. They were all people he knew, with whom in the past he had exchanged confidential information, whose goals were the same as his: to eradicate a hateful and life-destroying trade. The most senior of them, Liew Kim Poh, an unusually tall Chinese, was one of Adam's regular tennis partners. Now, Adam had to acknowledge that, out of a misplaced sense of loyalty to his High Commissioner, he had wilfully obstructed a Central Narcotics Bureau investigation.

Worse, he had concealed, and lost, material evidence. Throughout the detailed interrogation the three men remained courteous and soft-spoken, but he sensed their disbelief and disappointment.

"Look," he said finally, when there were no more questions. "I can't turn the clock back, and I'm not excusing what I did. But there is one positive thing. At least you now know where the heroin came from."

"Ah, yes," said Liew Kim Poh. "The man with the missing hand. Unfortunately, the Malaysians have so far been unable to trace him."

Was it possible that Kim Poh didn't believe him? No, he decided. It was a genuine expression of regret.

"I'm still puzzled as to what exactly Marina was supposed to be doing with the drugs," said Adam. "Her story about the courier at Changi just doesn't seem to fit with the amount she had on her."

No one spoke for a while. It was as though they were deliberating on his trustworthiness. Then Liew shrugged and said: "You might as well know what we know ourselves. Our intelligence suggests that Miss Singleton and her partner are novices at this game – and not very clever ones. Somehow or other they've managed to get their hands on a source of supply, and are trying to break into the market in Singapore as well as smuggle heroin through here to Australia. Our guess is that there was in fact a courier passing through Changi last week, and that's where the bulk of the consignment went. Our informant just gave us the wrong day."

"Your informant?"

"We had an anonymous phone call. We think it was from the same person who tipped us off about the Long Bar."

"But why was Marina carrying heroin around in her handbag?"

"We think she was planning to meet a local retailer later that night," said Liew. "As I say, they're amateurs. They were mad to bring the stuff into Singapore in the first place. I suppose they thought Miss Singleton's diplomatic status would protect her."

Adam could only agree with Liew's assessment. Most people trying to smuggle drugs into Singapore got caught, and the conviction rate was effectively one hundred per cent.

"Why did she plant the packet of heroin on Daniel Taylor?" asked Adam. "She told me some nonsense about having a dare with herself and then panicking."

"I've no doubt she panicked," said Liew. "But the business about a dare is, as you say, undoubtedly nonsense. She may have been about to meet a retailer and was surprised by the raid. She seems to be a rather stupid young woman."

"I think she's in way over her head," said Adam. "This man she's with obviously exerts strong influence over her."

"Well, let's hope she returns to Singapore soon and we can put a stop to all this nonsense," said Liew.

"I suppose she might risk coming back if she thinks I'm dead," said Adam. As he spoke, he wondered whether, for all her defects, Marina was really as cold-blooded as he made her sound. He was sure he had seen genuine alarm on her face the moment before his assailant had struck him from behind. And why had he not been finished off in the ditch outside Kuala Kedah? It had to be because of Marina's intervention. She was simply not capable of harming someone she knew and liked. On the other hand, he thought, if she *didn't* like you...

And then, suddenly, without warning, Adam resolved the puzzle of the name on the Bintan resort guest list, the name which had been troubling him since the previous evening. He saw Marina, sun-bronzed, beautiful and aggressive in her yellow bikini. And he heard her voice, contemptuous and hate-filled, as she responded to Adam's question ten days earlier about her father's whereabouts. "Probably off somewhere with his German bitch," she had said.

Adam became aware that Liew Kim Poh was speaking. "We shall need you to testify in due course, Adam," he said. "And we even may have to bring charges against you, although I fully understand that this will entail your government waiving your diplomatic immunity."

"Don't worry, I'll waive it voluntarily," said Adam, his mind on other things. "But I need to ask you a favour in return. There's someone I need to speak to urgently."

* * *

"Good morning, Miss Webster. I do so sincerely hope you had a delightful visit to your most revered parents in the City of London."

"Thank you, Siew Ling. Can I see Miss Bennett, please?"

"I will call her for you without any further delay."

Mary let Alison into the secure area.

"Adam will be coming in later, Mary," said Alison, as they went into Mary's office. "I just came to pick up the mail."

"I think Adam may have collected it last night, Alison," said Mary. She seemed distracted.

"Last night?"

"Yes," said Mary, sitting down and toying listlessly with a ballpoint pen. "Registry said he was in reading up on the kidnapping."

Adam had said nothing to Alison about being at the High Commission the night before. Did that mean he'd seen the letter and didn't want her to know he'd seen it? *Oh God,* she thought, *I must speak to him at once.*

Then she saw that Mary was crying.

"Mary, what's wrong?" she said.

Mary was silent for a moment. Alison sat next to her and put her arm round her shoulder. *Just as Janet did to me less than two weeks ago,* she thought – it seemed like a lifetime. "Tell me, Mary," she said. And Mary told her story, haltingly and in between outbursts of sobbing.

"Oh, Mary, poor you," said Alison when Mary had finished, feeling that her concerns about Adam now seemed so trivial. "But you still don't know if Muzafar is guilty of anything."

"They let me see him last night," said Mary, wiping her face with a tissue Alison had given her. "Just for ten minutes. He swore to me he was innocent. But how can I believe him when he lied to me about where he'd been all last week?"

"Do you love him?"

"Yes, of course I love him."

"Then you must believe him," said Alison.

* * *

"Thank you for seeing me at such short notice," said Adam.

Detective Inspector Ow gave a neutral smile. "The CNB were pretty insistent I do so," he said.

"I've looked at the list of people staying at the resort at the same time as the High Commissioner," said Adam.

"We interviewed all those who came from Singapore," said Ow. "None of them knew anything that looked worth following up."

"I think you should talk to Birgit Berger again," said Adam.

"For any special reason?"

"I think she may have been with the High Commissioner."

"Really?" said Ow, looking interested for the first time. "Why do you think that?"

"Because of something Andrew Singleton's daughter said to me at one stage," said Adam. "She seemed to think her father had a German mistress. Berger is the only German name on the list."

Ow turned to his computer and ran his fingers rapidly over the keyboard.

"We interviewed her on Tuesday," he said, looking into the screen. "She said she knew nothing."

"I think you should talk to her again," Adam said.

Ow frowned at the screen. "That doesn't seem to be possible," he said. "My boss has put a bar on any further interviews with Mrs Berger."

"Why would he do that?"

Ow turned to look at Adam. "It doesn't happen very often," he said. "Someone fairly high up must have intervened."

"Can I talk to your boss?"

"You think this is serious, don't you?"

"I think every possible lead should be followed up," said Adam.

"Come on then," said Detective Inspector Ow. "I'll see what I can do."

Detective Superintendent Chandra Dhanabalan was a bulky, grey-haired Indian with large tortoiseshell glasses. "I had a request from the Senior Minister's office," he said, in response to Adam's question. "They asked me – very nicely, you understand, – not to bother Mrs Berger again. Apparently she'd been upset by the persistence of our questioning. Her husband complained to someone close to the Senior Minister."

"So Mr Berger has friends in high places," said Adam.

"I was told he's exactly the kind of person the government is seeking to attract to invest and conduct business here," said Dhanabalan. "He has – and I quote – 'entrepreneurial skills, capital, technological capacity and the vision to make Singapore the hub of his global business'."

"Does that mean his wife is necessarily telling the truth?" said Adam.

Dhanabalan gave Adam a sharp look. "It means that, in the absence of evidence to the contrary, we're asked to assume that she is," he said.

Adam looked at his watch. "The High Commissioner is due to be killed in just under eight hours' time," he said. "Don't you think you should be exploring every possible avenue?"

"I'm told the Indonesians think they're getting close to finding him," said Dhanabalan. "Talking to Mrs Berger at this stage surely won't make any difference to a possible rescue." He saw that Adam was unmoved. "Alright," he said. "I'll see what I can do. But I can't promise anything."

* * *

Andrew remained locked in the cabin as the yacht travelled at speed towards whatever was now its destination. He had worked out from the position of the sun that their course was more or less due south. But since he had no idea of the route they had taken during the first two days of his incarceration, he had only the vaguest notion of where they might be.

His captor seemed to have been busy on deck all morning. Andrew had heard a number of things being tossed overboard and assumed he was getting rid of incriminating evidence. It occurred to Andrew to try to secrete a message of some kind in the cabin, but unless he wrote it in his own blood he had no means of doing so. Besides, what could he write which would be of any use? *Marina is my murderer? Look for a handsome, dark-skinned man who speaks fluent English and plans to commit the worst terrorist attack of all time?* (How much blood would that take?) No, his only hope was to conserve his strength and wait for an opportunity to escape.

Andrew's thoughts were interrupted by the opening of the cabin door. The man stood at the top of the steps, dressed, bizarrely, in a wetsuit.

"It's time," he said. "You get one last cigarette."

* * *

"Welcome back, Mr White. I am so pleased to see that you are in a single piece."

"Thank you, Siew Ling," said Adam, wondering again at the speed with which information found its way around the locally engaged staff network. But the question to which his mind was immediately directed was where his priorities now lay. He ought to take command of the High Commission and focus on the myriad responsibilities this entailed. But he could not be confident the police would be interviewing Birgit Berger again. If there was the remotest possibility she knew where Andrew Singleton was, he must try to speak to her himself.

Adam was met at the top of the stairs by Nick Childs and a man he did not know, but assumed was Patrick Young.

"Shall we just go into the meeting room a moment, Adam," the stranger said. His face suggested that his origins were Caribbean. The accent was south London, with a mildly incongruous hint of Irish.

Nick Childs seemed very uncomfortable. "You must be Patrick Young," said Adam. "If you want a meeting, come to my office in five minutes. I just need to sort a couple of things out first."

"No, we'd better go to the meeting room," said Young. Adam frowned. Who the hell did Young think he was? Then he began to understand, and nodded his acquiescence.

"I'll leave you chaps to it," said Childs, looking very unhappy.

The two men sat down. Young was immaculate in a white shirt and red-and-white spotted tie, but he had bloodshot eyes, as though he had not slept much the previous night.

"I'm sorry we should meet like this," said Young. "But I have instructions from London to inform you that you are suspended from duty pending disciplinary action in relation to possible criminal activity."

"No one said anything about this to me last night," said Adam.

"It took London a few hours to get their act together," said Young. "The instructions came in overnight."

"This is crazy," said Adam. "Today of all days, the High Commission needs me."

"London's view is that nothing anyone can do in Singapore is going to affect the outcome of the High Commissioner's kidnapping at this stage," said Young. "And the allegations against you are too serious to ignore."

"It's not a question of *allegations*," said Adam. "I'm not denying what I did."

The other man said nothing. Adam suddenly realised that things were even worse than he suspected. "I didn't see the whole file last night, did I?" he said. "You sent a personal telegram to the Deputy Head of Personnel."

Young kept silent.

"What did you tell him?"

"I said it was possible that you and Marina Singleton were working together in a drug ring," said Young.

"That's bollocks!" said Adam angrily. "I've just been with the CNB. They don't believe that."

"I just told it as I saw it," said Young.

Adam struggled to be fair-minded. The bare facts certainly looked bad. But what right did Patrick Young have to second guess the police investigation?

"Why are you doing this?" Adam said.

"I'm just trying to clear up the mess I was sent out to deal with," said Young.

"No. What you're doing is painting things as black as you can so you look good in London," said Adam.

For the first time, the other appeared to be roused. "I'd choose your metaphors more carefully, if I were you," he said. "Alright, yes. I do want to look good in London. When I'm up against over-educated, middle-class bastards like you I can't afford to wear kid gloves."

"Bloody hell," said Adam. "It's only a figure of speech, for crying out loud. And, for your information, my father was a railwayman."

"But he paid for your fancy education, didn't he?" said Young. "An only child, were you?"

"I was an only child because my father died when I was two years old and my mother refused ever to look at another man," said Adam, now very angry. "Not that it's any of your bloody business. My mother worked her guts off to get me through university."

Young seemed unprepared for this information. After a short pause, he said: "Look, it's nothing personal. I'm sorry. I didn't mean it to be personal. I'm a bit tired and it all came bursting out. But I have the instruction now, so there's nothing to be done about it."

Adam was conscious of time draining away. "Do they want me back in London?" he said.

"No. You're to remain at the disposition of the Singapore authorities."

Adam made a decision. "Okay," he said. "I'm suspended. I just need a few things from my office."

"I'm sorry," said Young. "I can't allow you to go there. We'll send anything personal round to the house in due course."

Adam began to protest, then thought better of it. At least now his immediate priorities had been decided for him.

* * *

The sky was almost without cloud and a light breeze rippled the surface of the sea. The yacht was now nearly stationary, riding gently up and down as it drifted through the water.

Andrew and his captor sat beneath the awning. On the table between them lay a packet of cigarettes. Andrew scanned the horizon, unsuccessfully, for some clue as to where they might be headed. The other sat, cradling the gun in his lap, just far enough away for Andrew to be unable to reach him with a surprise attack.

"I've just had a very satisfactory telephone conversation,"

said the man. "It would appear that I have everything I wanted. So, now you and I can conclude our business."

"Take your time," said Andrew. If the man had used a satellite telephone, and if the Indonesians were looking for him in remotely the right place, it was conceivable that help was already on its way. But the man must know that. He seemed to be playing some perverse game of chicken.

"We don't have that much time," said the other. "As you know full well."

The situation seemed unreal to Andrew. He forced himself to think about making a desperate lunge for the gun when the moment came, however unlikely the possibility of success.

"Have you guessed?" asked the man.

"It must be an attack with some kind of weapon of mass destruction," Andrew said. "My guess would be a nuclear device."

"Very good," said the other.

"That's it?"

"Part of it."

"A multiple strike?"

The man laughed. "You flatter me," he said. "Getting hold of one bomb has been difficult enough."

"So it must be the target that's significant," said Andrew. "The White House, presumably. Or maybe the Pentagon."

"Oh, no," said the other. "I need them intact for the second phase. I'm only planning to destroy Manhattan."

"I don't get it," said Andrew.

"We're using an Iranian bomb," said the man. "But we're going to claim credit on behalf of the North Koreans."

"You think the Americans will retaliate," said Andrew, sufficiently appalled at the prospect to forget, momentarily, his own predicament.

"They'll have no choice," said the other. "And what do you think the Chinese will do about that?"

"I don't believe you," said Andrew. "Even if the Iranians

have given you a bomb, how on earth are you going to deliver it?"

The other laughed. "Trust me," he said. "That's all under control."

"You're a lunatic," said Andrew.

"Come now," said the man. "I've done my very best to treat you in a civilised manner, within the obvious constraints of the situation. There's no need for cheap insults."

Andrew sat in stunned silence. What else was there to say? The man was mad. For all the urbanity and eloquence, for all the logistical cunning and meticulous planning, for all the high-flown philosophical rhetoric, underneath it all he was certifiably insane.

The other looked at his watch. "Well, there we are," he said. "We've run out of time." He lifted the gun from his lap and eased off the safety catch. "Would you prefer the head or the body?"

* * *

Alison was out when Adam returned to the house. He remembered now that she had said something about restocking the food cupboard. He went straight to the telephone directory. There were six people listed with the surname Berger, an indication of the large German business community in Singapore. He called them one by one, asking if he might speak to Birgit.

On his fourth call, to a number listed under Franz Berger, he spoke to a woman who sounded American. "Not again," she said. "People are always calling me in mistake for her. I'm Bridget, not Birgit."

"Do you know her?" asked Adam.

"My husband sometimes plays tennis with Dieter," she said.

There was no Dieter Berger listed in the book. "Do you have the telephone number, by any chance?" he said.

The woman's voice became wary. "Are you a personal friend?" she said.

"No," said Adam. "But I have an urgent message from someone who is." He had no idea where the thought had come from. It had sprung fully formed from his lips.

The woman sounded uncertain. "I don't think I should really give you her number just like that," she said.

"Of course not," said Adam. "But could you do me an enormous favour? Could you ring her yourself and say I have a message from Andrew?"

* * *

Gillian's telephone woke her just before dawn. It was Paul Burrows.

"The Indonesians have a precise location," he said. "The kidnappers used a satellite telephone and the Americans picked up the signal."

Gillian was wide awake and reaching for her clothes. "How close are they?" she said.

"There's a unit of Indonesian special forces on the way by helicopter. They're about an hour away at most."

"I'm coming in," said Gillian. "Do we know what the call was about?"

"It was pretty cryptic," said Burrows. "The experts are crawling over it now. Something about a stranger having delivered the goods."

* * *

Adam's mobile was somewhere in Malaysia, and Ali had taken hers with her. Adam calculated that he had at most five minutes to make a call without risking missing one from Birgit Berger – always assuming she would call. He rang Murray Parker.

"Adam!" said Murray. "Where've you been? How did it go in Malaysia?"

"Long story, Murray," said Adam. "I'll tell you over the beer I owe you. Meantime, I need some quick information."

"The press is at your disposal, as ever," said Murray.

"Do you know anything about someone called Dieter Berger?"

"I've heard of him," said Murray. "I think I may have met him at a German Chamber of Commerce reception."

"What does he do?"

"He runs some kind of global services company – counter-trade, special financing arrangements, that sort of thing."

"Have you ever met his wife?"

"No, mate, sorry," said Murray. He gave a dirty laugh. "Don't tell me you're looking for *another* girl?" he said. "I may have to have a quiet word with Alison about all this."

Adam had scarcely put the phone down when it rang again. The caller's voice sounded strained and she spoke very quietly.

"Mr White? I'm Birgit Berger. You had a message for me."

"Yes, Mrs Berger," said Adam. "I wanted to talk to you about Andrew Singleton."

"Do you know where Andrew is?"

"No," said Adam. "I was hoping you might be able to tell me."

"But you said you had a message from him."

"I had to speak to you," said Adam. "I'm sorry. It was all I could think of to say."

There was a pause. Then she said, "Who are you, Mr White?"

"I'm the acting British High Commissioner," said Adam, stretching the truth only as far as he needed to. "I thought you might have some information which could be of help in finding the High Commissioner."

"Why did you think that?"

"It was just a guess," said Adam. "You were with him in Bintan, weren't you?"

There was a long silence before she spoke. "Yes, alright," she

244

said. "I was there. But Andrew was fine when I left him. I've no idea what's happened to him."

"Is there nothing you can tell me which might be relevant?" said Adam. "It's literally a matter of life and death."

"I don't know anything," she said. "I really don't. Oh God, this is so awful."

"If you think of anything," said Adam. "Anything at all, just call me on this number. Or better still, call the police."

"But, Mr White, I don't know anything," she said.

* * *

With the gun pointed straight at him, Andrew felt a huge surge of adrenalin, which left him almost breathless.

"I'd prefer the body," he heard himself saying.

"Very well," said the man, "Although it will be all the same in the end."

Andrew experienced a sense of heightened awareness, as though his brain were intensifying his sensations to compensate for the fact that he had only a few moments to live. Every detail of the man and his diving garb were impressed upon his consciousness, as were those of the neatly folded sails along the rigid boom, the gently fluttering awning, the flag flapping lazily on the stern. He heard the idling engine and the lap of the waves against the side of the yacht, and, in the background, the faintest of sounds which he could not identify.

Looking past the man's head he saw the horizon, which was clear except for – except for what? There was something. Two somethings. He strove to make out what the two dots he saw in the distance could be, strove yet sought not to strive, lest his captor sense what he could see.

"You might answer one final question for me," he said, keeping his voice as level as he could. The dots were bigger now, the background noise a gentle throbbing sound.

"Be my guest," said the man.

"Who in the name of God does Marina know who could persuade the Iranians to part with a nuclear device?"

"Marina?" said the man. "Who said anything about Marina?"

Andrew stared, uncomprehending, at the man. "But I thought… " he said.

"You thought you were being punished for your wife's death?" said the other. "Well, I certainly enjoyed hearing your confession, but I'm afraid you rather jumped to that conclusion yourself."

The helicopters were now clearly visible, and the throbbing had become louder, but they were still several minutes flying time away. Andrew experienced an amalgam of hope and desperation, as he simultaneously struggled to assimilate the information he had just received.

"The question you should be asking yourself at this stage, is 'was she worth it?'" said the man.

Andrew continued to stare. Then, at last, he understood.

"Dieter Berger," he said. "Of course."

"I'd say she *was* worth it, myself," said the other.

The throbbing had elided into a clattering, chattering sound as the helicopters came within a kilometre of the yacht. Andrew's brain grappled with the words the man had just uttered. "What did you say?" he said.

The man moved closer, holding the gun levelled at Andrew's chest. "Birgit," he said. "A woman to die for, wouldn't you say?"

"Jesus Christ," Andrew said. "You're Hussein."

"Well," said the man. "It's not a name I use much these days."

The man looked over his shoulder at the approaching helicopters. Andrew lunged for him, but he had left it too late. The man fired and Andrew fell backwards, taking the flimsy chair with him.

He lay on his back on the deck. Kirsty reached through the window and took him by the hand, as though to lead him into the green fields and the mountains beyond. But then he could no longer see Kirsty, and after a while he saw nothing.

END GAME

CHAPTER 19

The tanks had capacity for two hours of steady swimming. After one hour, he surfaced briefly to look back to where a pall of black smoke rose from the horizon. He had timed the explosive charges with extreme care and was confident he had achieved the desired effect.

There was no longer any sign of the helicopters. But there would be reinforcements soon, probably by sea. He consulted the compass on his wrist and set course once more before submerging. One more hour under water and he would be far enough from the yacht to be able to jettison the tanks and travel safely on the surface. The inflatable dinghy in a pack attached to his waist was ready for the moment when he became too tired to swim. By then it would be dark.

He was swimming now at an easy, assured pace. He would need to make a mild correction to his route when he finally transferred to the dinghy. But he was confident of making landfall within a mile or so of the cache. Clothes, money, a false passport and pre-booked ferry and air tickets would bring him unnoticed back to civilisation. A couple of nights in a decent hotel to recuperate his strength, and then he would be ready for the next phase. Singleton had been right: it *was* a game. But he had not suspected how great a game.

He was sorry things had ended as they had with Singleton. In other circumstances, he would have done things differently. But the plan was paramount. This time, his personal predilections must come second.

* * *

The video sequence of the mass of blazing wreckage had appeared first, live, on CNN. Now, in a matter of minutes, it had spread across every one of the battery of television screens in the Emergency Unit, which were permanently tuned to the world's main television news services. The screens were silent; the sound from each was being monitored by analysts wearing headphones, each of them listening for the slightest nuance in the reportage.

In Paul Burrows's office, behind a half-closed door, Gillian King concentrated on the CNN coverage. (She had long given up wondering how CNN were always in the right place, at the right time. It was an inevitable fact of life.) A young female reporter based in Jakarta was describing the burning yacht as 'possibly the fiery grave of kidnapped British Ambassador Andrew Singleton'. The Indonesian authorities had reportedly issued only a brief statement to the effect that an attempted rescue had left a number of their forces killed or wounded. A full statement was promised later.

The official communications between governments had been equally terse. By agreement with all concerned, the rescue helicopters had maintained radio silence in their approach to the yacht. This had been broken, briefly, when the force commander in the leading helicopter had reported a body lying alone on the deck, and his intention of dropping a group of commandos to investigate. There had been no further communication from either helicopter for some twenty minutes or more. Then the Indonesians had received a garbled message from one of the helicopters about an explosion. They had despatched more helicopters and armed patrol boats, and promised to report as soon as they had further news.

So, this is how it ends, thought Gillian. *In an unholy mess. Oh, Andrew, you fool. It's not just you now, it's those poor, courageous soldiers. How could you be so careless, so arrogant, so driven by your crude physical appetites?* And yet, beneath her instinctive anger, she was already grieving. She saw him sweep his blond hair out of his eyes, she heard him mocking Marx and A. J. Ayer, enthusing about Truffaut's latest offering, relishing a Dizzy Gillespie solo. *I've got to get out of here before I lose control*, she thought.

Burrows's telephone rang as she was about to move. He picked it up on the first ring, listened for a moment and then handed the phone to Gillian.

"It's Michael Seng," he said. "For your ears only, apparently."

* * *

Alison returned to the house by taxi. She found Adam sitting in front of the television watching CNN. She joined him and they sat hand-in-hand, all thoughts on her part of intercepting her letter to Adam banished by the horror of what they were watching and hearing. Even the news of Adam's suspension made little impact on her.

There were now helicopters circling the wreck at a discreet distance. The CNN reporter was speaking of a further statement by the Indonesian authorities. Their special forces had lost one helicopter, which had been hovering over the yacht at the time of the explosion. All the occupants had been killed. A second helicopter had apparently been damaged but had managed to make its way back to base. No mention was made of the whereabouts of Andrew Singleton's body.

Alison and Adam watched as the smouldering remains of the yacht sank beneath the surface, sending one final belch of black smoke into the atmosphere.

"Well, there's no saving him now," said Adam. "I just hope he thought she was worth it."

"I don't understand," said Alison.

"He was with a woman," said Adam. "That's why he went to Bintan."

"How do you know?"

Before Adam could reply the telephone rang. Alison picked it up. It was a woman, a woman evidently in considerable distress.

"Please," she said. "My name is Berger. I must speak to Mr Adam White at once."

* * *

Marina and Pepe sat silently side by side in the Land Rover. They were somewhere on the outskirts of Kuala Lumpur – Marina did not know exactly where, or what they were doing there.

"Pepe, I think I want to go back to Singapore," she said.

"Tranquila, chica," he said. "We have a slight change of plan."

"I thought it would be only a few days," she said. "My father will be going crazy. He'll have called the police by now."

Pepe laughed. "He loves you so much?" he said.

"No," she said. "He'll be more worried about the car."

He shrugged. "You can go back tonight if you want. I've had contact with some people who'll take the stuff from us here. Less risky than Singapore." He looked at his watch. "They'll be here soon."

They sat in silence again. Marina did not know whether to be irritated or relieved. Was she being cut out? Why had Pepe got her to go all the way with him to Langkawi if she had no further part to play?

"Or you could come with me," he said.

"Where to?"

"Back home," he said. "To places where the cops can be bribed and they don't fucking hang you for dealing, *¡coño!*"

"I don't know, Pepe," she said. "I'm confused. I don't know what I want."

There was silence again. Then Pepe said, "Elena never told you, did she?"

"Told me what?"

Pepe did not answer immediately. Then he turned to look at Marina. "When I was a kid, my mother explained to me why people use Pepe as a nickname for José. It was probably bullshit – my mother was full of bullshit. But she told me it came from the bible. *P.P.* stands for *padre putativo*, which is what Joseph was to Jesus. Not his real father at all. So: Joseph, José, Pepe. Isn't that funny? It's Andrew who should really be called Pepe – not me."

Marina did not immediately understand. "What are you saying?" she said. "Are you saying… ?"

"You really are so stupid, Marina," he said. Then he looked up, as a car drew up alongside them. "Here they are now."

* * *

Andrew emerged from a long black tunnel of nothingness into a world of light and pain and knew, somehow, that he was in Singapore. The smell, the cleanliness, the sense of calm efficiency as the pretty Malay nurse leaned over to adjust his drip, all told him he could be nowhere else.

He had to tell them. He had to tell them what was going to happen. What had he told them already? He recalled a momentary flash of consciousness as he was lifted from the deck of the yacht by the men in camouflage. What had he said then? Something about a nuclear attack? Yes, he was pretty certain he'd said that. Had he mentioned New York? He couldn't remember. Then there had been darkness again, and he had dreamed of explosions and smelled smoke and then there had been nothing once more. For how long, this nothing? Hours? Days?

"I have to speak to someone from the government," he said. His throat was dry and he felt nauseous.

"We're here, Andrew," said the voice of Michael Seng.

Andrew tried to move, but the pain in his upper body was too severe. He became aware of several people seated round the bed. Some had tape recorders. Apart from Michael Seng, he recognised Quentin Asquith and the CIA man from the American Embassy, Jack Webb. The others he did not know.

"High Commissioner, we need you to tell us everything you know as soon as you can," said the CIA man. "We've already lost several hours we can't afford."

"You needed a rather delicate emergency operation," explained Seng to Andrew. "The Indonesians thought they'd better turn you over to us for that."

"That cost us two hours," said Webb, visibly irritated.

"If the High Commissioner had bled to death, you wouldn't have learned anything from him at all," said Seng mildly.

With enormous effort, Andrew told his story in as much detail as he could recall. He left out any reference to Elena, on the grounds that it was irrelevant and no one's business but his own. But he could not avoid acknowledging the affair with Birgit. He kept his eyes on Michael Seng's impassive face as he spoke, imagining only too easily the devout churchgoer's tactfully disguised disapproval of his behaviour. Occasionally he was prompted by specific questions from one or other of the people at his bedside, but for the most part his narrative was uninterrupted.

When he had finished, the group sat silently for a few seconds. Then Quentin Asquith spoke.

"I don't buy it," he said. "We have absolutely no evidence the Iranians have a bomb yet. Not even the Israelis think they have. Even if they did, they must realise the consequences if they made it available to terrorists. And how would they deliver it to the target?"

Webb gave Asquith a look which betrayed personal animosity as well as professional disdain. "We had people like you once who said terrorists couldn't fly planes into buildings," he said. "We don't take risks with this kind of thing any more."

Asquith removed his spectacles and polished them carefully with a handkerchief. "These would not, I assume, be the same people who said Saddam Hussein had weapons of mass destruction," he said.

"Yeah, well, we all got that one wrong," said Webb. "Not least MI fucking 6."

"Gentlemen, gentlemen," said Seng. "This is too grave a matter for this kind of professional jealousy. And I fear we are tiring the High Commissioner."

Webb shrugged his shoulders and stood up. "I'm going back to the Embassy to file a full report to Washington," he said. "If he comes up with anything more I want to know at once. In the meantime, you'd better pick up this guy Berger and squeeze what you can out of him. I'll get one of my people to give you a hand."

Andrew could feel unconsciousness claiming him again. "Don't touch Birgit," he murmured. "She's innocent, I know it."

* * *

Patrick returned to the High Commission with Quentin Asquith. Between them they drafted a flash telegram, for the Permanent Under Secretary's eyes only, reporting what Andrew Singleton had said. Asquith wanted to add a paragraph of sceptical comment, but Patrick insisted on a purely factual report, limiting his observations to the fact that, despite the absence so far of any collateral evidence, the Americans were taking the threat seriously. Asquith then withdrew behind his secure grille, where Patrick had no doubt he would send his own version of events on the intelligence network.

Patrick was glad it was well after office hours, which meant he would not have to indulge in any wide-scale dissimulation. Only he and Asquith knew Andrew Singleton was still alive, and there had been an air of mourning in the High Commission earlier

255

in the day. Even the normally voluble Chinese receptionist had seemed subdued.

Patrick set his features in a suitably solemn mode as he sent the Duty Registry Officer home. He felt doubly fraudulent, first because he hardly knew Singleton and, second, because the man was not even dead. Patrick had personally doubted the need to keep his survival secret. But the Indonesians and the Singaporeans, strongly supported by the Americans, had argued that the less the kidnappers believed they knew the better. How this fitted with arresting Dieter Berger had not been explained.

Patrick pulled the kidnapping files from the Registry and settled himself down in Adam White's office to read them for the first time in their entirety. For a few seconds he began to drift off into a reverie about Susan Hyde, but he caught the temptation in time and forced himself to focus on the files.

* * *

Birgit Berger had asked Adam to come to her house, explaining that she was nervous about being seen with him in public. Alison had at first wanted to accompany Adam, but he had thought her presence might inhibit Birgit from speaking freely. In the end, they had agreed that he would take Alison's mobile and report in by telephone as necessary.

Birgit was dressed in a simple cotton dress and sandals. She was in a terrible state. Adam could see that she was a beautiful woman, but her face was haggard from weeping and lack of sleep and she seemed, from the evidence of the ashtrays, to have been chain-smoking.

The Bergers' house was opulently furnished. Birgit led Adam through the main reception rooms, out to a subtly-lit terrace by a large, kidney-shaped swimming pool. Beyond the pool was a tennis court. In the corner of the terrace, on a low bamboo table, stood a portable television set, tuned in to CNN, but with the volume turned down. Birgit offered Adam a drink and fetched the beer he requested from a small refrigerator on the terrace. Her own glass looked to contain neat vodka and ice. As far as Adam could tell, they were alone in the house.

"My husband's away on a trip at the moment," she said, as though to explain the absence of other people, although Adam had said nothing. "Somewhere in Central Asia."

Adam remained silent. She was clearly working herself up to say something and he would not help by interrupting.

"He knew about Andrew and me," she said. "I don't know how, but he must have known for quite some time. I broke into his desk drawer and found a diary listing every trip I made with Andrew in the last few months."

"Are you telling me he had something to do with the High Commissioner's kidnapping?" said Adam.

Birgit was silent for several seconds. She finally spoke with a kind of shuddering sigh. "I think he may have had him killed," she said, squashing her cigarette in the ashtray and looking for another.

"My God," said Adam. "What makes you think that?"

"Dieter's used to getting what he wants," she said. "And keeping it."

"But even so… " said Adam.

"Believe me, Mr White," she said. "He would simply have regarded Andrew as an obstacle to be removed."

"Why haven't you been to the police about this?"

"I've been trying to persuade myself it couldn't be true," she said. "But now I know Andrew's dead, I can't deny it any longer."

"Then you should tell them now," said Adam.

She hesitated. "The truth is, I'm afraid," she said. "Dieter might tolerate temporary unfaithfulness, but he would not forgive me if I betrayed him."

"Then why are you telling me?"

"I want you to speak to the police for me."

"But I have no proof," said Adam.

"Take the diary," she said. "Invent some story about how you found it."

"Are you sure you want to do this?" said Adam.

She looked him straight in the eye. "I'm responsible for Andrew's death," she said. "It's the least I can do."

"When is your husband due back?" asked Adam.

"Tomorrow," she said. "He's travelling via Delhi. He comes in on the Air India flight first thing in the morning."

* * *

As far as the staff of the emergency unit were concerned, Andrew Singleton was dead. Their job now was to tidy up the files and close the unit down. Within the Foreign Office, only Gillian King and a restricted group of officials, including Paul Burrows, knew the truth, which was deemed too sensitive to risk further dissemination. The Foreign Office was, in any case, no longer in sole charge: what had been a simple kidnapping had become a full-blown crisis. The Cabinet Office briefing rooms had been secretly opened and staffed with hand-picked officials from all relevant Whitehall departments. The Chief of the Defence Staff had been pulled off an aircraft as he was about to leave for a tour of the Far East. The Prime Minister had cancelled a visit to Belfast.

But the truth was, as Gillian King knew, that matters were now largely out of British hands. The Americans were in the lead, and they would be deciding within the next twenty-four hours what action to take.

Gillian could still only guess what the Americans would do. From the flurry of exchanges between London and Washington in the last two hours it was evident that the State Department and the Pentagon were arguing very different courses of action, while the White House remained undecided. The Prime Minister had telephoned the President to urge restraint. But Gillian doubted the Americans would be in a mood for compromise. A pre-emptive strike against Iranian nuclear installations – or on Tehran itself – was the nightmare scenario. At best, Washington would issue an ultimatum to the Iranian Government before taking military action. But how would the latter respond? And what would the Americans do if they judged the response inadequate?

With Gillian's acquiescence, the Political Director had tried, unsuccessfully, to persuade the Foreign Secretary to involve his European colleagues in a joint approach to the Americans. Number Ten had vetoed the proposal. "They might just listen to us," said the Prime Minister's foreign policy adviser. "They're not going to listen to what they regard as a bunch of cheese-eating surrender monkeys." *So much for a European security and defence policy*, thought Gillian. *The first major crisis since Iraq, and it's the same old story. Either we rein the Americans back or we're riding shotgun again.*

The Joint Intelligence Committee was to meet in emergency session that evening to assess the situation. Gillian had cleared her diary for the rest of the day until then. She instructed her Private Secretary to accept no calls other than from the Foreign Secretary's office or from people who gave the relevant code word. The draft assessment was still under preparation within the Cabinet Office. But on Gillian's desk sat the entire set of Foreign Office papers pertaining to Andrew Singleton's kidnapping. If war was about to be launched again in the Middle East, the least she could do was brief herself directly on the facts.

* * *

It was late when Patrick Young finished reading the files. A number of things about Andrew Singleton's kidnapping and near-fatal wounding looked odd to him. He had better compare notes with Quentin Asquith first thing in the morning. In the meantime, it had been a heavy day and he needed, finally, to relax. He dialled Susan's home telephone number.

* * *

It took Adam some time to get hold of Detective Inspector Ow's home telephone number. Once again he had to perpetuate the fiction that he was the acting High Commissioner before he could persuade the young female detective on duty at police headquarters to relax her, very correct, reluctance to reveal the number.

To Adam's surprise, Detective Inspector Ow was entirely receptive to his theory about Dieter Berger's complicity in Andrew Singleton's kidnapping. "We have instructions to arrest him when he returns to Singapore tomorrow," he said. "I would have expected you to know about that."

"I didn't realise things had gone quite that far," said Adam, truthfully if somewhat misleadingly. What had changed? he wondered. What additional intelligence did the police have of which he was unaware?

"Incidentally," said Ow. "Have you been in touch with the CNB in the last three hours?"

"No," said Adam.

"Well, I'd better tell you then," said Ow.

Adam listened with growing incredulity. Late that afternoon, Marina Singleton and her companion had been discovered in an outer suburb of Kuala Lumpur. They were sitting in a parked green Land Rover Discovery with Singapore diplomatic number plates. Both had died from a single shot to the centre of the forehead.

CHAPTER 20

After speaking to the Central Narcotics Bureau, Adam telephoned the High Commission and got the standard recorded message. He telephoned the Duty Officer – Benjamin Kendall – and was given a semi-apologetic brush-off. "It's, like, nothing personal, Adam," he said. "I'm just not supposed to talk to you, that's all." Then Adam did what he realised he should have done first of all, and rang Mary Bennett.

"Adam!" she said. "Are you okay? First I heard you were hurt and then you were suspended from duty. What's going on?"

"Marina's dead," said Adam. "I need to get hold of Patrick Young as soon as possible."

"Oh, my God!" cried Mary. "What happened?"

"She was murdered," said Adam. "They found her body in Kuala Lumpur. I heard through the police here, but I can't raise anyone on the telephone in the High Commission in Kuala Lumpur at the moment. I wanted to be sure Patrick Young knew what had happened."

"He's staying at the Regent," said Mary. "Adam, is there anything I can do to help?"

"Just stay by the phone in case I need you, Mary," said Adam. He paused, then added. "Oh, by the way, I should have said this before. Ali told me about Muzafar. Don't worry, I'm pretty certain he's off the hook."

* * *

261

Patrick and Susan sat opposite each other in Susan's sitting room. He drank a beer. She had a mineral water.

"It's very late," she said. "You shouldn't have come."

"How can you say that?" he said.

"I'm sober," she said, casting her head down and speaking to the floor. "Nothing can happen, you understand."

"You were sober this morning," said Patrick. For some reason, he found this chaste and frightened Susan irresistibly seductive.

"That was different," she said.

"Different? How?"

"I don't know," she said. "In your hotel room. In the small hours of the morning – it wasn't real."

"Are you sorry it happened?" he said.

She blushed, and he felt even more aroused. Then she looked up, unsmiling. "No," she said. "It was lovely."

"Well, then," he said.

"I can't," she said. "I mustn't."

"What's the problem?"

She looked agonised. "It's everything," she said. "I've made a mess of everything. And now... "

"And now what?"

She seemed about to say something, then changed her mind. There was silence for a while.

"Susan," he said. "Come on."

"You're married," she said, abruptly, as though this was a new thought. "It's not right."

He could see that she was wavering, and he knew why. Their early morning lovemaking had been sensational, in a different league entirely from their drunken rutting of the previous evening.

"Maybe you should have a drink," he said.

"No," she said. "No drink." For several seconds she looked at him, helplessly, one hand clutching the gold chain at her neck, the other clenched at her thigh. He wanted her very badly now.

"No drink," she said again, as she reached with shaking fingers for the buttons of her blouse.

* * *

When the Regent Hotel receptionist said that Patrick Young was not in his room, Adam had to take a rapid decision. The person nominally in charge of the High Commission was incommunicado. The Duty Officer would not speak to him. Someone had to grip the situation, and it had better be him.

First, he rang Stan Murdoch in Kuala Lumpur, hoping that Stan would know nothing of Adam's suspension; thankfully he did not. Stan had just returned home from a call, followed by dinner, on a senior member of the Selangor State Government. He confirmed that he had only just learned of Marina's death. The Consul was preparing a report for the Foreign Office, and was in touch with the Singapore High Commission Duty Officer about informing next of kin.

"Her mother's dead," said Adam, relieved to learn that everything seemed to be in hand. "It would have to be her grandfather, I imagine. I think he lives in Panama. Do you have any idea who the other victim was?"

"His name was José García," said Stan. "He was carrying a Panamanian passport describing him as a businessman – I've no doubt that covers a multitude of sins."

* * *

The Joint Intelligence Committee met in special session, in a nondescript room in the Cabinet Office with cream-painted walls and a genteelly worn fitted grey carpet.

Gillian King's presence was unusual, if not entirely unprecedented. The Permanent Under Secretary was a regular consumer of the JIC's output, but the Foreign Office input came, as a rule, at a more junior level. Gillian had been obliged to make a number of placatory telephone calls to ensure that no feathers were unnecessarily ruffled.

The draft before the Committee was short and to the point. It described the reported plot to attack New York with a nuclear device, and summarised the collateral evidence. This consisted mainly of intercepts of telephone and email exchanges between suspected terrorists which might, or might not, be referring to the planned attack. There were also snippets of human intelligence describing second- or third-hand claims by known terrorists that a massive attack on a western target was imminent. The most specific intelligence had been provided by a friendly agency in a Central Asian country. It reported a deal, involving unspecified weaponry, recently struck between the Iranian Government and an unknown businessman thought to be based in South East Asia. The balance of the draft assessed the probability of the Iranians already possessing nuclear weapons and, if they did, of their being prepared to sell them to third parties. Finally, there was a carefully weighed discussion of whether a terrorist group would have the means of delivering and detonating such a weapon with the required degree of accuracy. The paper's conclusion betrayed the hand of a seasoned bureaucrat. It was that, for all the inherent improbabilities, the possibility of an imminent nuclear attack could not be ruled out with 100% certainty.

The Chairman, his calm expression masking his relative newness to the position, emphasised in his opening remarks the gravity of the situation. He explained that the assessment agreed by the meeting would form the basis of the briefing for the Prime Minister's next telephone call to the President, which was scheduled for ten o'clock that evening London time.

As soon as the Chairman had spoken, Gillian intervened. Before the meeting she had consulted the Head of MI6, who had agreed that she would speak initially for both of them. She had also spoken by telephone to a personal contact in the White House.

"I wonder, Mr Chairman, if I might make a few immediate observations which could save the meeting a good deal of time," she said.

The Chairman, who had, at one time, aspired to the position Gillian now occupied, nodded his assent silently.

"First, I should explain my presence here," she said. "The urgency of the situation is such that the normal policymaking timetable is inevitably compressed. Once this committee's assessment reaches Number Ten and COBRA there will be little, if any, opportunity to influence the situation. It is therefore imperative that we get it right."

Gillian paused to let her words sink in.

"The draft assessment addresses a number of crucial questions," she continued. "It evaluates the collateral intelligence and offers a judgement on the probability of a successful nuclear attack. What it fails to do – and this is as much my fault as anyone's, because the Foreign Office agreed the terms of reference – is answer the most important question of all. It offers no view of the reliability of the source for the original story."

"Are you suggesting the British High Commissioner is lying?" said the Chairman, his demeanour not quite as impassive as hitherto.

"It's possible," said Gillian. "Although I think it extremely unlikely. My concern is with the truthfulness or otherwise of his kidnapper."

The meeting was silent. A number of the participants stopped doodling on their pads and looked up at Gillian.

"From the very beginning this was an unusual kidnapping," she said. "The demand for the release of the Jemaah Islamiyah detainees was couched in dispassionate terms, free of any of the violent rhetoric we normally associate with Al Qaeda. We might have expected the demand to appear on a website, but instead it came via email. There was no brutal video, no ritual declamation. Just a single email with a photo attached."

"Are these things significant?" asked the Ministry of Defence representative. "Al Qaeda's a loose network. There's no reason why every terrorist group in the world should adopt the same methods."

"Maybe, on their own, these details might not seem important," said Gillian. "But, considered together with other factors, they take on greater weight. It was risky enough, for example, to send an email that allowed the Indonesians to establish the kidnappers' approximate location, and indeed to capture one of their number. How much more foolish was it to use a satellite telephone, which allowed the yacht's precise location to be identified?"

"All you seem to be saying is that these people were extraordinarily careless," said the Chairman.

"Well, if that were true, it would certainly diminish the probability of their being able to launch a successful nuclear strike on New York," said Gillian. "But I'm actually suggesting the contrary. I think they *wanted* to be found – at the appropriate moment."

No one said anything. The atmosphere in the meeting room had become perceptibly heightened.

"It's also strange that we have no details of how the nuclear device is to be delivered," said Gillian. "We know the target. We know who's allegedly providing the bomb. We even know the name of the intermediary. Why would this man, Hussein, not also speak of the means of delivery?"

Gillian paused, but no one spoke.

"I'll put it another way," she continued. "In the absence of any information about the method of delivery, where is the United States most likely to focus her action?"

Still there was silence.

"Then, there's the treatment Andrew Singleton received," said Gillian. "For the first two days he was treated very badly. But once the principal kidnapper was alone, the mistreatment ceased.

Singleton got decent food, coffee, cigarettes, a proper bed and so on. Why? Don't tell me his captor was afflicted by sudden compassion. There had to be a reason for building up Andrew Singleton's strength."

"And I have a feeling you're going to tell us what it is, Dame Gillian," said the Chairman.

"Let's consider also the wound suffered by Andrew Singleton," Gillian continued. "Singleton says he was offered the choice of a bullet in the head or in the body. But the kidnapper must have known he would choose the body. Anyone would in those circumstances. And what actually happened? The bullet was aimed at the upper right-hand side of Singleton's chest. It was a serious wound, and the High Commissioner lost a lot of blood. But it was unlikely to be fatal to a man in reasonable physical shape – someone who had been well fed and rested – so long as he received immediate medical attention. So, why didn't the kidnapper administer a *coup de grace?* Why didn't he put a bullet in Singleton's head to finish him off?"

The Chairman began to make a series of notes on his pad, but again no one spoke.

"Finally, there's the timing of the explosive charges on the yacht," said Gillian. "Andrew Singleton has told us he could see the rescue helicopters clearly just before he was shot. They can only therefore have been a couple of minutes flying time away. They will have been even closer by the time the kidnapper had fitted his breathing apparatus and jumped from the yacht – as we must now assume he did. How long would he need to get clear? Five minutes? Maybe ten. But surely not half an hour. Why delay for so long?"

The room remained silent.

"I'll tell you why," said Gillian. "Because he wanted the High Commissioner to be found alive and taken safely off the yacht. He wanted Andrew Singleton to tell us the story of his great plan of deception. He wanted us to believe that the Iranians were conniving at a scheme to direct the military might of the United Sates against North Korea." She turned to the CIA observer on the Committee. "In short, he wanted to trick the Americans into making a pre-emptive strike against Iran."

CHAPTER 21

It was barely light when the flight from Delhi touched down at Changi. Adam and the two plain clothes policemen waited unobtrusively in an office just off the fast-track immigration desk. Backup teams were posted at all exits from the airport terminal. Detective Inspector Ow had explained that, after due consideration, and following a high-level discussion with the Senior Minister's office, the decision had been taken not to board the aircraft and arrest Dieter Berger before he disembarked. He would, instead, be asked discreetly by the immigration officer to step into the office, where he could be taken into custody behind closed doors.

Adam had persuaded Detective Inspector Ow (who, miraculously, remained unaware of Adam's suspension) to let him accompany the arresting team. "You seem to know a lot more about Berger than I thought," he said to Ow, as the first passengers began to descend the escalators into the immigration zone.

"We gave his staff a good grilling yesterday," said Ow. "They confirmed the flight number Mrs Berger had given you. They also gave us a detailed itinerary for his recent trips. Two weeks ago he was in Iran and Turkey. Last week it was Afghanistan and Kazakhstan. This week it was Thailand and Iran again."

Adam had no idea what the relevance of this information was. "But what persuaded you to look at Berger more seriously?" he asked. "I thought he was off limits."

Ow looked at him somewhat askance. "Not any more," he said. "How could he be?"

Again, Adam had the feeling he was missing something important. But he did not want to arouse Ow's suspicions any further, so he just nodded.

The bulk of the passengers from the Delhi flight had now passed through immigration control. The advance guard of passengers on a recently arrived flight from Bangkok were beginning to join the steadily moving queue.

"Maybe he's not on the plane after all," said Adam.

Ow began to look worried. "Someone must have warned him," he said. But, at that moment, Dieter Berger appeared at the top of the escalator, dressed in a white linen suit and a pink open-necked shirt, a Ralph Lauren travel bag slung casually over his shoulder. He appeared ultra-relaxed and ludicrously well groomed.

"Cheeky bastard," said Adam. "He must have taken time out for a shower and a shave."

* * *

Day was breaking, but Patrick did not want to leave her.

Five years married to Buffy had made him used to living with a strong woman, someone who fought tenaciously for her rights. She had bullied him into escaping from Brixton, had urged him on to advancement despite his lack of formal education. She was the one who dreamed of their children becoming doctors or lawyers. Everything they did, even the act of conception, was directed towards fulfilling her social ambitions. They loved each other, of course. But their life together was arduous and the joyous element thinly spread.

Susan, by comparison, was fragile and innocently erotic. There was an air of suppressed tragedy about her which he could not resist. Even as he eased himself out of bed, he was tempted to

270

wake her and make love again. But he had already taken enough risks. It had to stop, and it had to stop now.

* * *

Adam slipped into bed beside Alison and nuzzled the back of her neck.

"Go away," she said, without moving. "You can't go off in the middle of the night to play detectives, and then expect to come back and have your wicked way with me." She rolled over. "What time is it anyway?"

"Seven-thirty," he said. "Berger's safely under lock and key, so that's one good deed for the day."

"That was quick," she said. "Did he confess?"

"No," Adam said. "He refused to say anything until his lawyer arrived. I'll phone in later to see what's happened. In the meantime I thought maybe I'd, you know, come back to bed for a bit."

"No way," she said, turning her back on him. "I don't want to see you again until you've got a cup of tea in your hand."

* * *

Benjamin Kendall was waiting impatiently in Adam White's office to tell Patrick of Marina Singleton's death as soon as he arrived. "We're trying to make contact with her grandfather," he said breathlessly. "He's living in Miami, but seems to be away travelling."

Patrick had to bite his tongue to avoid telling Benjamin that Marina's father was alive and lying in hospital no more than a mile or two from where they were standing. "What's happening to the body?" he said.

"It's staying in Kuala Lumpur for the moment," said Kendall. "The police are carrying out forensic tests. Once they're done, it's up to the next of kin what happens, I suppose."

Christ, thought Patrick, looking at the man's animated expression, *I think you're actually enjoying this.* "Okay," he said. "Keep me posted."

As Patrick switched on his computer, the telephone rang.

"Good morning one more time, Mr Young," said Siew Ling. "I have Detective Inspector Ow on the telephone line. He wishes to have some chat with Mr White. I have informed him that the latter is not currently being located in the High Commission."

"Put him through," said Patrick. *What now?* he thought.

Detective Inspector Ow sounded surprised that Adam White was not in the office, but Patrick decided this was no time for explanations. "He's not here just at the moment," he said. "If it's urgent, I can take a message."

"I wanted to let him know we've released Dieter Berger," said Ow. "His lawyer threatened us with legal action for wrongful arrest, harassment and defamation of character."

"I see," said Patrick, wondering what any of this had to do with Adam White. He was also wondering whether Detective Inspector Ow knew about Andrew Singleton: the Singaporeans had been keeping knowledge of his survival very restricted. He decided to play safe. "But didn't you have sufficient grounds to hold him for questioning?" he asked.

"We thought we did," said Ow gloomily. "But the word came down from on high not to detain him any longer unless we were confident we had evidence on which to base an immediate charge."

"As a matter of interest," said Patrick. "Who is Berger's lawyer?"

"Oh, he had the best," said Ow. "Chin Beng Seng."

"Yes," said Patrick. "Somehow I'm not surprised."

The conversation left Patrick puzzled, on two counts. What was Adam White's involvement in the arrest of Dieter Berger? And why had the Singaporeans not held on to Berger?

The second question was answered almost immediately, when

Registry rang to tell him there was a flash personal telegram for him.

He deciphered the telegram sitting at a machine squashed in the corner of the strong room. It had been despatched from the Foreign Office shortly after midnight in London. The threat of a nuclear attack on New York had now been discredited. The Americans would take no precipitate action against Iran, but would insist on redoubled monitoring of the latter's nuclear programme. The Singaporeans and the Indonesians were being advised of the position by the Americans. Patrick was instructed to take parallel action with the Singapore Foreign Ministry. A similar message was being passed on intelligence channels.

Patrick cursed his timidity for not endorsing Quentin Asquith's scepticism the previous evening, and for postponing discussion of his own doubts with Asquith until the morning. His uncritical account of Andrew Singleton's story would have made him look credulous in London. Not, he acknowledged, that this was of any importance in the context of averting major conflict in the Middle East. But it still hurt.

Patrick asked Sophie Smith to arrange an immediate appointment for him at the Foreign Ministry. The Americans would have got there first. No doubt Quentin Asquith had also already spoken to his intelligence contacts, so Patrick would be last in the queue to communicate with the Singaporeans. But instructions were instructions.

No wonder Dieter Berger had been released, he thought. The lies fed to Andrew Singleton might have been designed primarily to sow catastrophe in the Middle East. But it looked as though someone had also been doing their best to frame Berger.

* * *

"I suppose there are some advantages to being suspended from duty," said Adam, as he fondled the wisps of light brown hair at the back of Alison's neck. She snuggled closer and whispered into his chest. "You're hopeless," she said, feeling happier than she had for a very long time. Adam would sort this nonsense out. He was so transparently honest that people would understand that his intentions had been good. *Poor Marina*, she thought. *Poor Andrew, come to that.* They had not been her favourite people, but no civilised person could have wished their fate on them.

The doorbell rang and startled her out of her daydream. "I'll go," said Adam, swinging out of bed and reaching for a pair of shorts. "Drink your tea before it goes stone cold."

He was back in a moment, carrying a pile of mail. "Look what the driver brought us," he said, beginning to leaf through the pile. "Mostly bills from the look of it."

"Leave that, Adam," she said, possibly a little too fast. "I'll sort it out later. Come back to bed."

He hesitated momentarily, and then grinned, threw the letters on to an armchair and dived for her.

Alison squealed and wriggled away. A hairy arm reached round her waist and she turned towards him, laughing and protesting. The telephone rang.

"Bugger, bugger, bugger," said Adam, as he picked it up, still grinning. Then his face went serious. "Yes, of course," he said. "I'll come at once."

"What is it?" said Alison, the joy of the moment draining out of her.

"It's Birgit Berger," he said. "The police have released her husband." He shook his head in disbelief. "How could they do that?" he said. "The poor woman sounded terrified."

* * *

Andrew had spent a bad night, but he was feeling a little better when Michael Seng came to visit – until Seng explained the reason for his visit.

"I don't suppose any of your people have been able to get away to talk to you yet, this morning," said Seng. "So I thought I'd better tell you myself. It was all a hoax, Andrew, misinformation designed to lure the Americans into another Middle East adventure."

Andrew struggled to make sense of Seng's statement. "But he tried to kill me," he said.

"Apparently not," said Liew. "He just wanted it to look that way."

"But he let me see his face," Andrew protested. "I'll be able to identify him."

"He evidently thought it important you should believe he really meant to kill you," said Seng.

"He took an enormous risk," Andrew said.

"From your description of him, that was probably part of the enjoyment for him," said Seng. "But, in any case, a little plastic surgery would help him cover his tracks."

Andrew still could not comprehend the enormity of what Seng was saying. It had all been a charade? He had been duped into believing a total fabrication? He felt suddenly very feeble. "How can you be you sure of any of this?" he said, although there was no conviction in his question.

Seng made a gesture of modesty. "Who am I to gainsay the collective analytical powers of the United States and British Governments?" he said. "But, as it happens, I agree with their assessment. Not least, I should say, because I'm told it was my old friend Gillian King who halted the potential tide of hysteria."

Oh my God, thought Andrew. *Kirsty. What must she think of me now, after all this?* Then he thought of Birgit. "What's happened to Dieter Berger?" he said.

"The police have let him go," said Seng. "In the circumstances they had no grounds for holding him."

Andrew felt a sudden rush of apprehension. "Did he know why he'd been arrested?"

"Apparently not," said Seng. "He claimed complete ignorance of your kidnapping."

"But did he know I was having an affair with his wife?"

Was there the faintest hint of a wince in Michael Seng's expression as he replied? "The subject apparently didn't arise," he said, his tone professionally neutral. "By the time his lawyer arrived we knew about the hoax. So there was no real interrogation."

"I don't like the sound of this, all the same," said Andrew. "I have to make a phone call, if you don't mind, Michael."

"Andrew, is that wise?" said Seng. "Most people don't know you're still alive."

"For Christ's sake, Michael," said Andrew, careless now of the impact on Seng of his profanity. "If it's a hoax, the kidnapper knows I'm alive. And what difference does it make now anyway?"

* * *

The door to the Bergers' house was ajar. Adam pushed it open and walked into the living room. The room was empty. He walked through and out on to the patio by the swimming pool. Dieter Berger was sitting in a cane chair with his back to Adam, looking towards the pool. He was still dressed in his white linen suit. "Come and sit down, Mr White," he said, without turning his head.

"Your wife called me," said Adam, remaining standing.

"She's taking a rest," said Berger. He sounded as though he was thinking about something else. "In any case, I was the one who wanted to speak to you."

"What's this all about?" asked Adam.

"Please sit down," said Berger. Adam sat in a chair alongside Berger and waited.

Inside the house, the telephone began to ring. Berger ignored it. The telephone rang for thirty, maybe forty, seconds before it ceased. Then Adam heard the sound of a mobile telephone ringing on the floor above. Once again it rang for half a minute or so, then ceased.

Berger remained motionless. It was almost as though he had not heard the telephones. Now he turned his head towards Adam. His face was expressionless. "I want you to tell me why the police arrested me this morning," he said.

"Surely they told you," said Adam. "They believed you were in some way involved with the kidnapping of the British High Commissioner."

"That's it?"

"Isn't it enough?"

"It's totally ridiculous," said Berger. "Why did they believe that?"

Adam hesitated, and Berger spoke again. "Don't try to be discreet, Mr White. I know my wife was having an affair with Mr Singleton."

"Then why are you asking me?" said Adam.

"Well, first of all, I should like to know how the police knew."

"I told them," said Adam. And yet, he reminded himself, the police had already known enough to arrest Berger by the time he had spoken to Detective Inspector Ow.

"I see," said Berger. "And how did you find out?"

"It was a lucky guess," Adam said.

"Please don't insult my intelligence, Mr White," said Berger. "You must have had some reason for making such a guess."

Did it matter if he told Berger? Probably not, any longer. "It was something the High Commissioner's daughter said to me," he said. "Something about his involvement with a German woman. I remembered when I saw your wife's name on the resort guest list."

Berger raised his eyebrows at this information and appeared about to say something, but he checked himself. After a few more seconds of silence he spoke. "But you also got my wife to corroborate your – how did you call it? – 'lucky guess'."

"I tried," said Adam. Not knowing what Birgit might have said – or not said – to her husband, he did not want to create further difficulties for her. "But it wasn't necessary," he continued. "The police had already decided to arrest you."

"Well now, you see, this is exactly my point," said Berger. "Why did they do that?

Why indeed? thought Adam. The question had been bugging him too. And why had they then let Berger go? And what had Curly Jones of the American Embassy been doing skulking around police headquarters this morning and then disappearing with a brief wave of the hand after taking a call on his mobile?

"This is not just idle curiosity on my part, Mr White," said Berger. "My staff were interrogated yesterday. This is a serious matter for me. I have a spotless reputation in Singapore. I also have very complicated business arrangements that require me to maintain the trust of my associates in the various countries where I work. They will not like the fact that the police have been delving into my affairs."

"I'm afraid I can't explain that," said Adam. "I've told you. It was just a hunch on my part."

"A hunch supported, I understand, by entries in my personal diary," said Berger. "I wonder how you could have got hold of that."

Adam said nothing.

"It saddens me that my wife believed me capable of such a crime," said Berger. "And that she should be prepared to betray me."

"She didn't betray you," said Adam. "I told you. The police had made their decision before I spoke to her."

"But why, Mr White? What else do they think they know? Why are they harassing me?"

"I don't know," said Adam. "Why should I know?"

Berger sighed. "I suppose I should let sleeping dogs lie," he said. "But I'm German and we have a reputation for being very thorough. So I'm afraid I must ask you again. What do you know? And what do the police know?"

"I haven't the faintest idea what you're talking about," said Adam.

"Then why were you at the airport this morning?"

"Idle curiosity, I suppose," said Adam.

"You know something," said Berger, impervious to Adam's intentional irony. "You wouldn't have been there if you hadn't known something."

"Look," said Adam. "I'd never even heard of you until yesterday. What is there to know?"

Berger stood up and came over to where Adam was sitting. He leaned down, placing his hand on the armrests either side of the chair and put his face very close to Adam's.

"I don't have time for this bullshit, Mr White," said Berger. "If you know something, I have to act very fast. If the police know anything, I have to act even faster. So please tell me the truth. Now. Immediately. It will be better for everyone if you do."

Adam could see the slight bulge of sunburned flesh at Berger's collar, the beads of sweat on his nose, the tiny threads of red in the white of his eyes.

"I've told you," he said. "I don't know what you're talking about."

For a moment Berger appeared nonplussed. He moved away, his expression distant, as though he were engaged in some inner calculation. Adam waited, still puzzled by Berger's insistence that he reveal knowledge he did not possess. He shifted slightly in the chair to ease the seat of his trousers, which were damp with sweat. And it was then he saw the photograph.

It was framed in bamboo and stood, with a number of similar photographs, on the side table by his chair. It was of a group of fishermen, dressed for the most part only in shorts, proudly demonstrating their catch, a handsome sailfish. Dieter

Berger was in the centre, flanked on either side by two men, who also looked as though they might be German, certainly European. Next to the man on Berger's right was someone who could be Chinese, or possibly Thai. Next to him was another Caucasian. On the far left, and slightly apart from the group, was a Malay, the only man wearing a sweatshirt. He was also the only man not smiling. It was as though he did not quite belong. Perhaps he was the man who had driven the boat. He certainly gave the impression of being in a subordinate position. At first glance there was nothing special about the man. His face was bland, neither ugly nor handsome. He was neither young nor old, fat nor thin, tall nor short. A more featureless man would have been difficult to imagine. And yet, on closer inspection there was, in fact, something unusual about him. He had no right hand.

Finally, Adam understood what Berger expected him to know.

* * *

Alison had dressed and made coffee. But she could not drink it, or sit still for more than a few seconds at a time. She felt jumpy and apprehensive.

In his rush to get to Birgit Berger, Adam had left Alison's mobile on the bedside table. *This is all wrong*, she thought. *I said I'd never let him get into anything on his own again.* Adam obviously believed that Birgit Berger was in fear of her husband. Who knew what the man might be capable of? Adam himself could be in danger. Her Adam. She would never forgive herself if he came to harm. *Do something, Alison*, she said to herself. *Do something.*

Feverishly, she searched for Detective Inspector Ow's card. Adam had pinned it to the kitchen notice board. But what if Ow was not there? What if he refused to take any action? *You have to do something, Alison,* she said to herself again. *You're the one who has to do something.*

* * *

Patrick had barely returned to the office from his largely otiose call on the Foreign Ministry when the telephone rang.

"Excuse me, Mr Young. I have the assistant to Detective Inspector Ow who would wish to chat with you. He is Sergeant Ho Thiam Yew."

"Put him through, Siew Ling."

"But, sir, he is down below and wishes to ascend."

"Then send him up."

"I shall do so without any further delay."

Sergeant Ho wore rimless glasses and, like his superior, looked impossibly young.

"Detective Inspector Ow sends his apologies for not coming to see you himself, Mr Young," said Ho. "He's been called out on urgent business."

"Is there some new development?" asked Patrick.

"As you know, we've been trying to identify the person who told the kidnappers about the High Commissioner's trip to Bintan," said Ho.

"I thought you'd already arrested someone," said Patrick.

"Yes," said Sergeant Ho. "But we can't find any trace of him having made or received any calls in the period in question which might relate to the kidnapping."

"But couldn't he have used a public telephone or an Internet café or something?" said Patrick. "Or even met the kidnappers in person?"

"Maybe he could have," said Ho. "But the point is that we've now identified what we think is the critical call."

"And?"

"It wasn't made by Muzafar Nasser. It was made by a woman, calling from the High Commission switchboard extension."

Patrick looked at him in disbelief. "Are you suggesting… ?" he said.

Sergeant Ho looked almost apologetic. "I'm sorry, Mr Young," he said. "I shall have to ask the High Commission receptionist to come down to police headquarters to answer some questions."

* * *

Berger had been staring out over the pool. Suddenly he swung round, as though he had made a decision. He turned in time to see the expression on Adam's face. And as he looked from Adam to the photographs on the table beside him, he gave a short, ugly laugh.

"My God, how careless of me," he said. "You really didn't know anything, did you?"

Adam made a desperate bid to retrieve the situation. "How many times do I have to tell you?" he said. "I don't know what you're talking about."

Berger made a sound that sounded like a contemptuous hiss. He stood with his arms crossed, looking at Adam from a distance of about two metres.

"There are so many ironies in this situation that I don't know where to begin," he said. "You may, for example, be surprised to know that I had no idea until today about the High Commissioner and my wife."

"But, you said—"

"Oh, I realised something was going on," Berger interrupted. "All these trips my wife was making every time I was travelling were too much of a coincidence. But I didn't know who the man was." He curled his lip. "For all I knew, it might have been you." He looked thoughtful. "In fact, on reflection, I think you must have both been fucking her."

"Don't be absurd," said Adam angrily. "I've hardly met your wife."

"So you say," said Berger, pulling an automatic pistol from his jacket pocket and pointing it at Adam's heart. "But who will ever know that?"

Adam sat motionless, adrenalin flooding through him. "You're not going to shoot me in your own house," he said.

"All this is extremely irritating," Berger continued, ignoring what Adam had said. "I go to the most extraordinary lengths to keep my operation in Singapore totally clean. My company here deals exclusively with legitimate business, all my accounts are scrupulously kept, my taxes paid promptly and in full. It's true that a number of my deals involve what your government so euphemistically describes as 'defence equipment'. But none of it comes within a thousand miles of Singapore, and in any case it's almost all entirely legal."

"Almost all?"

"Oh well, you know," said Berger. "Occasionally one must offer a financial inducement to secure a signature on an essential document. But it all happens a long way from here. And by the time the transactions have found their way back through my subordinate companies overseas to my consolidated accounts in Singapore, these payments have been satisfactorily transmuted into 'handling charges' and agents' commissions'".

"But all of that wasn't enough for you," said Adam.

"Let's say I saw a business opportunity too good to miss," said Berger. "When you've built up a logistical and financial network as extensive and efficient as mine it seems a shame not to put it to the most effective use. And that means dealing in the highest value-added product."

"Heroin."

"I'm very proud of my operation," said Berger. "It's simple but effective. The chain begins in Afghanistan and Burma and extends down as far as Thailand. Then it moves offshore to – well, who knows where? I'm not interested in the complexities of the retail trade. Just so long as it comes nowhere near Singapore."

"But it did come to Singapore."

"Yes," said Berger. "That was extremely unfortunate. Everything otherwise had been running very smoothly."

"And then along came Marina."

"Well, more precisely, along came a small-time Latin American gangster called José García, who thought he could steal a slice of my business," said Berger. "He bribed one of my men into diverting supplies which were en route through southern Thailand."

"The man with the missing hand."

"I fear Mohamed is missing the other hand now," said Berger. "And his eyes and his tongue." He paused for a moment. "And his teeth," he continued. "In fact, I'd say he's pretty well unidentifiable now."

Adam said nothing.

"What Mohamed did was unforgivable," said Berger. "What García and the girl did was worse. They smuggled the heroin into Singapore. It was a disgracefully amateurish operation, which was bound to fail. And the trail would have led, in time, back to my own operation. Such a risk I could not afford."

"So you had them killed," said Adam.

"I didn't originally plan to kill the girl," said Berger. "Eliminating Mohamed and García would have severed any possible link with me. I'd have been perfectly happy for Marina to go to jail."

"You engineered the tip-off at Raffles?"

"Exactly."

"But how did you know she'd be there that night?"

Berger smiled nastily. "I think I'll leave you to work that one out for yourself," he said. "All I'll say is that everything became more complicated than I had intended – thanks to your untimely intervention."

"Jesus," said Adam, as he understood the implication of Berger's words. "If I hadn't saved Marina from being arrested, she'd still be alive."

"I fear so," said Berger. "And you might not be about to die yourself."

"Here?" said Adam. "Here in your house?"

"It's not ideal, I agree," said Berger. "In other countries I have people who do this sort of thing for me. But, as I've explained, my Singapore operation is totally clean. So I'm having to improvise a little."

"You think you can fake this as self-defence?" said Adam. "You're mad."

"I was thinking more of murder and suicide," said Berger. "A crime of passion, then an act of remorse."

"What the hell are you talking about?"

"First, you strangle my wife," said Berger. "The jealous lover discovers that his mistress has been betraying him with, of all people, his very own boss. Then he shoots himself."

"What a load of bollocks," said Adam. "There's no way you can make me strangle your wife." But as he spoke, Adam saw the mocking smile on Berger's face and realised that Birgit was already dead.

"I just need to get your fingerprints and DNA on the stocking," said Berger. He moved swiftly to Adam's side and thrust the gun into his ear.

"This appears to be Birgit's gun, by the way," said Berger. "Registered in her maiden name in Hamburg. She must have smuggled it into Singapore illegally, or at least that's what I'll tell the police. So with luck I should come out of this rather well, don't you think?"

* * *

Siew Ling had left with Sergeant Ho, chatting cheerily to him in Mandarin for all the world as though they were fellow students off on a school outing. But the word soon spread around the High Commission that she had been arrested for suspected complicity in the High Commissioner's kidnapping.

285

Susan Hyde appeared, distraught, in the doorway to Patrick's office.

"Robert Redford's just asked to borrow the Commercial Section receptionist to man the switchboard," she said. "What's happened to Siew Ling?"

Patrick closed the door and gestured to her to sit down. He was aroused by her agitation and felt his early morning resolution dissolving. "The police are asking her some questions about the kidnapping," he said.

"What sort of questions?" She seemed almost to be on the edge of breakdown. *Christ*, he thought. *That vulnerability.* She was irresistible.

He hesitated before replying. "Is she a friend of yours?" he said.

"Yes," she said. "She came with Sophie and me to Koh Samui. Why? What's that got to do with it?"

"This is confidential, you understand?" said Patrick. "The police think she may have told the kidnappers about the High Commissioner's travel plans."

"No, that's impossible," said Susan, now very distressed. "Why would she do that?"

"I don't know, Susan," said Patrick. "But the call to the kidnappers came from the High Commission switchboard."

"How can they know that?"

"Susan, you must know that the Singaporeans listen to everything," said Patrick. "This is one of the most closely monitored societies in the world."

"You mean they have a recording of the call?"

"Of course," said Patrick.

Her face was drained of all colour. When she spoke, it was almost a whisper. "Well then," she said. "That's the end of it, I suppose."

* * *

Adam had been raised as a Catholic, but had shed his faith at an early age. Sex and death, he had told Ali when they first met, was what he had believed in since his own mother had died. But it was no longer true, or at least it was not the whole truth. He now believed in love. He believed in Ali.

So he made now no inner appeal to God. Instead, he apologised to Ali for his stupidity. And he swore that, if some miracle were to save him, he would devote the rest of his life to her happiness. No more Foreign Office. No more overseas life. No more (for he had in fact read Ali's letter) sacrificing her career for his. They would settle where she was happy, close to her family, her friends and her work.

It was not the first time Adam had faced imminent death at the hands of a desperate murderer. But this time was different. This time he had not alerted the police in advance. This time there could be no last-minute rescue.

In a flash of inspiration he said: "You've got the gun on the wrong side. I'm right-handed."

"How very observant of you," said Berger. He pulled the gun round in one smooth movement and stuck it into Adam's other ear. He had moved too fast for Adam to be able to take advantage of the momentary reprieve.

"Goodbye, arsehole," said Berger. Involuntarily, Adam closed his eyes.

And then, inexplicably, Berger gave a sharp cry and fell backwards away from the chair where Adam was sitting. The gun clattered on to the polished marble floor. Adam sprang up and saw Berger lying on the floor, cursing and clutching the upper part of his right leg. He was staring, incredulous, at something protruding from his thigh. It was an arrow.

Adam heard Ali's voice, crying. "Adam! Adam! Are you alright?" and he laughed exultantly.

"Yes!" he cried. "Oh, bloody hell, you're brilliant, Ali!" And then he saw Berger squirming across the floor and reaching for the automatic. Adam took a swift stride and kicked the gun away with his left foot, following through with a right-footed kick to Berger's chin.

Ali was in his arms, and then the house was suddenly full of policemen. He saw Detective Inspector Ow speaking into a mobile telephone, and two uniformed men pointing guns at Berger's head as they approached with professional care.

"Thank God you're here, officers," said Berger weakly, hauling himself up on to one elbow. "I came home and found these people in my house. They attacked me – look what they've done to me. I think they may have harmed my wife."

"I hardly think so, Mr Berger," said Detective Inspector Ow, rapidly consulting his handheld computer. "The ERP records show that your lawyer's car, in which I know you were travelling, passed under the gantry on the Pan Island Expressway, less than a quarter of a mile from here, an hour and a half ago. Mr White's car passed under it only about forty minutes ago. And this young lady arrived minutes ago in a taxi – whose driver, incidentally, almost certainly broke the law by allowing her to travel while carrying a lethal weapon with intent to harm."

Berger was handcuffed and left where he lay. One of the uniformed officers telephoned for an ambulance.

"I was so worried," said Ali to Adam. "I called Detective Inspector Ow." She blushed very slightly. "I didn't tell him I was planning to practise my archery."

"Thank God you did," said Adam.

"Against all my professional judgement, I have to agree with you," said Ow. "From the look of it, we would have been too late to save you."

"I had no idea you were so good, Ali," said Adam, squeezing her shoulders.

"You don't know where I was aiming," she laughed.

"Berger's killed his wife," Adam said to Detective Inspector Ow. "You'll find her upstairs. He's also responsible for the murders of Marina Singleton and José García. And he's a big-time narcotics smuggler." He paused, puzzled once more. "But the one thing he seems to be innocent of is the kidnapping and murder of Andrew Singleton."

CHAPTER 22

By agreement of all governments involved, Andrew Singleton gave a press conference from his hospital bed at 0900 Singapore time on Saturday morning. Also present were the Permanent Secretary of the Singapore Ministry of Foreign Affairs, representatives of the Prime Minister and the Senior Minister, the Police Commissioner, the Indonesian Ambassador, the acting British High Commissioner and the High Commission's Press and Public Affairs Officer. By common consent, the American Ambassador had stayed away.

Andrew began by reading out a statement, the text of which had been cleared with all interested parties. He expressed gratitude to all those who had been instrumental in his rescue, and deep condolences to the families of the valiant members of the Indonesian armed forces killed or injured in the process. He also made clear his unconditional support for the Singapore Government's refusal to give in to the terrorists' demands, a policy entirely consistent with that of the British Government.

"High Commissioner, why have we only just learned the rescue was successful?" asked Liu Kuan Loong from the *Straits Times*. "We all thought you were dead!"

"The Indonesian and Singaporean Governments felt it better to keep the terrorists in ignorance," said Andrew. "Otherwise, information I provided to help with the search for the kidnappers might have been rendered useless."

"What information would that be, High Commissioner?" asked Murray Parker.

"I'm afraid that has to remain confidential," said Andrew.

"Then why are you going public now?" persisted Murray.

"I'd better let the Permanent Secretary answer that," said Andrew.

"We now know the kidnappers are aware the High Commissioner survived," said Michael Seng.

"How?" asked Murray.

"From intelligence sources," said Seng, his voice so silky it was clear there would be no point in further enquiry.

Several questions followed, about Andrew's experiences at the hands of the terrorists and his personal recollection of the rescue. Andrew responded in sober, factual terms. At the centre of his account, there was a gaping hole where the story of the nuclear hoax should have been. But no one in the know, least of all Andrew, had any desire to reveal that story.

Finally came the question he had been expecting. It came, inevitably, from Murray Parker.

"High Commissioner, Mr Dieter Berger was arrested yesterday on suspicion of murdering his wife. Does this have any connection with your kidnapping, by any chance?"

Andrew had not learned of the deaths of Birgit and Marina until late the previous day. Before then, the only member of the police force to know of Andrew's survival was the Police Commissioner (the officers originally investigating Berger having been told only that an unimpeachable source had linked him to the kidnapping). But the Police Commissioner himself had, remarkably, been ignorant of Marina's death. Michael Seng had also not known of Marina's death, because no one had thought to notify the Singapore Foreign Ministry. Even in the depths of grief and remorse, Andrew had felt bound to reflect that sometimes the Singaporeans' legendary efficiency deserted them.

It had been Patrick Young, after Berger's final detention, who had belatedly woken up to the omission and gone to the hospital to speak to Andrew. The news of Birgit's death had devastated Andrew, and yet he had feared, almost expected it. He still could not believe that Marina was dead.

"No," he said. "There's no connection at all."

* * *

Patrick sent the Press and Public Affairs Officer home and drafted the telegram reporting the High Commissioner's press conference himself. Then he tried calling Susan, as he had done several times the previous evening, but with no success. He walked back to the Regent Hotel, showered and changed into casual clothes and took a taxi to Susan's house in Ridley Park.

Patrick had calculated that he was unlikely to be in Singapore for more than a few more days. The Commercial Counsellor was returning over the weekend and would become acting High Commissioner on Monday. Jane Rosendale was almost fully recovered and planned to resume work the same day. Even if Adam White remained suspended, there would be enough staff to keep things ticking over now that the crisis was past. He had already had two emails from Peter Cole, asking when he might be free to reinforce another gap which had opened up in London as a result of re-structuring and a budget squeeze. So, casting aside his earlier resolve, he had decided to see Susan one more time.

There was no answer to his persistent ringing at the doorbell. He checked that Susan's car was in the drive and then went round to the back of the house. The garden was empty. He heard voices in the neighbouring garden and began to retreat immediately. He had no wish to broadcast the fact to strangers that he was calling on Susan. But he was too late. A tall, severe-looking woman called over the fence to him. "Can I help you?"

"I was looking for Miss Hyde," he said, somewhat redundantly.

"And you are?"

"Patrick Young," he said. "I'm temporarily in charge of the High Commission."

"Oh, yes," she said, her attitude softening marginally. "Nick's mentioned your name. I'm Sarah Childs."

"Is Susan at home, do you know?" Patrick asked.

"I've no idea, I'm afraid," said Sarah "We haven't seen her at all today."

"Oh well, not to worry," said Patrick. "She's probably sleeping in. I'll give her a call later on, perhaps. It was just a routine administrative matter."

Sarah looked at Patrick coolly. "If I see her, I'll tell her you were looking for her."

But, as Patrick later discovered, he had no sooner disappeared around the corner to begin his walk back down to Tanglin Road than Sarah Childs had persuaded her husband to produce the spare key to Susan's house and gone to investigate for herself.

The first thing she found, on the dining table, was an open laptop computer. The screen contained a rambling, near-incoherent message. Siew Ling, it said, was innocent of any wrongdoing other than gossiping to her friend about the High Commissioner's travel plans. For it was Susan herself who had revealed these plans to a man she had met on a trip to Koh Samui, two months previously. A man who had got her drunk and seduced her and then produced lewd photographs of her, which he threatened to make public unless she did what he demanded. She had thought he intended to use the information for the relatively benign purpose of revealing Andrew Singleton's suspected adultery to the wider world. She now knew that she had been deceived and must atone for her actions. Andrew Singleton had been killed because of her. And his only sin was one of which she herself was now guilty. She pleaded forgiveness of all those she had wronged.

Sarah fled next door to fetch her husband. Together they broke down the door of Susan Hyde's locked bedroom. They found her lying on the bed, dressed in a full-length night gown, the reddish brown curls of her carefully combed, shoulder-length hair stark against the chalky white of her face, an empty pill box on the bedside table alongside a half-full whisky bottle. "She looked, for all the world, like *The Woman In White*," said Sarah later. "Thank goodness we arrived in time."

If anyone thought it strange that Patrick left the police interview room so rapidly at this point in Nick and Sarah's story, they did not say so. For several seconds, he retched into the basin in the washroom. Then he turned on both taps and leaned heavily on the basin, watching, but not seeing, the water swirl down the plughole. He turned off the taps and lifted his head slowly to look into the mirror. The bile was bitter in his mouth. *It's not your fault*, he said to the reflection. *She thought she was an accessory to murder. She had actually been an accessory to kidnapping. It was nothing to do with the adultery. And in any case, she's alive.*

Would she say anything about him when she was well enough to talk to the police? It was unlikely – she was just too sweet-natured. *You've got away with it,* he said to the mirror. *Buffy will never know. No one will know. It's finished.*

But you know, another voice inside him said.

* * *

Adam, who remained suspended, had not attended Andrew Singleton's press conference. But Mary Bennett had telephoned him early on Saturday morning, as soon as the news that Singleton was alive had been given to all High Commission staff. Adam had decided he must see Singleton privately, as soon as possible.

"What's the news on Muzafar, Mary?" he asked.

"He's been released," said Mary. "I'm hoping to see him this afternoon. But did you know they'd arrested Siew Ling?"

"Never," said Adam. "I simply don't believe it."

He arranged the hospital visit for early afternoon. Shortly

before he left, he received a call from Patrick Young, with the shocking news of Susan Hyde's suicide attempt. But Young wanted to say more.

"Adam, I've behaved badly," said Young. "I want to do my best to repair things if I can. I'm sending a further report to London today about Marina. I'm going to make clear that my suppositions about you and her were wholly erroneous, and that you were acting at all times with honourable motives."

"Thank you," said Adam. "It doesn't alter the fact I was a bloody idiot, but it might help in London."

"Maybe we could meet for a beer or something later?" said Young.

"Sure," said Adam. "Come by the house around six."

Andrew Singleton was propped up on his pillows, half-dozing, when Adam arrived.

"I'm so very sorry for your loss, High Commissioner," said Adam.

"Thank you, Adam," said Singleton. He looked old. The tan had faded, the lines in his thin face were cruelly accentuated.

"I'm sorry for everything," said Adam, when he had told Singleton all he knew about Marina's fate. "But I'm especially sorry I didn't speak to you at once about Marina. None of this would have happened if I had."

"You meant well, Adam," said Singleton. "Marina was involved in an evil business. It was bound to end badly, sooner or later."

"But she wasn't an evil person," said Adam. "The man she was with tried to kill me. I think she did her best to stop him."

"You may be right," said Singleton. He seemed distracted, as well as tired. "I hope you're right."

Adam hesitated, not sure whether Andrew would want to talk further about Marina. "This man, José García," he said carefully. "The police think he was operating on his own. It's not clear how Marina became involved with him."

Andrew looked back at him, his face expressionless. Did he know Adam had guessed the truth? If he did, he chose to avoid the issue. "The name's familiar to me," he said. "I think he may have worked for Marina's grandfather at some stage."

Adam decided to steer the conversation on to less delicate ground. "For what it's worth, the police are pretty sure it was Daniel Taylor who told Berger when Marina was going to be in the Long Bar," he said. "His father and Berger did business together – legitimate, as far as we know. They were also tennis partners. Daniel used to play with them sometimes. Berger's people had told him exactly when Marina had brought the heroin into Singapore. He knew she was seeing Daniel and was able to ask Daniel about his plans for the evening without arousing any suspicion. There was always a risk Daniel would get arrested as well, but Berger didn't care about that. He was out to get Marina."

"He clearly didn't reckon with the depths of Marina's stupidity," said Singleton.

This struck Adam as a remarkably cold observation. "But you've lost your daughter," he said, cursing himself the moment the words were out. "I can't forgive myself for that."

Singleton seemed to be about to say something, but changed his mind. He too seemed to be searching for a less contentious matter to discuss. "Has anyone told you what this whole kidnapping business was about?" he said.

"No," said Adam. "I've been completely out of the High Commission loop for the last two days."

"Well, suspended or not, I think you deserve to hear the whole story," said Singleton.

When Singleton had finished, Adam sat silently for a while, piecing together in his mind fragments of conversations he had had in the last couple of days which now began to make sense.

"Well, it was certainly audacious," said Adam. "But it could easily have gone all wrong. You could have died and that would have been an end to it. Supposing the Indonesians hadn't found you in time. Suppose they'd been looking in the wrong place – searching the islands instead of only the sea, for example."

"Were they only searching the sea?" said Singleton. "How come?"

Adam laughed. "Well, you should know that," he said.

"I don't get you," said Singleton.

Adam wondered whether Singleton's medication had affected his memory. "They were searching for a yacht, Andrew," he said. "Because of the signal you sent us? The code, remember?"

"Signal?" said Singleton. "Code? I don't know what you're talking about."

CHAPTER 23

Mary awoke on Sunday morning in Muzafar's arms and thought, momentarily, that she was still dreaming. First light was seeping through the window and she could hear birdsong from the garden.

He smiled as soon as she opened her eyes and kissed her gently on the forehead. "I've been watching you sleep for the past hour," he said. "I think this is truly heaven."

She took his face in her hands and kissed him on the lips. "How could you think of leaving me?" she whispered.

"I told you, my darling, I was afraid for you, for your career," he said. "My cousin was a suspected terrorist. I was bound to come under suspicion as well. I felt it wasn't right to involve you in any of that."

"But you knew I loved you," she said. "It hurt so much, Muzafar."

He held her to him. "I was very foolish," he said. "I did not see how strong you would be."

They lay in silence for a while, looking into each other's eyes. Then Mary said: "Marry me."

He smiled again, a broad, glorious smile. "Oh, yes," he said. "Yes, yes, yes, yes."

* * *

Patrick had barely slept. The aftermath of the High Commissioner's kidnapping, the death of Marina Singleton

298

and Susan Hyde's attempted suicide had turned the High Commission into a madhouse. He had worked late into Saturday night, breaking only for an hour to go to make his peace with Adam White. He planned to work all day on Sunday. He was determined to do everything that needed to be done before the Commercial Counsellor, Vincent Greenfield, arrived.

He told himself that this intensive activity demonstrated professionalism, that it would be noticed in London, be good for his career. But the truth was that he was trying to compensate for his own past behaviour. He would fend off the press when they sought to fabricate a salacious dimension to Andrew Singleton's kidnapping. He would work on the High Commissioner's behalf for the rapid recovery of Marina's remains and a discreet and dignified funeral. He would strive for Adam White's exoneration. He would comfort and provide all practical assistance to Susan Hyde's widowed mother, who was due to arrive that evening from London.

In the scales of his conscience, these things weighed as nothing against what he had done. But he could not stop himself from doing them.

Buffy rang as he was stepping out of the shower. "It's a girl," she said.

"A *girl?*"

"Yes, Patrick. We've got a lovely little girl. Seven pounds four ounces."

He rapidly wrapped the towelling robe around him. "Why didn't you call me when you knew the baby was coming?" he said.

"Is that all you can say, man?" she cried. "How about a bit more enthusiasm!"

"Sorry," he said. "You caught me by surprise. That's great. I was so sure we'd have a boy again."

"She came so fast," said Buffy. "Not like Jamie. I had no time to call."

"We haven't thought of any girl's names," he said, still trying to absorb the information.

"I know what I want to call her," said Buffy. "It has to be Susie."

Was it his imagination, or could he still smell her on the bathrobe? Surely it had been replaced when the towels were changed? There was definitely something. Or was it in his mind?

"Are you still there, Patrick?" said Buffy. "What do you think?"

"If that's what you want, love," he said.

* * *

An unexpected fall of snow had dusted the spires of Oxford and created a fairy-tale picture of white and pale gold in the February sunshine. Gillian arrived early and opted to leave her chauffeur-driven car on the High Street outside All Souls. The temperature was hovering around freezing. The snow underfoot, which had so far seen little pedestrian traffic, was still crisp and white. Pulling up the collar of her coat, Gillian cut through Catte Street, past the domed, Palladian elegance of the Radcliffe Camera and the English Gothic mass of the Bodleian, and turned left into Broad Street towards Trinity and Balliol.

Roger Singleton had asked Gillian to look him up whenever she was in Oxford. When she had telephoned the previous day with the news of Andrew's survival, she had expected him to be surprised that she should be taking him up on his invitation so soon. ("I'm seeing an old friend in Banbury for lunch," she had said. "I thought I might drop in on the way for coffee.") But he had simply said he was pleased she had remembered.

She turned right, towards St Giles, and found herself at the entrance to his college. She consulted her watch, waited for one minute and then walked into the Porter's Lodge to ask for directions to Dr Singleton's room.

Roger Singleton was dressed relatively formally for a Sunday morning, in a grey suit, white shirt and college tie. He ushered her in and sat her in the one comfortable chair in the room, placing himself on an upright chair which he had brought over from his desk. There was no doubt it was a bachelor's room. There were no family photographs on display, or indeed paintings or ornaments of any kind. The books which covered most of the wall space were carefully catalogued, the papers on the desk were neatly sorted into separate piles alongside the computer and telephone. The furniture was sparse and of indeterminate age.

"It's only instant, I'm afraid," he said, handing her a mug. Gillian had a sudden picture in her mind of Andrew, even as a student, grinding Colombian coffee beans and lovingly brewing the coffee he would make at the end of their evenings together.

For a while they sat, silently, drinking their coffee. Finally, Roger spoke.

"I'm glad you came," he said. "I thought it would just be the boys in blue."

"I was curious about your motivation," said Gillian. "And I thought – maybe I was wrong – that you'd be more likely to speak openly to me."

He stared out of the window, down on to the snow-covered quadrangle. "I wish I'd had the guts to ask you out when we first met," he said. "Andrew was just too glamorous to compete with."

"We all have regrets about the past," she said. "But I hardly think that's relevant to what you did."

He looked back at her. "What I did?" he said. "I'll tell you what I did. I tried to restore sanity to a lunatic world."

"I'm still struggling to understand," said Gillian. "Your brother was nearly killed. You tried to start a war. That's not sanity."

He shrugged. "It was an extreme measure," he said. "But these are extreme times. The Americans have to be stopped. I thought this might be one way of doing it."

301

"By provoking a conflict in which thousands of innocent people would die?"

He became more animated now. "But don't you see?" he said. "The entire Islamic community would have been united as one against the United States. The Americans would have suffered such a catastrophic military and diplomatic defeat that they would have withdrawn from meddling in the world's affairs for all time."

"Even supposing that to be both true and desirable – which I do not for one moment accept – how could you justify the horrendous human cost?" she said.

"I think Stalin had the answer to that," he said. "Something about omelettes and eggs, if I recall correctly."

"Oh, really, Roger," she said. "Are you seriously telling me you were prepared to cause untold suffering in support of your personal political vision?"

"You don't think the Americans will cause untold suffering if they're not stopped?" he said angrily. "At least during the Cold War the Soviet Union kept them in check. It will be thirty years before China can fulfil the same role. We can't afford to wait that long."

"That's madness," said Gillian quietly. "And what about Andrew? Your own brother?"

He was cooler now. "Andrew led a debauched life," he said. "A little suffering was overdue."

"But he could have been killed."

"Oh, no," he said. "There was no danger of that. We'd calculated it all very carefully. It was only a shoulder wound."

"He was shot in the chest," said Gillian. "He lost a lot of blood. He could have died."

For the first time, Singleton gave the appearance of being disconcerted. "It wasn't supposed to be like that," he muttered.

"In any case, your carefully laid plans didn't work," said Gillian.

"No," said Singleton. "The Americans were smarter than we thought." He paused. "Or maybe it was you."

"This man, Hussein," said Gillian. "It would help your situation if you could give us some idea of how he might be traced."

"Oh, Kirsty," said Singleton, who had by now recovered his composure. "I do hope you're not trying to play 'good cop, bad cop' with me."

"Well, you'll certainly be subjected to considerably more vigorous interrogation after you've been arrested," said Gillian.

"Who by, I wonder?" said Singleton. "Your people? Or the Americans?"

"Technically, I rather think the Indonesians have first refusal," said Gillian. She paused, allowing Singleton to absorb this information. Then she continued. "But everyone will get their turn, of course."

Singleton laughed, dismissively. "It won't make any difference," he said. "I couldn't tell you even if I wanted. We deliberately severed all our links as soon as the operation began."

"But you know a great deal about him which could be helpful."

"Nothing you won't have worked out already," said Singleton. "He'd been my student. He was clever. But he was more than that. He was a natural conspirator. Perfect for my purposes."

"And a Moslem," said Gillian. "To add verisimilitude to the alleged plot."

Singleton gave a nasty laugh. "Yes, and I'm an Anglican," he said. "Oh, he may believe militant Islam is destined to crush the West. And he certainly wants to be on the winning side. But his real reason for indulging in terror is the terror itself."

"Did you know he'd had a liaison with the woman Andrew was having an affair with?"

"That was what made it so perfect," said Singleton. "She provided the link to this man Berger, who was the prime target for our disinformation."

Gillian glanced at her watch. She had asked the police for

half an hour's grace. They would be here very soon. "I still don't understand the nonsense about the code," she said.

"I was worried the Indonesians were looking in the wrong place," he said. "If they hadn't found the yacht in good time the whole plan would have had to be aborted."

"But it was a terrible risk," said Gillian. "You'd planned for Andrew to survive. It was bound to emerge you'd invented the story about the code."

Singleton did not reply immediately. When he spoke, it was in a mildly self-deprecating tone. "If the scheme had worked, that would have been of very little consequence," he said. "It was worth the risk." Then he smiled, almost mischievously. "Besides, I couldn't resist the temptation. It was a bit like signing a great work of art."

* * *

Andrew dreamed the vivid, anxious dreams of daytime sleep. Kirsty was there, and Dieter Berger. So too was Roger and the man, Hussein. Birgit and Marina he could not see, though he sensed their presence. But when he awoke, in pain again and with a parched throat, the images in his head dissolved into nonsense. The one thing of which he was sure was that, for once, he had not dreamed of Elena.

He lifted himself gingerly and drank some water from the glass by his bed, then sank back, his eyes closed once more. He had slept after a tiring session with Vincent Greenfield, who had insisted on coming to see him the moment he arrived back in Singapore. In his kindly, non-judgemental way, Greenfield had assured Andrew he would now take charge of everything and set the High Commission back on an even keel. The message he brought from London was that Andrew should return home as soon as he was well enough to travel and then take extended leave.

304

Extended leave, thought Andrew, opening his eyes again and shifting his weight on the pillow. *They're going to sack me.* Well, that was only to be expected, but it did seem something of an anti-climax when he might have gone out in a blaze of glory as an executed hostage.

"Excuse me, High Commissioner," said the Malay nurse. "You have a telephone call."

It was Gillian King.

"Hello, Kirsty," he said. "Are you calling to administer a formal admonishment?"

"No, Andrew," she said. "This is strictly personal. How are you?"

"I've been better."

"I'm so very sorry about Marina," she said.

"Thank you," he said. "Has Roger been arrested yet?"

"This morning," she said.

"He always took everything so seriously," Andrew said. "Even so… "

There was silence for a while. Then Kirsty said, "At least you're safe, Andrew. I just wanted to say… " She paused, then said, "I wanted to say how relieved I was you're safe."

"Thank you, Kirsty," he said. "That means a lot to me."

He might have said more, but there was no point.

"I'll see you when you get back," she said.

He dozed again and woke, once more convinced he had not dreamed of Elena. Was that ghost now truly exorcised? It hardly mattered, for now he had new, bitter memories from which he would never escape: his brother's secret hatred, Marina's wasted life, and the loss which would consume him with pain and remorse for all time.

Forgive me, Birgit, he thought. *Please, please, forgive me.*

* * *

Adam and Ali sat on their small terrace, holding hands and listening to the noises of the tropical twilight. Cicadas whirred in the undergrowth. A bullfrog called to his mate, with a sound like a braying donkey. The faint scent of anthurium and heliconia drifted in from the garden. In the distance a dog barked insistently at an innocent passer-by.

"I have an announcement to make," said Adam.

Ali turned her face towards him.

"Me too," she said, kissing him lightly on the cheek.

It was the first time they had sat together, alone and fully rested, since the dramatic events of the previous two days. Police interrogations, communications via the High Commission with London, and a conciliatory meeting with a remarkably humble Patrick Young had taken them late into Saturday night. There had been time for only a brief telephone call from Ali to her parents to assure them she and Adam were safe and well, whatever they might read in the tabloid newspapers. There had then been further meetings with the police early on Sunday morning, followed by another visit by Adam to the High Commissioner in hospital. While Adam then went to check that all was well with Jane Rosendale, Ali spent time on the telephone with Mary Bennett and Mimi Parker. When Adam returned, he spoke briefly to Murray Parker to thank him for all his help. "You still owe me that beer," said Murray. "Not to mention an explanation of your peregrinations." They had then eaten a sandwich, taken the phone off the hook and slept an overdue siesta.

"You first then," said Adam.

"I wrote you a letter from London," she said.

"I read it."

"I want to retract what I said," she said. "I want to try again, with you, in Singapore."

"No, Ali," said Adam. "I'm not going to let you do that. All my adult life I've pretty much had things my own way. It's time I put someone else's needs first."

"Well, that's tough," said Ali. "Because you'll have to bind and gag me before you get me on that plane."

"Don't be daft," he said. "I'm coming with you."

"What? No, Adam, you can't give up your career just like that."

"Look, Ali," he said. "It's no big deal, really. I'll have to go back to face disciplinary action anyway."

"But what will you do?"

"Live off your vast earnings, I hope," he said, laughing.

"No, be serious, Adam."

"Oh, they'll find some corner of the office in London to hide me away," he said.

The telephone rang. Ali left Adam on the terrace to go inside to answer it.

Five minutes later, she emerged from the house, her face like stone.

"My mother's had a stroke," she said.

"Your *mother?*"

"An hour ago. Daddy says it's serious."

"But I thought—"

"So did I. I just assumed… "

"Oh, Ali, I'm so sorry," he said, taking her into his arms.

"We were always so angry with each other," she said.

Adam held her close to him. After a while she began to cry, dry shuddering sobs which turned in time into wailing groans. He stroked her head and whispered meaningless words of comfort into her ear.

* * *

He sat in an Internet café in downtown Bangkok, reading the online version of the *Straits Times*. He had already skimmed through the main American and British newspapers and scanned the CNN and BBC websites.

It had not been a wholly satisfactory operation. He had warned the old man the Americans were unlikely to be that gullible, but it had been worth a try.

It was a shame about Birgit, but her murder had won him the real prize: the elimination of Dieter Berger. What did it matter if the Singaporeans hanged him for the wrong crime? One swift movement of the executioner's hand would remove the man who had stolen Birgit from him. More to the point, it would free up a large slice of the drugs business in South East Asia, into which his own operatives could rapidly move. There would be no more living from hand to mouth, no more haggling with inflexible paymasters. With drug money to spend, he could contemplate a more ambitious game: one of his own choosing.

He had wanted to kill Andrew Singleton; the way things had panned out, it would have made no difference. It still might not be not too late to remedy the omission. An operation on Singaporean soil would be impossible, but Singleton was bound to travel again in due course: if the Foreign Office did not withdraw him, he would probably go somewhere to recuperate. Susan was out of the game now, but Sophie would know where.